ALSO BY CHRIS ROBERSON

Novels
Voices of Thunder
Cybermancy Incorporated
Any Time At All
Here, There & Everywhere
Paragaea: A Planetary Romance
The Voyage of Night Shining White
X-Men: The Return
Set the Seas on Fire

Series
Shark Boy and Lava Girl Adventures:
Book 1
Shark Boy and Lava Girl Adventures:
Book 2

THE DRAGON'S NINE SONS

A novel of the Celestial Empire

CHRIS ROBERSON

SOLARIS

First published 2008 by Solaris
an imprint of BL Publishing
Games Workshop Ltd
Willow Road
Nottingham
NG7 2WS
UK

www.solarisbooks.com

ISBN-13: 978 1 84416 524 7
ISBN-10: 1 84416 524 8

10 9 8 7 6 5 4 3 2 1

A CIP catalogue record for this book is available from the British Library.

Designed & typeset by BL Publishing

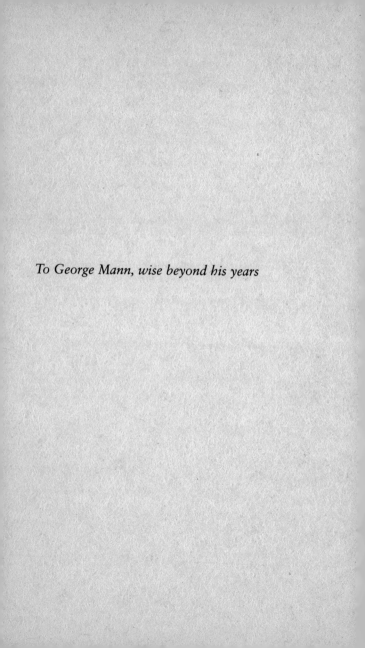

To George Mann, wise beyond his years

PROLOGUE

It was the fifty-second year of the Taikong emperor.

It was Water-Monkey year.

It was the twenty-eighth terrestrial year since man first walked on the face of the red planet, Fire Star (though measured in the longer years of Fire Star itself, the count was nearer fifteen).

It was the year 2052 of the long-abandoned Gregorian calendar, now only employed in religious rites in Europa and Vinland.

It was 4,689 years since the Yellow Emperor, Huangdi, whose reign-name had been Keeper of Bears, had invented the calendar, taught man how to keep track of the seasons, and instituted the Middle Kingdom.

It was one hundred-forty-seven years since the end of the First Mexic War, when the Dragon Throne clashed with the blood-soaked warriors of the Mexic Dominion.

It was the twelfth year of the Second Mexic War, and there was no end in sight.

CHAPTER ONE

On the bridge of the *Exhortation*, Captain Zhuan Jie gripped the armrests of his seat, and fought to keep from voiding his bowels when the Mexica's first salvo splashed across the nose of his spacecraft. A low-mass, high-velocity explosive projectile, the shot didn't have enough momentum to push the *Exhortation* off course, but its payload was hot enough to pit and crack the ship's ferroceramic hull. It burned so brightly that Zhuan was forced to squint, the bridge bathed in the blinding white radiance pouring through the forward viewports.

Over the sound of the ship's air-circulation system and the rattle and hum of the bridge controls, a groaning could be heard, as the kinetic energy of the impact was distributed through the ship's hull. The low-frequency squeal of metal on metal reminded Zhuan of nothing so much as the growl of a caged bear, trained but never tamed. A lifetime spent running from the life he never wanted, and still he couldn't escape the memories.

"Orders, my captain?" From his station along the bridge's forward wall, the steersman glanced over his shoulder, teeth gritted, searching for strength.

Captain Zhuan had been in the Interplanetary Fleet for more than half his life, and fighting the forces of the Mexica for more than half of that, but each combat encounter could for him just as easily have been the first. War in the vacuum of space was most often a question of waiting, of patrolling the dark void in search of an enemy one rarely found. In the more than twelve years of the Second Mexic War the captain had found himself in close combat with a Mexic vessel fewer times than the number of his fingers and toes. But his reactions to even those few experiences had been the same each time—the clenched gut, the cold sweat, the dry tongue thick in the mouth, the gripping hands—stark terror.

Little more than a boy at the time, Zhuan had enlisted in the fleet, then the emperor's Treasure Fleet to the red planet Fire Star, in search of a life of adventure, like the flying aces of the Imperial Navy of the Air during the first War Against the Mexica—the Spirits of the Upper Air, the Flying Immortals, the Golden Dragons. He had wanted to escape the life of his parents, spent training dangerous animals for the emperor's pleasure, the musky stench hanging on them all of their days like a shroud; there had been some irony, then, to the fact that he had first sailed into the black vacuum of space aboard *Jade Maiden*, the livestock carrier of the Treasure Fleet, her holds divided into stalls full of grunting, shitting beasts—goats, cattle, pigs—the smell always thick in his nostrils. Then, years later, the war had begun, and the emperor had militarized the now Interplanetary Fleet, and Zhuan had reason to curse his younger self for ever seeing anything of romance or beauty in stories of war.

Zhuan swallowed, and wished he could give the steersman and the rest of the crew the strength and steely resolve he knew they craved. But while he had always been an exemplary captain and sailor, he was a poor soldier at best, and struggled to keep from becoming completely unmanned in combat.

"Evasive," he finally responded, flicking a gesture toward the navigator and nodding in the steersman's direction. Then he turned to the weaponeer, seated between them. "Prepare main batteries to return fire."

The crewmen nodded their assent and turned to their duties. A less familiar eye might have mistaken the captain's momentary pause for a passing bit of indigestion, or a fleeting bout of disorientation as the ship changed position. But these crewmen had served with Zhuan in one capacity or another for some years, through several such encounters, and knew the captain's reaction for what it was.

From behind Zhuan's seat to the right, the communicationist cleared his throat, and the captain looked back over his shoulder in response. The communications officer's hair was worn in a long Manchurian queue that drifted in the air currents of the bridge's microgravity like weed floating at the bottom of a slow-moving stream. The tip of the queue barely avoided brushing the shoulder of the engineer, seated beside him.

"It's the *Pure Harmony* again, my captain." The communicationist cut his eyes from the controls of his station to the captain and back again, uneasily. "Do you respond?"

Zhuan glanced at the empty seat beside him. If the ship's minister of rites hadn't been taken ill with damp wind, the captain would already have been forced to observe protocol and acknowledge the hail long before now. But the *Exhortation*'s political officer had been confined to quarters by the ship's physician, leaving Zhuan with more than usual latitude. Still, the inevitable couldn't be forever delayed.

Zhuan nodded. "Pipe it in, communicationist."

Already today Zhuan had learned to dread the hiss of the speakers mounted in the ceiling overhead, and the voices that followed. The *Exhortation* had been returning from a patrol out on the edge of the red planet Fire Star's gravity well, a week's long reconnaissance searching for any sign of Mexic Dominion vessels. Having found none—thankfully—the ship had made the long journey back to the main body of the fleet, intending to enter a parking orbit before docking at the Zhurong moonbase for much-needed leave. But then orders came through from the flagship of the Interplanetary Fleet, the *Iridescent Cloud*, instructing Zhuan's ship to divert course and join an engagement already in progress. The *Exhortation* was the nearest ship to the location, and the best equipped to assist.

It had taken some time to reach the indicated coordinates, and on arrival Zhuan had found a pitched battle already in progress. A trio of Middle Kingdom vessels were in the process of engaging two larger Mexic warships. But while the Middle Kingdom ships outnumbered their enemies, the Mexica's armaments more than made up the difference. As they approached the battle, Zhuan momentarily refused to respond to the hails of the lead Middle Kingdom vessel, the *Pure Harmony*, feeling the familiar grip of fear, and while he delayed his response, the *Exhortation* was hit by a long salvo from the nearest of the Mexic warships, a fiery welcome to the fray.

"Commander the *Exhortation*," came the voice from the speakers, crackling with static.

"Captain Zhuan Jie receiving. Who calls?"

"Captain Skidjai of the *Pure Harmony*, ranking officer of this blockade. Glad you could join us, *Exhortation*."

There was a rough good humor to Skidjai's words, a camaraderie of men-at-arms that Zhuan often encountered with other ship's captains but did not, and could not, himself share.

"Blockade?" Zhuan repeated.

There was a burst of static, and through the forward viewports Zhuan could see the *Pure Harmony* painted with bright flashes of red and white as self-propelled explosives fired from the Mexic warships found their marks on her hull. The static faded and was replaced by the sound of imaginative cursing as Captain Skidjai hurled imprecations at the enemy while his weaponeer loosed a few rounds in their direction. Then Skidjai returned his attention to the *Exhortation*.

"So the *Iridescent Cloud* sent you all this way without a word as to what we're about?"

Zhuan shook his head, a meaningless gesture. "Our orders were simply to divert course and join the engagement."

Skidjai cursed again, to make even a veteran sailor blush. Zhuan wondered what had become of *his* minister of rites, to strain protocol to such an extent. "It's a simple matter, *Exhortation*. There's a Mexic launch vessel currently blasting up from the surface, thinking to reach escape velocity and head out into the void. The pair of blood-hungry Mexic bastards you see before you are here to run interference. Our job is to stop them, and to keep that vessel from getting past."

Zhuan glanced around the bridge, and saw the crew watching him expectantly, waiting to hear his response. He raised his eyes to the ceiling, fixing his gaze on the speakers, as though the captain of the other vessel lay hidden behind them. "Commander the *Pure Harmony*, are you aware that this vessel is a shanzhou-class patrol ship?"

A brief pause followed. "Understood and acknowledged, *Exhortation*. But you're the only vessel close enough to join in, so we've got to make do."

Zhuan bit the inside of his cheek. The shanzhou-class was designed to be low-mass, high-velocity, and maneuverable, and as a result didn't carry much in the way of armament. Even its defensive capabilities were comparatively slight, especially in contrast with the vicious Mexic warships they were facing.

"Move into interception position and await further orders. *Pure Harmony* out."

With an audible click the radio connection dropped and a sibilant hiss of static poured from the speakers.

"They've transmitted coordinates, my captain," the communicationist said from his station.

Zhuan forced himself to relax, and loosened his grip on his seat's armrests. His arms drifted up on either side, buoyant in microgravity. He took deep breaths through his nose, the ozone-tang of the ship's electrics stinging his nostrils, and then breathed out through pursed lips, willing his heartbeat to slow from its racing pulse.

"Navigator..." The captain began, then paused. The crew looked at him, unblinking, searching for resolve. Zhuan took another deep breath, in through the nostrils and out through pursed lips. "Navigator, receive coordinates from the communicationist and set course. Steersman, enter thrust and directional values. Engineer, retract control rods three-quarters, release the liquid hydrogen into the heating chamber, and iris the aperture for thrust."

The crew did as instructed, each to their task, and the *Exhortation* again shuddered into movement. As the craft's inertia shifted, Zhuan felt slightly queasy as his insides realigned themselves, the acceleration imparting something almost like gravity that pressed him fractionally back into his seat. Instinctively he checked the straps securing him into place, and then turned his attention to the forward viewports, as the craft changed orientation and the red crescent of Fire Star hoved slowly into view.

The aerial combat about which Zhuan had read as a boy, thrilling accounts of brave Middle Kingdom aeronauts who piloted their craft in dogfights against the lumbering but no-less-deadly airships of the Mexic Dominion's elite Eagle Knights, had been fierce and brief contests. Craft met in the skies above Vinland and Khalifah and Fusang, appearing suddenly out of cloud banks and strafing one another with tracer fire, each life and death struggle decided in a matter of moments.

Not so the vacuum combat of the Second Mexic War. The fission-engine-propelled craft of the Middle Kingdom and the Mexic Dominion were able to reach speeds that would have been unthinkable a century and a half before, but the distances involved swallowed those velocities whole, hungry for more. Captains could see their enemies' ships long before they got close enough to inflict any real damage on one another, and by the time they drew near enough that the target could no longer simply move out of the way of any approaching projectile, the encounters could prove all-too-brief. Sometimes, the craft got so close together that their crews learned first-hand the destructive potential of inertia when a few tons of steel and ceramic collided at thousands of kilometers per hour.

The launch vessel blasting up from the surface of Fire Star, in order to break free of the red planet's gravity, would have been traveling somewhere in excess of five kilometers per second. Whatever its mass, large or small, its momentum by the time it reached low orbit would be considerable. This was a calculation that Zhuan could not help performing, as the steersman nudged the *Exhortation* into position.

At a signal from the steersman, the engineer closed the aperture on the thrust chamber, and then fired the attitude rockets on the outer hull to reorient the ship one hundred and eighty degrees. When the nose of the craft was pointed back in the direction it had come, the aperture was opened for a short burst that burned off the remaining acceleration, and as the *Exhortation* drifted to a relative stop the control rods were reinserted into the reactor.

"Station keeping, steersman," Zhuan said.

"Yes, my captain." The steersman and the navigator exchanged nervous looks, steadying their hands on their controls.

The arc of Fire Star filled the viewports, a great red disc before them. Zhuan remembered the first time he'd seen it, a lifetime ago, engineer's mate on the *Jade Maiden*. He and the rest of the crew had spent one and a half terrestrial years down on the surface—nearly a full Fire Star year—before the Treasure Fleet returned to Earth. A year spent building habitats, constructing generators and atmosphere farms, falling in and out of love and gradually becoming a man. Then they had left it all behind and returned to Earth. By the time they had reached home, the emperor had rechristened it the Interplanetary Fleet and increased its number from the original ten vessels, only eight of which had managed to return from the red planet, until there were dozens of vessels ferrying colonists to Fire Star and returning with precious ores. Zhuan remained with the fleet, first as an engineer's mate, then as an engineer, and eventually, when the need for command officers outpaced the ability of the bureaucracy to supply them, he was given a command of his own.

In the next fifteen years, Zhuan made the trip to and from the red planet again and again, six times in all counting his original voyage with the Treasure Fleet. It was on his sixth voyage that he first heard the news of the Mexic attack on the colonists, and knew that things would never be the same again. In a single day he went from being an honest sailor who ferried hopeful families to a new world out in the void, to being the commander of a ship of war. But while he was perfectly suited for the former, the latter had always seemed like clothing tailored for another man, fitting him badly if at all.

A smudge appeared on the red disc before them that grew with each passing heartbeat. It was a black speck riding atop a plume of fire.

"Incoming from *Pure Harmony*, my captain," the communicationist announced.

Zhuan raised a single finger, pointing to the speakers overhead.

"*Exhortation*," came the voice of Captain Skidjai, laced with static. "Do you have visual contact?"

Zhuan nodded again, pointlessly, and silently cursed himself for the instinct. "Yes, we see it."

"Good. Now, I know you've not got much in the way of arms on that boat, but I want you to throw everything you've got at that thing. We need to stop it, whatever the cost." Skidjai paused. "Do you hear me, *Exhortation*? Whatever the cost. Throw anything and everything in that launch vehicle's path, up to and including your ship's hull."

Zhuan's fingers tightened on the armrests, and the crew turned to regard him with widened eyes. Suddenly unable to swallow, Zhuan opened his mouth and closed it again, before finally responding. "Sir? Could you repeat, please?"

"I said put yourself in the launch vehicle's path if you have to, *Exhortation*. If that's the only way to stop it, then that's what we have to do."

Zhuan saw the weaponeer catch the steersman's eye and mouth, "We?"

"But sir," Zhuan began, "the chances of survival after that kind of collision…"

"I said ram it, *Exhortation*." Then, in a slightly gentler voice, Skidjai continued. "Look, I know it sounds risky, but the shanzhou-class is rated for that sort of impact. It's at the upper limits of tolerance, but it should be survivable. Just break out your pressure gear and, should worst come to worst, you can always abandon ship and drift until a Middle Kingdom vessel is free to come to pick you up. If not *Pure Harmony* or one of the other two, then a tender from the main fleet."

Zhuan licked his dry lips, like dragging dead meat over sandpaper. "What's in that ship, anyway?"

A momentary silence. "I don't know, *Exhortation*. The orders come down from on high, and command says it's classified. But they want that thing grounded, and that's what we're going to do."

"We?" Zhuan was tempted to say to himself.

"We'll hold the Mexic warships off your back for as long as we can," Skidjai said. "They'll tear through us sooner or later, so we're counting on you to get this right the first time."

So there was the "we" Zhuan had been missing. The other ships in the blockade would be sacrificing themselves, if necessary, to provide Zhuan the opportunity to throw himself into the path of a rocket traveling at five kilometers per second. The impact would, at the very least, cost the launch vessel its inertia and keep it from breaking free of Fire Star's gravity well. And at worst...?

Zhuan glanced around the bridge. He looked at the steersman, in whose hands their survival would rest, if the two craft came into close contact. Zhuan had only served with one pilot who might have been able to pull off the kind of maneuver that Skidjai had outlined, but Steersman Ang had been arrested the year before and sent off to Baochuan to await sentencing. The current crewman to occupy Ang's seat was competent, no question, and his conduct above reproach, but he lacked Ang's finesse and gentle touch, and Zhuan doubted seriously that he could successfully complete that complicated a maneuver.

"More coordinates received, my captain," the communicationist relayed, as the speakers overhead fell to hissing static. The *Pure Harmony* carried a full complement of computators, who would have been busy calculating the trajectory and velocity of the launch vessel based on observations. Already, before Zhuan even gave the order, the sound of magnetic beads shuttling back and forth over greased metal rods could be heard, as the navigator worked his abacus, plotting out their course.

"Orders, my captain?" The steersman's hands rested on the controls, light as an *erhu*-fiddle player's on the strings.

In the viewport the black speck atop the plume of flame grew larger and larger still. Though it was flatly impossible, Zhuan fancied he could hear the sound of its approach, and in his mind it sounded exactly like the growl of a bear.

The weaponeer sat ready at the fire control station, knowing that there was little the weapons under his hand could do in the circumstances, but eager to try, nonetheless.

"It's the *Pure Harmony*, my captain," the communicationist reported from behind Zhuan. "They want to know why we're still at station keeping."

Zhuan closed his eyes, for a moment in red-lidded darkness as the light of the approaching vessel glared through the viewport. He thought back to those early voyages, the comforting silence of the long passage in the interplanetary gulf between Earth and Fire Star, and the peaceful solitude of the return voyage, the holds filled with ore, the passenger compartments standing quiet and empty. There had been a kind of serenity in that stillness that Zhuan had come to rely upon, in those years, when his youthful dreams of adventure and glory had been forgot, and he had found his true place in the universe. That was what the war had cost him; it had taken that serenity, and left only this inescapable fear in its place.

"Navigator." Zhuan opened his eyes, and cycled a deep breath in through his nostrils and out through his mouth. The crewmen turned to look at him, expectantly. None were eager to rush to their deaths, but they were loyal to the Dragon Throne, and willing to do whatever was asked of them. "Plot a heading away from the engagement. Steersman, get us out of harm's way."

The crew exchanged uneasy glances.

"Sir?" The steersman was the first to speak, head tilted to one side.

"You heard me," Zhuan repeated. "Get us out of here. Back to Zhurong. We're overdue for leave, as I recall."

The crew looked from one to another, unsure how to respond.

If the minister of rites had been at his post, he'd have removed Zhuan from command on the spot, and appointed another officer to take charge. But the minister was strapped to his bunk in the crew quarters with rheumatic distress, and none of the other bridge officers were rushing forward to take responsibility for deposing the captain, an action that, without the minister's blessing, would be mutiny. Of course, refusing to follow a superior's direct order in combat was tantamount to signing one's own death warrant. Ironic that the very protocol that Zhuan was breaking was the one which was now keeping him in command.

"Steersman," Zhuan's tone was suddenly threatening, his eyes narrowing. "You have your orders, sir."

"Yes, my captain," the steersman reluctantly answered, then turned back to his station.

As the Mexic launch vessel approached, now no longer a speck but a menacing tower of black, the

Exhortation began to move, not toward a collision but away from it.

"The *Pure Harmony* is hailing again." The communicationist sounded harried, defeated. "They're... they're not happy."

"I can imagine," Zhuan said with a smile. "Cut the receiver, will you, communicationist?"

As the nose of the *Exhortation* swung around, the disc of Fire Star slipped to one side, and the ships of the blockade came into view. To the port side, Zhuan and the others could just see the launch vehicle thundering by atop its fiery plume. To starboard they watched as one of the Middle Kingdom warships suddenly exploded in a gout of flame as the explosive projectiles of the Mexica burst through the hull, the blaze quickly extinguished as the ship's atmosphere boiled off into the cold vacuum.

The crew muttered to one another, quietly, their eyes cutting back to Zhuan. The captain hit the buckle that released the straps holding him to the seat, and drifted up and forward.

"Head us back to Zhurong," the captain repeated, as he maneuvered toward the hatch at the rear of the bridge that led toward the craft's main corridor. "Communicationist, I'm leaving you in command."

"Sir?" The communicationist raised his eyebrows, eyes widened with worry. "Where... where will you be?"

"In my quarters," Zhuan said, and passed through the hatch. "Awaiting the inevitable."

The heated hydrogen propellant, at the rear of the *Exhortation*, poured through the thrust aperture, pushing the craft along. The vibrations of its rumbling carried through the ship, and as Zhuan paused and laid his hand against the bulkhead, the sound of it was faintly audible, just at the edge of hearing.

To Zhuan, it sounded just like the growl of a bear who finds his cage door left open wide, and his trainer slumbering unawares just beyond.

CHAPTER TWO

Bannerman Yao Guanzhong sat on a metal bench, his legs in shackles, his hands resting on the table before him. Opposite the bench were two chairs, unusually ornate for so austere a chamber, which to all appearances were actually constructed of carved wood. Not formed plastics with imitation grain, but real sticks of dead vegetable matter worked into shape by knife, plane, and awl. On Fire Star, plants were a prized commodity, carefully cultivated in greenhouses, cherished for their ability to transmute carbon dioxide into breathable oxygen, and no one would have dreamed of chopping down a full-grown tree to make something as frivolous as a wooden chair. This pair must have been shipped from Earth, carefully packed in a cargo hold, a small luxury brought to this barren world.

The chairs were empty. Yao had been waiting for some time, but he was patient. He knew what was coming to him, and was in no mood to speed its arrival. It was quiet there, in the interrogation chamber in the heart of Fanchuan Garrison, deep in the Tianfei Valley, and Yao closed his eyes, for the moment reveling in the unexpected solace and stillness. Eleven terrestrial years Yao had been on Fire Star, fighting the forces of the Mexic Dominion on land, in the air, and in the vacuum, and silence was as precious a commodity to him as all the plants and trees in all the greenhouses in all of Fire Star. Out on the surface Yao was never without his surface suit, its elastic constriction countering the lower atmospheric pressure of the red planet, his chest encased in a hard-shell carapace, a helmet over his head. And even if sound traveled poorly in the thin Fire Star air, the sounds of Yao's own body were never far from his ears, the rhythm of his breath and the pounding of his heart rattling around his helmet. And in the vacuum above Fire Star it was even worse, enclosed in a bulky pressure suit, an island of noisy bodily functions, the silence of the void always just beyond his reach.

Fanchuan Garrison was pressurized, close to Earth-normal, and the circulated air heated to a comfortable temperature. The walls were constructed of a concrete formed from the reddish-orange sands of Fire Star itself, and had a vaguely pinkish tint to them. But they were thick enough to block any noise from passing through, either that from without passing in, or that from within passing out, and it seemed to Yao almost like being struck deaf, as the sound of his own steady breathing was swallowed by the empty space around him. In time, he began to hear a high-pitched whine, and for a brief moment worried that it signaled some incoming attack, like the whistle of incoming mortars that he had grown to know so well in his days patrolling the border with the Mexic Dominion in the Vinland province of Tejas. Then Yao forced himself to relax when he remembered that this whine was what silence sounded like, the hum of an empty room. It had been too long since last he heard it.

The silence was interrupted when the door behind Yao suddenly opened. Shackled to the bench by his ankles, Yao was unable to rise, as long training and protocol impelled him to do, and so he was forced to lift fractionally from the bench, leaning heavily on the table, turning from the waist to see who entered.

The older man and somewhat younger woman seemed to take no notice of Yao, but rounded the table and seated themselves in the wooden chairs, the man setting down a thick folder on the table before him.

Yao dipped his head, eyes down, waiting to be addressed.

The man wore the long dark surcoat and pants of the Eight Banners dress uniform. Yao had such a suit, packed somewhere in his personal belongings, but hadn't had occasion to wear it in... months? Years, perhaps? But while Yao's uniform was emblazoned with the image of a bear, insignia of a fifth-rank military officer, this man's garment spoke of a much more elevated standing. Embroidered across his chest was a *qilin* in a verdant field, fire bursting from the mythical beast's flanks, its teeth bared and horns sharpened to points. It was the insignia badge of a first-rank officer, hand-picked by the emperor himself. In all of Fire Star, so far as Yao knew, there was only one officer of that rank currently stationed, the commander of the Eight Banners himself, General Qiao Bi.

Yao had seen General Qiao only once, from a distance, and then in a surface suit. Some very powerful people must have been annoyed by the questions Yao persisted in asking, to merit a personal audience with the general himself.

So far, General Qiao had not looked at Yao, but had opened the file on the table before him, reviewing the tightly printed lines of characters on page after page after page.

From the corner of his eye, Yao regarded the woman sitting at the general's side. Unlike the general, who wore the ornate surcoat of a bannerman, the woman was wearing a plain gray tunic and pants, unmarked and unadorned. If Yao hadn't known better, he would have taken her for a merchant's daughter, or a clerk in a shop. But there was no road Yao could imagine that would have led a merchant or a clerk to the hidden heart of Fanchuan Garrison, and a seat beside the general himself. Yao suspected who the woman was, but was reluctant to even voice it in his thoughts, for fear of what it suggested.

The general continued to review the file. Yao knew this was solely for theatrical effect. The general would have known everything it contained before walking into the room. This was for Yao's benefit, establishing the balance of authority and power. The message was clear: Yao waited at the general's pleasure, and the general was far from pleased.

Finally, the general closed the file again, and folded his hands. Only now did he raise his eyes and look across the table at the bannerman shackled to the bench.

"Bannerman Yao Guanzhong?" The general voiced it as a question, as though there was any doubt. Yao bobbed his head once, a precise movement, indicating assent. "I am General Qiao Bi." Again, as if doubt could remain. "And this"—he turned fractionally in his seat and indicated the woman with the smallest of gestures, one finger lifting for the briefest of instants before falling again—"is Agent Wu." The general paused. "She speaks for the Eastern Depot."

Those few words were freighted with considerable meaning, and Yao's suspicions were confirmed. The woman was an Embroidered Guard, one of the emperor's secret police and intelligence gatherers. Soldiers like Yao spent their entire careers hoping not to come to the attention of an agent of the Eastern Depot.

So Yao's quest for answers had brought him beneath the gaze of the supreme commander of the Eight Banners and a representative of the emperor's secret police? Yao suppressed a sneer. Even if he had known where it would end, he'd have done nothing differently. Bad enough to have been forced to stand by and watch so many innocents killed, needlessly; he could not have left their deaths a mystery.

"Now," the general continued, tapping the file under his fingers, "your record is an impressive one, bannerman. Served with distinction for several tours along the border with the Mexic Dominion, before being transferred to Fire Star in the forty-second year of the Taikong emperor. For more than ten years your performance record has been spotless, with numerous commendations from your superiors for service above and beyond. But it would appear that you have been asking a great many questions of late, along quite inappropriate lines."

Yao bristled, but years of training kept him from voicing the first response that appeared in his thoughts. "Yes," he said at length, his voice straining. "I have been asking questions."

The general nodded, thoughtfully, and pursed his lips. "And yet your file indicates that you were ordered to abandon this inquiry by your superiors on at least two occasions."

"Three, actually, my general."

The general cocked an eyebrow, and the color started to rise in his cheeks. "Meaning what, precisely?"

"I was ordered by my superiors on three separate occasions to abandon the inquiry, my general."

Yao didn't intend the answer to be mocking, but it was clear the general took it as such. He fixed Yao with a hard stare. "And on these *three* occasions, did you fail to comprehend your orders in this regard? Were your superiors *unclear* in their instructions?"

Yao shook his head. "There was no confusion, my general."

The general regarded Yao for a moment, taking several deep breaths, wearing an expression suggesting a mental state not completely unlike sympathy. Finally, Qiao spoke again, breaking the silence. "The events surrounding the Shachuan Station Massacre were indeed tragic and unfortunate, bannerman." The general paused, moistening his lips and searching for the precise phrase. "But difficult decisions must be made in wartime, and this is no exception."

Yao's hands tightened to fists on the table's surface, but he remained still and silent.

"The attack on Shachuan Station cost many lives," the general continued, "but in the balance there was considerable gain." The general sighed, and pushed the file away from him, toward the center of the table's surface. "And it appears that, due to your insistence on overturning stones that should remain untouched, the Shachuan Station Massacre has claimed yet one more life."

Yao had no doubt whose life General Qiao meant. Contravening direct orders, as he had done, was a serious enough offense in its own right. But discovering what Yao had about the truth of the attack, and the orders associated with it, had led him to learn sensitive information several levels above his own security rating, an offense punishable by the severest methods.

Agent Wu of the Eastern Depot had remained silent throughout the exchange, sitting almost serenely beside the general, unspeaking. But now she leaned forward, interrupting Qiao with a gentle touch on his elbow. When she spoke, her voice sounded gentle and soothing, but Yao could hear steel hidden beneath. Yao remembered what he had heard about the training suffered by anyone inducted into the Embroidered Guard, and tried not to imagine what sort of person walked out at the other end of such an experience.

"Perhaps," she said, her voice like petals floating on still waters, hiding sharks circling beneath, "there is an alternative to execution." She treated Yao to a smile that chilled his blood. "Perhaps there is one final service that Bannerman Yao can perform for the Dragon Throne."

The general sat back, his arms folded across his chest, while Agent Wu began to explain. "Tell me, Bannerman Yao. What do you know of Xolotl?"

CHAPTER THREE

The cell was small, no more than a few paces to a wall, and in the last three days Zhuan Jie had memorized every square centimeter.

Cut into the western cliff-face of the Great Yu Canyon's high walls, Baochuan Station had been one of the first settlements on the red planet Fire Star, built on a thermal vent that supplied the structure with water and power. The station had been abandoned when the more advanced habitats of the Tianfei Valley were constructed, and stood empty for some years, but with the onset of the Second Mexic War nothing was left to waste, and Baochuan was reclaimed and put to other uses.

A lifetime before, a young Zhuan had helped construct the station, along with the technicians' corps of the Treasure Fleet, back before there was such a thing as the Interplanetary Fleet, when the Dragon Throne had naively assumed that Fire Star was its for the taking. Then the Mexica had attacked the colonists, more than a dozen terrestrial years ago, and the long conflict that the Middle Kingdom called the Second Mexic War began.

Zhuan was sure that the Mexica have their own name for the conflict. Presumably something appropriately blood-soaked and brutal. But if they did, he'd never heard it.

All those years ago, when he had only just met Thien Ziling and was groping toward something called love, not yet fully a man, Zhuan could never have guessed that Baochuan might one day house a military prison, or that he himself would be imprisoned there. But then, at that age, Zhuan would never have guessed that he would spend more than a quarter of his life waging war.

Zhuan had been taken into custody by the authorities when the *Exhortation* docked at Zhurong moonbase, clapped in irons, and escorted to a cloud-flyer that carried him down to the planet's surface, here to Baochuan prison, to await trial. And it was here that Zhuan had waited, the three days since.

He had little doubt what the verdict would be, and could well imagine what punishment his sentence would carry.

In his more charitable moments, Zhuan tried to fool himself that it was for the sake of his crew that he refused to ram the Mexic launch vessel, and that it was their lives he'd been saving. But in his darker moments, in the long hours of the night, it was not so easy to lie, even to oneself.

The cell reminded Zhuan of his berth on the *Jade Maiden*, the craft that had first carried him from

Earth to Fire Star. The light from the element in the cell's ceiling cast the same weak illumination, and the ever-present smell of the latrine trench in the far corner brought to mind the inescapable stench of dung from the stalls in the cargo hold. If Zhuan closed his eyes, it was almost as if he was back there again, in that cramped hull, still dreaming of adventure and romance, his thoughts not yet beaten into proper shape by reality.

There was no furniture in the room, just a thin pallet along one wall, a bowl of burnished metal for food, a bamboo flask for water, the latrine-trench cut into the concrete floor, and the heavy steel door.

Zhuan sat cross-legged on the pallet, his eyes closed, imagining that he was anywhere else but here. Imagining that he was anyone else but Zhuan Jie. He remembered a poem about a man and a butterfly, but could not recall the details. It would not be so bad to be a butterfly, Zhuan thought. A brief life of beauty, free from care, and ended before life went on too long. It sometimes seemed that Zhuan's life had gone on too long, as much as he was in no hurry to see its end. If he had died as a young man, and never known war, would it have been such a tragedy? Mightn't he have been happier to die while still a boy? But not before he first ventured into the void. No, not that. Those memories he would not trade for any happiness.

Zhuan's wandering reverie was interrupted by the clang of steel on concrete, as the door to his cell slammed open. He opened his eyes, sure that the end had come for him at last. Now it would be sentencing and summary execution for gross dereliction of duty. He hoped that it wouldn't hurt.

To his surprise, though, the guards who dragged him from the cell did not usher him to an audience with a disciplinary committee. Instead, he found himself being escorted to the hangar bay, where a military cloud-flyer shuttle waited. There he was trundled onboard, and shackled to the posts of an acceleration chair. There were four others already seated, like him wearing drab prisoners' tunics and pants. Three were strangers to Zhuan, but one was very familiar indeed.

Before Zhuan could make eye contact, a pilot vaulted into the cloud-flyer, a list in his hand. He checked the names of the five prisoners—Zhuan, Ang, Cai, Nguyen, and Paik—and once he was satisfied that he had the right men, he signaled to one of the guards. Together the guard and the pilot sealed the hatch, and then moved to the forward end of the cloud-flyer. The pilot began the preflight sequence, while the guard swiveled his chair to keep careful watch on the prisoners, in his hands a pistol, a saber at his side.

With a building scream, the cloud-flyer taxied out of the hangar, onto the runway set into the canyon floor beyond Baochuan prison. The craft began to accelerate down the runway, forcing the prisoners back into their chairs, while the rear-facing guard leaned forward fractionally, straining against the straps securing him in place. And when it sounded as though the whine of the craft's engines could grow no higher, no louder, the cloud-flyer lifted off the ground and was airborne.

Through a port in the side of the craft, Zhuan could see the outline of Baochuan prison as they banked to the south, looking like a series of irregular shadows on the canyon wall. Then the craft righted itself, and all that was visible through the ports on either side was cloudless pink sky.

Zhuan tried to catch the eye of the prisoner opposite him. He was thinner than he'd been a year before, when last Zhuan had seen him, and for a moment Zhuan supposed that it might have been another man, but when the guard had read off the list of names it'd been confirmed. Ang Xunhuo, one of the finest pilots and most dangerous gamblers Zhuan had ever met, who until late the previous year had been the steersman of the *Exhortation*. Then Ang had run afoul of the authorities while on leave on Zhurong, and Zhuan had found himself in need of another steersman.

But Ang refused to meet Zhuan's eye. Finally, his curiosity getting the better of him, Zhuan leaned forward. "Steersman Ang. What is this about?"

Ang turned and regarded him with a sly smile. "Not steersman any longer, my captain…"

"No talking!" The guard at the front of the cloud-flyer banged the heel of his pistol's grip against the inside hull of the cloud-flyer, resounding like a drum. "Or else!"

Ang rolled his eyes, almost comically, in the guard's direction, and shrugged. Then, holding his hands before his mouth, his wrists manacled together like all the other prisoners, he mimed sewing his lips shut.

Zhuan didn't know if the rest of the prisoners were as ignorant as he was about the purpose of this journey—or of what awaited them at its end—but from their expressions he supposed they are just as much in the dark. Ang was no help, either, having turned back to the window with a bemused grin, leaning over as far as possible to watch the reddish-orange ground slide beneath them, far below.

After the dim illumination of the cell in Baochuan prison, the bright glare of the midday sun through the viewports caused Zhuan's eyes to water, and he squeezed them shut. The sunlight warmed him, too, helping melt the chill that had set into his bones after three days in the bare concrete cell, and Zhuan felt himself beginning to drowse.

Drifting on the edge of wakefulness and slumber, Zhuan slipped into a kind of hypnagogic state, in which the distant thrum of the cloud-flyer's engines became voices, just at the edge of hearing, and he imagined that the other prisoners were talking secretly to one another, thinking that he slept. But the voices that he imagined were indistinct and vague, and though he struggled in his dreamy state to understand what they were saying, their meaning eluded him.

Zhuan was rousted to full wakefulness when the cloud-flyer landed with a noisy bump. Shaking his head, as though to knock his thoughts back into place, Zhuan looked out the viewport and saw familiar bunkers hulking to the west, which after searching his memories he finally recognized as Fanchuan Garrison, the seat of military command on Fire Star, and home to the commanders of both the Army of the Green Standard and the Eight Banners, and to the admiralty of the Interplanetary Fleet.

When the cloud-flyer had come to a rest, the hatch was opened from the outside, and a phalanx of Green Standard guardsmen greeted them from the pavement beyond.

One by one the guard who had ridden herd on them since Baochuan unshackled the prisoners from the acceleration chairs, and they were ushered out onto the pavement. One of the prisoners, a bear of a man whom the guard had identified as Paik Gui Jin, was snoring peacefully when his turn came around, and when shaken roughly awake by the guard seemed stirred to anger. So genial in his slumber, with his rest interrupted Paik seemed like another man entirely, and if not for the chains which still bound his ankles and wrists he might have done considerable injury to the guard. As it was, Paik was knocked to the floor of the cloud-flyer, and then dragged bodily out of the hatch by the guards beyond.

The Green Standard guardsmen took over custody of the prisoners from the cloud-flyer guard, and then escorted the five away from the landing strip, in through a heavily guarded entrance and along labyrinthine corridors and passageways to a long, narrow room buried deep within Fanchuan Garrison. There were three doors in the room, the one through which they'd come, one on the far wall, and one to their left. Along the unbroken wall was a low bench. The five prisoners were ordered to seat themselves on the bench and remain silent, while the guardsmen took up positions on either end, their weapons at the ready.

One of the guardsmen confirmed their names once more from a list, asking each man to identify himself. Then he took the list through the door opposite the bench, closing it behind him.

It was difficult to judge the passage of time in the windowless room, but Zhuan figured that it was close to an hour before the guardsman returned. He referred to the list still in his hand, and then called out for the prisoner named Nguyen Trang to step forward.

Nguyen stood, and kept standing for some time. He was one of the tallest men that Zhuan had ever seen, but not lanky in the slightest. As broad as he was tall, Nguyen was a mountain disguised as a man. But his face resembled that of a child, down to the somewhat childish expressions which flitted across it. It seemed that Nguyen was not one who filtered his thoughts or feelings, but who openly displayed his inner landscape in the contours of his face. He looked like a happy puppy when his name was called, eyes widening with excitement, but then seemed to recall the uncertainty of their position, and that wonder was replaced by naked fear.

As Nguyen took a step forward toward the doorway, his progress was interrupted. The man sitting beside him, whom the guard had identified as Cai Yingtai, was of average height, but thin and gawky, with large ears and a protruding laryngeal prominence, what the Vinlanders called an "Adam's apple." Wearing an expression of unsullied innocence, Cai hooked his foot out, and tripped Nguyen's first step. The man-mountain stumbled forward, hands out before him, and came crashing down onto the hard floor.

As Cai began to laugh at his little prank, Nguyen rushed up from the floor, hands as far apart as his manacles would allow, murder in his eyes. He lunged toward the small man still sitting on the bench, a wordless howl of rage on his lips. Only the intervention of the guardsmen on either side, dragging Nguyen off and away, saved Cai from a quick and painful death.

As Nguyen was escorted, at gunpoint, through the open doorway, Zhuan revised his opinion of the man-mountain. Not only the tallest man Zhuan had ever met, whose child-like face made plain every thought or feeling that passed through him, but also a terrible opponent capable of great violence when roused to anger.

A good part of an hour passed, and then Nguyen was led back out of the room. Rather than being returned to the bench, he was escorted to the other end of the hall, and ushered through the door opposite that through which they had entered. Then the man named Cai was summoned, and passed through the door also.

A short while later Cai came back out, and was taken through the door at the end of the hall, and Paik was escorted through. Then Paik came out and Ang went through.

Zhuan was the last left on the bench, and from this vantage he was able to see each of the prisoners as they were led back out of the doorway and escorted away. Their expressions were maddeningly unreadable. Cai came back from the room beyond with a stricken look on his face, and Nguyen seemed confused, but Paik had just looked bored on his exit. Ang, for his part, looked as though his mind was racing, looking for some way to turn the circumstances to his advantage. Zhuan had seen that look before, when Ang still served on the *Exhortation* and gambled with the other crew; it was the expression Ang wore when he held a losing hand that he was sure could still be bluffed into a victory.

Finally, it was Zhuan's turn. His name was called out by the guardsman at the door. Rising from the bench, Zhuan crossed the room to pass through the door and see what awaited him.

CHAPTER FOUR

"It's called the *Dragon*."

The rough-hewn man with the *qilin* badge of a first-rank officer stitched across the chest of his Eight Banners dress uniform slid a lithograph across the table to Zhuan Jie.

"Strange name for a Mexic vessel," Zhuan said, looking up from the image.

"It's our code name for the craft," said the man wearing the red surcoat of the Interplanetary Fleet's dress uniform, the insignia of a fleet admiral on his breast. "And it's no longer a Mexic vessel, to be precise. It's ours."

There had been three people seated across the table when Zhuan was led in. A general of the Eight Banners named Qiao, an admiral of the Interplanetary Fleet named Geng, and a woman introduced only as Agent Wu. So far the woman had not spoken, but the admiral paused and glanced at her before continuing, almost as if looking for permission.

"Came down after a firefight with a reconnaissance patrol," Admiral Geng said. "Impacted on Gonggong, with minimal damage to the craft's structural integrity. The crew weren't so lucky. Their radio had been shot out in the exchange, and they were unable to call for any assistance. The last of them died just as our salvage team was getting the hatch pried open."

"A salvage team of bannermen," General Qiao was quick to amend.

The admiral nodded in the general's direction, a conciliatory gesture. "As you say. In any event, once the bodies were cleared out, and as much of the blood as possible, our artificers went to work restoring the craft's systems to full functioning. As well as accommodating for the more..." He paused, grimacing slightly. "...brutal aspects of the craft's control mechanisms. The lead artificer reports that the newly christened *Dragon* should be vacuum-worthy in another two days' time."

Zhuan studied the image before him, the oblong, lozenge-shaped body, with looping armatures from the dorsal and ventral sides. A brutal design, so unlike the baroque curves of a Middle Kingdom vessel.

"What is this to do with me?" Zhuan looked up, his gaze taking in the three people before him.

The two men glanced at each other, then to the woman, before the general finally answered. "Have you ever heard of Xolotl?"

Zhuan shook his head.

The general's eyes cut to the silent Agent Wu, and he continued. "There have been rumors about a secret Mexic base for some time, fragmentary reports and whispers from the lips of dying prisoners. But until recently, we've been unable to ascertain the base's existence, much less its location."

"For years," Admiral Geng said, folding his hands on the table before him, "the strategists of the Middle Kingdom have wrestled with the question of precisely where the Mexic fleet is based. They don't come all the way from Earth for each sortie, clearly. But neither are they based on or around Fire Star. And yet time and again the Mexica are able to get warships in orbit around Fire Star, or attack ships of the Dragon Throne in the interplanetary gulf between the orbits of Fire Star and Earth. It's long been theorized that the Mexica employ some sort of orbital base, but all attempts to locate it have been stymied."

"Until now," said Agent Wu, with a slight smile. "Recently, the Eastern Depot received intercepted transmissions that proved to be coded Mexic communications. These were decrypted by the Eastern Depot's best cryptographers, and were revealed to contain information not only about the location of Xolotl, but also about its security protocols and pass-codes." Her voice unsettled Zhuan; sounding like honey and sweetness, with something toxic and sharp just beneath the surface. She treated Zhuan to a sweet-seeming smile, and then pulled another lithograph from the file before her, and flipped it across the table to him.

Zhuan leaned forward, keeping his hands in his lap. The lithograph depicted an asteroid, the image apparently taken at a considerable distance, if the graininess could be assumed to indicate high-magnification.

"Once we knew where to look," Agent Wu continued, "it was a matter of ease to find. Using a high-powered remote-viewing mirror, we were able to find out even more about the asteroid. It's over two kilometers in length, and follows an elliptical orbit around the sun, between the orbits of Earth and Fire Star. For months at a time it tracks very near Fire Star, just a few degrees off the red planet's orbital plane. The delta-v requirements to get from Earth to Xolotl, or from there to Fire Star, are comparatively low. Its close proximity to Fire Star makes it an ideal staging ground for the Mexic forces, and it is believed that Xolotl acts as the home base for the majority of the Mexic fleet and ground forces. They've even managed to put enough of a spin on the asteroid that the hollowed interior must have an appreciable gravity, somewhere around that of Fire Star."

General Qiao shifted forward in his seat, splaying his fingers wide on the table's surface, looking like a predator about to pounce on its prey. "This Xolotl is just the thing we've been after, all this time. If the forces of the Dragon Throne can successfully knock this rock out of the sky, we could deal a crippling blow to the Mexic Dominion's ability to wage war."

"Come to that," Admiral Geng put in, "if we take out Xolotl, we might end the threat posed by the

Dominion altogether, in the vacuum and on Fire Star definitely, and possibly even on Earth itself."

Zhuan frowned. "Again, and begging your pardon, but what is this to do with me?" He glanced at the dark shadow of the asteroid on the lithograph. "I'm not expected to *attack* this thing, am I?"

The general shook his head, chuckling. "Don't worry, sailor. We have some *real* soldiers picked out for that particular duty."

The admiral shot the general a sharp look, and seemed to bite back a response, before turning his attention back to Zhuan. "The strike team is already assembled. But we need someone to get them there."

Agent Wu extended a long finger, pointing at the lithograph of the lozenge-shaped Mexic craft. "Which brings us back to the *Dragon*," she said with a slight smile, "and your part in this enterprise."

CHAPTER FIVE

Bannerman Yao Guanzhong was in a crouch, his weight on the balls of his feet, his wrists resting on his knees, while the other three bannermen sprawled on the floor, their legs stretched in front of them, their backs to the cold concrete wall of the chamber. From this position, Yao could spring up in any direction, or dive to either side, if the circumstances required. It was vanishingly unlikely that the circumstances would require any such thing, but Yao'd had the habit drilled into him as a young boy, before ever enlisting with the Eight Banners, and could not shake the conditioning now even if he wanted to do so. As a child at his father's knee, Yao had learned that a soldier was always ready, even at rest, and one could never know when danger might arise. These were lessons Yao's father had learned from his own father, and so on back several generations. Theirs had been a soldiering family since the days of the Guangxu emperor and the First Mexic War, and Yao had been drilled in the proper etiquette and protocols since the moment he could speak, just as he had been drilled in combat and strategy since before he could walk.

The three men with him now had once worn the uniforms of the Eight Banners, though like Yao they were for the moment clad only in prisoners' garb, but there was little to their manner or attitudes suggestive of a soldier's training. One seemed as morose as a disaffected youth, while another was as twitchy as a rabid animal. The third exhibited the same placid serenity shared by holy men and imbeciles, and could as easily have been either.

Like Yao, all had been bannermen, and like him they were all now prisoners. Each had a death sentence on his head already or, like Yao, would have as soon as he got a formal military hearing. But all four men had been offered an alternative to the executioner's blade. If they succeeded in their mission, and destroyed the asteroid called Xolotl, each would receive a full pardon and an honorable discharge from the Eight Banners.

Yao knew that none of them would live to enjoy their success, if it came.

"I'm not going back to Earth," the morose young man finally said, breaking the long silence. "There's nothing for me back there."

No one had asked, and from their expressions the other two cared about as much as Yao did about what the young man did or did not have waiting for him on Earth.

"Look, bug..." began the twitchy man with the burn mark that ran across his nose from one cheek to the other, whose features had the look of Nippon to them, but before he could continue the morose young man cut him off.

"My name is Dea," he interrupted, haughtily. "Dea Chao Ru."

"As I was saying, *bug*," the twitchy man continued, "if I were you I wouldn't worry too much about where you'll be going when this is all over."

"And why not?" Dea's tone was angry but strained, laced with fear.

"Because if we fail, we die on the end of a Mexic warrior's blade, and there's little chance of coming back from that."

"And if we succeed?" Dea lifted his head, proudly. "What then?"

"Then there is even less chance of coming back alive, to Fire Star or Earth or anywhere else. Or didn't they explain to you what this was all about?"

"What's *your* name, friend?" Dea asked.

"Fukuda Uyeda." The twitchy man crossed his arms over his chest, defiantly, pronouncing his name as if it were a challenge.

"Well, Fukuda Uyeda, if you're so convinced this is suicide, why not just kill yourself and get it over with? Seems to me that you long for death like a lover's touch."

Fukuda's lip curled back from his teeth, and his eyes flashed. "Keep your mouth shut, bug."

Dea waved his hand, dismissively. "What are you but a son of a whore and a brother to pigs?"

Without warning, Fukuda launched himself across the floor, and grabbed Dea by the throat. As the younger man's face began to purple, his eyes widening as he batted without effect at the Nipponese man's arms, Fukuda sneered, the burn mark across his nose standing out stark white against his reddening skin, and his voice was a snake's hiss between his clenched teeth. "What did you say about my brother?"

Before Dea began to lose consciousness or Fukuda could think to batter the younger man's head against the pink concrete wall, Yao was across the floor, springing up from his crouch and launching himself at the two men. So focused was the Nipponese that he didn't notice Yao's approach until the bannerman had his arms locked around his throat.

"Let him go," Yao said in Fukuda's ear, scarcely above a whisper. "I won't ask again."

Fukuda seethed, whipping his head from side to side, jerking his shoulders and trying to shake Yao loose, but failing. With a grunt, he shoved Dea away from him, the younger man's head bouncing off the concrete wall, and then held his hands in the air. Fukuda opened his mouth to demand Yao release him, but his air passages were still constricted, and all that came forth was a strained hiss.

Yao waited an eye-blink, then in one smooth motion unwrapped his arms from Fukuda's throat and stepped back, out of the Nipponese's reach. Yao needn't have bothered, since Fukuda was more occupied with trying to regain his breath, his fingertips testing his bruised throat.

There was something slightly amusing about seeing both bannermen crouched on the ground, their hands at their throats, still purple-faced and bug-eyed, but Yao was hardly in a mood to smile. If Dea had been more wary, Fukuda would never have been able to lay hands on him; and if Fukuda had not allowed himself to be carried away with insensible rage, he'd never been taken in a headlock so easily, much less attacked a fellow soldier with so little provocation. Both might have worn the uniform of the Eight Banners, but they were hardly exemplary soldiers.

Which meant there was no reason to address them as exemplary soldiers. A proper bannerman wouldn't need to be reminded not to attack his fellows, but these men might need sterner warnings.

"If you keep this up," Yao said, eyes narrowed, pointing from one man to the other, "then I'll kill you both myself, and that will be an end to it."

"But I…" croaked Dea in objection, but Yao silenced him with a look.

"Have you no pride?" Yao shook his head in disgust.

Fukuda opened his mouth as if to speak, but then met Yao's steely gaze and reconsidered.

"What about you?" Yao said, turning to the third man, who sat still in placid contemplation wearing the empty smile of the holy man or the imbecile. "Have you nothing to add?"

As the man looked up and met his gaze, Yao saw that his eyes were amber. The man had the long nose and red-brown skin of an Athabascan, with a thin beard gone to gray, the hair on his head still black. "What is your name?" the man at last asked, his voice level.

"Bannerman Yao Guanzhong."

Something amused the man, who smiled behind his beard as he nodded in response. "I too am a bannerman, of course," he said, "though it is not my name. It is yours, though, I suspect." The man pulled his legs in, folding them under him, and then rested his hands on his knees. "My name is Syuxtun Haji. As for these discussions"—he gestured with an inclination of his head to Dea and Fukuda— "I'm afraid death doesn't interest me much, in recent days. The people say, 'We shall die and we shall live, and nothing but Time can destroy us,' but they speak without knowledge. In the words of the Prophet, 'It is God who gives you life, then give you death; then He will gather you together for the Day of Judgment about which there is no doubt.' All of us dies, sooner or later. What matter if it be here or there?"

Before Yao's mind could frame an answer, his thoughts were interrupted by the clang of metal on concrete, and a guardsman stood at the open door to their cell.

"Bannerman Yao?" The guardsman motioned to Yao with the rifle in his arms, the barrel trained at the bannerman's chest. "They're ready for you."

CHAPTER SIX

The bannerman who sat across from Zhuan Jie looked tough enough to take a bite of the steel table between them and spit out bullets. It was impossible to judge his age with any precision, but Zhuan supposed he was anywhere from a rough and worn thirty terrestrial years old to a well-preserved fifty. He was of average height, his nose slightly crooked from a badly healed break, with a scar that ran down the left side of his face like the track of a teardrop. But the bannerman didn't look like one who cried very often.

"Captain Zhuan Jie," said the Embroidered Guard, Agent Wu, who stood at the side of the table between them, a thick bundle of files in her hands. "This is Bannerman Yao Guanzhong. You will be sharing authority on this mission…"

"Your pardon, agent," Yao said, interrupting, "but I was given to understand that I was in command."

Agent Wu treated them both to a smile that didn't quite reach her eyes, and nodded. "You will be in command of the strike team, bannerman, and exercise absolute authority once you and your men are delivered to Xolotl. But this is a joint operation between all of the branches of the emperor's military, and Captain Zhuan"—she nodded in his direction—"has been elected to command the transport vessel. Onboard the *Dragon*, Zhuan will be the final authority."

The bannerman regarded Zhuan with his eyes narrowed for a long moment, and then nodded. "Received and understood."

"Splendid." Wu acted as if it had been a request and not an order, which both men knew to be an empty formality. "Now, the balance of your team has been selected, and I have their files here." She dropped the bundle of files onto the table between them. "Naturally, any sensitive areas in their service records will have been redacted. I'm afraid that I'm not at liberty to share all of the details concerning the reasons, but I can tell you that, like yourselves, each of these seven men had been... detained by the military authorities prior to their selection for this assignment. Bannerman Yao, I believe that you have spent some small amount of time with a number of these men, and may have interacted with them, but unless I'm mistaken Captain Zhuan will not have had the opportunity to speak to any of the others, though he did share a cloud-flyer flight with several of them." She paused, and then tilted her head back slightly, as if struck by a sudden memory. "That said, I believe

Captain Zhuan should be very familiar with one of them, at least."

Zhuan picked up the file upon which were inscribed the ideograms "ANG XUNHUO." He opened it, and saw thick black lines obscuring many lines of text. Beside an entry for a previous assignment, he saw his own name listed, along with the name and registry number of the *Exhortation*.

"The briefing is set to begin shortly," Agent Wu said, heading toward the door. "I will leave you to get better acquainted with each other and with these files, and will send for you presently."

The Embroidered Guard inclined her head fractionally before turning, an unnecessary observance of etiquette, and then rapped on the metal door. The guardsman on the other side opened it, his weapon ready, and then when she'd passed through closed it behind her, leaving the two men alone in the chamber.

Zhuan glanced over at the bannerman, who was busy investigating the files before them. Putting Ang's file aside, Zhuan picked up another and began to read.

"By my count, we have three murderers, a thief, a dealer in contraband, an insubordinate, and a conscientious objector."

Yao looked up at the sailor, who sat back on the bench, his arms crossed over his chest.

"Failing to take us into account," the bannerman answered. There was no file in the stack for the sailor sitting before him, and Yao found himself curious as to the reasons for Zhuan's imprisonment.

Yao had spent time with sailors before, and this Zhuan's manner struck him as different, not typical of those who served in the Interplanetary Fleet. There was something lax in his attitude, Yao felt. Zhuan's muscles had the softness that came with long years spent in microgravity, but it seemed that the softness extended to his character, as well as his appearance.

"Indeed," Zhuan said, guardedly. He paused for a moment before continuing. "I've served with the thief, Ang Xunhuo. Thief and gambler, to be precise. But he is also the finest pilot with whom I've ever served, and I have no doubts about his abilities to perform his duties, if his vices can be kept in check." He glanced at the files spread on the table. "I'm a poor judge of a soldier's worth, though. What is your opinion of the rest?"

Yao's shoulders raised in the shadow of a shrug. "Their records speak for themselves. The three bannermen, at least, have skills that should prove useful, though each is markedly lacking in discipline. Syuxtun's skills with language and communication should prove a valuable asset, as should Fukuda's expertise with demolitions. And if Dea's marksmanship scores are to be believed, I would not want to find myself on the business end of his firearm. As for the guardsmen..." Yao waved a hand at the other three files, those for Cai, Nguyen, and Paik. "They may simply be the class of men allowed entry into the Green Standard Army these days, for all I know. This war has taxed the resources of the Middle Kingdom, but even so..."

Zhuan gave a slight smile. "So the old rivalries persist?" He raised an eyebrow, in an expression Yao felt verged dangerously close to mocking. "Sailors don't trust guardsmen who don't trust bannermen who don't trust anyone, is that it?"

Yao controlled his reaction, and drew his lips into a tight line. "I do my duty, and judge others by their ability and willingness to do the same."

Zhuan's eyebrow rose even higher. "And was it the observance of your duty that brought you to this end?" The sailor wagged his fingers toward the files. "Leading a team of reprobates on a suicide mission, no doubt to escape some harsher punishment here on the ground?"

The bannerman bristled, teeth gritted. "Do you question my honor?"

Zhuan raised his hands in front of him, palms forward, and shook his head. "No, of course not," he said, in a tone that suggested the opposite. "Merely making an observation."

Yao raised his chin, and regarded Zhuan through narrowed eyes. "I am a soldier of the Eight Banners, and loyal to the Dragon Throne. Whatever the circumstances that led me to this pass, nothing has changed that."

"Duly noted." The sailor nodded, a placating gesture. "In any event, I wouldn't be so quick to dismiss the qualities of our three guardsmen of the Green Standard Army. One of them, Nguyen, is a mountain of a man, if perhaps with a child's face and mind, and I would prefer never to be the focus of his rage. And I saw Paik attack an armed guard while he himself was still unarmed and with bound hands and feet, so he certainly doesn't lack for courage. As for Cai, I can only say that in addition to the glint of mischief I saw in his eyes there burned the fire of intelligence, so he may be one who fights more with his mind than with his muscles."

Yao was silent for a moment, collating his thoughts. "And you?" he finally said, leaning forward. "What crime or sin did you commit out in the world that earned you this commission? Whom did you anger to merit the captaincy of a ship of no return?"

The sailor's eyes flashed angrily, and a cloud passed over his features. The laxness and easy humor Yao had seen in him suddenly faded, a steely resolve in its place, with something like fear firing around the edges. "You..." Zhuan began, then broke off, taking a deep breath. "You want to know why I...?"

Yao would never learn just what Zhuan had been about to say, as the sailor's words were interrupted by the sound of the steel door clanging against the concrete wall, as a pair of guardsmen entered, their weapons drawn.

"You are summoned," one of the guardsmen said, while the other collected the files from the table. "And be quick about it. I'm in no mood to anger an Embroidered Guard today."

Yao almost smiled, and followed the guardsmen out of the room, leaving Zhuan to trail in his wake.

CHAPTER SEVEN

Lithographs printed on transparencies were projected by bright lights onto the featureless wall of the chamber. General Qiao and Admiral Geng sat at either side, while Agent Wu walked in front of the image, a telescoping pointer in her hands, indicating areas of interest. She'd already covered the basics of the captured Mexic craft, the *Dragon*, and had changed the transparency to one depicting a lumpy, roughly cylindrical asteroid.

"This is Xolotl," the Embroidered Guard went on, tapping the end of her pointer against the wall, right in the middle of the projected image. "Up until a few weeks ago, it was nothing but an entry in a logbook in the Directorate of Astronomy in Northern Capital, just a numerical designation and a string of characteristics opaque to anyone not trained in the astronomical arts. And even the imperial astronomers didn't know much, just that it was an asteroid whose orbit crosses that of Fire Star but not of Earth, that it has a semi-major axis of 1.321 astronomical units, and that its absolute magnitude put its diameter at just around one kilometer and a third kilometer, give or take half a kilometer. Just one of thousands of near-Earth asteroids of the type, nothing of note or interest about it." She paused, and glanced around at the nine men seated before her, and smiled. "What a difference a few weeks can make."

Wu changed the transparency again. Now projected behind her was the image of a hollowed-out asteroid in cross-section. She walked to the other side, and as she did the image slid onto and over her body, distorting the lines, making it seem as if she were walking right through the wall of the asteroid like a ghost.

Yao wished that they *could* ghost through the walls of the asteroid, at that. It would save them a considerable amount of trouble.

"This is the interior layout of Xolotl, as best as military intelligence has been able to determine. The asteroid is a little over two kilometers in length, a little less than one kilometer wide, and is rotating on the longest axis. The spin appears to have been imparted by small attitude rockets mounted on the asteroid's surface, and fired periodically as the momentum bleeds off, and the rotational velocity would appear to be fast enough to impart approximately one-third of an Earth standard gravity to the asteroid's inner surface, roughly that of Fire Star."

Agent Wu indicated the concentric circles within the asteroid's cross-section.

"Xolotl is roughly cylindrical, as are the decks, which are nested within one another. The innermost decks would exhibit considerable shear forces, that close to the axis of rotation, so we have to assume that they are reserved for storage or engineering purposes, perhaps power generation. The hangar appears to be here"—she pointed to a blank area at one end the asteroid—"based on changes in reflective patterns visible to our high-powered remote-viewing-mirrors, but it is quite possible there is more than one hangar. After all, this is assumed to be the staging ground for the entire Mexic battle fleet, and that's a considerable number of craft to fit into a volume roughly one and a half cubic kilometers in size."

Another transparency slid into place, this one showing a diagram depicting a series of concentric circles, shaded different values of gray, shot through with lines and geometric shapes, with ideogram labels pointing to the various components. It looked to Yao almost like an astrologer's chart.

"This is the payload," Wu continued, "that you'll be transporting onboard the *Dragon*, and which the strike team has the responsibility for positioning at the asteroid's core."

Beside Yao, Zhuan sucked a breath in through his teeth, wincing almost as if in pain. Then, in a voice barely above a whisper, the sailor muttered, "Ancestors preserve us."

The bannerman was tempted to ask Zhuan what troubled him, but etiquette prevented him from speaking while the Embroidered Guard held the floor. As it happened, his curiosity was soon satisfied when Wu explained what the diagram represented.

"This is an implosion-type fission explosive device, with a destructive capacity in the eighty kiloton range."

There was a ripple of muttering around the room, and more than a few of the men grimaced or scowled as Zhuan had done. Yao gave the sailor an appraising look; it was not every man who could recognize a fission bomb from simply glancing at a diagram.

"Is that safe?" asked the guardsman named Cai, raising his hand to catch Agent Wu's attention.

The Embroidered Guard gave him a queer look, and then glanced up at the projected image. "Well, it *is* a bomb…"

As Cai shook his head, Bannerman Dea leaned forward. "I think what he's asking is, ma'am, is it safe to travel with a bomb like that?"

Agent Wu treated them to a thin smile. "There's a low level of radiation leakage from the fissile material at the heart of the device, to be sure, that even the best shielding couldn't completely stop, but that's a marginal risk, at best." She chuckled, without much humor. "Of course, if you detonate the device onboard the *Dragon* by mistake while en route, I think that radiation leakage will quickly become the least of your concerns."

The answer seemed not to assuage many of the fears festering in the room.

"But even with the destructive capacity of the device, you won't simply be able to drop it in the hangar and run," Agent Wu continued. "If detonated too close to the surface of the asteroid, the explosion will simply vent out into the vacuum, and while the resulting damage might cripple the station, it wouldn't be guaranteed to destroy it. Instead, the payload will have to be carried into the core of the asteroid before detonation. With the force of the explosion directed outward in all directions, the asteroid should be broken up into small enough parts, none of which will be of much use to the Mexica."

"And all of those parts hot enough that they'll glow on their own," Zhuan said, his voice sounding like it came from far away.

"That's the idea," Wu answered with an almost genuine smile.

From the sounds of the muttered discontent around him, it seemed to Yao as though the Embroidered Guard was quickly losing the room. She seemed to notice, as well, as she quickly replaced the transparency of the fission bomb with another, showing a pressure suit, a radio schematic, and a pair of firearms, one pistol, and one carbine.

"This is a special mission," Wu continued, apparently trying to brighten her tone, "and as such it calls for special equipment. You'll be checked out on all of this once you transfer to Zhurong moon-base, before boarding the *Dragon*, but this should give you a quick overview of what you can expect." She stabbed the pointer at the pressure suit. "Our artificers have developed a stealth suit for missions just such as these. Designed to reduce the wearer's thermal profile, they should be virtually invisible to infrared cameras. They carry the same armor rating as our typical combat pressure suits, but don't plan on taking too many hits before the hard shell begins to crumple."

She pointed to the radio schematic. "You'll all be equipped with scrambler radios. These are prototypes, the first to be put into the field. They broadcast over normal radio waves, but the transmissions sound like nothing but sunspot noise to any radio not equipped with a descrambler. You should still keep communications to a minimum, since your broadcast signals could still be tracked, but these should allow you to speak freely when you find it necessary." She next pointed to the two weapons, the pistol and the carbine. "We're not sure what sort of resistance you'll encounter, but we have to assume it will be considerable. The potential fields of combat involved could conceivably cover everything from one-third Earth gravity to zero-gravity, and pressurized climate controlled sections to cold vacuum. You'll all be outfitted with the same bladed weapons you use on Fire Star, but the tactics you employ on the surface to brace yourselves before firing your weapons, to counteract the low surface gravity, potentially won't be available to you on Xolotl. As a result, your standard firearms won't be of much use." A few rows up from Yao, the young bannerman named Dea pulled a face, crossing his arms over his chest defiantly.

"Taking this into consideration, our artificers have stepped up production of these new microgravity firearms. These are adaptations of similar technologies employed to varying degrees of success in recent years, and inherit much of the same limitations. The pistols fire low-mass, high-velocity needle-like flechette projectiles, frangible such that they shatter on impact so as not to puncture a hull. And the carbines fire rocket-propelled ammunition, each projectile leaving the barrel with low velocity before accelerating under its own power. The ammunition has a tendency to explode before…"

At the corner of the room, the admiral of the Interplanetary Fleet, Geng, cleared his throat, interrupting the Embroidered Guard. She looked over and caught his eye, and then nodded. She had evidently been about to outline all of the potential hazards of these microgravity weapons, which Yao knew only too well from personal experience, and Admiral Geng seemed to think that Wu shouldn't squander the faint goodwill the rest of her presentation had just engendered with the men. There were a few expressions around the room that suggested some of the men actually thought a new-model pressure suit and a fancy radio would allow them to come back alive from a suicide mission; it wouldn't do to smash those tenuous hopes by pointing out that they were just as likely to be killed by their own weapons as by the enemy's.

"I think that concludes this stage of the briefing," Agent Wu said, collapsing the telescoped pointer against the palm of her hand and then tucking it into a hidden pocket.

"I agree," General Qiao said, climbing to his feet. He'd done little but scowl since the nine men had been ushered into the room. "There are things to be done, and you won't do them while lounging around here."

With that, the general turned on his heel, marched to the door, and opened it. There were guardsmen waiting outside, at parade rest, and when Qiao snapped his fingers they filed into the room, ready to escort the nine.

"Admiral," Qiao said, with a short nod to his opposite number across the room. "Agent Wu," he continued, nodding in her direction, "this is your show from this point onwards." He spared a quick glance at the nine, and Yao felt his gaze come to rest on him. "Don't disappoint us, men, and don't disappoint the Dragon Throne."

Then the general was gone, shouldering past the guardsmen and out into the corridor.

Admiral Geng watched the general's retreating back for a moment, his expression unreadable, then turned to address the men. "A launch vehicle is waiting on the pad, to carry you to Zhurong and the rest of your mission orientation." Then the admiral signaled the guardsmen, and he followed the general out of the room.

"Come along, men," Agent Wu said, making for the door. "We don't want to keep the launch vehicle waiting."

CHAPTER EIGHT

As they were being strapped into the acceleration chairs, Zhuan looked around the passenger compartment of the launch vehicle, studying the faces of each of the men in turn.

"I hate this part," said Guardsman Paik, scratching at the stubble which dusted his upper lip and scowling. He spoke Official Speech with the slight accent of Choson, his tone languid. "Nearly thirty years we've been on this damned planet, and they still can't get an orbital elevator working yet?"

On Earth, every gram that went from the surface into orbit and beyond for years had been carried by costly launch vehicles, just like the one they now boarded, until roughly seventy years before when the Bridge of Heaven had become fully operational, an orbital elevator rising up from Gold Mountain in Fragrant Harbor. Work had begun on a similar tether, Heaven's Ladder, out on the highlands south of Tianfei

Valley only a few years after the first colonists arrived on Fire Star, but it was a costly and time-consuming construction project. The Bridge of Heaven had taken nearly two decades to construct, and on Earth all of the raw materials necessary for the project's completion had been relatively close at hand. On Fire Star, they either had to be brought from Earth, or located and subsequently mined on the red planet itself or from its moons and nearby asteroids. Even with such limitations and constraints, though, Heaven's Ladder had been more than half completed when the Mexica had first attacked the colonists on Fire Star, and though work had been able to continue intermittently in the following seasons, by the previous year the project had to all intents and purposes been brought to a complete halt, until the southern highlands could be completely pacified and secured.

However, none of these concerns seemed to have much bearing on the Chosonese guardsman's complaints, which appeared to devolve almost entirely on his own comfort.

"I lost friends defending the Heaven's Ladder worksite last year, oaf," snapped Bannerman Fukuda, whose Official Speech was laced with Nipponese inflections. "Perhaps their lives weren't price enough to pay for your comfort?"

Paik shrugged, and rubbed the close-cropped hair on his head with his palms. "Maybe if they were better fighters, they wouldn't have died and the damned elevator would be done by now, neh?"

If he'd not already been strapped into his acceleration chair, Fukuda would have launched himself at Paik. As it was, with murder flashing in his eyes, the

Nipponese began slapping the buckles on the seat's harness, freeing himself from its embrace, while Paik laid back in his seat, his hands folded over his broad belly, eyes half-lidded, as though daring Fukuda to make a move.

Zhuan had carried guardsmen and bannermen aboard the *Exhortation* more times than he could count, but they were seldom under his direct authority, instead being little more than passengers whom he ferried from one location to another. And so, he was unused to issuing orders to infantrymen and commandos. But though they were not yet onboard the *Dragon*, still these would be men under his command, at least until they reached their destination and that authority fell to Bannermen Yao, and Zhuan had no desire to watch the two of them attempt to kill each other before they even left the ground. Yao had yet to board the launch vehicle, being the last to mount the stairs, and the compartment was too cramped for any of their guards to accompany them, so that if Zhuan didn't move to intervene then no one would.

Zhuan was out of his seat before Fukuda had released the last of his harness's buckles, and the captain reached down to push the Nipponese back in his seat. "Stand down, bannerman," he said, his tone level but firm. "It isn't too late for you to make that appointment with the executioner's blade, after all. I'm sure we can find another demolitions expert with a spotty record who could be enticed to take your place."

Fukuda seethed, looking up through narrowed eyes at the captain, but kept his seat.

"And you," Zhuan said, whirling around and pointing a finger in Paik's direction. "Kindly stow your complaints and keep any opinions you might have about the relative merits of other soldiers, living or dead, to yourself, Guardsman Paik. You'd be far easier to replace than Bannerman Fukuda, so don't tempt me."

Paik's eyes opened fractionally wider, and his lip twitched for a moment into a shadow of a sneer, but then he closed his eyelids and feigned slumber.

"Problem, Captain Zhuan?" Yao appeared at the open hatch, with a pair of guards on the stair behind him.

"None, Bannerman Yao," Zhuan replied. As Fukuda began rebuckling his harness, the captain returned to his seat and began to do the same. "Just a minor difference of opinion." He nodded to Yao as the bannerman maneuvered through the cramped space to his own acceleration chair. "Nothing I couldn't handle."

As Yao dropped into his chair and began to settle the harness over his shoulder and legs, his gaze cut from the apparently slumbering Paik to the still-simmering Fukuda, and then back to Zhuan. "As you say, captain," he said at length, his tone suggesting he was less than entirely convinced.

As the bannerman turned his attention away, Zhuan stroked his long mustaches, and wondered why he felt the need to account for himself to Yao. After all, until the *Dragon* reached Xolotl, wasn't he himself in command? So why then did he feel that he would be forever looking for the approval of the bannerman, who was himself only in command of the strike team? What did it matter to Zhuan what Yao thought of him and his fitness to lead?

As the hatch was closed, sealing them into the passenger compartment, Yao spared a glance at the sailor who was to command the en route part of the mission, Zhuan Jie. At the moment, so far as Yao was able to determine, they were all under the direct authority of Agent Wu, who rode up in the launch vehicle's command center with the flight crew. But in short order Yao would find himself under Zhuan's command, and he was hardly sanguine about the prospect.

Yao found himself seated between Steersman Ang and Bannerman Syuxtun. While the sailor to his left fidgeted, uneasy in his seat, the bannerman on Yao's opposite side sat motionless and still, his eyes closed, muttering softly to himself. Straining to hear, Yao could just make out the words he was saying.

"In the name of God, most gracious, most merciful, praise be to God, the Cherisher and Sustainer of the Worlds; most gracious, most merciful; Master of the Day of Judgment. Thee do we worship, and Thine aid we seek."

Yao folded his arms over his chest, leaving the Athabascan to his prayers. While he'd never had much patience for beliefs himself, Yao didn't begrudge others whatever comforts their own might provide. If seeking the aid of supernatural forces helped Syuxtun allay any fears about their impending launch, or what would follow, who was Yao to judge?

Not that Yao had no fears of his own. While they were relatively secure within the confines of Fanchuan Garrison itself, once the torch beneath them lit and the solid fuel rockets of the launch vehicle carried them up from the planet's surface, all bets were off. Not a few launches had been lost in recent years to attacks by Mexic aircraft, though as often as not the launch vehicles had managed to take their Mexic attackers down with them in flames. The Mexica operated on Fire Star from temporary bases scattered all across Fire Star, hidden in the deep ravines of the Forking Paths labyrinth, or in the wide and unpeopled stretches of the southern highlands. The forces of the Dragon Throne managed to locate and attack these bases, from time to time, but the Mexica had the unerring and highly annoying ability to relocate quickly, so that any base that was eliminated was simply replaced immediately by another elsewhere. And taking into account the large stretches of land more or less completely controlled by Mexic occupation forces, this meant that any launch vehicle could easily find itself under attack from craft taking off from any number of Mexic strongholds in the hemisphere.

The deck beneath their feet began to shudder, the vibrations rattling their teeth in their heads, as the solid-fuel engines beneath them began to fire. By this time the launch gantry would have retreated, their guardsmen escorts with it, leaving the launch vehicle alone on the pad. A low rumble could be heard, like distant thunder, and Yao's ears popped as the passenger cabin completed its pressurization. The only viewports in the passenger compartment were high overhead, impossible to see through while strapped in their seats, but there would have been little to see outside had they been able to do so, just vast expanses of reddish-orange sand stretching out to the high walls of the Tianfei Valley in the distance, and the vault of pink sky overhead.

Finally the roar of the engines filled their ears, squashing out any sound, and had Yao not turned to see Syuxtun's lips moving soundlessly he would never have known that the Athabascan continued to pray. And when it seemed that the sound could grow no louder, and the vibrations threatened to shake their flesh loose from their bones, there was a sudden shift, and they were slammed back into their chairs as if by a giant invisible hand, as the forces of acceleration pulled at them, thrust fighting inertia, flattening them in the struggle.

A force several times that of Earth's gravity pulled at them, stretching the flesh of their faces taut against their skulls, and Yao felt his insides rebel as his internal organs were all dragged toward his lower back. Their acceleration chairs were angled backward, so that they faced more or less in the direction of the nosecone high overhead. Yao tried to close his eyes, but the pull of acceleration tugged the lids back open, and he stared at the ceiling of the chamber, teeth gritted.

The launch vehicle jolted and shuddered as the reusable fuel tanks fell away, jettisoned from the main body of the vehicle to fall back to the red planet's surface, buoyed beneath camouflaged pink parachutes, virtually invisible against the Fire Star sky. Then the second stage rockets kicked in, and the press of acceleration on them increased.

Yao knew that the velocity necessary to escape the gravitational pull of Fire Star was less than half that needed to break free of Earth's pull, and wondered as he always did when going aloft how men had managed to make so many repeat launches to Earth orbit in the days before the Bridge of Heaven. The long minutes needed to leave the surface of Fire Star were bad enough, but to endure greater accelerations for longer periods? It was difficult to fathom. Of course, perhaps the more than ten terrestrial years that he had spent on the red planet, more than five Fire Star years living with a gravity that pulled only a third as hard as that of Earth, might have colored his views.

Suddenly, when it seemed that the strain would never end, the forces pushing Yao deep into his chair finally ended, and he could feel himself growing lighter. The roar of the engines, which had blanketed the compartment in a wall of sound, gradually faded to silence.

This was one of the moments when a launch vehicle was at its most vulnerable; coasting into a low orbit, before firing the attitude-adjusting rockets that would orient it toward its destination. Once pointed in the right direction, the main thruster would be fired again, and then the vehicle sent hurtling to its eventual goal—in this case, the larger of Fire Star's two moons, Zhurong. Unlike vehicles designed to stay forever in vacuum, such as those which Captain Zhuan must once have commanded, a launch vehicle was an amphibious craft, intended to rocket up from and then return to the thin Fire Star atmosphere down in the gravity well, while at the same time capable of traversing short distances through the black void.

Amphibious craft of that sort were notoriously difficult to maneuver, their design having to accommodate aerodynamic forces that purely space-going craft could safely ignore. As a result, in this awkward transition period between the thin atmosphere below and the black void of vacuum above, the launch vehicle would be a comparatively easy target for a Mexic attack. The Mexica would need to have a vessel already in orbit to mount an effective assault, of course, which somewhat limited the risk profile, but Mexic stealth vessels were not unheard of, and could sometimes be found masquerading as debris floating in low Fire Star orbit, unnoticed until their weapons were aimed and ready, at which point it was typically too late.

This time, at least, fortune was with them, and the launch vehicle completed its reorientation without incident. Then the thrusters fired once more and the craft began to coast toward Zhurong at speed. Toward the moonbase, where the *Dragon* awaited.

CHAPTER NINE

Once the launch vessel was well on its way to Zhurong, Agent Wu's voice crackled over speakers in the ceiling, letting them know that they were free to move about the compartment until they reached the moonbase. Since the craft was moving at a constant speed, the compartment was in freefall, and as the nine men released the harnesses holding them into their acceleration chairs they drifted weightless up into the empty air.

While the compartment had been cramped when the vehicle was on the ground, and gravity had pinned them to one surface, in weightless conditions its volume was more than ample. The fixtures were utilitarian, to say the least, but it wasn't as if the men would remain onboard for long. Zhurong was somewhere just over nine thousand kilometers from the surface of Fire Star. Having attained escape velocity, five kilometers per second, the craft would now reach the moon in a relatively short amount of time.

Zhuan stretched his limbs, opening and closing his mouth in exaggerated movements to try to work feeling back into his acceleration-squashed lips and cheeks. A short distance off, the man-mountain Guardsman Nguyen hung in mid-air by one of the viewports, looking out into the night.

"Oh, look!" Nguyen's face split in a broad smile. He turned his head, his eyes seeking the nearest face, and saw Zhuan. "Come look at this," he called to the captain, and pointed a finger at the viewport.

Pushing off from the back of his chair, Zhuan drifted across the empty air, alighting next to the guardsman.

"Look at that out there," Nguyen repeated, and Zhuan could hear the echoes of Annam in his accent. The enormous man sounded like an over-excited child, eager to share some new discovery he'd made.

Zhuan peered out, and followed the line of Nguyen's finger. The red arc of Fire Star spread below them, and just above the horizon there flashed a bright light, blazing like the sun.

"What *is* it?" Nguyen's voice was breathless, anticipatory. It was as if he'd just been given a gift and wasn't yet sure what it was.

"Burning Mirror," Zhuan said, steadying himself with a handhold on the bulkhead while turning to face the guardsman. The structure had been knocked out of alignment the previous year by a Mexic orbital gunsling, and it had taken three ships and a crew of men nearly a month to get it maneuvered back into position before its orbit degraded badly enough for it to plunge to the planet's surface below. The *Exhortation* had been one of those ships, and Zhuan had got his fill of the mirror in those long weeks.

Nguyen looked up, his confusion evident, clearly not understanding the reference.

Zhuan smiled, and then nodded toward the viewport and the light beyond. "That's the south pole of Fire Star, and the light is an orbital mirror used to redirect the sun's rays onto the southern polar cap, to raise the surface temperature and thaw the carbon dioxide frozen there."

Nguyen nodded, glanced to the viewport for a moment, and then turned his head back toward Zhuan. "Why?"

Puzzled, Zhuan asked, "Why what?"

"Why do that... that thing?"

Zhuan quirked a smile. "Thaw the carbon dioxide?"

Nguyen nodded, eagerly, almost puppyish.

"A few reasons, really. Increasing the amount of carbon dioxide in the atmosphere, along with the introduction of halocarbons, will help produce a runaway greenhouse effect, gradually raising the surface temperature of the whole planet. And as the temperature rises, hardier plants will be able to survive out in the open, and not just in pressurized farms. Plants take in carbon dioxide and metabolize it, yielding pure oxygen. Assuming that sufficient amounts of nitrogen can be liberated from the nitrate deposits in the soil, given enough time the atmosphere would be breathable."

"Oh." Nguyen's brows knit, and he almost looked as if he were in pain.

"It makes the planet better," Zhuan amended, gently.

"Oh." Nguyen's confusion melted, and he nodded, smiling broadly. "That's good."

Zhurong was the larger and nearer of Fire Star's two moons. The other, Gongong, was roughly half its size and nearly three times as distant. Zhurong was so close to Fire Star, in fact, that it orbited below the synchronous orbit radius, moving around the planet faster than Fire Star itself was revolving. Twice a day it rose in the west and set in the east, unlike the smaller moon that tracked much more slowly from east to west. It was this characteristic that had led the early settlers to name them for the mythical god of fire and his son the water god who in ancient stories had battled across the heavens, hurtling themselves at one another.

The moon was irregularly shaped, with an almost negligible surface gravity, but a nontrivial percentage of its five-and-a-half thousand cubic kilometers of interior volume had been hollowed out and transformed into pressurized habitats, engineering facilities, and shipyards. Most of the base's staff and residents were housed in a pressurized ring that rotated at speed along a gimballed track bored through the living rock of the moon itself. With a radius of several kilometers, this ring was spun up to speeds sufficient to impart a little over one-third Earth's gravity to the living compartments, equivalent to that found on the surface of Fire Star. It was something like an enormous, multi-tiered subway train, its tail joined to its nose, spinning endlessly in the dark.

The rough surface of the moon bristled with defensive systems, turrets and cannons, and gunsling relays. The Zhurong base was one of the most heavily fortified stations in existence, and the time and expense of hollowing large sections of its volume were well justified by the relative security enjoyed by those sheltered within its walls. And by placing the repair depots and shipyards of the Interplanetary Fleet within immense underground hangars buried beneath the moon's surface, the Dragon Throne provided a safe haven for its artificers and technicians to work, secure in the knowledge that they were protected against all but the most destructive of attacks, and those few so unlikely as to be virtually impossible.

The notion of a secured base buried within living rock was apparently one that had also appealed to the Mexic Dominion, if the intelligence gathered by the Eastern Depot was to be believed.

Entry into the Zhurong base was gained through one of several large hangar doors, around which the outer defenses were concentrated. Traffic control was located in secured bunkers just beneath the moon's surface, viewing images fed through cameras mounted outside and communicating with any incoming vessels through coded radio transmissions.

As the launch vessel carrying the nine approached, traffic control exchanged signs and countersigns with the craft's pilots, confirming authorization codes and clearances, all in accordance with the most current security protocols. Finally, and only when traffic control was satisfied as to the craft's bona fides, the bay doors on the moon's nearest side began to open and the launch vessel was advised to maneuver into position.

Attitude rockets spurt quick gouts of heated gas in a syncopated rhythm, adjusting the craft's speed and orientation, and then as graceful as a bird in a blue Earth sky the vessel drifted in and through the open doors.

Retrorockets fired in short bursts, arresting the craft's forward movement, as the bay doors closed behind them. Another set of doors, heavily reinforced, also remained closed behind them, while from all surfaces of the large, red-lit chamber mobile turrets were trained on the craft. In the event that an enemy vessel might manage to penetrate this far into the moonbase's defenses, there was still this gauntlet to pass.

Another series of signs and countersigns, this time delivered over broadcasts so weak as to not carry beyond the rock walls of Zhurong into the space beyond, again ascertained and confirmed the identity of those piloting the craft. While it was vanishingly unlikely that the Mexica could intercept and decode the radio communications between traffic control and an incoming vessel, this additional layer of security was felt necessary on the slim chance that they could. The reinforced doors before them served to prevent any forward motion until this second series of checks could be performed, but since they were always closed while the outer doors were open, these inner doors also served to protect and obscure anything within from viewers outside. A Mexic vessel with a powerful enough remote-viewing-mirror could otherwise wait at station keeping out in the black void, and simply peer into the heart of the moonbase whenever the bay doors opened.

Finally, the secondary checks were completed and the pilots' identities, as well as those of their passengers, were confirmed. The inner doors began to open, and into the red-lit chamber spilt the bright white light of the shipyards within.

And it was here, from the viewports in the passenger compartment as the launch vehicle entered the massive hangar, that the nine got their first look at the vessel that would carry them to their destinies: the *Dragon*.

CHAPTER TEN

The lithographs which Zhuan had been shown in Fanchuan Garrison did not do the vessel justice. There was a certain brutality inherent in all Mexic designs, doubtless carried over from their cultural ethos, which demanded a never-ending series of sacrifices to their dark gods, a veritable river of blood that flowed beneath and around everything the Mexica had ever accomplished, and the newly rechristened *Dragon* was certainly no exception. Unlike the ships of the Middle Kingdom, with their baroque flourishes and careful artistry, so often designed to look like the fish of the seas or the birds of the air or more fanciful creatures only ever glimpsed in children's tales, accented with vibrant flourishes of color, the vessels of the Mexic Dominion were stark, utilitarian, and gray.

This was an ironic contrast to the armor worn by the soldiers of the two cultures, that of the Middle

Kingdom being relatively plain and unadorned, and that of the Mexic Dominion fashioned to resemble wild animals and demons and stranger creatures. Perhaps it was emblematic of the fact that, for all of its brutality, the Mexic Dominion was an egalitarian society, a meritocracy in which one rose to power and prominence on the basis of martial ability—specifically measured by the number of live prisoners one captured in combat—while the Middle Kingdom, though it measured the merits of its bureaucrats by scholastic examination, was a culture led by a hereditary ruler, whose authority flowed down through his forebears' bloodlines by grace of heaven itself. As a result, the Mexic Dominion could be seen to place more emphasis on the individual, and the Middle Kingdom on the collective culture, and each devoted its attentions in adorning those aspects it prized most highly.

The *Dragon* wasn't much larger than a cloud-flyer shuttle, about the size of the launch vessel that had carried the line from the surface, at least once the first stage and reusable fuel tanks had fallen away. The *Exhortation*, which Zhuan had commanded for so many years, had been a small patrol vessel, with a full complement of no more than a dozen crewmen, and yet it looked as if the *Dragon* would nearly fit into its cargo hold.

And *this* was the vessel that would carry the nine of them out into the black void, to the hidden Mexic base, a journey of far more than a week?

Zhuan knew from personal experience what happened to groups of men confined in close quarters for long periods of time. In the years in which he ferried colonists to Fire Star from Earth, an occasional technical malfunction would force them to abandon sections of the ship, and relocate the entire crew and all of the passengers temporarily into a limited volume of space. No matter how ideal the circumstances in such a situation—ample food, ample drink, functioning heat and air cycling— there inevitably came a point at which tempers wore too thin, and a single careless word or jostled elbow could result in a mêlée.

And those had been dutiful sailors of the Interplanetary Fleet and peaceful, well-meaning colonists, whom close quarters for long durations had turned into fierce combatants, every lip turned up in a snarl, each eye narrowed and wary. But for this coming voyage… ?

Zhuan glanced around the passenger compartment at the other eight men with him. With the exception of Yao, who seemed so rigid in his self-control he could have easily been a statue, and the Athabascan Syuxtun, who sat with a faint smile on his lips, his eyes half-lidded and expression peaceful, any of them looked to Zhuan as though they might turn their lip up in a snarl at any moment, and after a brief voyage of less than an hour, with more than sufficient space within the compartment to move around. What would such men, several of whom had already committed murder, become after weeks in the close confines of a craft as small as the *Dragon*?

Zhuan didn't know, but he had the uneasy suspicion that he was soon to find out.

* * *

Yao returned to his seat while the others hovered near the viewports, gawping at the Mexic vessel across the hangar. It was as if they had never seen one of the enemy's craft at close range before. Which, on reflection, he realized that some of them may not have done. Yao had been on enough missions in the vacuum above Fire Star, and had been part of a sufficient number of attacks on Mexic vessels, that there was no glamor or novelty left in such a sight for him. He had lost too many comrades in close quarters with the ships of the Mexic Dominion, and counted himself lucky to have survived the encounters. If he had any choice in the matter, he would not come so near a Mexic vessel again without the means in his hands to reduce it to dust, and his superiors' leave to do so.

But he had no choice in the matter, did he? Yao was here, had been selected for this mission, because his superiors had given him an order, and had known he would carry it out. The alternative would be disgrace, at least, and death by execution more than likely. And for what? For learning something he ought not to have known, for having the temerity to ask questions when he saw a gross injustice carried out before him. He burned now, thinking back on those days, and what might have happened if he had disobeyed orders and moved his men to intervene when he saw Shachuan Station about to come under attack. He could not have prevented the assault, to be sure, with just the handful of men in his squad against the overwhelming numbers of the Mexic horde. But in raising the alarm he might have alerted the station to the impending attack, and a number of the colonists might have been able to escape while he and his men harried the oncoming Mexica.

Instead, when he had radioed to his superiors that his squad had chanced upon a large number of Mexic forces massing to attack the Middle Kingdom settlement at Shachuan Station, deep in the Tianfei Valley, his orders had been to take no action, but instead to hold his position.

Yao had been flummoxed, unable to understand his superiors' reasoning. But while he knew that the orders could not be righteous, still he was too much the dutiful soldier to act against them. He radioed again and again for permission to deploy, to do some small part at least in protecting the innocents in the settlement below, but each time his superiors repeated the orders. Stand down and hold position. Stand down and hold position. Again and again, a senseless drone that in later months would haunt Yao in his sleep.

While the Mexica moved in and launched the initial waves of their attack, Yao and his men were forced to stand by and watch, helplessly. In those long minutes, countless innocents were killed. Yao could do nothing but radio again, reporting on the progress of the battle and begging his superiors for leave to move out.

Finally, and only after the attack had been underway for some time, Yao's squad was ordered to join with the Middle Kingdom forces en route from further up the Tianfei Valley. This was the final insult, added to the colonists' injuries, that Yao and his men had to divert *away* from the conflict some distance in order to join the main column, so that when they finally reached Shachuan, there were precious few lives left to save.

When the conflict was over, and the Mexica had withdrawn in victory, Yao had not rested until he discovered the reasons why his men had been ordered to take no action. He *had* to know why he had been kept from doing what he considered his duty. Yao continued to poke, and to prod, and to ask questions, using whatever influence he had after a lifetime of service and long years on Fire Star. Finally, after months had passed, and the Shachuan Station Massacre had receded in the memories of all but a few scarred and scattered survivors, Yao learned the terrible truth, much worse than he could ever have imagined.

And learning the truth, he could not unlearn it, and so he was led to his sad end, leading a group of cowards, murderers, and thieves on a desperate suicide mission with little chance of success.

And all because he could not bring himself to disobey orders when it would have saved so many lives by doing so.

CHAPTER ELEVEN

When the launch vehicle had docked, the nine were ushered out through the hatch into a pressurized umbilicus. Yao's ears plugged with the change in air pressure from ship to station, but by working his jaw he was able to get them to pop and the sound of the station came rushing in.

They were in the outer edges of the Zhurong moonbase, which were pressurized and heated but unmoving and essentially weightless. The main bulk of the base was housed in the rotating ring, and from where they floated in the receiving area the nine could hear the rumble of the ring on the track, the walls carrying the faint vibrations of the massive engines which kept the ring in motion. Had it been possible to build a station in the empty vacuum beyond, it could simply have been set rotating and that would have been an end to it, needing only periodic bursts from rockets on the hull to counteract any loss of momentum through collisions with meteoroids and other small debris; but the presence of the Mexic made the risks to a station in the vacuum simply too great, and so the hollowed moon was the more sensible choice, if a more costly one.

And while the moon's own gravity wasn't sufficient to stop the ring once it was set into motion, orbiting so close to Fire Star meant that Zhurong was awash in tidal forces which dragged at the ring in motion, and momentum was also being continually lost through the friction between ring and track. As a result, engines were necessary to keep the ring spinning. The force required wasn't nearly as much as that which would have been necessary to move a similar mass on Fire Star's surface, if such a thing were possible, or on the surface of the Earth, where it was undoubtedly impossible, but the requirements were still gargantuan.

Yao and the others were shortly joined by Agent Wu, while the flight crew went through their final docking procedures before handing control of the vessel over to the ground crew who would be responsible for refueling and preparing her for the return trip.

"Come along, men," Wu said, propelling herself toward a nearby corridor using handholds set in the walls. "The remainder of mission orientation awaits us."

The ten of them, Wu and the nine men picked for the mission, maneuvered down the corridor to a pair of sliding doors. It resembled an elevator, which in a way it was. Called an àccelerator, it was small for a room, but sizeable for an elevator, with sliding doors on the front and back walls and a series of loops set into the floor. Once the ten were onboard, the doors behind them slid shut, and a tinny recording playing over speakers in the ceiling advised all passengers to use the restraints provided to secure their feet to the floor. It took some doing, particularly for some of the Green Standard Army guardsmen who lacked the others' experience in microgravity, but in short order all ten pairs of feet were securely fastened to the ground. Then Wu hit a control on the rear wall, and the room began to move.

At first, the motion was almost imperceptible, as the passengers felt their insides shift slightly to the right. Then, a sound could be heard, a low wail that gradually climbed in pitch and volume, and the sensation of moving toward the left became more and more pronounced.

The accelerator was mounted on a smaller track outside that along which the habitat ring rotated, and could be independently spun up and down as needed. When anyone from the outside wished to enter the habitat ring, they entered the chamber, secured their feet to correctly orient them in the direction that something like gravity would shortly be pulling, and then the room began to spin along the track. When its velocity matched that of the habitat ring, a set of clamps on the outside of the accelerator affixed to anchor points on the outside of the habitat ring, and the room was transferred from one track to another. Then, when the doors on the forward wall slid open, the passengers found themselves looking out onto the outermost level of the habitat ring. Anyone wishing to move from the habitat into the outer sections of the base simply did the process in reverse, beginning with the accelerator anchored to the habitat and then riding it to a gradual stop and exiting in the weightless, unmoving sections beyond.

There was a similar conveyance mounted above the innermost level of the habitat ring, used to access the weightless sections located inside the track's circumference. In the days to come, the nine would come to know those sections intimately, as it was there that the training areas and firing ranges used by the military to drill its soldiers in microgravity combat and weaponry were situated.

But at the moment, all of the nine, with the exception of Zhuan and Ang, were somewhat queasy from the relatively sudden transition from virtual weightlessness to one-third Earth gravity. For her part, Agent Wu hardly seemed to have noticed the transition at all.

"This way, men," she said, leading them out of the accelerator and onto a broad thoroughfare.

The interior of the Zhurong station was like a miniature city, divided into segments and arranged in stacked levels. There were administrative offices, engineering sectors, training facilities, materiel stores, fabrication manufactories, dining and entertainment establishments, and living quarters, both the permanent residences of the station's staff and the temporary lodgings available for visitors, with widely varying gradations of amenities for a full spectrum of social standings and military ranks.

Zhurong wasn't a military installation, though it was at the complete disposal of the commanders of the various branches. It was an imperial possession, personal property of the Taikong emperor himself, like the colonial stations down on the surface of Fire Star. As a result, even on a war-footing as it had been these last years, Zhurong was home to as many bureaucrats as soldiers.

Yao was never so surrounded by civilians as when he visited the Zhurong moonbase, and the experience always left him feeling somewhat unsettled. He had been raised in a military family, his father and two of his uncles having been bannerman, just as his grandfathers on both sides had been. Growing up in Shandong, Yao had never questioned for a moment that his destiny, too, lay in the service of the Eight Banners. He had known of no nobler calling than to serve the Dragon Throne, to safeguard the empire, and enforce the emperor's will.

As soon as he was of an age, Yao had enlisted with the Eight Banners. He'd excelled at the rigorous training of the bannermen and, once he'd been fully vested, was dispatched to the far side of the world, to join the Banner stationed in Vinland. For the next several years, he had patrolled the border with the Mexic Dominion in Tejas, along the Big River, and though sightings of Mexic patrols were a regular occurrence, shots were seldom fired. Still, in those few times when action had been required of him, Yao had served with distinction and, when the somewhat sedate nature of the border assignment changed drastically with the onset of the Second Mexic War, he was prepared to rise to the challenge.

It was two years after the outbreak that Yao and the rest of his unit were reassigned from Vinland to Fire Star, two years in which the Middle Kingdom and the Mexic Dominion, so well entrenched on Earth after a century and a half of cold war, had simply glared at each other across borders, a state of stalemate was obtained on the ground while war raged in the heavens on and around the red planet.

But in all of those years, both as a child in Shandong and as a bannerman patrolling the Tejas border, Yao had never felt entirely comfortable around civilians, preferring the company of soldiers even before he'd been old enough to enlist. Perhaps it was that he found so many of them lax, both in their morals and in their manners. Having been raised in the certain belief that duty and personal sacrifice were the highest callings a man could answer, Yao could not understand the cozened bureaucrats who mouthed their eternal piety to the emperor, but whose principal concerns seemed to be their own comfort and personal advancement. Much less the merchants who offered only the thinnest shadows of obeisance to the emperor, and who spent their lives in the naked pursuit of profit and luxury, whether they ever managed to attain either or not.

For all Yao knew, civilians found soldiers just as difficult to understand. Perhaps a merchant's head began to ache when he tried to wrap his thoughts around the notion of duty being one's greatest motivator, and of thinking of others before thinking of oneself. Yao couldn't say. Even when he'd been a civilian, as a young boy, he'd thought as a soldier.

But, come to that, not all soldiers thought like soldiers, and there were many who wore the insignia of the emperor's armed forces while still thinking and behaving like merchants and bureaucrats. It was especially true of those impressed into service, or those who had been forced by circumstance to choose a life they'd otherwise never have led.

Looking around at the other eight men in the party, as they followed Agent Wu through the canyon-like corridor of the Zhurong habitat ring, Yao could not help but feel that most of these others were just such men, or perhaps even all. Bannerman Dea seemed to carry himself with a soldier's air, but there was something self-indulgently emotional about his manner as well, which suggested a romantic temperament that could prove fatal in a soldier. A battlefield was no place for grand emotional outbursts and wild passions, Yao knew from personal experience, and a soldier given to such extremes could be a danger to himself and those around him. Bannerman Fukuda had a soldier's steely gaze, but was too apt to fly into rages, which no unit could allow. And Bannerman Syuxtun seemed far too lax in manner and attitudes to have ever been vested in the Eight Banners.

Yao could not help a bitter smile. Even when judging the merits of this collection of reprobates and cowards, he instinctually looked at the bannermen as soldiers first, dismissing the others. But, in truth, the three other bannermen were no more or less acceptable than any of the other five, the Green Standard guardsmen and the Interplanetary Fleet sailors, their captain included, any one of them as bad as the next.

And these were the men he'd be trusting with his life, when they set out in the *Dragon* for Xolotl?

CHAPTER TWELVE

The accommodations to which Agent Wu led them were meager, but certainly no worse than the cell in which Zhuan had languished at Baochuan. There was a small private sleeping space for each of the nine, little more than a cubbyhole with a spongy pallet built into the floor, arranged along one wall in a three-by-three grid, with a ladder's rungs affixed to each of the upright walls on the open end. Such warrens were called "coffins" by those who were forced by standing or circumstance to use them, and the name was an apt one.

The nine coffins were stacked such that their open ends faced a cube-shaped room, in which there were shared toilet facilities, a circular table, a small larder, and nine plain metal chairs. The light in the room emanated from panels in the ceiling which burned at all hours, even though the moonbase observed a "day" and "night" despite the fact that no natural light reached the habitat's interior, and even though the sun that shone in the dark night beyond the walls rose and fell twice daily above the moon's surface as the red planet sped by below. It was now late night, and all around them the station slumbered.

"Rest here, men." Wu motioned them into the shared space, and indicated the door behind her. "You're free to move about in here as you wish, but you won't be granted access to the rest of the base unescorted. That door will remain locked from the outside, and can be opened only on my authorization." She pointed to the coffins along the far wall. "What you do with the next few hours is your business, but I recommend getting some rest. Mission orientation continues at first watch."

Zhuan saw the confusion on some of the guardsmen's faces, no doubt having difficulty transitioning from the twenty-four hour clock used on the planet's surface to the shipboard timekeeping of ten equal watches employed on the station. The first watch was equivalent to the beginning of the eighth hour after midnight, and lasted to the middle of the tenth hour, which was followed by the second watch which lasted from the middle of the tenth hour to the end of the twelfth, and so on. Whatever method one used, however one sliced the day into sections, the morning would come too quickly for Zhuan's taste.

Had it really been less than a day since he was roused from his cell at Baochuan and taken to Fanchuan Garrison, there given the choice of commanding this captured vessel or surrendering his neck to the executioner's blade? It seemed far, far longer a span.

Without pleasantry or preamble, Agent Wu turned on her heel and went back out the door, which closed behind her with a clang like a sounding cymbal, a resounding note of finality.

Paik appeared to be motivated by his appetites above all else, his hunger and his fatigue, and while the others moved warily into the shared space, keeping their eyes on one another distrustfully, the Chosonese guardsman simply crossed the floor to the larder, yanked the door open, and peered inside. In short order he was seated in one of the metal chairs, his feet propped on the table, with a bowl of dumplings in his lap, chopsticks in one hand and a bamboo flask of tea in the other, munching contentedly.

"I'm hungry," Nguyen said, licking his lips and moving to the now-open larder, shouldering Fukuda out of the way.

"Watch yourself, you great lummox," the Nipponese snapped.

Nguyen seemed not to mind, but continued on toward the larder.

"Do you leave nothing for the rest of us?" Ang sat down across the table from Paik, scratching his palm with the fingers of his other hand, a nervous habit with which Zhuan had become quite accustomed over the years.

Paik shrugged. "I'm hungry, I eat. You sit there scratching. If there's nothing left, that's your problem, not mine, neh?"

"I'm hungry," Nguyen said, looking up from the larder, "and there's no food."

Ang scowled. "So you *did* leave nothing for us, did you?"

Paik shrugged again. "Not my problem, is it?"

"What the devil are the rest of us supposed to eat?" chimed in Guardsman Cai, who still stood rooted to the spot by the door, where he'd been since they'd first come in. "Are they going to feed us again?"

"What does it matter to you, beanstalk?" Fukuda looked the lanky Cai up and down disdainfully. "You hardly eat at all, seems to me, so why should you mind?"

"Leave him alone," Bannerman Dea menaced, his hands at his sides, fingers limber, hovering above holsters that weren't there.

Cai flashed Dea an uneasy grin, the broad gap between his front teeth showing.

"Who asked you, bug?" Fukuda took a step toward Dea, lip curled. Syuxtun, who had been in the process of crossing the room, passed in front of the Nipponese, who redirected his ire at the new target. "And you, mudskin? What's your problem?"

"No problem of mine, bannerman," the Athabascan answered, holding his hands up, palms out, and angled toward the far corner. Once there, he took a moment, his expression thoughtful as if he were conducting some complex calculation, and then turned a fraction to one side, his hands at his side and his feet evenly spaced, and bowed his head. Then he raised his head, facing the empty space before him, brought his hands up to his ears, palms forward and thumbs behind his earlobes, and began to chant. "In the name of God, most gracious, most merciful, praise be to God..."

Zhuan nodded, finally understanding something about the Athabascan bannerman. He was a Muslim, then, whose calculations involved working out which way lay the Earth, and more specifically Mecca. And given that he recited the salat in Official Speech and not Arabic, he was likely a native of Khalifah, the nation on the western shore of Earth's western hemisphere, neighbor to Vinland and the Mexic peninsula, which had been established as a khalifate in honor of the Muslim admiral of the first Treasure Fleet to circumnavigate the Earth's oceans.

Khalifah had been a Muslim nation since the early days of the Clear Dynasty, when the Manchurians first came south and took control of the Middle Kingdom, but while the Khalifans had remained devoted followers of the Prophet these long years since, a progressive tendency in the young culture had led to certain liberalizing reforms, among them the allowance of native tongues in the daily observations. A center for art and technology for generations, Khalifah remained a devoutly religious nation, though the mullahs of earlier generations would doubtless have considered them all blasphemous heretics who prayed to God in heathen tongues and allowed their women to go about with their heads uncovered.

As Syuxtun began his daily observations, beginning the first of the four rakats of the Isha prayer, the other soldiers continued to agitate about their victuals, or lack thereof.

Fukuda had reached the larder, and inside found nothing but a jar of tea, a few empty bowls, a container filled with plastic chopsticks, and a stack of empty bamboo flasks. "So the oaf *does* eat the food our jailors would intend for all of us." The Nipponese snatched one of the chopsticks from the container, and spun around, holding it like a dagger. "Perhaps I'll need to cut the dumplings from his over-ample belly, and share them among the rest of us."

Nguyen wrinkled his nose, twisting his mouth in distaste. "I don't want to eat anything someone else already ate."

"He's not..." Dea began, then shook his head in frustration. "No one's making you, alright, friend?"

The Annamese man-mountain smiled down at the bannerman in relief.

"I thought I told you to stay out of my business, bug," Fukuda snarled.

Dea's lip curled back, his teeth gritted. "You wouldn't talk to me like that if I had my iron, or if you did you wouldn't be talking for long."

It took Zhuan a moment to realize that Bannerman Dea was talking about a firearm when he said "iron." Zhuan had never heard anyone outside of dramas about Vinlander gunslingers in the wilds of Tejas talking like that, and now that he thought of it, there was something of the gunslinger to the bannerman's stance, as well. Dea's hands hovered hungrily at his sides, grasping for the handles of pistols that weren't there, and his eyes were narrowed and wary.

"But you don't have a gun, do you, bug?" Fukuda sneered, and brandished the chopstick, waving its point in the air before it. It was plastic, and hardly sharp, but wielded against bare flesh in expert hands, even a blunt bit of plastic could do considerable damage.

The two bannermen faced each other, chests puffed, teeth barred, each waiting for the other to make the first move.

But it was another who took the opportunity.

Bannerman Yao's hand came down in a crashing blow on Fukuda's forearm, knocking the chopstick from his grip with a teeth-rattling impact. Then, as the Nipponese recoiled, Yao swung his right foot in a low, long arc, sweeping Dea's legs out from under him, sending him falling to the floor. Then, without losing the momentum of the sweep he continued to spin around until he was facing Fukuda, then planted his feet in a wide stance, and knifed his right hand forward in an open-fisted jab that caught the Nipponese in the solar plexus, driving the wind from his lungs. Fukuda staggered back, holding his battered arm to his bruised chest, sputtering, while Dea struggled to climb to his feet.

"Stay down!" Yao barked, pointing a finger at Dea, then back to Fukuda said, "Another move or word from you and the next blow won't be so soft."

The others stood silently by, watchful, all except Paik, who continued to munch on the dumplings speared from the bowl in his lap.

Yao took three long strides to the table's side, and as easily as he'd swept Dea's legs out from under him, kicked the chair out from beneath Paik. As the Chosonese guardsman went tumbling to the

ground, arms flailing in all directions, Yao effort-
lessly reached out and plucked the bowl from his
lap before a single dumpling had spilt over the edge.

Paik began to roar, in the midst of regaining his
balance and lurching to his feet, when Yao simply
stepped over and planted his foot on Paik's neck,
pinning him to the floor.

"This has all gone on long enough," Yao said,
raising his voice to a thundering volume without
ever giving the impression of yelling. "I'm not sure
what passed for discipline wherever you reprobates
last served, but I won't have it here. Not for an
instant." He tossed the bowl onto the table's surface, where it spun for several revolutions like a top
before finally coming to a rest. "The nine of us will
be spending a great deal of time together in the
coming days. There is a good chance, in fact, that
we'll be spending the rest of our lives together."

Most of them, Zhuan especially, understood that
when Yao said "coming days" and "the rest of our
lives" he was discussing the same span of time.
Nguyen, for his part, screwed up his face in confusion, but Zhuan was sure he would work it out,
sooner or later.

"There is every chance that we may die in the
course of our mission," Yao went on. "There is, in
fact, the highest probability that none of us shall
return from our coming voyage. And I understand
that, for some of you, the likelihood of your
impending death might make you less likely to
adhere to the strictures of discipline, and more likely to flaunt authority. But *you* should understand
this." He twisted his foot, pressing it harder into

Paik's neck, and Zhuan could hear the grinding of bone against bone. Tears streamed from Paik's eyes, as he struggled helplessly to get out from under Yao's foot. "I will not tolerate any insubordination, and any man who puts himself or his own interests above those of the mission will have me to answer to. That includes the survival of your fellows, even in such mundane matters as their daily nourishment." Again the twisting foot, again the bone-grinding sound and the tear-streaming eyes. "Put the lives of the men in jeopardy, and I will kill you myself. Then you needn't worry about whether death awaits on our mission, since you won't live long enough to find out."

Yao lifted his foot from Paik's neck, and the Chosonese curled into a whimpering ball, clutching at his bruised throat. Stepping over him, Yao reached into the larder, pulled out an empty bowl, a pair of chopsticks, and a bamboo flask that he filled with tea. Then he seated himself at the table, shoveled a few dumplings into his bowl, and then lifted one of them between the chopsticks to his waiting mouth. He took a large bite, and began to chew.

"Well?" Yao said around a mouthful of food. "Aren't the rest of you going to eat?"

The others exchanged quick glances, then hustled over to the larder to equip themselves and joined Yao at the table. Nearly half of the dumplings had already gone down Paik's gullet, but there was still enough left in the bowl to satisfy their immediate needs.

Zhuan was the last to sit, even after Fukuda had taken a seat and Dea and Paik had picked themselves up off the floor and slunk over to the table. The only open seat was that just opposite Yao, and Zhuan slid into it, with only a flask of tea in his hands. He sipped it, feeling the hot tea warm him as it slipped down his throat, and regarded the bannerman across from him.

"To your health, captain," Yao said with a thin smile, raising his own flask to his lips.

"And yours, bannerman," Zhuan replied with a nod.

There was a bitter undercurrent to the bannerman's toast, Zhuan knew. Like him, Yao had recognized that, while the fray had erupted all around them, Zhuan had not reacted in the slightest, had not spoken a word against it. Zhuan knew now that Yao had delayed his response, allowing the encounter to run its course far longer than he might have preferred, while waiting to see if the captain would respond. They were not yet onboard the *Dragon*, and so neither man was in command, with all nine falling under Agent Wu's responsibility, but Zhuan realized now that Yao was testing him, gauging his fitness to lead, taking his measure as a leader of men.

What, then, if Yao should decide once they had already set sail on the *Dragon* that Zhuan was not fit for command? What might the bannerman do then?

Zhuan glanced around the table at the pained expressions of Dea and Fukuda, and the wicked bruises already visible on Paik's throat, and feared to find out.

Chapter Thirteen

The next morning, as the recorded chiming of bells rang through the station's common areas, heralding the start of the day's first watch, mission orientation began.

When the door to the nine's temporary quarters slid open, Agent Wu stood beyond, flanked by a pair of strangers. One was a sailor, a woman wearing the light-colored tunic and pants of an Interplanetary Fleet duty uniform, while the other was a man in the dark-colored fatigues of Eight Banners combat dress.

Together now for nearly a day, and forced to slumber uneasily side-by-side in the cramped warren of coffins, the nine were now being broken into smaller groups, to make the most efficient use of the small time remaining before the *Dragon*'s scheduled departure.

Captain Zhuan Jie, Steersman Ang Xunhuo, and, somewhat surprisingly, Bannerman Syuxtun Haji, were to accompany the sailor, who would escort them back through the accelerator to the shipyards beyond the habitat ring, where they would be familiarized with the controls of the captured Mexic ship, the *Dragon*.

Meanwhile, Bannerman Yao and the others were to be escorted by the soldier and Agent Wu to the firing ranges in the microgravity training facilities deep in the moon's heart, inside the innermost level of the rotating habitat, there to be familiarized with the new weaponry with which they would be issued for the mission.

Yao and Zhuan exchanged a glance as their respective groups were led away from their sleeping quarters, their expressions mutually unreadable.

Yao and the others climbed to the highest and innermost level of the habitat ring, where they were just close enough to the center of rotation that they began to feel tidal forces tugging their heads and feet at different rates. There they boarded an accelerator, twin to that which had brought them to the habitat ring the day before, and rode it to a gradual stop, slipping from one third Earth gravity to near weightlessness once more, finding themselves at last at the outer edge of the immense network of corridors and chambers that constituted the deepest core of Zhurong. These, some little more than caves rimmed by undressed stone, were the principal place where bannermen honed their skills in vacuum and microgravity combat, kept safe and secure by kilometers of rock in every direction. Most of the corridors and chambers were pressurized, like those through which Agent Wu and the unknown bannerman now escorted them, but some were sealed off without any atmosphere at all, simulating conditions in the black void of space.

Like all of the bannermen, Yao had spent time training at the Zhurong facilities more times than he could count, these last years. It was felt by the commanders of the Eight Banners that their greatest enemy was complacency, and that the most difficult challenge faced by the bannermen was the atrophy of their unused tactics and skills. Bannermen typically spent months and years in a single assignment, whether on ground patrol down on the surface of Fire Star, or serving with marine forces onboard Interplanetary Fleet vessels, or piloting aircraft through the thin, pink skies of the red planet. As a result, even if bannermen were left on consistent assignments, they were periodically sent to retrain on all those skills they didn't employ on a daily basis. So ground-huggers like Yao were temporarily reassigned to Zhurong to practice their microgravity combat skills, and refreshed on the operation of the Eight Banners' aircraft, while vacuum-based soldiers were periodically asked to complete a full reassessment course in the training facilities located in the rotating Zhurong habitat ring, which closely simulated conditions on the planet's surface. Eight Banners aeronauts, while rarer than the much more numerous Interplanetary Fleet fliers, were still from time to time required to complete both retraining courses, gravity combat and microgravity combat.

However, the resources of the entire imperial military were stretched thin by the long-running nature of the present conflict, and as a result it had been nearly two years since Yao'd had occasion to return to Zhurong for reassessment and remedial training. From the way that they quickly adapted to microgravity, it appeared that Dea and Fukuda had more recently completed the training, or else were simply more naturally talented at adapting to changes in gravity.

For their part, the three guardsmen of the Green Standard Army seemed to take somewhat longer to get their feet beneath them, as the saying went. Yao had not noticed their lack of agility in microgravity the day before, whether in the launch vessel or in the outer corridors of the moonbase, but he attributed that to the fact that both the vessel's passenger compartment and the moonbase's outer corridors were relatively small and narrow, the walls, floor, and ceiling never more than a few arms' lengths away, and so they had been able to bound and rebound off the walls and ceiling as necessary without drifting too far from the rest of the group.

By contrast, the network of corridors and chambers at the heart of Zhurong was massive, given the appearance of being even larger by the winding and sinuous nature of many of those corridors. Entering the immense juncture between several corridors, one of the guardsmen at least, Nguyen Trang, began to drift away like an errant balloon in a high wind, and only the timely intercession of their bannerman escort saved the guardsman from losing sight of the rest of the party altogether.

Surprisingly, though, on second glance it appeared that Guardsman Cai Yingtai had begun to maneuver through the microgravity corridors and chambers with an effortless deftness and aplomb. If he'd had a momentary difficulty transitioning to weightlessness, it had quickly passed. Yao could not begin to guess the reasons, but imagined that Cai was one who had not spent a great deal of time in microgravity over all, so that it was not instinctual to him, but that he had only recently been in weightless conditions, perhaps for a relatively extended period of time.

Yao didn't have time to reflect on what the others' microgravity aptitudes or lack thereof suggested about their backgrounds, as their progress through the weightless corridors was stopped short when Agent Wu and her bannerman companion pulled themselves to a halt outside a large circular hatch. The ideograms inscribed around the hatch's circumference revealed that a firing range lay beyond, and though the tell in the metal cage affixed to the hatch's frame was unlit, indicating that the range was presently untenanted, Wu impressed on each of the men the need for care when entering, as live rounds were employed within.

A short while later, Yao and the other five men floated in an irregular sphere, facing Agent Wu and the bannerman, who had produced a large metal case from somewhere and was now extracting a pair of weapons, one a small, somewhat fragile looking handgun, the other a considerably more rugged carbine. Both had the unfinished look of prototypes and the bulky profile of microgravity weapons.

Yao, who'd had more than his fair share of experiences with dangerous and unreliable weapons designed for use in weightless and near-weightless conditions, managed to suppress a shudder, but just barely.

"Attend, men," Agent Wu said, motioning for their attention. "Bannerman Hughes has consented to give you an introduction to these new arms, with which you'll each be equipped on the coming mission." She turned her head in his direction, careful to move her left arm in a slow spiral, counterbalancing the motion and keeping herself from going into a spin. "Bannerman Hughes?"

The bannerman nodded, his fair hair shorn close to the scalp, looking almost white against the ruddy skin of his face and neck. When he spoke, his Official Speech was tinged with an accent Yao identified as being Briton, which was somewhat surprising. While fairly common in the ranks of the Green Standard Army, natives of Briton, or of any other Europa nation for that matter, were somewhat rare in the Eight Banners. This Hughes must have been a considerable talent, to earn such a commission.

"Look, guys, there's two ways I can go about this," Hughes said, addressing the men with an easy, perhaps overly familiar air, and a rugged smile. Whatever talents the man might possess, proper etiquette was obviously not included. But then, Yao had found such breaches of protocol not entirely uncommon among Europans. "I can explain too much, and you'll feel like a group of school children on a tour. Or I can explain too little, and sooner or later you'll find yourself in a firefight not knowing how to clear a jam in the firing mechanism. Better to err on the side of caution, as the old saying goes, and hope that too much can be enough. Agreed?"

The bannerman looked around at the six men floating before him, waiting for some response, and didn't continue until a few heads bobbed their assent.

"Fair enough. Now, when you're down in the gravity well, on the surface, you can use the same firearms we all learned to use back on Earth, right? Assuming that you brace yourself correctly before firing, so that the recoil doesn't knock you on your backside. But even so, the low gravity of Fire Star limits the amount of kick a firearm can provide, since there are limits to how much momentum even a properly braced shooter can absorb. Right?"

Again the pause, waiting for the ripple of nodding heads.

"Right. So in vacuum, firearms have been problematic these last years, to say the least, and close combat weapons like blades and cudgels even more commonly employed than they are down on Fire Star. That's all well and good, if the other side is restrained by the same limitations—and assuming that they don't have a gun mounted somewhere in range with enough mass behind it to absorb the momentum—but if you end up facing a disproportionate number of hostiles, then there's a good chance that blades and cudgels aren't going to do the trick. Which is why, since the outbreak of the

Second Mexic War, the military has been trying to perfect recoilless firearms that can be used in any conditions." He gestured with the weapons, one in either hand. "Which leads us to these."

Hughes held up the smaller of the two, the handgun.

"The flechette pistol is the first. It doesn't inherit the problems of previous microgravity weapon designs, but it comes with a few of its own." Hughes released his hold on the carbine, leaving it to float beside him, then with his free hand reached over and removed a clip from the pistol's handle. It slid out, a small metal container about the size of two of Yao's fingers side-by-side, a narrow box with squared-off edges. "The fletcher gets around the action-reaction problem with extremely low mass projectiles. When they're fired, there's a push back on the shooter, but the larger mass is able to absorb the momentum without imparting any appreciable movement." Hughes slid his thumb over the top of the clip, and then caught a slender piece of flashing silver between thumb and forefinger. It was no larger than a needle, and seemed to be fractionally wider at one end than the other.

"The fletcher has a considerably high muzzle velocity, quite a bit more than the weapons you might have used in the past, which is where the punch comes from. Low-mass, high-velocity. Even so, it takes quite a few hits to put anything like a dent in your target, so don't spare the shots. And you needn't worry about a stray shot puncturing a hull. The needles are entirely frangible, and will shatter on impact with anything much tougher than clothing. So point and squeeze and hope to get off enough rounds to bring the target down. But don't just spray and pray. The flechette pistols can only hold a short charge before needing to be replenished, so as soon as your fletcher is out of juice you've got a good while to wait before it's ready to go again." Hughes held up the fletcher and pointed at a tiny light-emitting diode inserted where the handle met the barrel, which now glowed bright green. "When that tell glows red you're out of juice, and when it glows green you're good to shoot."

Slamming the clip back into the handle, and checking the safety, Hughes tucked the flechette pistol into his belt and then snatched the carbine from midair.

"Which brings us to the rocket carbine." The carbine was shorter and bulkier than the rifles which were standard issue to guardsmen and bannermen alike, no longer than the length of Yao's arm from shoulder to wrist. "Now, this one is more like what you might be used to, if you've had any experience with microgravity weapons before." Hughes paused, and glanced around at the six men. "*Have* any of you had experience with rocket ammunition?"

Five heads stayed still, but after a long moment Yao finally nodded.

Hughes met his eye, and a silent exchange passed between the two bannermen. "So you ran into the usual problems, I take it?" Hughes finally asked.

Yao nodded, his lips drawn into a tight line. "I managed to keep all my fingers, but just barely." He paused, and then added, "But one of the men in my unit wasn't quite so lucky."

"Lost his fingers?" Hughes asked, with evident concern.

Yao shook his head, expression dark. "His life."

Hughes pursed his lips, wincing in sympathy, before continuing. "Well, this new batch is better than the old ones, but that's like being the tallest midget in the room. Which is to say, these won't blow up in your face *much*." Hughes worked a lever mounted on the carbine's stock, and a small dark shape was ejected out the other side. He snatched it from midair, albeit carefully, and held it up for everyone's inspection. It resembled nothing so much as a miniature version of the launch vessel that had carried them up from the planet's surface.

"The projectiles are rocket-propelled. The carbine itself doesn't do much more than get the ammunition pointed in the right direction and give it a little push to get it going. Once the shot clears the barrel, the triggering mechanism inside the projectile is supposed to fire off the rocket and push it up to a considerable velocity before it hits the target." He paused, and then added, meaningfully, "*Supposed* to, I said. Only problem is that the projectiles tend to be inaccurate over anything but the shortest of distances, and to make matters worse, even if they fly true, the things are prone to explode before reaching the target." He glanced in Yao's direction, a shadow passing over his features. "Sometimes they even explode before leaving the barrel, which is an experience I wouldn't recommend to anyone."

Hughes slotted the rocket-propelled projectile back into the carbine, and then slung it over his shoulder. Turning from the waist, he managed to rotate a fraction, then arrested his movement with short waves of his arms. He pointed at the distant end of the long, narrow firing range, where targets had been affixed to the thick sponge-like backing lining the wall. The backing was designed to absorb the kinetic energy of anything short of a mortar shell.

"The artificers are still finishing the fabrication of the weapons for this mission, so we've only got three each of the fletchers and rocket carbines, but before we're done today I want all six of you completely checked out on their operations, firing and loading, and what sort of jams you might encounter and how to fix them."

While Hughes spoke, Agent Wu kicked over to the nearest wall, where Hughes's metal case still floated. Opening it, she pulled out a pair of the fletcher pistols, which she snugged in pockets on either hip, and then carbines which she slung over her shoulder. Finally she tugged pouches of ammunition from within the case, and headed back to Hughes's side.

"Now," Hughes said, looking over the six, "who's going to be first?"

Each of the six fired enough rounds from both the pistol and carbine that their accuracy reached acceptable levels, though some took longer to reach that point than others. And each was drilled in the steps needed to clear the carbine's breech and to eject any jammed needles in the fletcher. Field-stripping and cleaning was considered a low-priority skill for the mission, at least according to Agent Wu, but Hughes demonstrated the procedure, just in case the information would prove useful, a kind of thoroughness that Yao appreciated.

Of the six, Yao was surprised to discover that he was not the most skilled marksman. He'd seen Bannerman Dea's shooting scores in his military records, back in Fanchuan Garrison, but had assumed that there had been some exaggeration on the part of the training officers, since marksmanship of that high caliber was a rare quality indeed.

By the time Dea had emptied the fletcher's clip of needles, Yao was satisfied that the training officers had not exaggerated. If anything, they might have understated the case.

Still, despite his almost unerring ability to put a shot dead-center in the target, time after time, there was something comical about the way that Dea handled the firearms. For one thing, when shooting the flechette pistol, he insisted that he begin each time with the fletcher in a holster at his side, and when Hughes called the order to fire Dea would draw the pistol in a fluid, lightning-fast movement and then fan his free hand over the pistol's reset lever, an unnecessary motion since simply squeezing and holding the trigger would result in an uninterrupted burst of automatic fire. Then, when he'd finished, he would raise the pistol to his lips and *blow* across the end of the barrel, smiling self-indulgently.

He acted, for all the world, like a character in a cheap drama, or in the pages of a tenth-tael terrible, a cartoonish figure of a gunman stepping straight out of lurid tales of the Tejas frontier. It was some-what unnerving, seeing someone with that kind of well-honed ability playacting at being a Vinlander gunslinger.

Even so, cartoonish or no, it was clear that Dea knew his way around firearms. Despite himself, Yao couldn't help but feel that their mission's chances of success had just raised in his own esti-mation, if only fractionally.

There was still the question of the ship, of course, and whether they would be able to reach Xolotl at all. But that was Zhuan's concern, not Yao's, for which the bannerman counted himself lucky.

CHAPTER FOURTEEN

While Yao and the others were being introduced to the intricacies of prototype microgravity weaponry, the rest of the team was escorted by Specialist Sima to the shipyards where the *Dragon* floated at anchor in near weightlessness.

There was a trace of Hunan pronunciation in the sailor's Official Speech, which Zhuan had ample opportunity to identify as she led them through the corridors of the habitat ring to the outer accelerator, and from there back to the hangar where the nine had first seen the captured Mexic vessel the day before.

Sima demonstrated a conversational focus, and a lack of observance of appropriate social protocols, which Zhuan had encountered many times among technicians and ships' engineers. It was a certain personality type, seemingly inborn, which combined a savant-level ability to understand extremely complex information with an almost complete inability to navigate in social situations. Zhuan had been tipped off by the fact that Sima seldom if ever made eye contact when speaking, and his suspicions were confirmed during the long trip from the habitat to the shipyards, in which Sima did not so much converse with her charges as lecture them. People who exhibited such traits, Zhuan had found, made invaluable artificers and technicians, and a ship could count itself lucky to have one as her engineer, but Zhuan had learned to avoid being trapped in confined spaces with them, if at all possible.

From their expressions, it was clear that Steersman Ang and Bannerman Syuxtun were quickly learning this lesson, as well, if they didn't know it already.

"We were able to get the craft's life support systems fully operational in short order," Sima was saying, as the accelerator slowed to a stop, "even though none of the bolts and fasteners the Mexica use are anything like the gauges we employ, so we had to machine all of the replacement components by hand. The artificers were too busy mapping schematics to be able to machine the components and so I ended up having to do all of them myself.

"That wasn't any trouble, since I started machining parts when I was a girl in Changde and couldn't find the components necessary to replace my father's thresher. The manufacturer had gone out of business while my grandfather was still a boy, probably because they used proprietary components and when their machinery broke down in the field only authorized technicians could repair it. So my father was sure that he would have to purchase a new thresher, which would have taken up too much of our family budget for my brother to continue taking his *erhu* lessons, and all mother ever talked about was what a fine fiddle-player my brother was shaping up to be, and that it would break her heart if he were forced to give it up. My brother said that he would rather be…"

"Specialist Sima?" Zhuan interrupted, raising a finger. "You were talking about the *Dragon*'s life support systems." At least, that was what Zhuan thought she had been talking about.

"Yes," Sima said, giving him an annoyed glare, "I was getting to that. Now, we were able to get the life support systems operational once I had finished machining all of the appropriate replacement components—bolts, fasteners, and such—but the *real* problem came in getting the ship's controls into anything like a useable state. That and the mess, of course."

Zhuan had dim recollections of Admiral Geng mentioning something to him about the ship's "brutal" control mechanisms, back in Fanchuan Garrison, but the admiral had not gone into any detail. Zhuan had counted himself lucky at the time, since he'd heard dark rumors about the rites the Mexica performed before each launch, and could only imagine what Geng had meant.

Sima went on talking, looping around anything resembling a point, like a carrion bird circling in the sky over a potential meal that hadn't yet had the decency to die, only occasionally diving in long enough to nip at the subject at hand before soaring back up into the upper reaches of vaguely associative topics.

Zhuan gathered that much of her discourse was internalized and repurposed quotations from other speakers, particularly anything that touched on feelings or emotional responses. Sima talked a lot about things that upset other people, or situations in which others would be "heartbroken" or "overjoyed," but she treated the trivial and grave with equal importance, apparently not seeing the distinction between someone's slight disappointment at their midday meal arriving to the table a few moments late, and the sorrow of a parent over the loss of a child. Again, though, this was consistent with the personality type she exhibited, so it was nothing that surprised Zhuan, however disconcerting it may have been.

Reaching the shipyards, Sima broke four sets of pressure suits out of a storage locker, and directed Zhuan and the others to don them. Though they would be ferried to the *Dragon* in a small, pressurized tug, which maneuvered through the near-weightless expanse of the hangar propelled by short bursts of compressed air, and though the *Dragon* itself was completely pressurized and airtight, there was always the chance that something would go amiss in transit, whether a docking umbilicus slipping loose its moorings or an inadvertent evacuation of atmosphere in a cycling airlock. In the interests of safety, as was the standard protocol in all imperial hangar facilities, they would all go dressed in pressure gear.

These were not the pressure suits used by troops in combat, which would be heavily armored and rated to withstand small arms fire. Instead, these were rugged, unadorned workmen's utility suits, with reinforced joints at the elbows and knees, compartments for small tools and loops for larger ones to be fastened, and bright strips of reflective coating on the shoulders, back, and chest, in the event that the wearer should drift inadvertently into the path of an oncoming vessel.

Clear plastic helmets surmounted the suits, affixed to heavy metal collars, giving the wearer an unobstructed view in all directions. Beneath the wearer's chin was a microphone pickup, while speakers were mounted on either side below the ears. And unlike the combat variety, these suits were equipped with only a simple binary control for the radio—off and on—along with a channel setting. While combat suits could be reconfigured to transmit on a wide spectrum of wavelengths at a variety of signal strengths, and to transmit everything from plain speech to encoded transmissions, all that the wearer of a utility suit could do was determine whether or not they wanted to talk and listen, and on which channel they'd be broadcasting.

Crammed into these bulky and uncomfortable utility suits, the four entered a pressurized airlock, and from there climbed into a small tug vessel, barely large enough for them all to fit. As it was, only Sima got to sit, positioned at the forward end of the cabin near the simple, unadorned controls, while Zhuan and the others clung to webbing affixed to floor and ceiling to keep from jostling into one another while drifting in microgravity.

Since the tug cabin was pressurized, sound carried, though somewhat muffled by the thick plastic of their helmets, for which Zhuan was hardly grateful. If the cabin had been airless, he would have been able to shut off his suit-radio and be spared a few moments of Specialist Sima's endless discourse, but as it was he was at her mercy.

However, as Sima maneuvered the tug around, and the profile of the *Dragon* drifted in view of its forward viewport, Zhuan forgot all about her seemingly endless catalog of minor annoyances and technical trivialities. As the sight of the blunt-nosed craft filled his vision, thoughts of other Mexica craft filled his thoughts. He remembered the hot flush of panic, the cold grip of fear, the inescapable terror that assailed him each time he went into combat. He'd managed to steel himself against that terror, and do his duty regardless of his own feelings, every time but one. And that one time, the single instance in his long career in which he chose his own safety over blind loyalty to command, had brought him to this point. Now, it was no longer even an option to turn and run, since fleeing from this fate would only lead him directly under the path of the executioner's blade. His only chance of survival, and a dim hope it was, lay in the possibility of the successful completion of their mission.

"I did warn you about the mess," Specialist Sima said as they drifted through the docking umbilicus into the pressurized interior of the *Dragon*. As she'd explained at some length en route, the Mexic vessel had been constructed to different standards than those employed by the Middle Kingdom, and as a result the *Dragon* could not dock directly to one of the service armatures, as the ships of the Interplanetary Fleet customarily did. The only consolation, she said, was that if the Mexica captured a Middle Kingdom vessel and tried to dock it in one of their own facilities, they'd run into the same difficulty.

It was simply another hallmark of Sima's inaptitude at social interaction that she could speak so blithely about the potential capture of a Middle Kingdom vessel by the forces of the Mexic Dominion. Because, while the Middle Kingdom might imprison or execute its prisoners, as the circumstances and the particulars demanded, the Mexica employed far harsher treatment of those Middle Kingdom subjects unfortunate enough to fall into their hands. Which, ultimately, was the source of the "mess" to which Sima referred.

The interior of the *Dragon* was dimly lit, though Zhuan wasn't sure if that was by design or because the Middle Kingdom artificers were maintaining it on reduced power consumption. But even through the twilit gloom, Zhuan could make out rust-like stains which could be found here and there on the bulkheads and decks, especially clustered around the control mechanics of the command center.

"We worked for days," Sima explained, her eyes shifting around the room, unwilling or unable to meet anyone's gaze, "but we couldn't get the stains cleaned off. Not entirely, anyway. A cleansing agent that included citrus extracts in a solution of bleach and water was the most effective we tried, but even that couldn't get the most stubborn marks to come clean."

For the moment, Zhuan was glad that Sima did not make eye contact, as he was unsure how well he'd have been able to marshal his expression if he was forced to look her in the eye. He understood that, with her constellation of personality defects, she could hardly be blamed for so casually discussing cleaning products in the face of the horror those stains represented, but that didn't stop him from being somewhat disgusted with her, all the same.

"Is that…?" Ang began, and pointed to the bulky structure at the forward end of the narrow command center, a six-sided block with tapered sides, surmounted by a wide flat surface almost as wide as the distance between the tips of Zhuan's outstretched arms. It resembled nothing so much as a sleeping platform of some kind, except that the surface, covered in circuitry and ridges which combined in fantastic shapes and designs, was stained an almost uniform shade of reddish-brown, so dark as to almost be black.

"That's the starting mechanism," Sima explained, glancing over somewhere in the vicinity of Ang's left shoulder before looking back to the platform. "That's where the majority of the rites would have been performed."

The four of them, Specialist Sima and the three men, hovered in the midst of the ship's command center which, aside from the fantastic designs on the fixtures and the horrors suggested by the dark stains, looked more or less the same as every ship's bridge on which Zhuan had ever served. There was a seat for the commanding officer, and stations for each of the command crew. Just what each station controlled, Zhuan could not say, since he was unable to read the Mexic language of Nahuatl, but then that was why Syuxtun was with them, since he could.

"The artificers have been able to bypass the hemoglobin-sensing trigger mechanism, so that the ship can be started and operated normally. But they were unable to change the system's core programming, and their bypass is acting as a surface level patch only. In the event that the system was cycled and defaults restored, the bypass would be overwritten and the hemoglobin-sensors brought back online."

This was what happened to prisoners of the Mexic Dominion. This was why Zhuan had always faced his encounters with the Mexica with the cold grip of terror clenching his insides. This was why it was thought better to die in combat with the Mexica than to fall still living into their hands.

"We'll be sending a small supply of blood to the refrigeration unit, in shock-resistant containers," Sima went on, motioning toward the steps leading down from the command center to the cramped living quarters of the ship, "in the event that a restart returns the system to default. You shouldn't need it, but should have it on hand, just in case. Otherwise one of you would need to open a vein, and I don't think you're taking a physician on the mission, unless I'm mistaken, so that could always lead to potential infection, and if one of you is anemic or has difficulty with clotting that could be an even more serious problem. And of course the amount of blood required to trip the hemoglobin sensors is not inconsiderable, and under less than ideal circumstances that in itself could prove life-threatening."

Sima kept talking, but Zhuan found it difficult to focus on her words, his eyes riveted to the platform at the forward edge of the command center, and the dark stains on it. The circuitry and ridges on the platform surface combined to form a fierce tableau, an image of the Mexic moon goddess being cut into pieces by the warrior god of the sun. The platform was not a separate component, like the altar used by the minister of rites onboard a Middle Kingdom vessel, where the crew gathered to invoke the Celestial Consort Tianfei at the outset of each new voyage; this was an integrated part of the bridge controls, without which the rest of the ship would not function. And the circuitry and ridges on the platform's surface were not purely decorative, but incorporated sensitive instrumentation capable of detecting the presence of an iron-containing, oxygen-carrying metalloprotein called hemoglobin. Without hemoglobin, the ship would not function, and the *Dragon* would not fly.

There was only one place that the Mexica got their hemoglobin, and it wasn't from shock-resistant containers in refrigeration units.

Syuxtun floated in midair by Zhuan's side, looking stricken. "How many? How many lives ended here?" he asked in a hushed voice, his jaw set and eyes narrowed. His voice did not quaver, as Ang's had a moment before, and as Zhuan was sure his own would if he were himself to speak, but instead hinted at reserves of strength belied by the bannerman's almost serene manner. If he was in fact a native of Khalifan, as Zhuan had surmised, and had grown up in the shadow of the Mexic Dominion, what might Syuxtun have seen as a younger man to light the fires which Zhuan now saw burning in the bannerman's eyes.

"It's hard to say with any exactitude," Sima said, treating Syuxtun's rhetorical statement of disgust as an honest question, unable to see the difference, "but given the age of the ship and the amount of organic material we cleaned away, I'd say anywhere from the high hundreds to the low thousands, possibly more." She paused, and pointed at stains on the ceiling. "A great many of the rites would have been performed when the ship was spun up, with centrifugal gravity, and so the spilt blood would have been collected by the runnels on the sacrificial altar, but some would have been performed when the ship was in weightless conditions, such as it is now, in which case whatever blood not drawn into the altar's sensor apparatus would have floated freely in globular form in the cabin until collected by suction-cleaning-devices or the like."

Zhuan tried to shut out the clinical way in which Sima cataloged the systematic slaughter and disposal of helpless prisoners. He had never understood how the Mexica had managed to become a world power, centuries past, with their blind allegiance to the blood-hungry gods of their forefathers, but somehow they had managed to integrate their brutal beliefs with their gradually increasing technological sophistication. And so rather than being stymied, their development retarded by their societal imperative to capture and sacrifice human victims to their inhuman gods, the artificers of the Mexica had found ways to incorporate those ritualistic requirements. When the Mexica had been for a generation part of the Middle Kingdom, the practice of human sacrifice had been banished; then when the Middle Kingdom was ousted, the practice was revived and systematized. Now, each vessel of the Mexica, whether operated on land, sea, air, or vacuum, employed an ignition system keyed to the presences of just-spilt human blood, and there were no Mexic craft that would operate without a human sacrifice performed onboard at regular intervals.

At the rear of the command center, opposite the sacrificial altar, just above the hatch leading down through the deck to the living quarters beneath, there was a pair of narrow metal cages, about the dimensions of the coffins in which Zhuan and the others had slept the night before. Zhuan didn't have much patience for stories of ghosts and hauntings, and didn't believe in such a thing as the supernatural, but glancing at those imposing cages, he found it hard not to hear the screams which must once have echoed from them, in the not-too-distant past, as innocent prisoners—captured subjects of the Middle Kingdom—awaited the moment that they would be dragged across the command center, strapped to the sacrificial altar, and gutted with an obsidian blade, all for the greater glory of the blood-hungry Mexic gods.

Zhuan's insides felt like they were made of ice, and he was forced to wonder: Would he continue to feel the cold grip of terror throughout the long voyage to Xolotl, or could he hope that eventually he might be inured to the horrors around him?

CHAPTER FIFTEEN

There followed three days of training and drills, as the trio of Zhuan, Ang, and Syuxtun were familiarized with the controls of the *Dragon*—with special attention to steering, propulsion, and communication—and Yao and the others practiced their marksmanship with the new weapons and went through exhaustive combat drills in a variety of terrains, everything from weightless hard vacuum to pressurized centrifugal gravity.

The goal, Yao knew, was for the men to perform as a cohesive unit, to operate collectively in theater with a minimum of spoken commands, to learn to anticipate one another's reactions and act accordingly. But while it was clear that several of the other five men might be passable combatants in their own right—Dea was incomparable with a firearm, Fukuda was a vicious hand-to-hand fighter, and Nguyen could take an astounding amount of punishment before hitting his knees—as a group they had yet to cohere. It was not surprising, Yao realized, since these were hardly model soldiers, but criminals and cowards who had only been saved from summary execution by the high command's urgent necessity; still, all of them had been soldiers, of one type or another, so must have been able to follow orders at some point.

Zhuan was having better luck getting his team acquainted with the *Dragon* and her controls, though the experience was no less frustrating than Yao's, for all of that. The original plan was that Zhuan and Ang would be familiarized with the Mexic language to the point where they could operate the ship's controls without Syuxtun's constant intercession as translator. But despite days of work, the two men could not make much headway, the meaning behind the perplexing glyphs of the Mexic ideography remaining stubbornly opaque. In the end, a compromise was reached, and strips of adhesive inscribed with the Middle Kingdom ideograms were affixed over the controls. It meant that, if Ang wanted to locate the switches controlling pitch or yaw, roll or thrust, he had merely to scan for those characters, rather than struggling to remember what the stylized rabbit or snake or flint glyphs meant.

Finally, on the fifth day since the nine were first gathered together in Fanchuan Garrison, they found themselves called to a large chamber, with Agent Wu on a dais before them. Arranged on platforms around her were a pair of pressure suits, each of a different design, and a spherical object constructed of dull brushed steel a little bigger in diameter than a helmet. The steel sphere rested on a tripod of legs welded to its lower body, and near the top, just below a visible seam in the metal, were handles of looped metal.

Agent Wu dispensed with any pleasantries quickly, giving the men cursory compliments on their progress in recent days, and her high opinions about their fitness to complete the mission before them. None of the men seemed overly concerned about Wu's opinions one way or the other, regarding their fitness or any other topics, and her compliments rolled off them like water off a duck's back. But they sat silently, all the same, out of deference to her position and everything it suggested.

Yao and Zhuan exchanged glances, and each could intuit that the other shared his thoughts: there was something unnerving about empty compliments coming from a woman who could, on the authority of the Eastern Depot, have any of them executed on the spot. And, her friendly demeanor aside, both men knew that, if the window of opportunity to reach Xolotl were not so small and growing smaller by the moment, there was every chance that Wu would simply execute the lot of them and start over with a more pliable group. Fortunately for all of the nine, a more pliable group was not readily available, and the window of opportunity was growing smaller with each passing hour, and so the summary execution of the group was a slim possibility at best.

Still, there was always the chance, so it didn't pay to evoke the agent's wrath, assuming she had any to evoke.

Having reached the end of her prepared pleasantries, Agent Wu moved on to introducing the
equipment arranged before them.

"We're calling this, for lack of a better term, a
stealth suit." She indicated the pressure suit, which
was arranged in its various constituent components
on a platform to her left. "It's built up from a standard combat pressure suit model, with significant
alterations to the design. For one thing, the col-
oration of the hardshell armor and fixtures."
Unlike typical combat suits, which trended toward
lighter metallic shades and tones of rust red, this
suit was completely covered in a flat, matte-black
laminate. It reflected back none of the ambient light
in the room, but seemed more like a solid shadow
than a physical object. "Designed to absorb all light
in the ultraviolet spectrum, against a black back-
drop—the night sky of the void, for example—it
will be virtually invisible to the naked eye. There's
still the infrared end of the spectrum to consider,
and that's where this comes in." She pointed to a
series of small ridges which were built over the
exhaust vents on the rear of the suit. "These baffles
are designed to dispel and cool any residual heat
from the system. It's not one hundred percent efficient, and the suit can still be spotted by infrared
cameras against the cold vacuum, but if worn in
environments anywhere at or above the freezing
point of water the suit should be rendered essentially invisible to infrared scanners. Intelligence
indicates that the best paths to maneuver through
the Xolotl station may be ventilation shafts, in
which case the stealth suits should be perfect. In the

event that you have to move through vacuum, just hope that the lights are down and nothing but naked eyes are pointed your way."

She lifted the suit's helmet, the plastic of the faceplate tinted so dark as to be almost black in itself. Rotating the helmet, she held it forward, the opening at the bottom toward the men. "That's the scrambler radio we mentioned during your first mission briefing." She reached in and flicked a nub of metal protruding from the inside rim of the helmet. "Like your microgravity weapons, the scramblers are prototypes, never before used in field conditions."

She paused, and smiled broadly. "But don't worry, I'm sure the artificers have worked out all the bugs by now. In any event, the radios broadcast over regular frequencies, just like those you're used to, but unless your signal is picked up by a radio equipped with a descrambler, all that anyone will hear is static, sounding like nothing but sunspot noise. Your broadcast signal itself can still be tracked, and if you stay online long enough your position could be triangulated, assuming the enemy has enough radios deployed around you, so you should keep your communications to a minimum. But when you *do* communicate over the scramblers, you should be able to speak freely, rather than in code, since the enemy is much more likely to be able to break any spoken-word cipher you're employing than the scrambled transmission, and if the enemy manages the latter it's a safe bet that they'll have managed the former, as well."

She moved to the platform on her right, upon which lay the components of another suit, of a quite different design. "Some of you might find this more familiar than will others." She lifted the helmet for the suit, which was constructed to resemble a stylized jaguar, tawny-yellow with black spots, with the faceplate set in the creature's open mouth, framed by wicked teeth as long as a man's finger.

Not a few of the men suppressed shivers on seeing the helmet, with varying degrees of success. There was scarcely a man or woman serving in the imperial armies and navy of the Dragon Throne who had not encountered one of the elite warriors of the Mexic Dominion, the Jaguar Knight, though not all who did lived to recount the tale.

The military divisions of the Mexica were different from those adopted by the Middle Kingdom. The forces of the Dragon Throne were divided into infantry trained for surface combat— the Army of the Green Standard—marine forces trained to operate in all environments—the Eight Banners—and the Interplanetary Fleet—as at home flying in vacuum as they were in the air, especially after absorbing the men and equipment of the now-decommissioned Imperial Navy of the Air some years before. By contrast, the military of the Mexic Dominion was a single body, reporting through a unified command structure, with men and women assigned to the various functions on an individual basis, by dint of their personal aptitudes and experience. It was sometimes difficult for onlookers from the Middle Kingdom to fathom, but it seemed it was not unusual for a Mexic warrior to begin as an infantryman, later to be transferred to a marine company of commandos, and end up finally as an aeronaut. The rank and role of the individual could be determined by the type of armor he wore, and especially by its adornment.

The Jaguar Knights were an elite body of Mexic warriors who stood near the pinnacle of a military hierarchy that dominated an entire society. From birth, Mexica were trained to be fierce combatants, and each child's umbilicus was ritually burned and then buried under the consecrated ground of a former battlefield not far from their capital city, Place of the Cactus. Testing throughout childhood gauged the child's aptitudes, and training was tailored to the individual's strengths and weaknesses accordingly. Coming of age, Mexica were sent into battle, and rose through the ranks by capturing prisoners in combat. Eventually, if the young warrior survived enough conflicts and distinguished himself through a sufficient number of kills and captures, he would be inducted into one of the orders. There were many such groupings, but the two pre-eminent warrior orders were the Eagle Knights, comprised of aeronauts who had garnered a requisite number of kills in air or space, and the Jaguar Knights, warriors who had captured a high number of enemy combatants on land, sea, air, or vacuum.

There was another warrior elite of the Mexic Dominion, the House of Darkness, which served the Great Speaker of the Mexic Dominion much as the Embroidered Guard served the Dragon Throne. But the servants of the House of Darkness were not simply secret policemen and intelligencers, like the agents of the Embroidered Guard, but were likewise torturers and ritual executioners. Those who came under the obsidian blades of the House of Darkness were sacrificed in the name of all the gods of the Mexica, but especially to the honor and glory of the flayed god, Xipe Totec.

"There were three Mexic pressure suits in the downed *Dragon*," Wu went on, "which our technicians were able to recover from the wreckage. They were considerably damaged in the crash, but using components scavenged from other fallen Mexica on Fire Star and in orbit, they have been able to restore the suits to full functioning. As you're well aware, we have at best only an approximate schematic of the interior of Xolotl with which to plan this mission, based on the intelligence from intercepted Mexic transmissions and the little we've been able to... extract from captured prisoners."

Zhuan shivered, and remembered that, in some respects, perhaps the Embroidered Guard were not so different from their opposite numbers in the House of Darkness, after all, and realized he had no interest whatsoever in learning precisely how that intelligence had been "extracted" from the Mexic prisoners.

"And since we have only an approximation of the asteroid's layout," Wu continued, "there is simply no way that we can account for all contingencies. And so, in the event that a more subtle approach is needed, subterfuge rather than an all-out assault, we have equipped these captured Mexic combat suits with the same scrambler radios as your stealth suits. Nothing has been done to modify the thermal profile of the Mexic suits, I'm afraid, since any such modifications would too greatly alter their outward appearance and eliminate any potential gains from subterfuge. Likewise, the fittings and junctures are the original Mexic designs, and so the components will not be interchangeable with suits of Middle Kingdom manufacture." She set the jaguar helmet down on the platform. "If fortune smiles, you'll have no need to use these suits after the initial stage of the mission, and any such limitations will be moot. But in the event that they are needed, there will be three Mexic suits onboard available for your use."

She turned from the Jaguar Knight suit, needlessly dusting her hands off, and stepped nearer the spherical object on the final platform. The brushed steel of its surface glinted dully in the room's bright light, but it seemed to radiate a coldness into the space around it.

Zhuan was sure he was not the only one to hope that cold was *all* that the sphere was radiating. It had been a few days, but he would have been able to recognize the design even if he hadn't been shown a schematic of the device during their first briefing.

"And this, finally," Wu said, standing with her hand hovering just a finger's width from the top of the sphere, "is your payload. Its code name, 'Dragon's Egg.'" She quirked a slight smile. "It was suggested by the artificers that a more appropriate name might be 'Cuckoo's Egg,' after that bird's habit of depositing its own unborn offspring into the nests of other birds, but the military command rejected the suggestion as lacking a certain...

gravity, perhaps?" Her smile widened for a fraction, and then began to fade. She continued, all business. "As I indicated in Fanchuan Garrison, the Egg is an implosion-type fission explosive device, with a destructive capacity in the eighty kiloton range."

Wu reached over and began to unscrew the top section of the sphere, casually, and several of the men gasped, while others rose involuntarily to their feet.

"Don't be alarmed," Wu said with genuine amusement. "This is just the housing and controls. The contents, and especially the fissile material, won't be inserted until just before the Egg is transported to the *Dragon*'s hold."

Sighs of relief rippled through the room, as everyone settled back into their seats.

"Now, the arming of the device is quite simple, and should be familiar to any of you who've operated standard model time-delayed explosives in the past. But just as we can't be completely sure of the layout of Xolotl, we can't be entirely sure which of you will be on hand in the mission's final stages, and so we want all of you to be checked out on this equipment." She cast a glance in Zhuan's direction. "That goes for you and the rest of the flight crew as well, Captain Zhuan."

Zhuan nodded, unsmiling.

"Now, this is the timing mechanism here"—she pointed to a series of dials—"and this display shows how much time remains. The Egg is quite heavy," she paused, and attempted to lift the sphere by the handles, able to shift it only fractionally, "and will take two men at least to maneuver it.

Once you get into the microgravity environment at the asteroid's core it should be easier to move, and then one set of hands should be enough, if necessary. Now, this is how to arm the explosives and set the timer."

Wu went through the procedure, first once, then again. Then, after she had reviewed all of the essentials, she called each of the nine to the front of the room to demonstrate their understanding, step by step.

When it came to Zhuan's turn, he found himself strangely unmoved by the experience of being so near a fission bomb, even one which wasn't yet capable of exploding. It wasn't until he had a chance to reflect, once he took his seat again, that he was able to work out why he was not moved. It was because, deep down, Zhuan knew that he would never have to worry about how to arm the explosive or set the timer, or any of the dozen mundane steps Wu drilled them on. He would never have to worry about that, because Zhuan knew without a hint of uncertainty that he would be long dead before that stage of the mission was reached.

CHAPTER SIXTEEN

On the morning of the seventh day, just as the bells were chiming the start of the second watch, the nine men were strapped into their acceleration chairs onboard the *Dragon*, waiting clearance to slip her moorings and maneuver through the shipyard hangar toward the massive lock, and from there to the empty void beyond.

Great care had been taken to get the captured Mexic vessel into Zhurong without their enemies discovering it had fallen into Middle Kingdom hands, and the success of the present mission hinged on the Mexic Dominion accepting that the *Dragon* was just what she appeared to be, when approaching the Xolotl asteroid base. And so, were the *Dragon* to be spotted leaving the Zhurong hangar at this early stage, by Mexic patrols with high-powered remote-viewing mirrors, then the game would be up, and the mission would be a failure even before it had begun.

To provide a distraction, and divert the attention of the Mexica away from the moonbase, if only for a short while, the Interplanetary Fleet had been massing at higher orbits for some days, preparing for an assault on the Mexic warships which had been identified drifting out near Gonggong, the smaller and more distant of Fire Star's two moons. Since early the night before, the Middle Kingdom vessels had been maneuvering into position, and at the chiming of the morning's first watch had launched their assault.

There were only a small number of Mexic warships in the flotilla, but well armed enough that they likely considered themselves more or less immune from attack, since any assault on them would be a costly one for the forces of the Middle Kingdom. But the risk to the ships and their crews had been determined an acceptable one by the admiralty, in exchange for the safe passage of the *Dragon*.

Strapped into his chair, awaiting orders to cast off moorings, Captain Zhuan could only imagine the danger those ships were now facing, all on his behalf. And the irony of his situation did not escape him, nor did the biting memory of that Middle Kingdom blockade ship going up in a guttering gout of flame while on his orders the *Exhortation* retreated to safety. It didn't matter that he was now likely sailing toward his own doom, out on that hidden Mexic asteroid; what mattered was that lives were now being lost, were being *paid*, so that his own life could be safeguarded, at least for a little while.

Finally, the word to disembark crackled over the ship's radio, and Zhuan and Ang manned their stations while the moorings slipped free and a pair of tugs pushed and prodded the *Dragon* toward the exit-lock. The great doors parted for them, and then the tugs puttered back into the hangar while they closed. At a signal from Zhuan, Steersman Ang worked the controls that gradually retracted the rods from the reactor in the pod at the *Dragon*'s stern, and then as the outer doors of the lock began to cycle open Zhuan prepared to give the order to open the aperture for thrust.

There was not room on the cramped bridge for all of the nine crewmen, and so five of the men were strapped into acceleration chairs bolted to the deck down in the living quarters. In addition to Zhuan in the captain's chair and Ang at the steersman's station, there was Syuxtun at the communications controls, and Bannerman Yao at the station which must have been intended by the *Dragon*'s original designers as a place of honor reserved for the ship's executioner.

At the forward end of the bridge hulked the sacrificial altar, now untenanted, still marred here and there by the dark blood stains that no amount of cleaning would ever scrub off. And at the rear of the bridge, pressure suits now hung in the cages once meant for sacrificial victims.

Deep in the belly of the *Dragon*, at its most protected and well-armored core, lay the Dragon's Egg, the fissile material carefully inserted just prior to boarding, safely swaddled in thick cushioning designed to absorb any impact short of the ship crash-landing.

As the doors gradually opened, little by little, like the jaws of a fierce beast widening to swallow its prey whole, the ship juddered with the contained pressure in the propellant chamber, heated to impossibly high temperatures and desperate to race out through the thrust aperture. The metal of the bulkheads and deck picked up the vibrations and began to hum, audibly, a low thrumming noise just at the edge of hearing.

Even in this strange place, strapped into an uncomfortable chair in a chamber whose walls would forever be stained by the lifeblood of all those lives wasted here, there was something that tickled the back of Zhuan's thoughts, something just beneath his notice that engendered an undeniable sensation of... familiarity?

Just as the doors opened wide enough for the *Dragon* to exit, and the admiralty reported that their distraction had served its purpose, the eyes of any distant Mexica no doubt trained on the fierce conflagration high overhead, Zhuan at last realized what was so familiar, and felt a sense of dread seeping through to his bones.

It was the thrum of the ship's engines. It sounded exactly like the growl of a bear on the prowl, just before pouncing on its prey.

CHAPTER SEVENTEEN

The asteroid recorded in the logs of the Directorate of Astronomy as Orbital Object 991216, which the Mexica had christened Xolotl, circled the sun once every five-hundred fifty-four and three-quarter days. Its orbit had a relatively low eccentricity for an asteroid of its class, nearly a perfect circle, and for more than half of its orbit it tracked very near the orbit of Fire Star, which circled the sun at a more sedate pace, completing a revolution once in every six hundred and sixty-eight and a half days. Circling at different rates, there were years in which Fire Star and Xolotl tracked more closely together than others, but even at their greatest variance the delta-v requirements to reach Fire Star from Xolotl or vice versa was much less than that required to reach Earth from either of them. The asteroid's proximity to Fire Star, and the relatively low cost in fuel consumption for the trip, made it a perfect staging ground for the forces of the Mexic Dominion.

This year, the fifty-second year of the Taikong emperor, planet and asteroid came nearest each other in the terrestrial spring, and orbited virtually in sync with one another for the rest of the terrestrial year. Only now were the two bodies beginning to drift apart. On Earth, it was now the month of the Rat, toward the end of autumn in the year of the Water-Monkey, sun currently in the Heavy Snow position in the sky. On Fire Star, according to the twenty-four-month calendar adopted by the Middle Kingdom artificers in the early years of colonization, it was the month of Dongzhi, the depths of Fire Star winter, with the vernal equinox and the onset of spring still months away. Of course, at this early stage of the terraforming process, Fire Star was still essentially a dead, cold world, and the variations from one season to the next were scarcely perceptible. It was cold enough to freeze a grown man to death in moments on the surface in the height of summer; that it might be a few degrees cooler in winter hardly made much difference.

Xolotl and Fire Star were drifting apart from one another, and given the difference in their orbital periods it would be some years before they were this close to each other again, not until the terrestrial year of the Hare, the eighteenth Fire Star year. The success of the *Dragon*'s mission depended on the accuracy of the intercepted pass-codes and protocols, and the longer it took Zhuan and his team to reach Xolotl, the greater the chance that those pass-codes might have been updated in the interim.

There was always the chance that the Eastern Depot might intercept a subsequent transmission and, decoding it, produce another set of pass-codes, but the risk that they wouldn't was considered too great. Thus the urgency with which the team was assembled and sent out into the void; every day that passed simply served to increase the likelihood that the mission would be a failure before it even began. As it was, there was scarcely time to get the crew trained and the ship prepared before they were sent out into the void, and by that time the travel time to Xolotl had extended to more than a week. Nearly nine days within the dark, blood-stained hull, hurtling through the black.

The *Dragon* had evidently been originally designed for a small crew of no more than four or five, a scout ship intended for high acceleration and maneuverability. If not for the fact that all Mexic Dominion vessels, by design, included storage space for sacrificial victims, there would not have been room for the entire nine-man team. As it was, their living quarters were cramped, to say the least, and each man was granted only a tiny mass allowance for any personal items.

Naturally, as all nine men had been incarcerated for days, weeks, or months before being brought to Zhurong and, from there, to the *Dragon*, it wasn't as if they had large numbers of personal items on hand to begin with. Rather, each had only those items he'd been allowed to keep on his person when imprisoned in the first place.

Most of the men had nothing to call their own, which suited them well enough. Zhuan, for example, had put very little stock in material possessions since he left his parents' house for the last time as a boy, and Yao, raised with military discipline, had been taught that the only thing a man truly possessed was his own honor, which had always been enough for him. A few of the others, though, had squirreled away little curios when they had been imprisoned, whether because they hid them or because some guard had taken pity on them, and these few items they prized as treasures more rare than gold. These, naturally, they had brought along with them onboard the *Dragon*, not even bothering to entertain the notion of leaving them behind.

But the close quarters and cramped conditions, combined with the few scattered treasured possessions brought onboard, were a sure recipe for disaster.

It didn't start with the game of big-and-small, though that was the inciting incident. No, so far as Zhuan remembered the trouble really began near the end of the first day of the *Dragon*'s voyage.

Once the ship was underway, the counterweight had been extended on a tether from the dorsal side of the craft, and attitude rockets fired to set the *Dragon* to rotate. It took several revolutions to build sufficient rotational velocity, with the heavy counterweight and the bulk of the ship both revolving around a point midway along the tether, but by the second revolution the crew onboard the *Dragon* could already feel something like gravity tugging at their bones. When the rotational velocity was great enough, the attitude rockets stopped firing, and the *Dragon* kept on spinning, end over end as it hurtled through the void, traveling at the constant velocity imparted by the engine's burst of thrust. And in the confines of the cramped craft, the centrifugal forces pressed the crew to the deck with a force equivalent to a third Earth gravity, roughly the same as on the surface of Fire Star.

It had been the better part of a day since the crew had last been able to maneuver around aided by centrifugal gravity, having been either in the near-weightless areas of the Zhurong base, the corridors, locks, and shipyards, or in the weightless compartments of the *Dragon*. During the initial bursts of acceleration they had been pushed back into their chairs for a time, the rear of the cabin effectively becoming the "down" direction, but once the ship picked up speed the additional acceleration bursts were comparatively minor, and the sense of weightlessness returned.

Now, they were able to move freely about the crew quarters, walking instead of floating. And it was here that the problem began.

"Where is it? Where *is* it?"

The crew had gathered in the common area of the crew compartment, at the beginning of the sixth watch, to eat the evening meal. Now that the ship had centrifugal gravity, eating from the sealed containers of rice and fish would be easier, and the bamboo flasks of tea could be handled like cups, with their tops removed, instead of through vacuum-sealed straws.

"Where is it?" Bannerman Dea was on his feet, patting his thighs and chest alternately, becoming increasingly frantic and distressed.

All of the nine were wearing one-piece black suits, with pockets sewn onto the thighs, chest, and upper arms, and all but Paik wore slippers on their feet, the latter instead going barefoot, despite the vocal objections of some of the others on being exposed to the sight of his gnarled and callused feet, to say nothing of the pungent aroma.

Evidently, Dea was checking his pockets for something, and failing to find it. It wasn't clear what he was attempting to locate, only that it was clearly something he considered extremely valuable.

"Where?" Dea slammed his fist down on the table, and glared at those seated around it.

Zhuan glanced over, and saw Yao looking at him, expression unreadable, and decided it was time to act. Now that they were onboard the *Dragon*, and had not yet reached Xolotl, he was the absolute authority on the ship, and would be best served by acting the part.

"Where is *what*, bannerman?" Zhuan asked, crossing his arms over his chest and putting as much force behind his words as possible.

The look in Dea's eye suggested that he knew that he was acting somewhat irrationally, recognized that he was overcome by whatever passions moved him at the time, but that he was unwilling or unable to do anything but surrender to it. "A wallet," he said, and held his hands up, his fingers making a rectangular shape, thumb to thumb and fingers outstretched at right angles. "About this size. Made of leather." He paused, and then held his hand up, forefinger and thumb a centimeter or so apart. "About this thick," he said, as though to distinguish it from any leather wallets of other various thicknesses they might have come across in the ship.

Zhuan had seen the wallet Dea meant, the day before, when the nine were going through the final pre-flight checks in the Zhurong station. There had been a brief battery of medical examinations—a perfunctory final precaution on some form or checklist, one assumed, since it could scarcely have mattered to the admirals and commanders if the men they were sending on a suicide mission had a cold or fever when they flung themselves into the enemy's lair—and then the nine had been outfitted with plain, unmarked worksuits and slippers, similar to those Zhuan had worn for years on Interplanetary Fleet vessels but now without any of the standard insignia or adornments. This was a matter of plausible deniability, perhaps, some symbolic gesture that said that the operation on which the nine were being sent was not a standard or even "sanctioned" military operation; more than likely, it was simply a question of none of the three military branches wishing to take the blame should the mission prove a failure, though Zhuan was sure they would each rush to take the credit, if it were instead a success.

In any event, while the men were being outfitted, Specialist Sima came by to mass out any personal items they wished to bring onboard the *Dragon*. Zhuan'd had none, and so had sat by, more or less patiently, while the others brought their effects to Sima to place on the scale. Ang had brought a trio of bone dice, though how he had managed to keep them in Baochuan, Zhuan had no desire to learn.

Syuxtun had a small book, bound in green leather with gilt letters stamped on the spine and cover. Dea had a small leather wallet, no more than a hand's width across and a little more in length. Sima did not open the wallet, nor did Dea offer to display its contents, but its mass was considerably below the threshold allotted to the bannerman so it hardly seemed to make any difference.

Dea had slid the wallet into one of the pockets sewn into his suit at the thigh, and that was the last that Zhuan saw of it.

"I've not seen it since we boarded," Zhuan said, as soothingly as possible. "Is it possible you misplaced it?"

"No!" Dea snapped. "It was secured in my pocket when we left the habitat ring, and I made doubly sure that the pocket was fastened before we boarded the accelerator."

"So that it would not drift off in microgravity." Zhuan nodded.

"Just so." Dea slapped his hand on the table's surface.

Zhuan glanced meaningfully at the pockets on Dea's either thigh. "And yet both appear to be unfastened and open."

Dea grit his teeth, his lip curling back. "Yes," he said, his tone strained. "That's my point exactly."

"What?" Cai asked from the far side of the table, confused. "That you left your pocket unfastened and your wallet floated off?"

"No!" Dea whirled to face the guardsman. "I *didn't* leave my pocket unfastened. Someone *else* unfastened it later."

Cai expelled a dismissive burst of air through pursed lips, and shrugged. "So you say…" he mumbled, and returned his attention to his meal.

"Captain," Dea turned back to face Zhuan, his jaw set, "my personal possession has been stolen. What do you intend to do about it?"

Zhuan sighed. "Did you see anyone steal it?"

Dea glowered, but shook his head.

"And have you seen anyone else with it in their possession?"

Again, Dea shook his head, angrily.

"Then I'm afraid there is no actionable offense before us." Zhuan rested his hands on the table, on either side of his bowl, and regarded Dea sympathetically. He'd been forced to arbitrate situations just such as this countless times over the years, as the master of a ship, and knew the protocols and procedures involved like a litany. "If you are not in a position to swear out a formal complaint, I'm afraid there's little more that I can do at this point."

Dea looked around the table, eyes narrowed to suspicious slits. "Certainly there is," he insisted. "You could have them all searched."

Zhuan shook his head, somewhat sadly. "If it were ship's property in question, perhaps," he allowed. "Or some component essential for the mission. But I'm afraid I'll not authorize a full search for a misplaced and non-essential personal effect."

"Non-essential?" Dea's eyes blazed. "Not to me it isn't!"

"Calm yourself, bannerman, and that's an order." Zhuan understood how the young man felt. Whatever was contained in the wallet was valuable to him, at least, even if it made no difference to Zhuan. But he had served on enough ships to know that one did not order a full strip and cavity search of an entire crew for such a relative trifle. To do so was to invite mutiny. However, it wasn't as if there weren't other options available to him, other avenues to ferret out a thief, if theft it was. "This is neither the time nor the place for histrionics."

Dea was hardly mollified, but he was soldier enough to accept Zhuan's orders, at least for the moment. He seated himself at the table, though he refused to eat, but cast suspicious glares around the table like bullets fired from a gun, his wary eye resting on each in turn.

Zhuan was not unsympathetic, having been in similar straits himself as a young man, and ventured to add some reassuring words.

"Try to take solace in the fact that this is a small ship, Bannerman Dea, and that none of us is going anywhere for the next eight days. In the event that your possession has been mislaid, inadvertently, it is sure to turn up. And, in the event that it *was* stolen..." He paused, and glanced meaningfully around the table, his eyes lingering for a moment on Ang, who seemed so relaxed as to have been carved from ice. "Well, in my experience, such matters have a way of working themselves out in the end, and it is rare that any offense committed on a ship, whether misdemeanor or high crime, goes undiscovered for too long."

As it happened, it would be only the next day, when the big-and-small game took a sour turn that Zhuan would be proved right.

CHAPTER EIGHTEEN

Steersman Ang had used the little mass allowance permitted him to bring onboard the *Dragon* three small six-sided dice, cubes of carved bone, each with black dots burned onto five faces and a single large red dot on the sixth. Once the ship was under-way, and spun up for centrifugal gravity, there was little to do but review the mission briefs and go through combat drills, and since Ang's role in the mission would be more or less complete when the others' were just beginning, he took little interest in such matters. Instead, as soon as there was suffi-cient gravity for his dice to roll across the deck-plates instead of rebounding and drifting through the cabin in microgravity, he produced his dice and began to roll.

Throughout that first day, it had seemed almost a nervous habit, rolling dice all on his own, without any purpose beyond the action itself. But watching him, Bannerman Yao suspected that there was a purpose beyond that which was evident, and glancing at Zhuan's expression the bannerman could see that his suspicion was shared.

Throughout the first day of their voyage, whenever his attentions weren't required at the steersman's station, Ang would be in the corner of the crew's common space, seated along the bulkhead on the deck, rattling his dice along the deck-plates, scooping them up, and throwing them again.

Then, near the beginning of the fourth watch in the mid-afternoon of the second day, Ang's purpose was gradually revealed.

"Are you going to put those things to use?" Paik had demanded, sullenly, "or are you just going to bat at them like a kitten with a dead rat?"

Ang had smiled, and looked up at the Chosonese guardsman. "What did you have in mind?" He glanced around the sparsely furnished common area and shrugged. "It isn't as if any of us have money with which to gamble. Or do you have taels of silver stitched into the lining of your tunic?"

Paik crouched down before the place where Ang sat, and scooped up the dice before the steersman could reach them. "Perhaps not money, but other comforts besides. Our food rations contain allotments of wine, neh? Lacking purse or coin, perhaps we roll for cups of wine, instead."

Ang arched an eyebrow, and nodded, as if gradually convinced. "A few rounds of big-and-small, perhaps?"

Yao had been there, reviewing the approximate schematics of Xolotl on the big table in the common area, and had seen the whole exchange, and it was clear to him from the moment that Paik opened his mouth that Ang had planned the thing all along. A short while later, when half of the crew were gathered around that bare spot of floor, cursing and cheering as the dice did or did not roll in the combinations on which they'd wagered, Yao saw that the steersman had very carefully maneuvered the whole encounter, as skillfully as a hunter lying in wait for prey. And it didn't escape Yao's notice that, more often than not, the dice rolls seemed to come up in Ang's favor.

He was still at the table, continuing to review the schematics, when things finally went sour. Seated in a rough circle were Ang, Paik, Fukuda, and Dea. The steersman had marked out a grid on the deck-plates using a bit of chalk, and the gamblers placed their wagers on the various possible combinations of dice rolls by placing markers of torn paper on the various squares. The dice were rolled around in one of the dinner bowls from which they'd eaten the night before, and sent skittering across the deck.

While the four in the corner rolled and cursed and cheered, Guardsman Cai came up to the table where Yao worked. "Bannerman?" Cai's manner seemed uneasy. "Well..." he shuffled his feet, chewing on his lower lip like a scolded child.

"What is it, guardsman? Better results today?" Of all the men on the mission, Cai's results on the firing range back on Zhurong had been the poorest, and Yao had exercised his authority as commander of the strike team to order the guardsman to practice with the flechette pistol on the makeshift firing range they'd erected in the ship's long, narrow hold below decks. Given the frangible nature of the fletcher's ammunition, even if he shot as poorly as he'd done on previous occasions, he'd not be able to do any real damage to the ship.

Cai shrugged. "I suppose," he said, equivocating. "I hit the target once or twice." Cai had not been much of a soldier, if his military records were any indication, and had landed in Baochuan after the cloud-flyer on which he was a passenger had crashed, and when salvaged from the wreckage his baggage had proved to have a fortune in contraband opium concealed in hidden compartments. He'd awoken from a coma in a military hospital to discover that his short, and apparently lucrative career as a courier for the opium syndicate had come to an unfortunate end. "The thing is..." Cai went on, then left off, glancing around the room.

Yao looked back up from his schematics, which had occupied his attentions. "Well? Spit it out, guardsman."

Cai leaned in, conspiratorially, and in a low voice said, "Are you having anyone else practice? Somewhere else, I mean? Because, when I went to put the fletcher back in the arms locker, after I was done, I saw that someone had taken another of the pistols out since I opened it last. But there was no one else down in the hold but me."

Yao raised his eyebrow. The arms locker hadn't been secured, but the crew was under orders that no one was to break it open except under his authorization. Of course, onboard ship, Zhuan had the authority to access the stores, but would he have?

What interest would the ship's captain have in a firearm?

He didn't have the opportunity to ruminate further on the matter, as shouts from the corner of the cabin disrupted his train of thought.

"You rutting cheat!"

Yao was on his feet before another word was spoken, in a tense stance ready for action, but didn't move until he had a chance to see what was happening. The gamblers had struck a tableau, with Fukuda wild-eyed and snarling, grabbing Ang's wrist in a vice-like grip, while Paik looked on half-lidded with boredom, and Dea sat cross-legged, his hands in his pockets. The dice on the deck before Ang were all rolled so that the single red dot on their sixth face was showing. Yao knew little about games and gambling, but knew enough to recognize triple-ones, an incredibly rare combination to begin with. When he saw the chalked-off grid, and the fact that Ang's marker rested on the square for triple-ones, he realized the odds were not just incredible, but nearer to impossibly against the likelihood.

It was Fukuda who had shouted, worked into a white-hot rage, and now Ang who answered for himself. "What... what do you mean?" He managed to look genuinely surprised, perhaps even dismayed. "Cheat?"

"Got greedy, didn't you?" Fukuda snarled, and then stood, dragging Ang to his feet. "You were happy losing a few rounds for all those you won, until I wagered all of my wine ration for the trip. Then you couldn't turn away."

"But... but I don't know what you mean," Ang pleaded, but as he spoke he turned his body to the side, as though trying to conceal something on his right side. "I didn't..."

Fukuda didn't let him finish talking, but spun him around, and then reached out and ripped open the pocket on Ang's right hip. "You palmed the dice and swapped another set. I *saw* it."

Sure enough, as the pocket's flap came tearing away from Ang's worksuit, another trio of dice clattered to the floor. Yao didn't want to begin imagining where Ang had been hiding those. But along with the dice came a few other bits and bobs, including a few pieces of paper, a small folding knife, a rolled length of twine, and a leather wallet.

Fukuda's concern was still about the dice, and he threatened to throttle Ang to get a confession from him. Paik sat sleepily on the deck, scarcely paying attention at all. Yao's attention was drawn by the leather wallet, and he remembered what Dea had said about it the night before. But before the bannerman could turn and see how Dea was reacting, the younger man was already on his feet.

"I knew it," Dea said through clenched teeth, leveling the flechette pistol in his hands at Ang's chest. "I *knew* that someone had stolen it."

Seeing the gun, Fukuda and Ang stopped their struggling, and the Nipponese deftly released his hold on Ang's arm and inched away. Paik, for his part, remained motionless, eyes wary. At Yao's side, Cai began to sidle backward toward the corridor.

"Pick it up," Dea said, his lip curled, showing his teeth. When Ang remained motionless, he stabbed forward with the fletcher's barrel and repeated. "I said, pick it up."

Ang held his hands up, palms forward. "Look, I don't want any trouble. Okay, I found your wallet. Okay, but I didn't..."

"Pick. It. Up."

Ang waved his hands, blanching. "Okay, okay! I picked your pocket, but hey, it was all... It was a joke! That's right! It was a kind of joke. I didn't mean any harm."

Dea slid the safety off, and thumbed back the release lever. "If you don't pick that up and hand it to me in the next three seconds, I'm going to drop you with a dozen of these needles in your throat."

"Okay, okay!" Ang scrambled, plucking the wallet up from the floor and holding it out to Dea, stretching his arm as far as it would go, holding his head and body back as though Dea were a fire whose flames would burn if he got too close.

Dea snatched the wallet from his hands, and in a deft one-handed motion shook it open. Then, using his forefinger and thumb, he pulled a square of paper from within and let the rest of the wallet fall to the deck. From his vantage point, Yao could see that the square was a lithograph. It was hard to tell from that distance, but it looked to be a portrait of a woman or a girl.

To this point, Yao had held back, waiting to see how things would play out, but watchful of any opening. As soon as the lithograph pulled free from the wallet, Yao saw his opening. Dea stood as if transfixed for a moment, his eyes on the small image, for the first time taking his eyes off Ang.

Yao now took the opening. He leapt forward, his feet clearing the deck as he sailed through the air, wordlessly. He tackled Dea, trying to knock the pistol from his hand, but while he succeeded in bowling the young bannerman to the deck, Yao wasn't able to get the pistol out of his grip before Dea fired off a round. As Ang started screaming, a blood-curdling howl, Yao and Dea grappled on the deck. In a matter of a blink of an eye, Yao managed to grab hold of Dea's gun-wielding arm, pointing the pistol's barrel harmlessly toward the bulkhead. And then, applying pressure with his thumbs to the tendons in Dea's wrist, Yao was able to wrench the pistol from his grasp.

Holding the pistol by the barrel, Yao leapt to his feet, jumping clear of Dea's struggling arms and legs. He snapped his fingers at Cai, who hadn't yet reached the corridor. "See to his wounds," he ordered, pointing at the still-screaming Ang. "And get him to shut up or I'll shoot him myself."

Yao had seen that the fletcher had only fired a single needle, and that Ang was clutching his shoulder. More than likely, he knew, it was little more than a graze. Still, shipboard weapons fire, and on a fellow crewman, was serious business.

Wielding the pistol, Yao stood over Dea, his expression stern. "Mind telling me why that picture is worth the life of one of your crewmen, Bannerman Dea?" It had not escaped Yao's notice that, the whole time they struggled on the deck, Dea had not let go of the small lithograph.

Dea pulled himself up into a sitting position, and with his arms resting on his knees, held the lithograph before him, carefully clutched in both hands. He studied the image, as if seeing it for the first time.

"Well?" Yao gestured with the pistol, and as punctuation nudged Dea hard with his toe.

Dea looked up from the image, and sighed. Then his lip curled back again into a slight, perhaps somewhat wistful sneer. "Do you know how I ended up in this fool's brigade, bannerman?"

Yao tilted his head slightly to one side. "Killed a man, as I understand it."

From the corner of his eye, he could see Cai tending to Ang, while Fukuda lounged at the table and Paik rested on the floor, leaned back on his elbow. The sound of the altercation must have carried, as Captain Zhuan and Syuxtun now stood in the open hatchway. Nguyen was the only one not to have made an appearance, which either meant that he was off somewhere asleep, or that his hearing wasn't as good as the others.

"That's right," Dea finally answered, ruefully. "Know why?"

"Why what?" Yao narrowed his eyes.

"Why I killed him?"

Yao shrugged. "Son, I don't know why most people do any of the things they do, and I'm not about to start guessing with you."

Dea chuckled, humorlessly. "Probably a wise choice." He turned the picture over in his hands, and for the moment seemed lost in thought.

Captain Zhuan came to stand beside Yao, careful to keep some distance. "Who's the girl?" he asked, keeping his tone level, pointing to the lithograph.

Dea's face lit up in a bright smile, counterpoint to the darkness that still clouded his eyes. "Isn't she a vision?" He gazed down at the image, and then turned it around and held it up for the others to see. Now Yao had a better look at her, he could see the picture was of a girl of perhaps seventeen or eighteen terrestrial years old, with the dark hair and eyes of the Han, but a touch of Chosonese to the shape of her nose and jaw line. "Her name is Lei Xiaoli, and she's the only girl I'll ever love." He paused, and looked up at Yao and Zhuan. "It was her brother I killed. And that's why I'll never get to see her again."

CHAPTER NINETEEN

"I suppose you could say I was doomed from the start."

The crewmen had moved to more comfortable positions around the common area, while Dea told his tale. Ang's shoulder, which had been bloodied little more than a bad splinter would have done, had been cleaned and dressed, and he sat in the corner of the room, looking daggers at Dea while trying not to attract Fukuda's attention. The others were seated around the table, some with tea and some with cups of wine in hand, with Dea sitting with empty seats on either side. Yao had the pistol laid on the table before him, having gone to secure the arms locker before continuing his interrogation. Or, to be more precise, the captain's interrogation, since upon his arrival in the room this matter had come under his authority.

This was something of an informal hearing, with a soldier's commanding officers questioning him about an offense—in this case, the unauthorized removal of a firearm from ship's stores, and the extremely unauthorized weapons fire that followed—but the other crewmen seemed just as interested to hear what Dea had to say. Perhaps it was that each man had arrived at the same end, in a sense, and each was curious to hear the paths by which the others had come. Or perhaps it was just that they were bored, and there was precious little else in the way of entertainment available to them.

"I was born in Jiangsu province," Dea began, "but grew up in Zhili in the outskirts of Northern Capital. My father was a bureaucrat with the Imperial Bureau of Armaments, and so was responsible not only for the manufacture of firearms, but also that of keys, locks, hammers, needles, screwdrivers, and scissors. When I was young, it was assumed that I would study for the imperial examinations and follow my father in joining the imperial bureaucracy. But I was of a more... romantic bent. Throughout childhood I had seen all manner of weaponry, whether brought home by my father, or during impromptu—and often unauthorized—tours of the manufactories of the Bureau of Armaments. I suppose you could say I was seduced by the romance of the gun. I haunted theaters showing dramas of Vinlander gunslingers in the wilds of Tejas, from the days when it was still a lawless frontier between the Commonwealth of Vinland and the Mexic Dominion. And every coin that passed through my hands

I spent on yellow-backed tenth-tael terribles, and I read every one of those stories until the pages were falling away from the spines.

"I spent all of my free time at the gun ranges, practicing my skills with rifle and pistol. I suppose, in retrospect, that I was one of those incurable romantics who feel that there are no frontiers left on Earth, with all of the land divided neatly between the Dragon Throne on the one hand and the Mexic Dominion on the other. It seemed to me that only the red planet Fire Star offered the chance for a man to prove his mettle, to live by his wits and his skills with a pistol alone.

"Naturally, my father didn't agree, but over his objections—and my mother's tears—I enlisted with the Eight Banners as soon as I was of age. I think that the recruitment officers weren't sure about me at first, and probably thought me the pampered son of a bureaucrat come out to play soldiers. But once I got out on the range and they saw my marksmanship scores, they didn't ask anymore questions. When I completed bannerman training and was fully vested, in short order I was bound for the red planet.

"I only took one personal possession along, which was only a fraction of our mass allowance. It was a pistol, plated with acid-etched silver, with carved ivory panels on the handle. It had been a gift from my father. He'd had it made for me especially by the manufactory, and sent it along with a brief and somewhat restrained note. I got the package just before I shipped out, and it seemed a fitting farewell. From that day on, I wore that pistol in a holster at my hip, whenever circumstances allowed.

"Now, one would think that, as soon as I reached Fire Star and saw first-hand the wages of war, that my foolish young notions of romance would have been ground underfoot. But no. On the contrary, the constant danger and adverse conditions only served to strengthen my romantic conceptions. I didn't just survive those first combat experiences, I reveled in them. Getting to use that ivory-handled pistol, quick-drawing just like those Tejas gun-slingers, mowing down blood-hungry Mexica one after another after another? That was the dreams of my childhood, given flesh and reality.

"Of course, since the only people I was shooting were Mexic warriors in full surface suits, made up to look like animals or monsters or suchlike, faces hidden behind tinted faceplates held in the beaks of terrifying birds or in the gaping mouths of stylized skulls, I was never forced to address the fact that these were people I was shooting at, not just targets. Each body that dropped was just another notch on my belt, not another human being, not a living person. I never had to look into their eyes, never had to admit what I was really doing.

"Then I found myself shooting a man whose face and eyes I could see, and my notions of romance went up in smoke.

"It all began when my unit was assigned to protect a group of colonial refugees. They were a group of families whose homesteads had come under heavy Mexic attack in recent days, and they were being temporarily housed in a supply depot before being moved to safer accommodations. Some of the families were opting to return to Earth, after seeing the fruit of an entire generation's labor destroyed in the war, with no end in sight.

"Now, we were fresh from active combat, and were on reduced duty as guards for the supply depot and the refugees living within. The duty wasn't any kind of challenge for us, but it was the closest we'd come to any kind of leave in months, and so we weren't about to complain. And besides, this was the nearest most of us had come to women in a long while, and though our orders were to avoid fraternizing with the refugees, more than a few of the men in the unit sought out the company of the unmarried or widowed women among the displaced colonists.

"Not me, though. I took the opportunity to practice my marksmanship. It wasn't that I didn't like women. I just... I found the leering glances that some of my less couth comrades threw at the civilian women distasteful. It just didn't seem appropriate. That is, until I met Lei Xiaoli.

"She was a farmer's daughter, youngest member of one of the first families to colonize Fire Star, who had worked an atmospheric greenhouse on the northern lowlands for longer than I'd been alive. I was... I think I was in love with her from first glance. After that moment, whenever my duties didn't require me to be elsewhere, I was there at her side. And Xiaoli—even though she'd never been more than a day's journey from her family's farm, she knew poetry, she knew songs—for some reason she seemed to return my affections.

"At first, it was a kind of bliss. Xiaoli's parents, still distraught over the loss of their greenhouse farm, were too preoccupied to notice my attentions, and my superiors were too busy relaxing to bother punishing the infraction. Unfortunately, the same couldn't be said for Xiaoli's older brother, Lei Sheng. He had noticed, no question, and was all too ready to do something about it.

"To be fair, Lei Sheng had seen the way the other bannermen had used and abused the affections of the other refugee women, and he didn't want to see his sister get hurt. So he forbade Xiaoli to have anything to do with me. But by that point, she was as much in love with me as I was with her, and she ignored her older brother's command. And things went on, much as they had. Until that one night, when everything came to an end.

"Lei Xiaoli and I were in the pressurized section of the depot, in the shadows behind some storage canisters, helping each other to keep warm, when Lei Sheng appeared. He'd found an antique carbine from somewhere or other, and waved it in my face. He told me to steer clear of his sister, or he'd take care of me once and for all.

"It was... It was like I'd just stepped into the pages of a tenth-tael terrible, or one of the old dramas, cast in the role of the Vinlander gunslinger. And suddenly... It doesn't excuse anything, quite the contrary, but it was as if I was a child again, playing those games as I'd done so often, only this time for real.

"Xiaoli was shouting at her brother to leave us be, but I felt like I had the matter well in hand. I loosened the ivory-handled pistol in its holster, and told Xiaoli to stand aside. Maybe she knew what I intended, maybe not. But when she'd tearfully retreated a few paces, I told Lei Sheng that I would continue to see his sister, that we were in love, and that there was nothing that he or anyone else could do about it.

"Sheng waved that carbine rifle around as if he had not the first clue what to do with it, and told me that if I thought there was nothing he could do, then I was mistaken.

"I held my hands limp at my sides, taking care to brace myself against the low gravity, and told him to take his best shot the first time, because he wouldn't get another. Just like the hero from one of those old yellow-backed stories, damn my eyes.

"Lei Sheng raised the carbine and started to aim, but before he could squeeze the trigger, I filled my hand and shot him dead-center in the chest.

"It wasn't until Sheng's body started to fall, and I heard Lei Xiaoli begin to scream, that I realized that I wasn't the hero of a tenth-tael terrible, and that this wasn't any kind of game.

"All I remember is Xiaoli cradling her brother in her arms, as his life poured out over the ground, her cheeks tear-stained, looking at me as though she'd never seen me before. It was in that moment that my romantic visions were finally shattered, as I watched Lei Sheng die. Not a monster, or a demon, or a faceless Mexic warrior, but a man just like me. And I had killed him

"When the other bannermen arrived, I didn't put up a fight. My superiors might have been willing to turn a blind eye to fraternizing with a civilian refugee, but murdering a civilian who was under the unit's protection? That was a capital offense. And it had been murder, pure and simple. With my skill with the gun on the one side, and Lei Sheng's fumbling inexperience with that antique on the other, it had been no contest. And I'd known that, even if I hadn't wanted to admit it to myself until it was too late. There was just some part of me that wanted that duel, wanted the shoot-out over the love of a woman, like all those Vinlander gun-slingers down in those Tejas border-towns. And because of that, I lost everything."

Dea looked up at the others around the table, the lithograph held in his hands.

"I never saw her again, after that. I don't know if her family stayed on Fire Star or returned to Earth. This picture she gave me is all I have left of her, all I have left of the things I lost, and I'm not giving it up for anybody. And if anyone tries to take it from me"—he glared at Ang, who cowered in the cor-ner—"I'll kill with pistol or bare hand, if it comes to it, and not feel the slightest guilt. I'm already filled with guilt as it is, and have no room for any-more."

CHAPTER TWENTY

A short while later, Captain Zhuan and Bannerman Yao conferred on the bridge, while the rest of the crew remained below decks. Aside from periodic checks to ensure that the ship's automated controls were keeping the *Dragon* on course, there had been little reason to visit the bridge since the previous day, and most of the men seemed quite happy to keep as much distance between themselves and the sacrificial altar at the front of the command center as possible.

Yao still had the purloined flechette pistol with him, tucked into his hip pocket, the safety fully engaged, while in his other pocket he kept the key to the lock which secured the arms locker below. He stood, at parade-rest, regarding the captain coolly.

Zhuan, for his part, sat in the captain's seat, fingers laced, deep in thought.

"No," the captain said at last, breaking the silence. "There's nothing else for it. We've got to lock him up."

Yao was unable to prevent a slight sigh from escaping his lips, though he was able to keep his head from shaking side to side.

Zhuan raised an eyebrow. "Don't you agree, bannerman?"

Yao seemed to struggle with some internal conflict, and grimaced. "Permission to speak freely?"

After a moment, Zhuan realized he hadn't answered. He waved his hand, in an inviting motion. "By all means, bannerman. I'm curious to hear your opinion."

The bannerman sighed again, slightly, taking a moment to gather his thoughts. "I understood your reasons for letting Bannerman Dea's general accusation about the theft of his property slide by without investigation."

"To initiate a crew-wide search at this early stage of the voyage, especially for something as relatively inconsequential as personal property, would only serve to engender resentment, which could fester over time into the desire to mutiny."

Yao nodded. "Your thinking paralleled my own. Without any evidence of wrongdoing, save the article's absence, there were insufficient grounds to act."

Zhuan narrowed his eyes. "But now?"

After a pause, Yao answered. "Having no wish to question your authority in the matter, I wonder if you aren't mistaken in your judgement on how to address Dea's subsequent infraction."

"Ah." Zhuan unthreaded his fingers, and laid his hands on the seat's armrests. "You think that he shouldn't be punished?"

"No," Yao said, shaking his head. "Or rather, that his infraction merits reprisal, but that the cost of that punishment, both to the crew and to the mission, outweighs the benefits."

"I'm not sure I follow." Zhuan leaned forward, his expression set. "The man removed a firearm from ship's stores without authorization, and then fired that weapon on a fellow member of the crew, *onboard* my ship. Protocols for shipboard conduct dictate summary execution for that kind of offense. I think that my decision is far more lenient. Perhaps even *too* lenient."

Yao took a deep breath before responding. "Obviously, you are better versed in fleet protocols than I am, and I wouldn't dream of contradicting you on that point, but unless I'm mistaken those protocols are designed to govern a ship of war sailing under normal circumstances." Yao paused, and glanced around the bloodstained gloom of the Mexica control center. "These are far from normal circumstances, and arguably not even a ship of war."

"So you argue for leniency?" Zhuan's eyebrow rose again, in surprise.

Yao nodded. "These men need to train and to drill if we are going to have any hope of completing our mission. Having one member of the strike team clapped in irons and secured in a storage space for the duration of the voyage only impedes our chances of success."

Zhuan crossed his arms over his chest. "Bannerman Yao, I must admit that I'm surprised."

"Surprised?" Now it was Yao's turn to cock an eyebrow.

"You've struck me as a man who follows orders, as the kind of soldier that lives and dies by the code of conduct. And yet here you are arguing to me, of all people, to abandon protocol."

Yao's lips pulled into a line. "I follow orders," he said, his voice low but level, "and I abide by a code of conduct. But protocols and codes can't be allowed to interfere with the successful completion of our orders. I am a practical man, not a slave to protocol."

Zhaun chewed the inside of his cheek thoughtfully. "So if your orders were in conflict with your code of conduct, you'd opt to jettison the conduct and follow the orders?"

Yao opened his mouth to respond, but nothing came out. He closed his mouth again, and tilted his head to one side. "I..." He shook his head. "No," he said at last. "In the past, I have allowed orders to countermand conduct, but no more. I am a man, first and foremost. I won't be ordered to do something that runs counter to what I believe to be right."

"And in this instance?" Zhuan's mouth twitched in the shadow of a smile.

"This isn't a question of right or wrong," Yao objected. "It's a question of practicality. Of benefit and loss. And there's simply nothing to be gained by imprisoning Dea."

"Nothing but the smooth operation of this ship," Zhuan countered. "Which is *my* sole responsibility and obligation to this mission, I'll remind you."

The bannerman shook his head, somewhat sadly. "You've given me permission to speak freely, captain. Now allow me to speak frankly." He leaned in fractionally, and lowered his voice, as though confiding a secret. "You know the kind of men with whom we share this ship. You saw their military records, redacted or no. And you know as well as I that this will not be the first such infraction in the course of our journey. Now, as I see it, we have two alternatives. One is to follow your protocols for shipboard conduct and, by the time we reach Xolotl, every one of these men will be clapped in irons and locked into a closet. The other is to allow me the latitude to handle these matters on my terms, without recourse to incarceration." A slight, grim smile tugged the corners of his mouth. "Believe me, there are things I can do in the name of training and drills that will more than satisfy your desire for punishment, honoring the spirit of your protocols if not to the letter."

Zhuan regarded him thoughtfully for a moment before nodding. "Very well. I'll follow your lead in this matter." He leaned forward further, his jaw set. "But I won't have members of this crew shooting at one another, do you understand me? If another of those reprobates opens fire anywhere but under controlled circumstances in your 'firing range,' frangible ammunition or no, I'll exercise my authority and opt for the harshest possible response."

Yao nodded his assent. He turned to walk back toward the hatch at the rear of the bridge, to return below decks and address the men. Before he'd taken two steps, though, he paused, and turned back to face Zhuan. "Captain, there's one final matter I wished to discuss."

"Yes, bannerman?"

Yao gestured to the controls at the forward walls of the bridge, and specifically to the steersman's station with the controls all labeled with strips of adhesive. "I have only a basic understanding of ship operation, and that little understanding limited to craft of Middle Kingdom design. In the days remaining on this voyage, I'd like for you to familiarize me with the *Dragon*'s controls."

Zhuan gave him a quizzical look. "I have no objection, bannerman. But may I ask why?"

"Because I don't like to enter a room I don't know how to exit, and don't like to board a boat I don't know how to drive. There hasn't been time before now to learn the basics, but there's only so much training I can drill into the men in any given twenty-four-hour period, and rather than spend the rest of them sitting on my thumb, I'd just as soon learn a few new skills." He paused. "Just in case."

"Just in case?" Zhuan repeated.

Yao nodded. "Just in case something happens to you, or Ang, or both."

Zhuan's mouth hung open. "Is… is that a threat, bannerman?"

Shaking his head, Yao was quick to answer. "Not in the least, captain. You've got me standing between the bridge crew and the rest of these reprobates, and I consider it one of my primary functions to keep any harm from coming your way. But I've been on too many missions that went from gold to dung in the final hours to think that nothing could go wrong, and I want to prepare for any contingencies."

The captain considered it for a long moment, and then nodded. "Fair enough, bannerman. Meet me back up here after the evening meal, and we'll start going over the basics."

Yao bowed, deferentially, inclining his head to indicate a courtesy offered to a superior by a subordinate. "By your leave, o captain."

CHAPTER TWENTY-ONE

The rest of the second day and most of the third passed more or less without incident. Yao drilled the strike team as long as seemed practicable, and when he wasn't with them was studying the mission briefs and the schematics, or else up in the bridge learning the rudiments of the Mexic controls. Steersman Ang knew more about the controls, by this point, than Captain Zhuan did, but would have made a poor tutor, it was decided, and so Zhuan offered the instruction. Syuxtun, when he was not drilling or busy with his daily devotions, was often called to the bridge to help Yao and Zhuan puzzle out some aspect of the ship's control systems which had not been adequately covered by Middle Kingdom labels.

The rest of the crew, for the most part, was left to their own devices in their personal time. Ang seemed to have little interest in enticing the others into another game of big-and-small, and even if he had tried it seemed unlikely that any would have taken him up on it. As it was, it was clear that no one involved had any inclination toward honoring the wagers won or lost in the previous game, especially considering that Ang had been caught swapping a loaded set of dice, and that the discovery had led ultimately, if indirectly, to the steersman catching a needle in the shoulder.

Which was not to say that Ang did not complain loudly and at length about his "grievous injury," as he called it, at least when Bannerman Dea was not in earshot, but once it had been established that it was scarcely a flesh wound, the rest of the crew paid him little attention.

With few things to occupy their minds, the majority of the men quickly lapsed into boredom. And the combination of such men, in such a confined space, with sufficient quantities of boredom was a certain recipe for disaster.

The first sign of trouble was the sound of bellowing rage from the lavatory. There were no circumstances in which such a noise coming from behind those doors would presage anything good.

But when Guardsman Nguyen burst out, stark naked with head and shoulders covered in blood, roaring like a bear caught in a trap, it was clear that things were about to get much worse.

Much of the detail in the military records which Bannerman Yao and Captain Zhuan had been shown about the other seven men had been redacted, deemed as too sensitive for their review by military command. As a result, the two did not know the specific circumstances under which most of the men had been originally incarcerated, and that had led to their selection for the current mission. There was sufficient detail remaining, though, usually about prior infractions, for them to develop a general opinion about the type of men with whom they sailed.

Guardsman Cai, they knew, had been arrested for dealing in contraband, an illicit activity which might not have ever been discovered had Cai not been unfortunate enough to take passage on a cloud-flyer destined to be shot down by enemy fire. But while that arrest had not been Cai's first infraction, it had been the first of its type. All of the other disciplinary notices in Cai's record had centered around other, seemingly more harmless activities.

Cai had something of a comical appearance, thin and gawky, with large ears and a protruding "apple" in his throat. Perhaps that was what had pushed him into playing the clown, from earliest childhood. In fact, he might well have missed his calling performing in a troupe of tumblers. Instead, the child of a farming family in Hunan province that lost their allotment after an extended drought, Cai had joined the Army of the Green Standard. But from his record, it seemed clear that he would not have made much of a farmer, either, so perhaps the loss to his family was not as great as it otherwise might have been.

In the notes appended to a disciplinary hearing, Cai reported to auditors that as a boy he had shaved the family dog as a prank, and later rigged his mother's broom to set alight as soon as she pushed it across the floor. While still in the Green Standard training camp on Taiwan Island he was reprimanded several times for pranks he played on other recruits, swapping boot-black for tooth polish, salt for sugar, removing the bolts from bunks so that they collapsed under the recruits' weight as soon as they laid down. Foolish, childish games and pranks, any one of which, taken by itself, was considered a minor infraction at worst, punishable by additional chores or otherwise odious duties, but which taken together indicated a persistent personality quirk largely unsuited to following commands.

Upon reaching Fire Star, where evidently he had been recruited to act as courier for an opium ring, Cai's behavior had improved, presumably because he was too worried about his illicit activities being discovered to allow himself to indulge his love of pranks. And while incarcerated in Baochuan prison, there had been scarcely little opportunity for such foolishness. But now that he was onboard the *Dragon*, at relative liberty for stretches at a time, and worse still growing bored like the others, Cai evidently found the perfect opportunity once again to play the prankster.

And that was where the trouble began.

An advantage of the ship's rotation, spinning on a tether opposite the counterweight and conferring centrifugal gravity on the crew compartments, was the ability for the crew to complete their toilet under more or less normal conditions. When the ship was effectively weightless, they were forced to resort to bathing only with damp sponges, and using a complicated suction apparatus to hose away their bodily wastes as necessary. Even when cleaning their teeth they weren't allowed to spit, for fear that free-floating globules of saliva might get into the ship's air intakes and muck up the electronics.

Under centrifugal gravity, though, the auxiliary plumbing fixtures were unlocked, and the crew were free to shower in an enclosed stall. They could sit and answer nature's call and allow gravity to carry away from them what otherwise they'd be forced to suck away with hoses. And they could spit into washbasins to their heart's content.

Of all the crew, Guardsman Nguyen seemed to delight the most in the lavatory facilities. They were simple, even austere by any normal standards, but to Nguyen they seemed the height of luxury. While the other crewmen groused and complained about the unfamiliar Mexic knobs and controls, or the low pressure of the shower or the tepid temperature of the water, Nguyen beamed, ecstatic, taking showers sometimes two or three times daily, while the others bathed once daily at the most, only every few days in most cases.

It was only natural, then, that Nguyen would be the butt of Cai's joke, though to all appearances the man-mountain had not been singled out for the treatment. If anything, when the prank was sprung, Cai's laughter at his carefully orchestrated joke quickly faded when he saw the anger on the giant man's blood-streaked face. But by then it was too late.

The prank had been a relatively simple one, which had taken some careful planning to orchestrate. In the same refrigeration units that held the crew's perishable comestibles, there were a pair of shock-resistant containers, clearly labeled with Middle Kingdom ideograms. There was no mistaking what was within: human blood.

There were, in all, several liters of blood, brought onboard by the Zhurong shipyard technicians against the possibility that the artificers' bypass of the Mexic hemoglobin sensors might be lost in a system restart. The chance was a slim one, all things considered, but the mission planners had not wanted to leave the crew in the position of needing a human sacrifice in order to get the *Dragon*'s systems up and running.

For a prankster of Cai's tastes, though, a supply of human blood in easy reach was simply too great a temptation to ignore.

The trick had been to get the containers into the lavatory without anyone seeing, and then to open the access panels in the bulkhead to get at the recessed plumbing. Once he'd done that, it was a matter of relative ease to disconnect the water leads, and then to connect them to makeshift spigots atop the containers of blood. By crawling partway into the wall, and then reaching up as far as he was able, he secured the containers, spigot down, to the ribs of the ship a half-meter above the shower closet's ceiling. Then he simply climbed back out, replaced the access panels, and went back to the common area to wait for the trap to be sprung.

The combination of the containers' internal pressure, and the pull of the centrifugal gravity, would draw the blood down through the leads, and out through the shower nozzle, spraying whomever spun the knobs. There was the risk that the blood might congeal, if allowed to sit in the relative warmth for too long, but the labeling on the outside of the container indicated that an anticoagulant had been added, which meant that so long as the shower was turned on within the next ship's day, it should still be liquid enough to flow.

Unfortunately for Cai, the next person to stand beneath the shower's nozzle and turn the knobs was the man-mountain Nguyen. And far from being merely annoyed by an unanticipated and unwanted shower of blood, Nguyen had reasons of his own for losing all reason and flying into an animal rage at the sight of so much blood, as the others were to learn.

None of which the others knew until later. All that they knew was that, bellowing like an enraged bull, completely naked and covered in blood, Guardsman Nguyen had rushed out into the common area, murder in his eyes. And though nearly all his reason seemed to have fled, when he saw Guardsman Cai laughing while the rest of the crew looked on in abject confusion, Nguyen was rational enough to know who to blame.

Then reason seemed to flee Nguyen altogether, for as he rushed forward, intent on killing Cai with his bare hands, he shouted at the top of his lungs, "I won't let you hurt her again!!"

And then the trouble had well and truly begun.

CHAPTER TWENTY-TWO

It took five of them to pull the naked and blood-soaked Nguyen off Cai, Zhuan and Yao both grabbing one of his arms, Syuxtun and Dea his legs, and Paik with his arm around his throat. Steersman Ang, for his part, had beat a hasty retreat to the bridge as soon as Nguyen came rushing into the crew compartment, and was not seen again until the crisis had passed.

While Zhuan and Yao kept shouting orders for Nguyen to stand down, one into each ear, the man-mountain seemed oblivious to them all, intent only on throttling Cai and shouting again and again that he would never let anyone hurt "her" again, whomever "her" was.

Cai's face was purple shading to blue, and it was clear that whatever humor his prank had held for him had quickly faded. He batted ineffectually at Nguyen's massive hands, his eyes bulging, struggling unsuccessfully for a breath.

Finally, and just before Cai lost consciousness entirely, Yao and Zhuan managed to pry Nguyen's fingers from around the prankster's throat, and together with the other three men succeeded in hauling him bodily off of Cai.

Pinned down, taxing the strength of five men to keep him from renewing his attack, Nguyen's rage gradually ebbed, and instead of murder there came a kind of lost sadness in his eyes. Eventually he went slack against the grips of the five men restraining him, and slipped to the deck in a heap, head in his hands, the blood which remained on him beginning to dry in brownish rust-colored rivulets.

And then Nguyen began to talk.

None of them had ever heard the man-mountain speak more than a few sentences at a time, and rarely more than a handful of words. But now, gored with another's blood and with his murderous rage replaced by a deep sorrow, his shoulders shuddering with racking sobs, he spoke in a torrent, a gushing outpouring of words, unprompted, and the others struggled to make sense of it.

The story was disjointed, confused, and it was only with concentration and careful attention that the others were able to parse out its meaning.

Nguyen Trang had been born thirty years before in Annam, and had never known his father, it seemed. He had either died before his birth, or while he was still an infant, the story was unclear. His mother was still young and attractive enough that she was able to find work at a brothel, and so Nguyen's formative years had been spent there, surrounded by women who had chosen the only work their poor circumstances allowed them, and the men who paid for the privilege of using the ladies for their own pleasure.

Nguyen suspected in later life that his mother had lied, that she had in fact been employed at the brothel before he was born, and that his father had not been an honest laborer as she had always told him, but instead one of the ill-mannered and foul-smelling patrons of the brothel. Nguyen liked to think that his mother was not lying, after all, since the alternative was too painful to contemplate. He had always been a slow child, pudgy and round, and had been tormented for his simple-mindedness by the brothel's patrons. But while it stung, it was balanced by the fact that, in effect, Nguyen didn't have one mother but a dozen, cozened by the perfumed ladies of the brothel for as long as he could recall.

As he grew older, Nguyen grew larger, becoming a mountain of a man by the time he was in his teenage years. But if he grew large enough that he was no longer physically tormented by the brothel patrons, still he was the target for their jeers and jibes.

As Nguyen's mother grew older, her ability to earn her keep at the brothel diminished in proportion with the gradual loss of her looks. She and Nguyen had become as much part of the brothel as if they were family, though, and so work was found for her, mending and washing the bedclothes and garments of the ladies, and Nguyen helped out where he could, repairing broken shingles and hauling furniture. It was a peaceful kind of life, and perfect for a boy whose few thoughts were slow ones, and who wanted only peace and comfort.

Nguyen was in his late teens when it all went wrong.

He decided the winter before that he was in love with one of the newest ladies at the brothel, a delicate flower of a girl. And while the girl did not return his affections, she was kind to him, treating him like a stray dog that had followed her home. One hot summer night a bureaucrat came to the brothel. He was an irregular patron, but was still well known to the ladies. His tastes were darker than most, and it was only in brutality that he could be satisfied. Whenever he visited the brothel, the next morning one of the ladies sported wicked cuts and bruises that would take weeks to heal. But the bureaucrat paid well for the service, and was well connected enough that anyone who raised their voice publicly against him would quickly find themselves jailed on trumped-up charges, or worse.

On this particular occasion, the bureaucrat chose the girl, whom Nguyen loved, for his evening's entertainment. Nguyen wasn't happy about it, but the girl soothed him, assuring Nguyen that nothing bad would happen. Then, in the night, the bureaucrat screamed out, and when the ladies came rushing in they found the girl dead. The bureaucrat was stricken, babbling apologies. He sobbed, saying that it had been an accident, that things had just got away from him.

But when Nguyen rushed in and saw the bruised, bloodied form of the girl on the floor, with the fat little bureaucrat standing over her, his detumescent member hanging limp between his fat little legs, the stain of his spent seed smeared across the dead girl's face, the boy'd had no patience for apologies or excuses.

Nguyen flew into a rage, and pummeled the man to death with his bare hands. The ladies of the brothel tried to stop him, but he brushed them away like flies. Finally, the bureaucrat was dead, tossed aside like a broken doll, and Nguyen cradled the dead girl in his arms.

By the time his mother arrived, it was all over, and too late.

The ladies all knew that it didn't matter whether killing the bureaucrat had been justified or not. With the dead man's connections, his killer would be executed for sure, regardless of the circumstances. Nguyen would meet the executioner's blade, and that would be an end to him.

Nguyen's mother took him by the arm and led him sobbing from the girl's room, leaving the ladies to see to the bodies. She cleaned and dressed his bloodied and bruised knuckles, and then led him out into the still-dark morning. As they walked through the streets, she told him that she'd always tried to protect him, tried to keep him from harm, but that she couldn't shield him from the consequences of the night's actions. The only thing she could do was to send him someplace where the danger hopefully wouldn't follow. But the people to whom she was taking him would be able to take care of him, and tell him what to do, when to eat and what to wear. Nguyen should do what he was told, and everything would be alright.

When the recruiting office of the Green Standard Army opened that morning, Nguyen Trang and his mother were there waiting. Nguyen's mother helped him sign the enlistment papers, kissed his cheek, and then hurried away back to the brothel. Nguyen never saw her again.

The next day, he was sent to Taiwan Island for training, and if he didn't do terribly well with tactics and strategy, he excelled in physical training, and could seldom be beaten in hand-to-hand combat. He was assigned to the infantry and sent off to Fire Star, where he served without distinction or reprimand for years. But it wasn't to last.

A few months before, on leave in Fanchuan Garrison, Nguyen had chanced upon a guardsman raping a female support staff member in the showers, and for Nguyen it was as though he were back in the brothel, years ago, and the girl and the bureaucrat were once more before him.

When the red rage passed, and Nguyen could reason again, the girl was huddled sobbing in the corner, while the guardsman lay dead on the floor at his feet. The showers were still pounding, washing the blood clean from Nguyen's hands, almost like a benediction.

And that was the end of Nguyen.

Though the woman he'd saved had testified in his defense at his hearing, Nguyen was still convicted of the crime of murder, and sent to Baochuan prison to await execution. But the executioner's blade never fell, and weeks later he found himself packed into a cloud-flyer and sent back to Fanchuan Garrison, there to be told there was one more task left to perform.

Of course, Nguyen did as he was told, just as his mother had instructed, as a dutiful son should. Which led him here, to this cold dark ship out in the void, once more in a shower with blood on his hands, and in that moment, in his sudden mindless grief, it was as though that night were repeating all over again, and he had one more chance to get things right.

CHAPTER TWENTY-THREE

They had nearly reached the end of their journey without further incident when the ship rebelled against them.

In the days since they had managed to calm, clean, and dress Nguyen, persuading him not to kill Cai Yingtai after all, none of the crew had assaulted any of the others—not physically, at any rate—and it looked for the moment as if they might reach Xolotl without first killing one another. Of course, their deaths likely waited for them on the Mexic asteroid, so it came as small comfort, but within the cramped confines of the *Dragon* they took what solace they could.

Then the *Dragon* herself had turned against them, or so it seemed, and their brief run of good fortune came quickly to an end.

The first stages of the procedure had gone smoothly, without a hint of the trouble that would follow.

They had reached the point in their plotted trajectory at which the *Dragon* needed to decelerate, in order to match orbits with Xolotl. If they continued on their current heading at their present velocity, they'd end up missing the asteroid altogether, overshooting its position.

Which presented a problem when the thrust aperture refused to open. And though that was enough to doom the mission to failure as it was, preventing them from reaching their goal, it quickly proved to be only a relatively minor concern, in comparison to an even greater threat.

"Rutting pile of dung!"

Steersman Ang slammed the heel of his palm against the control housing, his lips curled into a snarl. Then he hissed, shaking his hand as though he could fling from him the pain of the impact.

"Steersman, report," called Captain Zhuan from his seat at the center of the bridge.

"Rutting thing is still not rutting working!" Ang raised his hand again, as though to slam it once more against the controls, then thought better of it before bringing it down.

"Details, Steersman?"

Ang shot the captain an angry look and gave a ragged sigh. "The thrust aperture is still not rutting opening, captain. That detail enough for you?"

Zhuan resisted the impulse to smile. Ang had served under him for some years on the *Exhortation*, until he'd been arrested on Zhurong trying to pilfer an admiral's purse—though he was a committed gambler, Ang was clearly not above thievery, if the opportunity presented itself, as the recent escapade with Dea's wallet had proved—and while the man was the best pilot that Zhuan had ever seen, his observance of appropriate protocols, to say nothing of general etiquette, left a great deal to be desired.

Zhuan pushed himself off the captain's seat, and drifted toward the engineering station, opposite the steersman's seat on the other side of the hulking sacrificial altar. In preparation for the deceleration maneuver, they had fired the attitude rockets to slow and stop the ship's rotation, and retracted the counterweight. With the ship traveling at a constant velocity, and without the rotation to impart centrifugal gravity, the crew compartments were once more under weightless conditions. Had Ang not been securely strapped to his seat when slapping his hand against the controls, the resulting reaction would have been sufficient to push him away and toward the bridge's ceiling; as it was, it had resulted in little more than stinging pain and a slowly purpling bruise.

Reaching the engineering station, Zhuan secured the straps over his shoulders and around his waist, and then checked the dials and readouts.

"The aperture still registers as closed," Zhuan said, more musing aloud than conversing.

"Which is what I said, wasn't it?" Ang snapped back, nostrils flaring.

"Belay that," Zhuan said gently, understanding the tension which goaded the steersman, but also understanding the need to maintain discipline. "Let's take it by the numbers, steersman, step by step. You are certain you've toggled the correct commands?"

Ang sighed dramatically, then turned back to the controls. The Mexic approach to ship's operation was quite different from that employed on Middle Kingdom vessels. Instead of a single battery of controls for each function, the Mexica instead had an array of toggle switches, which could be configured in a near-infinite variety of combinations to control any number of different functions. It seemed counterintuitive and unwieldy to Zhuan at first—and he knew that Ang still contended it was the work of madmen—but the captain had gradually come to see the appeal. Since the switches on the steersman's station, for example, controlled all aspects of steering and propulsion, one need only glance at the state of the switches themselves, and assuming sufficient familiarity with the controls, one would know in an instant exactly the current state of the systems.

The only drawback to the approach was that the switches indicated only those commands that had been entered, and not the results of those commands. To match reality to ideal, one needed to consult the readout dials above the switch array, and at the moment, those told a very different story.

"Everything is as you ordered, captain," Ang said, his tone strained but level. "On your mark, once rotational velocity reached zero, I reoriented the ship with the bow pointing back along our trajectory. Then, after retracting the control rods from the reactor three-quarters, I released the hydrogen propellant into the chamber, and toggled the combination to begin opening the thrust aperture." He snarled, and hit the controls again, though this time with considerably less force. "Only the rutting thrust aperture is not rutting opening."

Zhuan nodded, studying the dials. "Which explains why we're still weightless." If the ship had begun decelerating, they'd once more have felt the pull of something like gravity, with relative "down" again being the rear of the cabin.

The captain chewed the inside of his cheek idly, deep in thought. Ang continued to check the switches, and finally threw up his hands in surrender.

"That's an end to it, I give up," Ang said, exasperated. "It's like the system's just frozen up, and doesn't seem to be responding at all."

Zhuan tapped his fingers against the housing of the engineering controls, and nodded. "That's probably exactly what happened. Could be a short somewhere in the system, preventing the instructions from relaying appropriately to engineering." He sighed, and then unbuckled the straps securing him to the chair. He pushed off, and began to navigate toward the hatch in the deck leading down to the common area. "I'm going to get Syuxtun up here to take a look at the controls. There may be something in the Nahuatl that we didn't translate that can help us." He glanced back over his shoulder at the steersman. "Shut off the propellant to the chamber and reinsert the rods into the reactor while we wait. We don't want to risk it getting too hot in there when there's nowhere for the propellant to go."

Ang grunted his assent, and bent over the controls. A moment later, just as the captain was about to drop through the hatch, the steersman swore loudly again. There were no histrionics this time though, no slamming of fists or banging of panels.

"Um, captain?" Ang looked up, his face ashen, eyes wide and mouth hanging open. "What was that you were saying about getting too hot?"

"Hmm?" Zhuan raised an eyebrow, stopping his motion through the hatch by grabbing hold of the edge of the deck before falling through. "What's that?"

The steersman glanced at the controls, and then back at the captain. "*Everything* is frozen. Propellant release, control rods, *everything*."

Zhuan's eyes widened now, in response, and his hand tightened in a white-knuckled grip on the hatch's edge.

If the control rods could not be reinserted into the reactor, and the propellant could not be thrust from the chamber, then the engine would grow hotter, and hotter, and hotter. And unless they were able to reverse the process, and allow the system to cool, it would only be a matter of time before the reactor entered thermal runaway and, ultimately, meltdown.

In which case the problem of overshooting Xolotl by a few kilometers paled in comparison.

CHAPTER TWENTY-FOUR

"Bannerman Syuxtun?" Captain Zhuan drifted near the ceiling of the common area, his hand resting gently on the nearest bulkhead.

The bannerman knelt against the deck, his legs secured in place with straps, head bowed and resting on the deck-plates.

For a moment it looked as if Syuxtun hadn't heard him, but then sat up, hands on his knees, eyes on the deck before him.

"Syuxtun?" Zhuan repeated, conscious of the fact that he was intruding.

"God is great," Syuxtun said, and then bent again from the waist, palms and forehead against the deck-plates. "Glory to my Lord, the Most High. God is great."

Sighing, Zhuan pushed off from the ceiling, drifting across the empty space and alighting on the floor next to where the bannerman knelt. Before rebounding back toward the ceiling, he grabbed hold of the edge of the table, whose legs were bolted to the floor, and managed to retain something almost like a standing position.

Again Syuxtun sat up, but still did not raise his eyes.

"Bannerman, there's a matter on the bridge requiring your attention." Zhuan kept his voice low, sounding urgent while hopefully avoiding any sense of panic. At the moment, he had no intention of advertising their situation to the rest of the crew, and the fewer who knew their present circumstances the better. Otherwise hysteria might sweep the ship, and with men such as these, who could say how they would react? At the moment, only he and Syuxtun were in the common area, but sound carried some distance through the hatches and corridors of the ship, and he didn't want his voice overheard. He'd left Ang in the bridge, to explore every possible course of action to alleviate the situation, but it seemed only a matter of time before the steersman gave up trying and came below decks to wail about their troubles to the rest of the crew. If at all possible, Zhuan intended to have a solution in hand before they reached that point, but from the way things stood, it wasn't looking likely.

Syuxtun opened his mouth as if to speak, but instead of answering the captain, he said, "All greetings, blessings and good acts are from Thee, my Lord.

Greetings to you, O Prophet, and the mercy and blessings of God.

Peace be unto us, and unto the righteous servants of God.

I bear witness that there is no god except God.

And I bear witness that Muhammad is His servant and messenger."

Zhuan bristled, but controlled himself. Once, when he was a child, he'd harbored beliefs in the supernatural, in gods and goddesses which lived beyond the curve of space, and looked down on the works of man in much the same way that he watched dramas at the theater. But in his first years in space, out in the black, silent void, he had come to the sure and sincere belief that there was nothing but nature, and that man was a part of nature. For years after, he believed that nature was, at least, on the whole a benevolent force, and that there was some comfort to be had in that. After the outbreak of the Second Mexic War, though, and the horrors Zhuan had witnessed in the years that followed, he'd come to revise his opinion. He'd been entirely too forgiving of nature, he realized, and entirely too optimistic about reality in general.

Which wasn't to say that he didn't still observe the mandated rituals, as prescribed by the emperor and enforced on virtually every ship of the Interplanetary Fleet by the ministers of rites. But these were mere displays of loyalty and fidelity, and the object of such devotions was not the Celestial Consort Tianfei, or the Duke of Zhou, or the Yellow Emperor, or Dark Raven, or any of the other worthies invoked in the rituals, but the emperor himself upon the Dragon Throne. Still, it was one of the few pleasant aspects of this present voyage that there was *not* a minister of rites onboard, and Zhuan could be somewhat lax in the observance of the prescribed rituals. When they had performed none after the abbreviated rites performed at the *Dragon*'s launch, none of the other crew had seemed much to mind.

Of the crew, in fact, only Bannerman Syuxtun exhibited much in the way of devotion. Perhaps, Zhuan had observed, the Athabascan's piety more than made up for the others' evident lack of belief.

Zhuan felt certain that he had been more than tolerant of Syuxtun's beliefs to date, but he was damned if he was going to let the man's blind adherence to his devotions put the rest of the crew in jeopardy.

"Damn it, Syuxtun, on your feet or I'll have you clapped in irons!" The captain's voice did not raise in volume, but increased in intensity, seething through gritted teeth.

The Athabascan looked up for the first time, and regarded the captain with his amber eyes. Zhuan felt he'd finally got through to the man, and was inwardly relieved he'd not have to order him punished, and eagerly leaned down to help the man up.

"O God," Syuxtun said, his voice even and low, "be gracious unto Muhammad and the people of Muhammad, as you were gracious unto Abraham and the people of Abraham. Surely you are the Praiseworthy, the Glorious."

Zhuan's teeth gritted, his face flushing red. "Did... did you not *hear* me?"

Breaking eye contact with the captain, Syuxtun looked over his right shoulder, then his left shoulder. "God's peace, blessings, and grace be on you."

The captain's hands closed into fists at his side, as Syuxtun undid the straps securing him to the deck, and pushed off with the slightest of gestures until he floated up into something resembling a standing position. With a tiny wave of his arms he brought himself around, facing the captain, and ducked his head in the bow due to a superior officer. "Your pardon, o captain. I believe you said something about the bridge?"

Zhuan didn't explain any of the details of their situation to Syuxtun yet, only told him that there was some problem with a malfunctioning control and he hoped that Syuxtun's ability to read Nahuatl glyphs might help them find a solution. The bannerman had nodded, deferentially, and said that he would be happy to assist however he could.

The hidden streak of defiance which Zhuan had glimpsed in the moment his eyes had locked with Syuxtun's, as the bannerman ignored his orders and continued with his devotions, was nowhere to be seen, now that the prayers had come to an end. Zhuan was forced to wonder whether he'd simply imagined that spark, or if there was something more specific about the encounter that had engendered it, and that the moment, having passed, was now gone.

The common area of the crew compartment had remained untenanted other than by Syuxtun and Zhuan throughout their brief exchange, but when they were halfway to the hatch which led above decks to the bridge, Bannerman Yao entered from the opposite side, followed by the others. Evidently they had been below decks in the narrow hold, in the makeshift firing range, practicing with the microgravity weaponry, Syuxtun having been excused in order to observe his devotions. Yao had apparently returned the weapons to the secured locker on their way above decks, as had become his standard practice, and all six men who now drifted into the common area, rebounding weightless off bulkheads and ceiling, were unarmed.

Entering the common area, Yao could at a glance tell that something was amiss. The captain was skillful at concealing his thoughts, but Yao had spent his entire adult life learning to study the strengths and weaknesses of any situation, surveying any terrain, and that included a man's facial expressions. And what Zhuan Jie's face was currently expressing was that something was seriously wrong.

"I had hoped to drill the men in centrifugal gravity combat situations," Yao said, as Zhuan maneuvered across the floor to the hatch leading to the bridge. "When might we expect the rotation to resume?"

Zhuan cast a quick glance at Syuxtun, and then met Yao's gaze. "Just a short time longer, it is hoped. A minor technical difficulty." He then turned and pushed off the floor, angling for the hatch. He motioned for Syuxtun to follow.

Yao nodded, thoughtfully, and then said, "Have I your permission to accompany you, captain?"

Glancing back, Zhuan hesitated, and Yao could see that the captain had no desire to grant his request. At the same time, though, it was clear that the captain was struggling to find grounds on which to refuse.

"If you must," Zhuan said at last, and then floated up through the hatch and out of sight.

As the others settled to their ease around him, Yao kicked off the floor and followed the captain toward the bridge, wondering what the trouble was, and whether it had anything to do with the fact that the ship hadn't yet resumed rotation. And, now that he stopped to consider it, was it getting hotter onboard, as well?

"I'm sorry, captain, there's nothing else I can do."

Bannerman Syuxtun looked up from the control manual, while Zhuan and Ang floated nearby. Yao drifted near the ceiling, taking it all in.

"What do you mean, there's nothing you can do?" Ang demanded, wringing his hands. "Nothing! Surely there's something in all those rutting glyphs that tells you what to do."

Syuxtun shook his head, sadly, and shrugged. He was seated at the steersman's controls, strapped into the seat, with a spiral-bound manual open across his knee. The pages, rigid sheets covered in transparent plastic, crawled with lines of Nahuatl ideography, stylized representations of animals, objects, and so on. There were such manuals stowed beneath each of the control stations on the bridge, detailed instructions on the station's operations.

Since the writing was worse than meaningless to Zhuan and Ang, they'd all but forgotten the manuals were there, but once Syuxtun had been apprised of their situation, he'd immediately suggested that they consult the texts. It was hardly surprising, since Syuxtun's specialty was language and communication, not avionics and engineering, and only natural that he would seek a solution in the written word.

Such a solution, though, did not appear to be forthcoming.

"It's as I said," Syuxtun insisted, holding up the manual and pointing to a string of glyphs on the middle of one plastic-coated page. "When the systems enter this kind of lock-up, the only way to restore full functionality is to cycle the power and reinitiate the system."

"What part of *this*"—Ang thumped a hand against the sacrificial altar beside the steersman's controls, barely managing to keep from spinning off to the ceiling by bracing with his other hand against the back of the engineer's station chair— "don't you *understand*?"

Syuxtun narrowed his gaze. "I understand perfectly, steersman," he said, tight-lipped. "But that understanding doesn't change our situation in the slightest."

"What is it?" Yao said, pushing off the ceiling and drifting down to rest nearer the other three, bracing himself by grabbing hold of the armrest of the captain's seat. "What's the difficulty?" He looked from face to face. "Why not simply restart the system, as the manual says?"

Ang and Syuxtun exchanged a quick look, and then turned to Zhuan, deferring to the captain to explain.

"It's the bypass the artificers built into the hemoglobin sensors," Zhuan began, after a moment. "Specialist Sima explained to us that, if the systems were restarted, then the bypasses would be lost. A reinitiation has the effect of restoring the core programming, which would overwrite the artificers' patch, and then the hemoglobin sensors come back on line."

Yao glanced to the looming bulk of the sacrificial altar, still shadowed with rust-colored bloodstains, and then back to the two cages at the rear of the bridge. Had the *Dragon* still been manned by a Mexic crew, those cages would not have held pressure suits, as they did now, but live captives. And in addition to those kept on the bridge, there were stalls down in the hold where Yao had set up his firing range, in which the Mexica would have kept "spares" in case of emergency.

"So after restarting the system, the only way to get things back up and running…?" Yao trailed off.

"Is to pour blood on that," Zhuan said, indicating to the altar with a nod.

"But didn't the artificers pack a supply…?" Yao began, but Zhuan interrupted him with a shake of his head.

The captain's mouth was drawn into a tight line. "All of it went down the shower drain when Cai played his prank on Nguyen the other day."

Yao's eyes widened, if fractionally. "But that would mean…"

The captain nodded. "It means that someone is going to have to bleed."

CHAPTER TWENTY-FIVE

"Very well, men, you have your orders."

There was nothing else for it. The machinery that controlled the ship's automated systems, including navigation and propulsion, would need to be powered down and restarted. The question of whose blood would be spilt over the altar to satisfy the hemoglobin sensors, which would allow the systems to complete their startup routine, was one which Zhuan wasn't yet prepared to answer.

"Bannerman Syuxtun," the captain said, drifting toward the hatch which led below decks from the bridge, "you're with me. Bannerman Yao, I can count on you to assist Steersman Ang?"

Yao nodded his assent.

"Then there's no reason to delay any longer," Zhuan went on, grabbing hold of the edge of the hatch. "Remain in contact via the shipboard radio"—he pointed to the microphone-speaker arrays mounted beside each of the bridge control stations, and on the armrest of the captain's seat— "and report on regular status updates. The radios are on a separate circuit, and powered by the ship's batteries, so they should remain operational throughout the procedure. Restart should take…?" He glanced at Syuxtun, who had the engineering manual tucked under his arm.

"Two hours, captain," Syuxtun responded.

"The better part of a watch, then." Zhuan consulted the chronometer he wore strapped to his wrist. "In which case, since we're now just into the third watch, we should have the process complete just before the fourth watch begins. Agreed?"

The other three men nodded.

"Let's get to it, then."

As he went below decks, passing through the common area of the crew compartments on his way to the engineering section, it occurred to Zhuan to question the advisability of leaving Yao alone with Ang, or rather Ang alone with Yao. The two men's temperaments could not have been more dissimilar, and Zhuan had not failed to notice the looks that the bannerman had given the steersman after the theft of Dea's wallet had come to light. Clearly, while Yao had argued for leniency in the matter of Dea's purloining a firearm and discharging it onboard, he had been less than entirely pleased with the punishment Zhuan had decreed for Ang. Since the steersman was literally irreplaceable under present circumstances, Zhuan had opted for little more than a verbal reprimand. So that while Yao was playing the cruel taskmaster, driving Dea in the combat drills to the point of complete exhaustion daily, the man who had driven Dea to his desperate act returned to his duties—and his leisure time— without even a rap across his knuckles. If Ang had been under Yao's authority, Zhuan knew, the steersman would not have got off quite so lightly.

So leaving the two together, the captain feared, might mean trouble.

However, he had an ulterior motive for leaving Yao with Ang. The bannerman might be of some assistance to the steersman in the coming procedure, to be sure, but the principal benefit would be that Yao would be on hand to ride herd on Ang, and to keep him from leaving his post and revealing the truth of their situation to the rest of the crew. At present, only the four of them knew how close they were coming to the meltdown of the ship's engines, and the fact that the only thing that would save them would be for one of the crew to open a vein. Ang was simply too untrustworthy for Zhuan to rely on him to keep that information to himself on his own recognizance, but with Yao there to make sure that the steersman didn't leave the bridge and, more importantly, didn't open his mouth, the chances seemed much greater.

Passing through the common area, Zhuan was careful not to give any indication of trouble to the other five crewmen, for fear that the knowledge might send them into a panic. And having stressed the importance for secrecy at this stage to Syuxtun, he was pleased to see that the Athabascan was perfectly able to conceal his thoughts and feelings, when necessary. As the two men drifted through the room, the other five lounged in the common area, drinking tea from sealed vacuum flasks of bamboo, or munching on balls of rice that floated weightless around their heads like miniature moons, or just lounging, still fatigued and sore from the morning's combat drills.

The engineering section was located below the ship's hold, and as they moved down from one deck to the next Zhuan caught a glimpse of Yao's makeshift firing range, and the targets he'd mounted at the far end, roundels marked out on insulated crates strapped to the bars of the Mexica's "spare cages." Then they continued through the hatch that led further down still, and came at last to the engineering level.

At the forward end of the engineering section, in a heavily insulated and shielded crate, was strapped a large six-sided case, nearly a meter on each plank. The sides of the featureless case were matt-black, starkly unreflective, absorbing all of the light which struck them. But if the sacrificial altar on the bridge above decks radiated cold, as though haunted by the spirits of all those who had met their ends on its ornate surface, this featureless black block seemed to generate heat, as though presaging all of the lives it had yet to take.

Of course, it *was* radiating, at least a nontrivial amount. Even the thick shielding that the artificers had incorporated into the design was not sufficient to completely block the occasional spray of subatomic particles from the fissile material at the heart of the sphere buried deep within the Dragon's Egg. This was the principal reason why it was located down here, as far from the living space of the crew above decks as possible. And to keep it as far as practicable from the heat of the ship's reactor, it had been positioned at the extreme forward end of the ship.

With the black case at their backs, Zhuan and Syuxtun advanced to the rear of the engineering section, where the primary controls could be found and, beyond the meter-thick bulkhead, the reactor itself was located.

But as thick as the bulkhead was, and with as much shielding and insulation separating them from the reactor itself, with each step forward the two men could feel the heat increasing, moment by moment.

If they did not shut down the reaction within the ship's reactor soon, and vent the heated hydrogen propellant out into space, it would be too late.

The procedure itself was simple, but time-consuming.

Under normal circumstances, the ship's systems could be cycled down and up from the bridge, with the use of a handful of switches. But with the systems frozen and the switches inoperable—which was the reason the cycling was necessary in the first place—the normal procedures would be useless. Which was why two of them had to be below decks, manning the engineering controls by hand, while Ang remained on the bridge to reset the switches at the appropriate time.

It fell to Zhuan and Syuxtun to go through and reset all of the breakers in the electrical system, to clear any potential shorts that might have caused the lock-up in the first place, and then remove power from the ship's systems so that the controls could cycle down. There were hundreds of the breakers, it seemed, and if the manual was accurate, it would take a considerable amount of time to reset them all. However, the breakers were in such a confined space that no more than two full-grown men could fit inside, and so there was nothing to be gained from enlisting the services of the other crewmen.

So Zhuan and Syuxtun squeezed themselves into the small space, opening off from the main engineering compartment, little more than a closet lined on all sides with breakers. And they set to work.

"I can't help but notice, Syuxtun," Zhuan said, when the silence became too great to bear, "that you don't seem much to belong in the company of these others."

"Captain?" The Athabascan didn't turn around, but kept his eyes on his task, resetting one breaker, then another, then another.

"This is a crew of reprobates, bannerman, as I'm sure you've noticed. With the possible exception of Bannerman Yao, and I've yet to work out just why he was selected for this assignment. Perhaps he just offended the wrong people."

"And you, captain? If you don't mind me asking, why were you selected for this mission?"

Zhuan's breath caught, and in his thoughts he was back to that day, reliving the moment when his cowardice at last got the better of him. "I... I refused to follow an order."

"Well." Syuxtun chuckled, good-humoredly but with a bitter undercurrent. "Then we have that in common."

Zhuan reset a breaker, and then turned to regard Syuxtun, his eyebrow raised.

Syuxtun was silent for a long moment, still refusing to turn and meet Zhuan's eyes. Then he sighed, shook his head, and began to speak.

"My parents were Khalifan Muslims, Athabascans of Chumash extraction," Syuxtun began, "and before I was born they instituted a school near the border between Khalifah and the Mexic Dominion, where they taught the children of Mexic children whose parents, whether defectors or dissidents, had illegally crossed the border seeking sanctuary. Most often these were Mexica whose politics differed from those of the Dominion's ruling elite, or whose name had come up on the sacrificial lists but who had decided that their lifeblood was too valuable to spill in appeasement of the distant and brutal gods of the Mexica.

"I grew up among the children of those Mexic refugees, playing the childhood games of the Mexica, learning to speak Nahuatl as well as any native. Which is not to say that I was not loyal to the Imam Council and a true son of Khalifan, nor that I was not a dutiful Muslim and follower of the Prophet. My parents were devout, and motivated by a sense of charity to help those less fortunate than themselves. And as I grew older, I felt called to join in their mission, and helped at the school as best I was able, until it came time for me to go on the pilgrimage to Mecca, but once I had earned the right to be called Haji I returned to my place at the school.

"When I was nearing the end of my third decade, I married one of the other workers at the school, a woman named Precious Flower. We had grown up together, as she had been one of the students at the school while still a child. Precious Flower had been born within the borders of the Mexic Dominion, but on defecting to Khalifah her parents had converted to Islam, inspired by my parents' example, and had raised her as a dutiful Muslim daughter.

"We were happy, for a short while. But we had only been married a short time when the news reached Earth of the Mexic attack on the Fire Star colonists. We continued to teach at my parents' school, trying to put such dark thoughts from us, but every day brought word of some new depredation, of families being taken prisoner and used by the Mexic warriors as sacrifices for their blood-thirsty gods. And as I heard these stories, I could not help but look at the faces of my young Mexic charges and imagine them in similar danger. Or worse, imagine them as those Mexic warriors themselves, had their parents not had the strength and resolve to escape from the Dominion's tyranny.

"The next spring, my wife announced that she was pregnant. What should have brought joy to my heart only increased my despair, as the conflict on Fire Star continued and worsened by the day. I had lived my entire life in the shadow of the Mexic Dominion, and knew too well what they were capable of doing. What if worst came to worst, and the forces of the Dragon Throne were unable to halt the Mexic advance across Fire Star? What if, in some nightmare scenario, the Great Speaker of the Mexica were to be emboldened by success on the red planet, and look to continue his conquest on Earth? Would the Jaguar Knights one day surge across the border into Vinland and Khalifah to the north, and Fusang to the south? How soon until my students were placed in harm's way? And not just them, but my own unborn child?

"I anguished, praying to God for guidance. In the end, I decided there was only one course that lay open to me. I could not sit back in safety and comfort, looking to strangers to safeguard my security and that of my family. The responsibility was my own. And so, after a tearful and lengthy embrace with my wife, now swelled with child, I went down to the recruitment office and enlisted with the Eight Banners.

"By the time my son Fareed was born, I was already on my way to Fire Star.

"At first, I was concerned that my being a follower of the Prophet would prove a difficulty, but I needn't have worried. Though Muslims are still a minority in the Eight Banners, and likely always will be, I was far from the only one, and my superiors did not interfere with my daily devotions. And though it was sometimes difficult for me to reconcile the orders I was given with the strictures of the Quran, the Imam Council itself had deemed that faithfully following orders in the service of the Dragon Throne was not a sin, so long as the orders themselves were righteous.

"I served for the next eleven years, on and above Fire Star, unable to return home. I came to know my son only through crumpled lithographs which came to me by post, always months or even years out of date by the time I saw them. When he grew older, my son wrote to me himself, over and over again, always asking when his father was coming home. And while I wrote back to my family as often as I was able, I was sure that the imperial censors redacted most of my missives anyway, so perhaps my explanations and apologies never reached him. In any case, in time the frequency of the missives from my son slowed, and then stopped altogether. My wife still wrote to me, as she always had done, telling me about the daily doings at the school, and then about the death of my father, and then that of my mother, and finally her missives, too, stopped arriving. The silence was only explained some months later when I received a brief and impersonal note from my son, now being raised by distant relations in the north, informing me that my wife, my beloved Precious Flower, had died, and that the school my parents had spent their lives building was being closed for good.

"Having gone off to war in order to protect my family and the children in my charge, I now found myself alone. My family was now only myself and a son who was no better than a stranger to me, and likely despised me for abandoning him and his mother all those years ago. I sacrificed everything, and what had it got me?

"I continued to serve the Dragon Throne, but my faith, I'm sorry to admit, was shaken. Not only my faith in the emperor and his war, but in God

Himself. I continued to observe the daily devotions, but as if by rote, without any true passion for the words of the prayers. And as my faith flagged, so too did my conviction that the orders I received were, in fact, as righteous as I once had thought. I had become, in recent years, a communications expert, by dint of my familiarity with the Nahuatl language, and so requested a transfer out of an active combat unit into a more secure rear-echelon position. Nahuatl-speakers were always needed to monitor Mexic transmissions, and I reasoned that I would be less likely to be put into a situation where I might be asked to do something with which I disagreed, if I served each day armed with a radio receiver instead of a firearm and blade.

"I was wrong.

"For a period of some years, I spent all day at a radio receiver. And when my services were not required sending and receiving communiqués for the Eight Banners command, I moved up and down the frequencies, searching for Mexic transmissions. I often found them, but those I discovered were most often encoded, in which case I was responsible simply for recording the transmission and then handing the record over to intelligence to analyze. I was often commended for my work, and in fact received a citation just shortly before I was arrested. If I understand correctly the sequence of events, one of the coded transmissions I intercepted was the Mexic message which, when decoded, revealed the location and nature of the asteroid base Xolotl. Some irony, then, that I should find myself here, don't you think?

"In any case, far from being removed from conflicts between my beliefs and my orders, it was as a communications officer that belief and orders came at last into irreconcilable conflict.

"It seems that a Mexic division had taken a group of Middle Kingdom colonists prisoner, and had loaded them onto a Mexic launch vessel. The commanders of the Eight Banners issued an order to the ground-to-air batteries that the launch vessel was to be shot down before it could reach escape velocity. But when that order came through my hands to transmit to the field, I refused.

"I objected, raising the concern that the commanders' plan would cost innocent lives. I was informed by the commanders that, as it was too late to retake the prisoners, innocents would die anyway if the launch vessel reached escape velocity, since they were doubtless bound for Mexic sacrificial altars. By shooting it down before it left Fire Star, we would at least deprive the Mexica of their prize.

"I understood the commanders' reasoning, but could not accept it. I would not allow my hands to be bloodied, and could not in good conscience give the order that would cost so many innocent lives. The commanders reminded me that I would be guilty of dereliction of duty if I refused a direct order, and I told them that I had joined the Eight Banners to protect children and families, not to order their deaths. Then, before they were able simply to order another communications officer to take my place, I brought the entire communications system offline. By the time the system was back up and transmitting again, the launch vessel had reached low orbit.

"I was clapped in irons and dragged from my post. I expected to be executed for what I had done, but found that I was not bothered by the thought. What *did* surprise me, though, was the realization that, in some strange way, the encounter had restored my faith, not in the emperor or in the orders of his generals, but in God and his strictures. Like their plans, men are imperfect, I came to realize, but God and his will are not, and we cannot blame the Almighty when we discover that men are fallible.

"As for the launch vessel, I understand an attempt was made to stop it once the craft reached orbit, but that one of the ships of the blockade turned away just before ramming it, and the Mexica continued out into open space. So the prisoners lived, at least for a short while longer, because of my inaction. I only wish that there had been something I could have done to save them altogether. I… I try not to think about what might have become of them in the days since."

CHAPTER TWENTY-SIX

Syuxtun carried on resetting the breakers, one after another, but Zhuan found himself unable to continue for a time, mulling over what the Athabascan bannerman had said.

If Syuxtun's story was to be believed, and Zhuan saw no reason to doubt him, then the launch vessel which the *Exhortation* had failed to ram—likely saving the lives of all those onboard both craft— had been the selfsame launch vessel which Syuxtun had refused to order blasted out of the sky by ground-to-air batteries. If Zhuan had followed his orders, and moved to block the launch vessel's trajectory, then Syuxtun's sacrifice would have been for naught.

And so, in a sense, both men were responsible for saving the lives of the Middle Kingdom prisoners on the Mexic launch vessel, but while one had done so motivated by the highest principles and firmly-held beliefs, the other had been motivated only by the desire to save his own skin. Syuxtun was a martyr, in the finest sense of the word, sacrificing his career and very likely his own life, since his actions assured him an appointment with the executioner's blade, all in exchange for the safety of others. Zhuan, on the other hand, was a coward, who had turned away from battle at the final moment, ensuring that those who died when one of the other ships of the blockade was destroyed did so in vain.

Zhuan was shamed, standing in such close proximity to such a noble spirit. But, at the same time, the captain couldn't help but feel a certain lightening within. After all, hadn't his actions on that fateful day meant that his own karma was not stained with the deaths of the innocent prisoners onboard? He hadn't known that he was preserving innocent lives, and those of Middle Kingdom subjects at that, when he allowed his cowardice and fear to override any sense of duty he might have felt, but in the final analysis might action not be more important than intent? Could he pretend that it was, even if he did not believe it?

Elsewhere, other thoughts were likewise turned to matters of action and intent, though for quite different reasons.

Steersman Ang was attempting, for the fourth time since they'd been left on the bridge alone together, to engage Bannerman Yao in something like friendly conversation. The fourth attempt was proving no more successful than the three previous had been.

"I never wanted to be a soldier, me," Ang said, floating cross-legged in midair above the steersman's station, like a somewhat underfed Buddha. "But it beat the alternatives, I suppose. Them being fishermen, first off, like my father and uncles and brothers, long days and dangerous days and nights spent smelling of fish. Working themselves dead of exhaustion just so they could spend a few taels down at the tavern of a night, and see their wives and children only in passing." He shook his head. "Not for me.

"Of course, my career of choice wasn't completely free of dangers, either, come to that. But oh, how I loved the clatter of the mahjong tiles and the sweet taste of making some mark's small fortune my own, all on the turn of his poorly considered wager. But it was a simple slide from gambling to a bit of thievery, from taking another's hard-worn wages over a game of chance to taking an unwatched purse off some fat merchant's belt. But then I fell in with a rougher crowd, and was tapped as lookout for a robbery that went sour when men I hardly knew killed a watchman who surprised them in the act. So I ran off and joined the Interplanetary Fleet, thinking that things would blow over by the time I got my first leave. In training it turned out I had a talent for steering, and found myself assigned Steersman's Third Mate.

"Three terrestrial years later I was back on Earth, now Steersman's Second Mate, with my bags packed and my purse full of coins I'd won off the rest of the crew in transit. But when I rode the Bridge of Heaven back down to Fragrant Harbor, whose is the first face I see but one of the thieves from that botched robbery. And who does he and the rest of his mob blame for it being botched, for not sounding the alarm that the watchman was coming in the first place?" He pointed at his own nose. "Too right they do. So I gave him the slip, and it's back up the elevator with me, back onto the ship, and nevermore am I to see home.

"I figured on jumping ship the next trip back, finding some way to slip through Fragrant Harbor without getting spotted, making my way to Europa, maybe, or Vinland. But when my boat was next in transit to Fire Star, the word came over the radio that the Mexica had attacked the colonists there. The war started, the Interplanetary Fleet was militarized, and all leave was cancelled until further notice. And that was an end to me. Years more, eventually ending up as steersman on the *Exhortation* under his nibs, Captain Zhuan, who wasn't a bad sort, if a bit humorless. But then I got nabbed in Zhurong over an unfortunate bit of business, and here I find myself."

Ang shrugged, glancing around the bridge.

After a long pause, he turned to Yao, who sat in the captain's seat, strapped in place, arms on the armrests and expression impassive.

"How about you, bannerman?" Ang asked, cheerily. "How did you come to ship out on this little suicide mission of ours?"

Yao looked up, and met Ang's eyes. "Are you going to be done talking anytime soon?"

The steersman scowled, but nodded. "Sure, sure," he said, sullenly. "I'm done, I'm done."

* * *

Yao checked his wrist chronometer, impatiently. It felt as if it had been hours already, but there was some time to go yet before the end of the third watch, when the process would be complete. Captain Zhuan had radioed a short while before, to say that he and Bannerman Syuxtun were nearly finished with the work of resetting the breakers, and would send word as soon as were done. Then Ang would enter the commands necessary to power down the bridge systems, and once Zhuan had done the same down in engineering, they could initiate the procedure to get everything back up and running.

Of course, at that point, the question of whose blood would be spilt on the altar would need to be addressed, but that was Captain Zhuan's lookout, not Yao's, and he was content to let the captain make the decision.

Ang had started talking again, after only a few moments of silence, and Yao did his best to tune out the steersman's drone, with little success. Closing his eyes, Yao knew who he would select to donate their lifeblood, if the choice were his.

The hiss of static from the radio interrupted Ang's monolog, and Yao tightened his hands on the armrests of his seat, ready to hear the captain's report that all was in readiness. Instead, Yao was surprised to hear the unsuitably child-like voice of Guardsman Nguyen crackling from the speaker, instantly recognizable.

"Um, hello?" Nguyen's voice was laced with static, sounding as if it were coming from hundreds of kilometers away, and not just one deck down. Just one more reason, Yao reflected, to prefer proper Middle Kingdom technology to that of the Mexic Dominion; he hated to imagine what voices transmitted from hundreds of kilometers away would sound like over the Mexic radio system.

"Bannerman Yao," he said, announcing himself. "Nguyen, what is it?"

"Wait, what?" The man-mountain was clearly confused. "No, Yao's not here. That's who I'm calling for. This is Trang. Nguyen Trang."

Yao sighed, while Ang made monkey faces at the speaker, highly amused. "No," he said, shaking his head, "this is Bannerman Yao, receiving. What is it that you—Bannerman Nguyen—want?"

"Oh." The child-like voice over the speakers sounded relieved. "Well, you might want to come down here."

"Where is 'here', and why?" Yao asked.

"In the common area," Nguyen clarified. There followed a loud crashing sound, blaring over the speakers, which Yao could dimly hear unaided drifting up through the open hatch. "You probably want to hurry."

"Why?" Yao repeated.

"Because someone'll probably be dead already if you wait too long."

Only later would Yao learn what had led to Nguyen's call to the bridge, once he'd had an opportunity to question the others in the aftermath of what followed. Like most disagreements of the sort, it had started simply enough, and then veered wildly out of control in short order.

The root of the trouble, as near as could later be determined, came when Guardsman Cai made an off-hand remark about their prolonged condition of weightlessness, and the condition it reminded him of.

"I am light-headed from all this floating," he had said, or words to that effect. "Light. Headed." He had grinned at the others, who still lounged in the common area of the crew compartment. "Must be all the blood racing from my brain, right? Eighteen-hells, the last time I felt like this was the first time I smoked the poppy back on Taiwan Island." He had paused then, and chuckled. "Maybe all of the time since has just been an opium dream, you think? Maybe I'm still just a new recruit, back in Green Standard training, and I never went to Fire Star, never smuggled poppy, never crash-landed and got banged up, or anything. Maybe when I come down"—he fairly giggled—"I'll open my eyes and it will be as if none of it had ever happened."

It was a innocuous statement, taken out of context, the likes of which Yao had heard young soldiers say any number of times over the years. Though wine was permitted to soldiers in small quantities when off-duty—and larger quantities when on leave—intoxicants such as opium were strictly prohibited. And while it was rare that one came upon a soldier who had not sampled such substances while still a civilian, it was hoped by command that use of contraband substances ended once one enlisted in the service. The number of soldiers brought up on disciplinary charges every year, after being caught under the influence, though, put to lie to that slim hope.

Typically, though, when a soldier casually mentioned previous experiences with mood altering substances on the prohibited list, those listening either responded with comments based on their own experiences or, which was more likely, ignored the speaker altogether.

On this occasion, though, one of the listeners took exception, rather violently.

"What did you say?" Bannerman Fukuda was reported to have said, his teeth clenched.

Cai laughed again, still drifting in midair. "I said, maybe it will be as if none of this ever happened. Wouldn't that be great?"

"No." Fukuda had shook his head, his expression humorless. "Before that. About the poppy."

"Oh." Cai nodded. "That I smoked it, or that I smuggled it?"

And that was when the trouble had begun to worsen.

Fukuda had been crouching near the deck, his foot hooked around one of the chairs, which had all been secured to the deck-plates before the counterweight had been retracted and the ship's rotation halted. In a brief moment, grabbing hold of the chair's back, Fukuda unhooked his foot, crouched lower, and then like an uncoiling spring pushed off from the deck, hurtling through the empty air directly toward Cai, his hands outstretched and grasping.

The two men collided in midair, and before Cai could call out or ask what grieved Fukuda, the Nipponese had wrapped his hands around Cai's neck, squeezing off his air passage, shaking his head back and forth violently.

"My brother died of smoking the poppy, dealer in death! If not for your kind, you and those like you, Keimi would still be alive now!"

Fukuda's teeth were gritted, his eyes narrowed to slits, and in the opinion of one observer at least, it was possible that he might have begun to cry. If nothing else, his normally controlled and even voice was strained, almost to breaking, his angry and urgent words sounding almost like sobs.

It might have ended there, with Fukuda squeezing the life from Cai in a rage, with no one moving to intervene, but for the simple fact of physics. There were three other men in the common area, scattered around the room. The collision when Fukuda struck Cai had done little to burn off the momentum the Nipponese had generated when launching himself off the deck-plates, and that remaining inertia now carried them forward, spinning end-over-end at a high rate of speed. And, as luck would have it, napping directly in their path, his hands folded over his ample belly and his eyes closed tight, snoring gently, was Guardsman Paik.

And then, the trouble was well and truly started.

And it was shortly after this point, as the now-awakened and enraged Paik sought to revenge himself on whomever had disrupted his slumber, that Yao entered the scene.

The crashing Yao heard over the speaker, before leaving the bridge, had evidently been caused by the chair which still rebounded from wall to wall, burning off momentum. From the ragged state of its legs, it looked to have been ripped up from the deck while still battened down, and then hurled through the air. The one who threw it would've had to have been braced against the floor in order to impart that much momentum to the object in weightlessness, since otherwise the force would have been distributed between the object thrown going forward and the person throwing being pushed in the opposite direction.

Judging by the tiny spheres of arterial blood which were drifting like errant moons through the empty air, though, the chair had struck its target, and burned off some of its momentum colliding with Fukuda's face before continuing on to bounce off the walls.

Only later would Yao learn what had precipitated the mêlée, and on entering the common area, all he knew was that three of the men under his command had fallen to loggerheads. He'd left Ang on the bridge, waiting for the captain's word to proceed with the system shutdown, and while he trusted the steersman had the technical expertise to complete the task, Yao would if possible have preferred to be on hand to make sure that nothing went awry. He himself lacked the mechanical skills necessary to do the job himself, but then Yao had always been good at motivating others, whatever the circumstance.

So it was Yao that greeted the unruly behavior of the men with an even poorer humor than he might have otherwise done, and he would never conscientiously tolerate this sort of indiscipline in the best of circumstances.

The three men in the air had all been trained in microgravity combat techniques, as was evidenced by their movements and tactics. But of them one man, Cai, was clearly only battling to extricate himself from the situation he'd unknowingly caused, and the other two seemed blinded by emotion, their instincts blunted. Paik, for his part, was a creature of awoken fury, lashing out with punches and kicks, using the walls, deck, and ceiling as springboards to launch himself at Yao, striking a blow, and then careering off in the other direction, to land once more, gather up energy in crouched legs, and spring back upward and repeat the procedure again. Yao, who still had one hand wrapped tightly around Cai's neck, used his legs and his free arm to ward off Paik's blows, while at the same time fending off Cai's mostly ineffectual attempts to batter his arm away. But while Paik was blinded by rage, Yao seemed distracted by something else entirely.

At that moment, it hardly mattered to Yao what motivated the men to act as they were doing. His first duty was to subdue them, and worry about causes and effects in the aftermath. Assuming, of course, that any of them survived; which, considering how much hotter it was within the crew compartment than it had been just a short while ago, was still a question to be decided. There was always the chance that Zhuan's plan to reset the ship's systems would fail, for some unguessable reason, and all their troubles would be brought to a speedy end in a nuclear meltdown.

For the moment, though, Yao had to operate on the assumption that the ship would be saved, the mission able to continue, and it was his responsibility to see to it that the men were in a fit state to carry out their assignment, when the time came.

Yao was unarmed, as were the other three men. But it hardly mattered, as there was no reason to take recourse to the arms locker. If Yao was unable to subdue three soldiers of this caliber bare-handed, he had no business being their commander.

Close-quarter-combat protocols prescribed five escalating levels of conflict, beginning with verbal commands and continuing up through the minor application of contact controls like elbow grabs, to more elaborate holds and blows, to defensive tactics, and on to the use of deadly force. A strict reading of the protocols would indicate that Yao was required to order the three men to stand down, then attempt a series of contact controls, before finally moving on to the use of force. But Yao had not survived as long as he had, and risen as high in the ranks of the Eight Banners, without gaining the understanding that there were some protocols that were best suited for theory and training, and other procedures that were better followed in the field. And one of those more practical procedures was the ability to determine the appropriate level of conflict response without ascending the escalating levels one by one.

In a situation such as this, in which blood had already been spilt and tempers already fanned to flames, verbal commands were rarely more than a waste of time and breath, and minor contact controls like grabbing elbows were likely to do little more than delay the inevitable. In such situations, with more than one active combatant requiring pacification, the prudent response was to move directly to the use of defensive tactics, the level categorized as Bodily Harm.

Yao only hoped that the situation did not escalate
further, to the next and final level: Death. The mission could probably survive the loss of one of the
men, if Yao were forced to use extreme measures,
but more than that might seriously jeopardize their
chances for success.

Yao quickly prioritized the targets by threat level,
and then moved into action.

Paik, since he was the most mobile of the three
and the most likely to bring injury to a noncombat-
ant, was the first priority. Fortunately, as he was
momentarily careering off the wall, he was relatively easy to subdue.

Using much the same technique that Paik had
employed, Yao crouched low against the deck,
steadying himself against the table's edge, and then
straightened his legs with a snap, springing up and
into the air at speed. He launched himself not at
where Paik was, but at where Paik would be. The
guardsman saw him coming, but was unable to do
anything about it, having already oriented his body
to strike at Fukuda, who hung on the far side of the
room, not having the time to twist and turn his
body in mid-flight.

Yao had calculated his trajectory perfectly, and
mused for a moment that perhaps he'd missed his
calling, and should have become a steersman like
Ang. But he knew, even then, that his talents lay in
a different direction. Then, just as he shot ahead of
Paik, he snapped out a quick one-knuckle-punch,
catching Paik in the infraorbital nerve, just below
the nose, one of the principal pressure points. It was

a risky strike, for a variety of reasons: hitting so near the mouth, there was a chance that the target might bite; and, of course, there was the risk that, if the blow was too hard, death could result. But with a precise and measured strike, as Yao had used, the worse that would occasion would be a bloody nose, perhaps some broken cartilage, followed by considerable pain and loss of consciousness. So it was that, with blood streaming, eyes rolling up in his head, Paik continued sailing across the empty space of the common area, insensate.

The blow had changed Paik's trajectory such that he was no longer heading right for Fukuda, but angling off to one side. Yao, for his part, continued on toward the ceiling, doubling from the waist and reorienting one-hundred-eighty degrees as he went, so that when he hit it was feet first. He buckled his legs, absorbing the impact, and then kicked off again at an angle, directly toward Fukuda.

Fukuda had come to rest near the far wall, still gripping Cai's throat in one hand, but his grip must have lessened as his emotions surged, for the guardsman had yet to lose consciousness, though his face was flushed purple and eyes bulging. So long as Yao was able to effect Cai's release in the next few moments, it was likely that the guardsman would live, though with considerable bruising on his throat.

From the corner of his eye Yao had seen Fukuda glance back and see him collide with Paik, so he knew that the Nipponese was aware he had entered the fray. But as Fukuda's grip had weakened, so too had his combat readiness, so that now he seemed scarcely to care who or what was around him. He continued to rail at Cai, but his words were now interrupted by racking sobs, and in addition to the errant moons of blood which streamed from the gash on his forehead, from where the hurled chair had struck him, there were now added tiny satellites of tears, little droplets of salt water that flowed from his eyes.

"You killed him," Fukuda was howling, his rage now all but completely lost in sorrow. "You killed my brother, and I wasn't there to save him."

Hurtling in from above and behind Fukuda, Yao changed his tactics at the final moment. He had intended to strike the sciatic nerve just above the left buttock, hard enough to stun but not cause complete respiratory failure, and then continue with a palm-heel strike to the brachial plexus origin at the side of the neck, immobilizing Fukuda momentarily and causing him to lose full functioning in the arm holding Cai. A standard fourth-level Bodily Harm response. But en route, Yao downgraded the situation, to scarcely a level two, categorized as Resistant. At this stage, in fact, it appeared that Fukuda was practically Compliant.

Instead of striking Fukuda in the lower back and then pivoting to deliver a blow with the heel of his palm to the Nipponese's neck, Yao reached out a hand to arrest his forward movement, using the wall against which Fukuda had pushed Cai. And then, when his momentum had been completely absorbed, he reached out and laid a gentle hand on Fukuda's shoulder.

"Let him go, bannerman," Yao said, his voice low but level. "Whatever else Guardsman Cai has done, he never killed your brother."

Slow as a glacier advancing over a plain, Fukuda loosened his grip on Cai, and when his fingers had relaxed enough, the guardsman pulled away, grabbing his bruised throat and coughing painfully.

"No," Fukuda said, his voice coming from somewhere far off, turning his head to look at Yao with mournful eyes. "I know he didn't kill my brother," he admitted. "*I* did."

CHAPTER TWENTY-SEVEN

Captain Zhuan heard the rumble of conversation as he came up the companionway from the engineering section. He and Syuxtun had just completed the preparations necessary to complete the system shutdown and restart, and he was on his way to join Ang on the bridge for the final steps of the procedure. He'd given little thought to what the rest of the crew were up to, since he and the Athabascan had gone below decks, but he hardly expected anything like the chaos he found on entering the common area.

Broken pieces of furniture drifted in midair, while the light glinted off little rotating droplets, dark ones that looked like blood and clear ones that might have been sweat, or tears. Guardsman Paik bobbed limp and unconscious near the ceiling, rivulets of red drops streaming from just beneath his nose, while Guardsman Cai clutched his throat on the opposite side of the chamber, sputtering red-faced and wincing. Dea and Nguyen, neither bloodied nor bruised, clung to handholds on the far wall, their attention on the pair that now drifted near the center of the room, Bannerman Yao and Bannerman Fukuda.

The Nipponese Fukuda was curled up, his knees hugged to his chest, words spilling out of him in a torrent, while Yao floated just above him, resting a hand on Fukuda's shoulder.

"I left home to get away from my father," Fukuda was saying, and he reached up to touch the burn mark which ran across his nose from one cheek to the other, "but I left my brother behind. If I'd been there, maybe he wouldn't have taken to the poppy, maybe he wouldn't have smoked so much his body just quit, maybe he'd still be alive today."

Yao's expression was surprisingly tender, and he squeezed Fukuda's shoulder, a comforting gesture. "A man can spend his life worrying about what might have happened, had he acted differently in the past," the bannerman said, his voice pitched so low Zhuan could scarcely hear him, "or he can concern himself with how he might act in future, and what might follow as a result."

Fukuda looked up, meeting Yao's eyes. "When I learned of Keimi's death, when my father's missive finally reached me, years later, the first words I heard after reading it were those of my superior officer, whose criticisms of my discipline and behavior echoed the words of my father when I was still a boy. And because I could not revenge myself on my father in those days, my strength not equal to the task, I took my revenge on that officer, and killed him with my bare hands, there and then." He glanced at the still-sputtering Cai, who drifted in midair a short way off. "But killing that officer did nothing to hurt my father, or avenge my brother's death, but only landed me in irons."

Yao nodded. "Looking to the past leads one only to self-pity; by looking to the future, we honor the memory of those who have gone before us."

A long silence followed. "Perhaps," Fukuda allowed, at last. "Perhaps you're right."

As the two men left off talking, continuing to regard one another for a time, it seemed that the moment had passed in the common room, and the tension seemed to dissipate. Zhuan would have to ask Yao later what had led to the tableau upon which he had stumbled, assuming that they all survived long enough to tell the tale.

"Your pardon, men," Zhuan said, pushing off the rim of the hatch and sailing further into the common room.

The others had clearly not seen his approach and, startled, turned to face him, all but Paik, who continued to list unconsciously against the ceiling.

"Just a small disagreement among the crew, o captain," Yao explained, spiraling his arms to reorient himself to face Zhuan. "I have addressed the matter."

"Received and understood, Bannerman Yao."

It was clear that there were questions, or one question at least, that Yao burned to ask. He glanced around the room, checking the faces of the others, apparently wondering how much to say, and how to say it.

"Captain?" Yao began at last, deferentially. "If I may ask, how do... matters in engineering progress?"

Zhuan knew what Yao was really asking. He wanted to know whether the time had come to spill blood on the sacrificial altar and, if so, whose blood would be spilt.

"Bannerman," Zhuan responded with a request of his own, holding out his hand, "I wonder if you wouldn't mind opening the arms locker? I find myself in need of a knife."

It was nearly the beginning of the fourth watch before everything was ready to begin. Things would have been prepared sooner, but it had proved impossible to keep the news of their situation from the crew any longer, when Ang appeared at the hatch leading from the bridge, and announced that if the captain didn't get the system restarted soon they'd all be cooked alive in their skins, shortly before the ship was blown to pieces.

Zhuan had been forced to give a brief speech to the men, except for the still-unconscious Paik, and the general consensus was that it would be better to reach Xolotl and entertain at least the slim hope of success and survival, than to simply give up and wait for the overheating reactor to boil them all alive. And so the men had steered clear while Zhuan and Yao fetched what was necessary and made their way to the bridge.

Now that the others had been informed, there were duties to which other hands could be turned. Dea and Cai were sent below deck to engineering, to assist Syuxtun in getting the system properly cal-ibrated once everything was back online, those two chosen because Zhuan determined their technical aptitudes were probably the best suited to the task. As a demolitions expert, Fukuda likely had the dex-terity and nuance needed for the work, but he was still raw from his recent emotional breakdown and outbursts, and the captain had quickly decided that it would be best not to put their lives so soon into the hands of a man still struggling to bring his rag-ing emotions under control.

Paik awoke from his enforced slumber while the final preparations were being made, with a bloody nose and a headache, but after Nguyen explained to him in the simplest of terms what he had missed while unconscious, Paik had simply shrugged, dry-swallowed a couple of analgesics from the first-aid kit and, after strapping into an acceleration couch, folded his arms and tried to go back to sleep. He told Nguyen to wake him if they weren't all killed in a nuclear meltdown.

Zhuan made his way to the bridge, the sheathed knife hung at his side, while Yao followed with the first-aid kit in hand. Fukuda and Nguyen followed, though there was nothing for them to do and little room for them, but the captain was hard pressed to keep them out, and lacked the energy to try. He had them strapped into the acceleration chairs at the communications and weapons stations, to keep them immobile and out of the way, and then turned to the business at hand.

"Are you certain this is how you wish to proceed, captain?" Yao asked, holding the first-aid kit in one hand, steadying himself against the edge of the sacrificial altar with the other.

Zhuan nodded. "Mine is the least essential position, at this stage of the journey. Steersman Ang can pilot you the rest of the way, and Bannerman Syuxtun can handle communications with the Mexica once the *Dragon* reaches Xolotl. You and the rest of the strike team will need to be in the best possible condition to deliver the payload on our arrival." He gave a half-smile that didn't quite reach his eyes. "In all likelihood, I'll get by with only a scar."

Yao shook his head, his mouth drawn into a tight line. "You told me how much hemoglobin is necessary to set off the altar's sensors. I've seen men lose that much blood and not get up again afterwards."

The captain responded with the ghost of a shrug, and drew the knife from the sheath. "Then we'd better hope that my blood clots, then, eh?"

From the steersman's station, where he was strapped into his seat, his eyes on the readout dials monitoring the reactor temperatures, Ang said, "Any time you're ready to begin will be fine with me, captain." He shifted, nervously. "It's getting pretty hot back there."

Zhuan nodded, but turned to the radio set nearest him and toggled to transmit. "Captain Zhuan to engineering. Bannerman Syuxtun, do you receive?"

"Syuxtun here," crackled the voice from the speaker.

"Is everything set down there?"

"Set and ready, captain."

The captain smiled grimly. "Wait for the signal, Syuxtun."

"Received and understood."

Zhuan toggled the radio back to receive.

"Alright, men," he said, glancing around. "We might as well begin."

There were straps bolted to the deck just before the sacrificial altar. When the *Dragon* had been crewed by Mexica, these would have been used by the ship's ritualist, possibly an agent of the House of Darkness itself, to remain in place at the altar when the ship was in microgravity or weightless conditions. The surface of the altar was covered with circuitry and ridges that combined in bas relief to form the image of the Mexic moon goddess, in the process of being cut to pieces by the warrior god of the sun. At the four corners were reinforced metal shackles, where the sacrificial victim would have been secured by their wrists and ankles.

The hemoglobin sensors incorporated into the altar's surface were positioned at the base of small intake vents, which drew air into them with minor amounts of suction. If any fluid were brought in close contact with the surface, the suction would draw the fluid drop by drop into the vent, and from there into contact with the sensors.

If the ship were operating under centrifugal gravity, it was enough that the victim be bled directly above the altar, but if the ship were in microgravity or, worse, weightless conditions, then the victim's bleeding form would have to be pressed down against the altar's surface.

There were diagrams on the plastic-coated pages of the manuals Syuxtun had found, indicating the proper stance the ritualist should adopt, accompanied by lists of Nahuatl glyphs which spelled out the prayers which should be recited, and which showed how the obsidian knife should be forced down and into the victim's body, ideally pressing through to the other side, to open a wound on the side nearest the altar's surface. It was generally understood that blood would drift in globules and droplets in all directions from the cut, propelled by the pumping action of the victim's still-beating heart, but there were vacuum hoses mounted in the walls and ceiling of the bridge which could be used for clean-up after the sacrifice was performed.

In all, it was a gruesome, gory business. And yet it was one which was carried out on the bridge of every ship of the Mexic fleet, every time they went out into the black void.

Zhuan would use the straps on the deck-plates to keep his body in place, but had no intention of employing the shackles for any use whatsoever. And since the bridge was presently weightless, he would not be able to simply spill his blood on the altar, but would have to force an open wound against its surface, for as long as necessary.

Less than a meter away hung Bannerman Yao, the first-aid kit open in his hands, bandages and antiseptics at the ready. As soon as the tells on the altar's surface indicated the hemoglobin sensors had been tripped, Yao would rush forward to clean and bandage Zhuan's hand, while Ang completed the start-up routines, aided by Syuxtun and the others in engineering.

Zhuan stood at the altar, hand outstretched, palm up, the knife held ready just a few centimeters away. He thought about all that Syuxtun had told him, while they had worked at resetting the breakers down below. He thought about that shipload of Middle Kingdom prisoners, who had got a few more days or weeks or months of life because he had refused to ram the launch vessel with the *Exhortation*. Like Syuxtun, he disagreed with the commanders who had written those prisoners off as dead the moment they fell into Mexic hands; where there was life, there was hope, and there always remained the chance, however slim, that they might somehow be rescued, sometime down the line.

But while Zhuan hoped that his inadvertent good deed balanced the cowardice and fear that had motivated him, he knew that it could not. He had done the right thing for the wrong reason, unlike Syuxtun who had been driven only by the noblest of motivations. The Athabascan had even left a life of comfort and security back on Earth, leaving behind him a loving wife and son and students who needed him, sacrificing his own happiness for the safety of those he loved. But why had Zhuan left home? Not out of any noble sense of self-sacrifice, but only to escape the life of drudgery he saw before him, training bears and lions and tigers for the emperor's amusement, like his father had, and his father before him. Zhuan's forebears had lived lives of service, putting themselves into harm's way out of a sense of obligation to their emperor. Zhuan had gone into space seeking only romance and adventure. It hardly mattered that he'd found little of either; he hardly deserved more.

So now, through happenstance and misadventure, and no choice of his own, Zhuan found himself faced with the choice of sacrificing his own comfort for the sake of others, willingly sustaining an injury and the accompanying pain to save the lives of those under his command. And while he wasn't willing to throw away his life by ramming the *Exhortation* into the Mexic vessel as ordered, perhaps if he knew of some greater purpose his death would serve, he might one day be willing to choose differently, in a similar circumstance. But today, at least, his death was not necessary, so long as Yao hadn't been right about him bleeding out. No, today, all that was necessary was pain.

And if pain was the price for the survival of his ship and crew, that was a cost Zhuan was willing to bear.

The knife's blade was like a freezing cold whisper across Zhuan's palm, and for the briefest instant he was surprised that it didn't hurt in the slightest. Then his nerves caught up with what his eyes were seeing, and he hissed as the stinging pain slammed into him.

Careful not to lose his grip on the now-bloodied knife, Zhuan turned his wounded hand over, and brought it palm-down onto the surface of the altar. The ridges and whorls of the bas relief bit into the long cut, probing the tender flesh within, and he seethed through gritted teeth. The pain continued to throb up his arm, in waves. He squeezed his eyes shut, willing himself not to pull his hand away too soon, not to call for Yao's help with the antiseptics and unguents.

An eternity followed. Zhuan began to feel light-headed, and when he opened his eyes, his vision swam, tears streaming out in salty drops that drifted around his head like wandering satellites.

His pulse roared in his ear, like a bellowing beast, and he closed his eyes again, feeling the room spin around him. Then he felt a strong hand gripping his shoulder, and a voice shouting in his ear.

"That's enough, captain! That's enough!"

Zhuan opened his eyes, and turned to see Yao hovering next to him, in his other hand bandages and tubes of antiseptic ointment. "Did the sensors…?" the captain began, his voice sounding as though it were coming from somewhere far away, then trailing off, lacking the energy to finish.

"The tells are lit," Yao said, pointing to the light flashing above the altar. "We're back in business."

Zhuan tried to smile, and thought to lift his hand away from the altar's surface, but when he looked down, his palm was a red ruin, a wicked black gash surrounded on all sides by red. Then he closed his eyes, and darkness rose up to swallow him.

CHAPTER TWENTY-EIGHT

By the time the captain regained consciousness, his wound had been cleaned and dressed and, more importantly to him, the system error which had frozen the controls had been corrected.

Zhuan awoke to find himself strapped into the captain's seat. He had only been unconscious for a few short moments, he learned, but in that time the ship had been removed from immediate danger. Working in concert, Ang on the bridge and Syuxtun and the others in engineering had successfully opened the thrust aperture to vent the already heated hydrogen propellant, then reinserted the control rods to lower the reactor temperature. The burn off had pushed them slightly off course, but not so far that it couldn't be addressed by a minor correction once they began to decelerate.

Fukuda and Nguyen were still strapped into the seats at the bridge controls, watching Zhuan expectantly, the Nipponese with what appeared to be a newfound respect. Zhuan held onto the seat-back at the engineering controls, while Ang made some final calculations on his magnetic abacus and minute changes to the toggle switches before him.

"Your orders, o captain?" Yao asked, when he saw that the captain had regained full consciousness.

Zhuan looked up from his hand, neatly bandaged with military precision by Yao. His hand still throbbed beneath the clean dressings, which already were beginning to shadow with the blood seeping out from underneath, but the pain felt more distant, more controllable, no doubt due to the slight anesthetic quality of the analgesic antiseptic that Yao had applied.

In response, the captain turned to the steersmans station. "Let's try this again, shall we?" Zhuan managed a tight smile. "Orient the bow to Xolotl, as before, and prepare for a deceleration burn." He glanced around the bridge, and with good humor added, "But if the system locks up again, I'll be looking to one of you brave souls to volunteer and put your hand to the altar. Once was quite enough for me for the time being." He held his wounded hand aloft, and managed not to wince as the dressings pulled tight across his palm.

Nguyen looked worried for a moment, then laughed a little when he saw that Zhuan was joking, while Fukuda actually chuckled. For his part, Yao regarded the captain with a smile, as he strapped himself into the acceleration seat at the engineering controls, and prepared for deceleration.

"Engineering reports that they are strapped in and ready for deceleration, o captain," Ang reported, pointedly ignoring the comment about volunteers for the sacrifice, on the off-chance that the captain had not been joking.

Zhuan put his hand back into his lap, and nodded. To his surprise, for the first time, this gang of reprobates and criminals was actually beginning to feel like a proper crew. That their minor victory in escaping death only ensured that they would reach their destination, where untold Mexic warriors no doubt waited to do the job instead, was a bitter irony on which he tried not to dwell.

It was less than two days later that the *Dragon* first made radio contact with Xolotl, and a short while after that when they first made visual, through the high-powered remote-viewing mirrors mounted on the outer hull of the ship.

The first exchange of pass-codes, signs, and countersigns, was completed without any indication of trouble. Then, once the ship's identity was established by flight control, they were asked to account for their whereabouts in the previous weeks, and explain why they were now approaching Xolotl.

Bannerman Syuxtun sat at his place at the communicationist's station, bulky headphones over his ears, leaning into the microphone set into the controls, speaking a seemingly endless stream of Nahuatl words and phrases, then pausing while hearing the response, then speaking again.

None of the others on the bridge knew more than a word or two of Nahuatl, but none dared to speak to one another to ask what Syuxtun might be saying, for fear that their talking might be picked up by the microphone and transmitted, however laced with static, to the flight control operators on Xolotl, and if the approaching vessel was discovered to have people onboard conversing in Official Speech, the common language of the Middle Kingdom, their chances of passing as a Mexic crew would be dashed.

The cover story, as supplied by Agent Wu back on the Zhurong moonbase, and devised by the finest minds of the Eastern Depot, was that they were the original crew of the Mexic patrol vessel, who instead of crash landing on the Fire Star moon Gonggong, as had actually occurred, had rather experienced ship-wide system failure, in communications and propulsion specifically, that had prevented their returning to the Xolotl base before now.

It was a fairly thin cover, without many supporting details, but the Eastern Depot had decided that the fewer details to the story, the fewer chances for Syuxtun to make some mistake in the exchange. And, based on the initial contacts at least, that theory seemed to have been sound. When the Athabascan finally dropped connection with Xolotl's flight control, cutting off all transmissions from the bridge before turning to address the captain, he reported that the *Dragon* had been given clearance to approach the asteroid base on their present course and velocity.

It was as if all of those on the ship had been holding their breath, so great was the sigh of relief that followed Syuxtun's announcement. Their mission plans had thus far brought them success, carrying them this far across the black void, and now, to all appearances, convincing the Mexic flight control that they were the legitimate crew of a Mexic patrol vessel.

In approximately one and a half days, they would reach Xolotl, and the crew would then see how well the rest of the mission plan went.

The counterweight had been retracted, and the interior of the *Dragon* was weightless as the ship covered the remaining kilometers to the asteroid. But it hardly mattered, as everything onboard was battened down, and the men were all secured in their seats, ready for action.

All nine wore pressure suits, and all nine were armed. The mission directives called for only seven of them to leave the ship once the *Dragon* docked at Xolotl, but the parameters were flexible, given the number of uncertain variables in the plan, and the men had been instructed to be prepared for anything.

Three of them wore captured Mexic pressure suits, as the mission plan called for limited interaction with the base personnel before the rest of the strike team exited the ship, and while wearing the captured suits the men would be better able to pass for Mexica, at least for a short period. As a result, Bannerman Syuxtun, who now occupied the communicationist station, wore the armor of a Jaguar Knight, as did Guardsman Cai who was strapped into an acceleration chair down in the common area. Bannerman Yao, who was now secured in the engineer's seat on the bridge, wore the armor of an Eagle Knight. The other six, including Captain Zhuan and Steersman Ang at their stations on the bridge, wore the matte-black stealth suits designed by the Middle Kingdom artificers for the mission.

Each of the men, Zhuan included, had one of the flechette pistols at his waist, and one of the rocket carbines slung on his back. When they had been suiting up and arming themselves in the common area, the men had carried out little rituals, preparing to go into battle. Some had muttered prayers, or tried to strike bargains with whatever supernatural agencies might be listening in. Others invoked good fortune by rubbing good luck charms, as when Ang fondled a small coin he wore on a necklace. Others remembered loved ones distant or lost, as Bannerman Dea did when he took out the lithograph of his lost love, her name on his lips like a prayer, "Lei Xiaoli." Even Yao seemed to go through certain rites, checking and rechecking the action of his knife in its sheath, his pistol in its holster.

Zhuan had no rites to perform, no habits he followed before going into battle. Not unless one counted the twisted-gut feeling of terror that gripped him, as he numbly climbed into the matte-black armored pressure suit. Or the awkward way he handled the fletcher, having only fired the weapon on three separate occasions during their training on Zhurong and the journey to Xolotl. As for the carbine, he scarcely even knew how to hold it, and only managed to get it secured across his back with difficulty. But the knife which he fastened to his right thigh in a magnetic sheath, was the same one that he'd used two days before to open his veins and feed the blood-hungry hemoglobin sensors in the sacrificial altar. A blade he knew how to handle, just fine.

Now, all the rituals were through, and the men were suited and armed, strapped into place and waiting for the final phase of the mission to begin. The mission payload, the Dragon's Egg, had been removed from its shielded case down in the engineering section and strapped down to the deck-plates in the midsection, near the airlock. The plans called for Syuxtun to provide the final countersigns and pass-codes to gain docking clearance, and when the *Dragon* had docked in the hangar bay within the asteroid base, the members of the strike team wearing the Mexic armor would exit first. If it was necessary to engage in verbal communication with the base personnel in those first moments, Syuxtun would take point, while Cai and Yao, who had been selected for their vague facial resemblance to Mexic phenotypes—at least close enough that through their helmets' tinted faceplates they could pass at first glance as Mexica—had been instructed in the use of short Nahuatl phrases that would cover them for a few moments at least. Then the other four members of the strike team would remove the straps securing the Dragon's Egg to the *Dragon*'s deck, and with Paik and Nguyen carrying and Dea and Fukuda providing cover, they would exit the ship through the airlock. With all seven members of the strike team out in the hangar, they would deal with any initial resistance, and then proceed as quickly as was practicable through the base to the core of the asteroid to plant the Dragon's Egg, prime the explosive and begin the automated countdown. Then, assuming all other mission objectives had been met, the strike team would be able to look to their own survival, retreating to the hangar where Captain Zhuan and Steersman Ang were to keep the *Dragon* prepped and ready for take-off. The chances of the strike team reaching the vessel, or of the *Dragon* managing to exit the hangar bay, were remote at best, but the mission plan allowed for the possibility that the men might escape Xolotl with their lives, however unlikely that would be.

Those were the mission parameters. And the first elements of the plan were successfully accomplished without incident. Speaking a string of liquid Nahuatl syllables which were all but incomprehensible to everyone else on the bridge, Syuxtun managed to convince Xolotl ground control that the ship and its crew were precisely who he'd said they were, and the *Dragon* began its final approach. There was another Mexic vessel ahead of them, a larger transport ship, and the men onboard the *Dragon* were able to observe the docking procedures before following the steps themselves.

The asteroid which the Mexica called Xolotl was longer than it was wide, and was spun on its longest axis, imparting centrifugal gravity to the interior. The hangar was located on one of the asteroid's short ends, at the pole of its rotation, so that in docking the incoming ship had only to fire its attitude thrusters to match the asteroid's rotation and then, once it was synchronized, fire a quick burst from its main propulsion to push forward and through the hangar doors. Once inside the hangar the ship was maneuvered by tugs toward the outer wall of the asteroid, where the rotation created a centrifugal force roughly one-third that of Earth's gravity, equivalent with the surface of Fire Star.

Ang and Zhuan watched through the forward viewports as the Mexic transport went through the approach and docking procedures, and then Syux-tun relayed ground control's clearance to dock. Attitude thrusters nudged the *Dragon* into position, and then set her rotating. When the rotational velocity was sufficient Ang fired a quick burst from the *Dragon*'s engine and the ship began to drift toward the open hangar doors.

As the ship moved through, it felt to Zhuan as if they were flying into the open maw of some immense predator, willingly allowing themselves to be swallowed whole. And, as the *Dragon* moved into the darkness beyond, the bay doors closing behind them, he realized that he was not far wrong.

Once the tugs had pushed the *Dragon* into position, they began gradually to accelerate the ship until it was moving in sync with the rotating "floor" beneath them, which when they had first entered the hangar had been an unbroken circular "wall" nearly a kilometer away on all sides, on which was positioned countless Mexic warships of all sizes and varieties. Finally the *Dragon* was gently lowered onto an elevated gantry, which was designed to recoil to cushion the impact of the ship's sudden weight as it came into contact with the station's centrifugal gravity. Then the gantry lowered, and the *Dragon* finally came to rest on the floor of the immense interior hangar bay.

Unlike the hangar on the Zhurong moonbase, which was pressurized and heated but weightless, the hangar bay on Xolotl enjoyed the same centrifugal gravity as the rest of the station, while likewise being pressurized and heated. Had the crew wanted, they could have opened the airlock and exited through the hatch in nothing more than their black worksuits and slippers, and suffered nothing worse than a momentary pop in their ears as they acclimated to the change in air pressure. Of course, if they had exited in their worksuits and slippers they'd likely not have lasted very long, if the warriors out on the deck were any indication of the welcome they'd receive.

The plan called for the three men in the captured Mexic suits—Yao, Syuxtun, and Cai—to exit the *Dragon* almost immediately upon their arrival, to reduce the chance that the Mexica might discover their ruse before the strike team had an opportunity to mobilize. But looking through the forward viewports from the bridge, those onboard the *Dragon* could see that matters might be somewhat more complicated than they'd anticipated.

"That's a lot of warriors," Ang said, whistling through his teeth.

Yao shook his head. "Not a lot," he corrected, "but enough."

There were maybe half a dozen Mexica in armored pressure suits just a few meters outside the

Dragon's airlock, armed with firearms, or clubs lined with obsidian-blades, or truncheons. Yao's first instinct had been that the Mexica were there to apprehend the crew of the *Dragon*, but on second glance it was clear that their attentions were focused elsewhere. On the next landing pad of the hangar bay, in fact, on the Mexic troop transport which had preceded the *Dragon* into the station.

"Is there a problem, Yao?" Bannerman Dea was climbing up onto the bridge through the open hatch from the crew compartment below.

Yao knew why he had come, since the mission plans called for himself and Syuxtun to remain down in the crew compartment with others, preparing to go out the airlock. And he knew why Dea had addressed him directly, and not Captain Zhuan, as he would have done while they were still in flight. Now that the *Dragon* had landed at Xolotl, Zhuan's role in the mission was complete. Yao was the authority from this point forward.

"It's a bit crowded out there, that's all," Yao explained, his voice muffled by the reinforced faceplate of his helmet. He pointed to the viewport as Dea approached. "I'd like to wait for them to clear out before we move, if possible. If they haven't gone in a few minutes, though"—he glanced at the wrist chronometer he held in his hand, then tucked it back into an external pocket on his suit's carapace—"we may have to move anyway."

Dea nodded, the gesture mostly hidden by his own stealth suit's helmet, and came to stand beside Yao. Syuxtun was still at the communicationist's station, monitoring ground control broadcasts, while Zhuan and Ang stood at another viewport, looking out on the same scene from a different angle. Fortunately, all of the viewports were heavily tinted and shielded, to protect against the sun's unobstructed glare in the void, and while those onboard could see out, those outside could not easily see in.

The warriors out on the hangar floor came to attention, their weapons at the ready, as the transport's hatch opened with puffs of condensation, and the telescoping gangplank slid down to the floor. Whatever the reason for the warriors' presence, it was on that ship. But was it some sort of honor guard, receiving a Mexic dignitary?

Yao narrowed his eyes. He'd seen honor guards more times than he could count, and unless the Mexic Dominion held very different attitudes toward its leaders than the Middle Kingdom did, he was sure this was no honor guard. In such situations, the soldiers are on hand to display their weapons, not brandish them. And these were not highly decorated soldiers, if their suits' lack of adornment were any indication, but were rank-and-file soldiers. No, far from being an honor guard, these warriors were on hand for another reason entirely.

First down the gangplank came another Mexic warrior who, unlike those on the floor in their plain armor, wore an armored pressure suit of such elaborate design and decoration—painted black and spangled with stars, his helmet rising in a cone, on his arm a shield embossed with a delicate spiral design—that he must have captured a considerable number of prisoners in his military career. And he walked with the surety of one who expected to receive further accolades still. Which would explain the reason for the armed guard.

Yao's suspicions were confirmed with the next figure appeared on the gangplank. Not only was she not armored, and clearly no soldier, she wasn't Mexic, but was clearly of Han ethnicity. She had the look of someone's grandmother, and though she was clearly terrified, she met the blood-hungry gazes of the guards below with a proud bearing. She must have moved too slowly, though, because as her bare feet touched the smooth floor of the hangar, one of the plainly armored guards stepped forward and shoved her to the ground, shouting something Yao couldn't hear through the thick viewport.

Before the old woman could climb to her feet, another Middle Kingdom subject came down the gangplank, less proud in bearing than she had been, a young man, perhaps not yet out of his second decade. And after him, a young boy, and then an older man, and then another woman. All of them clearly subjects of the Dragon Throne, if their clothing and ethnicity was any indication, and the way they were treated by the guards proof enough that they weren't citizens of the Mexic Dominion.

"They're prisoners," Ang said, with pity, glancing toward the two cages at the rear of the bridge.

Captain Zhuan nodded. "Probably taken off a Middle Kingdom vessel en route between Earth and Fire Star. They likely attacked and disabled the ship, boarded her and took the crew and passengers by force, and when they'd got everybody back onto the Mexic vessel had put the torch to the Middle Kingdom ship." He spoke as if he'd heard more such stories than he cared to remember.

Yao's lips drew into a tight line. "Damn," he said under his breath. This was a factor they'd not considered. The Eastern Depot's plans had assumed that there would be some Middle Kingdom prisoners on the ships docked at Xolotl, and maybe even some held on the base itself, but the assumption had been that the strike team would not encounter any such prisoners face to face, and their deaths when the station was destroyed would be considered unavoidable and acceptable losses.

Like, Yao knew, the deaths of the strike team themselves.

But having see the faces of the innocent men, women, and children that his mission would consign to the flames was something for which Yao had not been prepared, and now he was finding it difficult to write their loss off as acceptable.

"We're not just going to leave them to die, are we?" Ang said, his voice strained, compassion from an unlikely source.

Before Yao could answer, the sixth and last of the prisoners descended the gangplank. It was a woman of Han extraction, little more than a girl, perhaps eighteen or nineteen years of age. She was unremarkably attractive, the same sort of girl that Yao had seen countless times in colonies and farms across the face of Fire Star.

The sight of her, though, evoked quite a different reaction from one of the others on the bridge.

"Xiaoli!" Dea shouted, pounding his fist against the viewport's reinforced glass. "Lei Xiaoli!!"

Yao turned to face the young bannerman, who grabbed his elbow in a vice-like grip and refused to let go. Through the tinted faceplate of his stealth suit, Dea looked wild-eyed and on the verge of tears.

"It's her!" Even muffled by their respective faceplates, Dea's voice thundered in Yao's ears. "Do you hear me? It's the woman I love. Lei Xiaoli!"

Still holding Yao's arm, Dea turned back to the viewport, and reached up to rest his free hand against the glass in a tender gesture.

"We've got to…"

And that was the last thing Dea said. It was as though a light had gone on behind his eyes. He dropped Yao's arm, and turning on his heel raced back toward the hatch, drawing his fletcher from its holster as he went.

Syuxtun managed to tackle Dea to the floor before Yao could even react, stopping the young man from barreling down the hatch and racing out through the airlock. Even as good a shot as he was, rushing out alone into the hangar, into the midst of all those armed Mexic warriors, Dea would have been lucky to last a matter of seconds.

"It's all right," Yao said, crouching down and grabbing Dea's shoulder as the younger man began to cry, his shoulders shaking with the sobs.

"We can't just leave her out there!" Dea wailed.

"Don't worry, we won't," Yao answered. Straightening, he turned to face Zhuan. "I think our mission parameters have just changed, o captain.

This isn't a suicide mission any longer. It's a rescue operation."

CHAPTER TWENTY-NINE

Captain Zhuan and Bannerman Yao were alone on the bridge. The captain had sent Ang down to the common area to apprise the others of their situation, and Syuxtun was with Dea, keeping him calm and preventing him from rushing out of the *Dragon* to the aid of the woman he loved.

"Are you certain about this course of action, bannerman?"

Yao, still dressed in the Eagle Knight armor, stood near one of the viewports, looking down on the scene below.

"As sure as I am of anything, o captain."

Syuxtun had reported to ground control that their ship had experienced a coolant leak in its reactor, and that the ship's engineer was busy getting it secured. Assuming that Mexic Dominion hangar procedures were anything like those on a Middle Kingdom base, the ruse would keep the ground crew from boarding the ship until the engineer gave the all-clear, which would give Zhuan and the others some breathing room to work out their next step.

"I'm surprised, I'll admit," Zhuan said, carefully. "Our mission objectives on this subject were quite clear."

Yao nodded, scowling. He'd removed the Eagle Knight helmet, now carried under his arm, and rubbed the bridge of his nose with the thickly gloved fingers of one hand. "Yes, Agent Wu was precise, as I recall, that the destruction of Xolotl overrode any other concerns, including preserving the lives of the strike team or of any other Middle Kingdom subjects we might encounter."

"And yet... ?" Zhuan raised an eyebrow, the faceplate of his own helmet swiveled up, the air somewhat chill on his exposed face.

"And yet those were mere hypotheticals," Yao countered, with growing passion. "It's one thing to disregard the lives of innocents you'll never have to face, but seeing them here in the flesh..." He waved his hand toward the viewport, and the hangar beyond, where the prisoners were now being escorted at gunpoint to an elevator of some sort in the near distance. "It's quite another matter entirely."

"Sufficient to lead you to abrogate your responsibility and disobey your orders?" Zhuan's tone suggested an almost idle curiosity, as though they were discussing abstract hypotheses.

Yao looked back to Zhuan and the two men locked eyes. "I told you before, captain. I am a man, first and foremost, and I won't be ordered to do something I believe to be wrong, or be held from doing what I know to be right."

"And so you are bound to rescue those prisoners, instead of destroying this base?"

"No." Yao shook his head with finality. "In addition to destroying this base. Our primary objective will still be met. Too many lives depend on our success. But I won't sacrifice a single innocent life in that goal's pursuit, and we'll get those prisoners off this station before it's destroyed, one way or another."

Zhuan nodded, a faint smile tugging the corners of his mouth. "Good. That is precisely my thinking on the subject. And, since we are still onboard the *Dragon* and the strike team has not yet deployed, I am technically still in command. If you hadn't agreed with me, I would've had no choice but to exercise my authority to force you to comply."

Now Yao smiled in reply, slyly. "Well," he said, good-humoredly, "you could have tried to force me, at least."

"It will be a tight fit, but we can manage it."

Zhuan and Yao had joined the others in the common area, where they had very nearly finished formulating their new improvised plans.

Yao glanced around the chamber at the faces of the others, studying their expressions.

"And have we sufficient propellant for a return journey, steersman," Zhuan went on, "assuming the addition of that much mass?"

Ang thought for a moment, brow furrowed, and then nodded. "Just barely," he finally answered. "It should be mostly balanced by getting rid of the payload. We won't be able to pick up much acceleration from the initial bursts, so the return trip will be longer than the outward journey, but so long as our air and food supplies hold out, that won't bother me."

Yao tried to suppress his own reaction, tried not to let his emotions show in his expression, but he knew he couldn't hide his thoughts entirely. The others seemed to think that they all might be leaving Xolotl with their lives. How could they allow themselves to be quite so deluded?

He'd got the impression, as the *Dragon* made her final approach to the Mexic base, that the other men, like him, had accepted their own deaths as the almost inevitable outcome of their mission. But something had happened in the last few moments to change that. Had it simply been the announcement that they were now to concern themselves with the rescue of the Middle Kingdom prisoners? Had the mere fact that they were now concerned with saving the lives of others given them greater optimism about their own survival?

Yao harbored no such illusions. His most fervent hope was that a few of the crew would survive long enough to return the prisoners to the ship, and that someone able to man the controls survived to fly the *Dragon* back to Zhurong. Ang seemed the most likely candidate for the latter task, which was why Yao had convinced Zhuan that the steersman should stay behind on the ship while the other eight men went out into the asteroid base to accomplish their revised mission objectives. Of course, Yao himself had likely learned enough about the operation of Mexic ships in his tutorials en route with Zhuan that he could do the job himself, but Yao knew that the chances of him returning to the ship at all, much less in a condition to pilot the ship, were vanishingly slim at best.

Which was why Yao had to suppress a smile when the others worried about whether there would be sufficient room onboard the *Dragon* during their return voyage, with the addition of six prisoners as passengers. As though it was a question that would ever need answering. As it stood, if as many as one or two of the crew returned to the ship, with Ang still onboard to fly her, then Yao would consider that aspect of the mission a success.

There was still, of course, the other mission objective, which had survived from the original formulation of the plan down to the new improvisation they had devised.

The Dragon's Egg.

They would divide into two teams.

The first team, composed of Yao, Fukuda, Paik, and Nguyen, would be responsible for transporting the Dragon's Egg to the core of the asteroid, planting it, and setting the timer. Yao would remain in the Eagle Knight pressure suit he now wore, and would scout ahead, running interference as necessary with any Mexica they encountered. His command of Nahuatl would not be sufficient to get him through more than the most rudimentary of encounters, but coupled with the Mexic armor with its tinted faceplate, under ideal circumstances he knew enough to allow him to get close enough to any base personnel to remove them as obstacles. If possible, he would use his dagger or the saber he wore at his side, since even the muffled sounds of the flechette pistol's firing would carry for some distance through the base's corridors.

The other team would be composed of Syuxtun, Cai, Zhuan, and Dea. Syuxtun and Cai were already clad in the captured Jaguar Knight pressure suits, and the captain and Bannerman Dea would remove their stealth pressure suits and go dressed in their plain black worksuits and slippers. Zhuan was loath to leave the ship unarmored, but it was necessary to establish their cover story, which Syuxtun would be providing to any Mexica that they encountered. The story would be that Zhuan and Dea were two Middle Kingdom subjects that were taken prisoner from the remains of a disabled Middle Kingdom scout ship, and Syuxtun and Cai would ostensibly be in the process of escorting them to wherever in Xolotl the prisoners were held. If all went to plan, this would be the same location to which the six prisoners, Lei Xiaoli included, had been escorted. On their arrival Zhuan and Dea would arm themselves with the fletchers secreted on their person, and the four men would effect the rescue of the six prisoners.

The teams would be able to communicate with one another using their scrambler radios, but communications were to be kept to a minimum, if at all possible.

Ang, for his part, would remain onboard the *Dragon*, keeping her prepped and ready for takeoff.

With any luck, the story about leaking coolant which Syuxtun had provided to the ground control would keep any of the hangar's work-crew from boarding the ship until the others could return with the rescued prisoners.

That was the intention, at any rate.

As with so many things, though, the reality fell far short of the ideal.

CHAPTER THIRTY

Zhuan felt the cold weight of the holstered flechette pistol pressing into the small of his back, and the smaller nub of the scrambler radio. The bulge was nearly entirely concealed by the fabric of his work-suit, which billowed somewhat at the waist. To reach the weapon or the radio, he would have to unfasten the stays on the front of the suit, and reach around his side to the small of his back. It would be cumbersome, and not a maneuver he could quickly perform, but a short amount of experimentation had proved that there was no other place on his body where the items could effectively be concealed.

Dea, it was clear, was less than happy about the arrangement. Zhuan could see, looking at the younger man, that the bannerman would have been more satisfied to wear his fletcher on a low-slung holster, like a Tejas gunslinger. As it was, with the pistol and radio for the moment inaccessible within the folds of his worksuit, Dea's hands twitched, as though desperate for some activity.

Zhuan knew Dea's hands would be more than busy enough in short order, if things went as expected.

Syuxtun and Cai were to play the part of their Mexic captors, bringing prisoners back to the asteroid base in order to receive accolades from their peers and to progress incrementally up the Mexic military hierarchy.

The four men stood at the airlock, ready to disembark. The second team remained in the common area, preparing the Dragon's Egg for travel, waiting for the hangar to empty of personnel.

"Are you ready, men?" Zhuan asked, glancing at the others.

Dea's jaw was set, his expression grim and determined, and he managed only a curt nod. The other two men, their expressions obscured by their helmets' faceplates, were somewhat more difficult to read.

"We are ready, o captain," Syuxtun said, his voice low but level.

"I don't know…" Cai began, then broke off. "I'm not sure…"

"Don't be afraid, brother," Syuxtun said, soothingly. "As the prophet says, 'Short is the enjoyment of this world; the Hereafter is the best for those who do right.'"

Cai looked at him, his confusion evident even through the tinted faceplate. "I have no idea what you just said."

"It means," Syuxtun explained, "that life is fleeting, and to do your duty is to do right. God's call to self-sacrifice is never unjust. And what do you gain from fleeing death, after all? 'Wherever ye are, Death will find you out, even if ye are in towers built up strong and high!' If you fear death you will not escape death by being afraid. Instead, face it boldly when duty calls."

"Oh, thank you, great sage," Cai said sarcastically, sounding near to the point of breaking, "I feel much better about everything now."

Zhuan stepped in, laying a hand on Cai's armored shoulder. It was somewhat disconcerting, to see the faint image of the clearly frightened young man's face within the open maw of a fearsome jaguar's head. "We have a duty to perform here, guardsman. And lives are depending on you rising to that challenge."

"I don't know what I'm doing here." Cai's voice was strained. "I've hardly even been in combat before. I worked in the quartermaster's division, doing material inventories and courier runs. I don't belong here."

"None of us belong here, guardsman," Zhuan said, tightening his hand on Cai's shoulder, a largely symbolic gesture since his grip wasn't likely to be felt through the armored pressure suit. "Syuxtun should be home with his son. Dea should be off reading poetry to this young woman of his. And I..." He paused, thoughtfully. "Well, perhaps some of us belong here, at that."

"I'm scared, alright," Cai shrugged away from Zhuan's grip.

"I understand fear, Cai." Zhuan leaned in close, his voice lowering. "And I'm not too proud to admit that I've allowed terror to get the best of me a time or two, myself. But there are people depending on us, not just the rest of this crew, but those innocent prisoners out there. And if you allow yourself the luxury of giving in to your fear, it will be just as if you killed all of them yourself."

"You... you're scared?" Cai asked, his expression open and child-like.

"Cai, I am rutting terrified," Zhuan said. "But that's not going to stop me from doing what I have to do."

Until he had spoken the words to Cai, Zhuan hadn't known them to be true. But they were. He was terrified, which hardly came as any surprise. What was less expected was the fact that, for the first time in his memory, Zhuan felt in complete control of that fear. It was there, an icy hand gripping his innards, but he didn't feel as if he had to rush away, fleeing for safety, nor did he feel as if he might collapse into a pile of jangled nerves at any moment. He was determined to do the job in hand, come what may. The ever-present fear was inescapable, almost a living part of him, but Zhuan felt as if some new element had been added to the equation, some unexpected strength welling up from within. It was a kind of resolve Zhuan could not remember possessing, but which he was not about to question now.

While Zhuan and his team prepared to exit the airlock, Yao was with the others in the common area, making the final preparations for their own deployment.

Their original mission brief had called for an essentially straightforward assault on the asteroid base as soon as the strike team had disembarked from the *Dragon*. The three captured Mexic pressure suits were intended only to allay any suspicions about their true identities for the brief span it would take for the other four members of the strike team to exit the ship. But a frontal assault such as the Eastern Depot had planned was certain to put the base's own security forces on high alert, and while Yao was confident in the team's abilities to punch a hole through those forces, though perhaps at the cost of their own lives, there was little chance that any of them would return to the ship in the aftermath in those conditions, much less with a half-dozen civilians in tow.

The idea had been suggested of waiting for the prisoners to be brought safely onboard the *Dragon* before the strike team set off with the Dragon's Egg. The problem was, the security forces were likely to be alerted soon after Zhuan's team freed the prisoners. And with the base already on high alert before the strike team set out, their chances of reaching the core of Xolotl with the explosive device were greatly diminished. They would, in essence, be sacrificing their original mission objective in order to accomplish the new one they'd adopted.

The best chance of success for both missions, it had been decided, was for both teams to set out at roughly the same time. The rescue team would leave first, with Zhuan and Dea playing the prisoners of their escorts Syuxtun and Cai. And once they were safely clear of the hangar bay and had sent back the first reports about the station's layout and security, then the demolition team would set out, led by Yao in the armor of an Eagle Knight, with Nguyen and Paik lugging the Dragon's Egg itself and Fukuda bringing up the rear.

Yao finished checking the action on his fletcher, and then slid it back into the holster at his right hip. Then he loosened the saber which hung on a sheath on his left side. Neither was regulation Mexic issue, and on close inspection would reveal him not to be the Eagle Knight he presented himself to be, but in Yao's experience the variety of weaponry used by Mexic warriors was broad enough that the inconsistency in his appearance would not be immediately noticeable, and by the time anyone was close enough to notice that he wore a Middle Kingdom blade at his side, then he would be close enough to draw the saber and use it, which would serve as an effective end to the immediate problem.

Fukuda, for his part, looked completely out of place on the Mexic base. His pressure suit, with stream-lined contours and tapering heat vents, was flat matte-black, and when he was out of direct light he had a tendency to blend into shadow. In movement he could be easily discerned, but if he stood motionless in a darkened corner, he would be difficult to spot. The Nipponese was busy with his own weaponry as well, having finished his final check of the Dragon's Egg controls. Fukuda was their designated demolitions expert, and while all members of the strike team had been checked out on the bomb's basic operation, none of them were as conversant with it as he was.

"My family manufactures fireworks, did I tell you?" Fukuda addressed Yao in a surprisingly conversational tone. "For generations the Fukuda name has been a watchword for intricate pyrotechnic displays." With his faceplate raised, Yao could see a somewhat wistful smile creep across Fukuda's face. "I spent my childhood assisting my parents in preparing fireworks, timing explosives, arranging displays. Burned myself more times than I could count." He wiggled his gloved fingers before his face, then pointed to the white scar which ran across his nose. "Of course, the last burn wasn't my fault at all." He sneered. "My father whipped a white-hot brand against my face, to bring to a sudden end one of our endless and heated arguments. He was a cruel tyrant, my father, a martinet, and I'd had the temerity to raise my hand to him when he told me for the millionth time that I was worthless, undisciplined, a failure." Fukuda chuckled, ruefully. "Still, I got my last blow in, before leaving the house forever. My brother didn't understand why I was leaving, asked when I was coming home, but…"

Fukuda broke off, looking into the middle distance for the moment, his attention drifting from the controls beneath his hands.

Yao stepped forward quickly, gently pulling Fukuda to his feet, and his hands away from the bomb's controls. "Bannerman, do you need a moment?" he said, concerned. The last thing they needed was for their demolitions expert to be swept away on a tide of memory and regret, and in some passionate moment imperil them all.

"What was it you said, Yao? A man can spend his life worrying about what might have been…?"

"Or he can concern himself with how he will act in the future," Yao said, completing the thought.

Fukuda nodded. "That was it." He paused, and then said, "There is a young boy among these prisoners, you said?"

"There is," Yao allowed.

The Nipponese pursed his lips. "That is… good," he said, nodding again. He glanced down at the Dragon's Egg, then straightened, coming to attention. He raised his hand in salute. "The payload is prepped for travel, bannerman, and I'm ready to move when you give the word."

Yao returned the salute with a grim smile. "Let's go see about that future, shall we?"

CHAPTER THIRTY-ONE

As the *Dragon* had been pushed into position by the tugs, Zhuan had for the first time had the chance to get a grasp on the scale of Xolotl. Now, stepping out through the airlock, feeling naked and exposed in nothing more than his worksuit and slippers, he was forced to confront that scale head on.

Xolotl was only a fraction of the size of Zhurong in terms of outer dimensions, a rough cylinder two kilometers long with a circumference of just over one-and-a-half kilometers compared to the oblong Fire Star moon over twenty-five kilometers long and more than twenty wide. But while the asteroid would have been dwarfed next to the moon, the Mexica had made impressively good use of Xolotl's interior. The body of the asteroid had apparently been nearly completely hollowed out, if the hangar was any indication. The space he now stepped out into was larger than any single chamber on

Zhurong, larger by orders of magnitude than any of the hangars in which the Middle Kingdom's Interplanetary Fleet was housed.

Looking straight up, Zhuan could see the far "wall" of the hangar, nearly a kilometer away, which was really the same floor on which he now stood, continuing in both directions and meeting itself on the far side. An immense floor more than one-and-a-half kilometers long and nearly a quarter of a kilometer wide, on which were arranged countless Mexic warships.

The immense space swallowed any echoes, and the sounds that reached Zhuan's ear were muffled and faint. The last of the prisoners from the Mexic transport on the next landing gantry had been led to a doorway in the nearest wall, and Zhuan could now faintly hear that door closing shut after them. It took a moment's consideration to remember that he was standing on the inner wall of the asteroid's longer side, and that the door he now faced led deeper into the cylinder, toward the asteroid's far end.

The intelligence reports of the Eastern Depot had suggested that the asteroid's interior was divided into cylindrical decks nestled one inside the other. It certainly made sense, as it would be the most effective use of the available space, but until he passed through that door, Zhuan would not know for certain whether Agent Wu's estimates had been correct.

As large as the hangar floor was, and as many ships were in evidence, the only one presently being tended by ground crews in the near vicinity was the troop transport from which the prisoners had been led. The next nearest ship around which support staff moved was some considerable distance away, well out of earshot.

With Syuxtun in the lead, playing the part of their Jaguar Knight captor, Zhuan and Dea in the middle as the dejected prisoners being led to the slaughter, and Cai bringing up the rear in his Mexic pressure suit, the four men made their way across the hangar floor to the doorway. Zhuan had to resist the urge to continue to glance back at the ground crew tending to the troop transport; as soon as they were out of sight, whether within the transport or disappeared around the other side, Yao and his demolition team were prepared to move out with the Dragon's Egg.

The quartet reached the door without incident. They didn't risk speaking, so as not to break cover, but Syuxtun paused for a moment and glanced over his shoulder at Zhuan, as if seeking assurance. Tight-lipped, Zhuan nodded, indicating the door's opening mechanism. Visibly steeling himself, Syuxtun reached over and opened the door, and there was no turning back.

It had been hoped that they would follow so soon after the six prisoners and their escort that they could remain in sight and simply tag along after them, waiting for the prisoners to be transferred to some sort of holding facility. Once there, Zhuan and the others could put their rescue plans into effect. Those plans, though, were highly notional, and were all but abandoned the moment that the four men stepped through the door from the hangar.

Zhuan wasn't sure what he'd expected the interior of the station to be like. Certainly the hangar, essentially featureless and immensely large, had given little indication how the habitation areas of the station might look. But on seeing the reality, Zhuan was forced to admit that he'd expected it to be much like the hangar—large and featureless. He'd anticipated something like an enormous building filled with little white rooms connected by unadorned corridors, sparsely populated by Mexic warriors in full battle dress.

His feeble imaginings had fallen so far from the mark that it was difficult not to laugh at himself. Xolotl wasn't a building, it was a small city, compacted into an even smaller place. And it was far, far from featureless.

In retrospect, Zhuan realized, it should have been obvious. Place of the Cactus, the capital of the Mexic Dominion, was the largest city in the western hemisphere, and one of the largest cities in the world, rivaled only by London, Al-Qahirah, Delhi, and of course Northern Capital, the largest of them all. And while Zhuan had never been there, he'd seen countless lithographs of Place of the Cactus and other Mexic cosmopolitan areas, the skylines dominated by immense step pyramids, the canals with their petal-covered boats, the market places and the flower wars and the ball courts. Mexic cities were a riot of colors and textures, crowded with people and animals, alive with music and noise. And though it was a city crammed into a hollowed asteroid floating out in the black void of interplanetary space, Xolotl was a Mexic city nonetheless, and was no different.

There was a ceiling, but it was dozens of meters overhead, and painted a light shade of blue that closely resembled the sky, that color that seems to disappear from view when not viewed directly, like blue-painted water-towers on the horizon. And rather than arranging space within the station as rooms in an immense building, the artificers of Xolotl had instead created them as separate structures with their own walls and roof. So that it was exactly as if one had stepped from a hangar on a space station onto the streets of a Mexic city somewhere. There in the near distance rose a stepped pyramid, its pinnacle standing some dozens of meters above the ground-level, nearly touching the sky-blue-painted ceiling. And it *was* ground-level, Zhuan realized, and not the floor. There was almost no sense at all of being in an enclosed space. Ironically, this was largely due to the fact that the buildings on all sides obstructed one's view; in the hangar, where one could see in all directions for a kilometer, it was inescapable that one was in a single large room, where here, by contrast, the fact that buildings rose on all sides allowed one the illusion that an unbroken horizon might extend somewhere just out of sight.

But neither were these city streets deserted. Unlike the sparsely-populated featureless white rooms of Zhuan's half-formed imaginings, these streets were closely packed with men, women, and children. *Children*, on a military station.

Later, when they had a moment's peace to themselves and were able to speak freely, onboard the lift that carried them to the level where the prisoner pens could be found, Syuxtun explained to Zhuan about the castes and callings of those they saw around them on the streets of Xolotl. At first glance they had seemed to Zhuan as little different from the families found in the colonies and farms of Fire Star, or even those back in Northern Capital itself. But as Syuxtun explained, Zhuan's first impressions had been far from accurate.

This was a purely military station, Syuxtun later confirmed, based on his observations of the Mexica they encountered. Xolotl's population numbered somewhere in the thousands, and included support personnel, administrative staff, priests and ritual-ists, student-warriors and warrior-instructors, and troops on leave—but no civilians.

There were women, to be sure, but none of them were married or, in fact, marriageable. The only females onboard Xolotl were *auianime*, or courte-sans, women who tended to the sexual appetites of the warriors. They were easy to spot, and Syuxtun had known them for what they were at a glance. Unlike civilian women, who when unmarried wore their hair long and loose, or when married braided their hair into two plaits coiled around their heads, with the ends sticking up like twin horns above their eyebrows, courtesans wore their hair cropped in a bob and dyed a purplish black. And while most Mexic women abhorred cosmetics, courtesans lightened their bronze-brown skin to a pale yellow shade with a special ointment prepared from ocher, stained their teeth red with cochineal, and painted their hands and neck with ornate designs.

Too, Syuxtun had been able to explain to Zhuan that the children he'd seen had hardly been the innocent and carefree offspring of station personnel, as the captain might have expected. These were young men and boys who had been trained from birth to kill. And while the hair worn in long queues at the back of their heads suggested that they hadn't yet captured a prisoner in battle, since children were not allowed to cut their hair until they did, they were still warriors, all the same. Though technically still students of either the House of Youth, where the rank and file warriors were trained, or the House of Learning, where future priests and captains received their instruction, these boys were considered sufficiently trained and mature to be sent into battle, though typically under the command of an adult warrior. And though the hand that pulled the trigger on the fire-lance or that swung the obsidian club might have been smaller, those the student-warriors killed would hardly have cared that their attackers had been youths who hadn't yet grown their first facial hair.

But Zhuan knew none of this when he first walked out onto the streets of Xolotl. All he knew at that moment was that, paradoxically, he had walked out from the cold blackness of the void into the hot, crowded closeness of a densely populated city, one comprised entirely by his mortal enemies, any one of whom would have been only too happy to rip his still beating-heart out of his chest for the greater glory of their blood-hungry gods.

Their goal was to remain unnoticed for as long as possible, and if they were unable to follow the six prisoners by sight it would be for Syuxtun to divine the direction they would have taken. As it happened, Dea gave away the game almost before it had begun.

The street scene they had initially faced had swelled with people, pigtailed youths and purple-haired and red-teethed courtesans, warriors in full pressure suit armor or in simple quilted mantles, priests in resplendent finery and officers in feathered cloaks with jeweled labrets through their lower lips and jade ear-plugs through their lobes. And yet, as crowded as the street had been, they had amazingly caught a brief glimpse of their quarry in the near distance. The six prisoners with their warrior escort were mounting the high stairs of a stepped pyramid that rose above the street, a hundred meters or more away from where Zhuan and the others now stood.

Zhuan didn't know for certain the reason the six Middle Kingdom subjects were being led up to the pyramid's summit, but based on his scant familiarity with Mexic culture he could only imagine one possible use to which they could be put atop a pyramid: as human sacrifice. The image of the stepped pyramid, its sides stained nearly black by centuries of spilt blood flowing down from the altar above, was a familiar one; the daily news throughout the Middle Kingdom had been filled with such images for years, whenever a story on the Mexic Dominion was run, on the off-chance that readers might have forgotten why the Mexica were the enemies of the Dragon Throne.

But if Zhuan assumed that the prisoners were being marched up the pyramid to their immediate death, he was not alone.

"No!" Dea shouted, looking in wide-eyed horror at the distant pyramid and the small shapes shadowing its steps. "Xiaoli, no!"

It was to their mission's benefit that the worksuits the two men wore were so difficult to get on and off, or Dea might have succeeded in pulling his fletcher pistol out from the small of his back before being subdued. And had he produced the weapon and begun firing, then it was likely that Syuxtun's following gambit would never have worked.

Lucky, too, that when Dea began to rave it was in Official Speech, which none of the Mexica around them seemed able to understand.

As soon as Dea began shouting, Zhuan's instinct to command took over, even if he was himself meant to be playing the part of a prisoner. "Belay that, bannerman!" the captain called over, his voice a loud whisper. But Dea had ignored him, and continuing to shout, had rushed forward, tearing at the stays on the front of his worksuit, desperate to reach the flechette pistol snugged at the small of his back.

Zhuan's first impulse was to race after the young man and bring him to heel, but a quick glance at the Mexica whose attention Dea's outburst had captured suggested to Zhuan that it wouldn't be the wisest course of action. To the milling crowd of Mexica, Dea looked to be nothing more than a prisoner who was shouting madly while trying to escape his captors. If Zhuan were to follow, a man of Han extraction likewise wearing a suit in the Middle Kingdom fashion, he would doubtless have been thought another prisoner attempting to escape, and then Zhuan would have been dealt with as harshly as Dea would soon be.

Syuxtun didn't need any additional instruction from the captain, but took to his heels in pursuit of Dea, while Cai stepped forward and, with a brief bit of whispered coaching from Zhuan, reached over and took hold of the captain's elbow, as if forcibly restraining him from fleeing as well.

Syuxtun's intention was to catch up with Dea and subdue him, playing the part of the escort retrieving an escaping prisoner, before Dea did anymore to disrupt the illusion that they were anything but what they presented themselves to be. Unfortunately, even if the reduced pull of Xolotl's centrifugal gravity, one-third that of Earth, Syuxtun's bulky pressure suit put him at a disadvantage, and Dea was able to outstrip him by lengths.

Again, if Dea'd had a weapon in his hand, things might have ended much worse for all of them, but as it stood he was unarmed, and gave no indication that he had any weapons secreted on his person. And so he was treated more like one would a misbehaving pet than a dangerous fugitive.

The man who had stepped in Dea's path was a portrait in ferocious martial finery. A feathered cloak hung on his shoulder, his chest bare beneath a broad necklace, with his hair shaved to a scalp-lock on the top of his head and a feathered head-band around his brow, with glittering jade ear-plugs dangling within his lobes and a wicked-looking labret piercing his lower lip. In his hands he carried a long wooden club, the edge lined with small obsidian blades, while around his waist was tied the pelt of a spotted ocelot. This was a captain of the Jaguar Knight order, whose regalia suggested he had taken quite a few live prisoners captive on the battlefield. Seeing Dea rushing through the thoroughfare, the officer had apparently decided this presented the opportunity to add another number to his score.

Dea didn't see the Jaguar Knight until it was too late. When he raised his hands before him in an ineffectual defensive posture, the Jaguar Knight simply lunged forward, using the blunt back of his obsidian club to swipe Dea's feet out from under him, then driving his shoulder forward into Dea's sternum, knocked him backward. Off balance, his arms pinwheeling on either side, Dea landed with an audible thump on the pavement underfoot. Before he could even attempt to struggle to his feet, the Jaguar Knight had planted a foot on his chest and then swung his obsidian club around, the sharpened edges of black glass stopping only a fin-ger's width from his throat.

Syuxtun reached his side just before the Jaguar Knight halted his club's swing, just before the black glass blades were about to cut through Dea's throat.

Lips snarling beneath his prominent hooked nose, the Mexic warrior had spoken a dozen or so syllables to Syuxtun, none of which reached Zhuan's ears, though he doubted he'd have understood them if they had. Syuxtun, adopting a submissive posture, head lowered, answered more briefly. The Jaguar Knight continued to scowl, looking displeased with Syuxtun who, if the armor the Athabascan wore was to be believed, was his brother-in-arms, a fellow member of the Order of the Jaguar. Then the Mexic officer had lifted his foot from Dea's chest, propped his obsidian club onto his shoulder, and then strode off haughtily, pausing only to toss a few more syllables back in Syuxtun's direction.

Before the Jaguar Knight passed out of sight, Syuxtun shouted after him, the only word of which Zhuan understood was the Nahuatl for "prisoner." The Jaguar Knight, without slowing, had pointed with his obsidian club at the stepped pyramid ahead, speaking a short word or two over his shoulder, and then disappeared from view into the crowd.

Syuxtun returned to where Zhuan and Cai stood. And though the Athabascan held onto Dea's arm as part of their pose, playing the escort recovering the recaptured prisoner, it was clear that his need to restrain Dea from running was a real one. The Mexica in the street around them looked with some scorn at Syuxtun; it was hardly surprising, since to all appearances he'd just been rebuked by a superior officer for the crime of letting a prisoner in his charge get loose and run away, and for a martial society like the Mexica, there were few offenses more odious than earning the opprobrium of one's superiors.

Zhuan covered his mouth with his hand, making as if he were scratching his nose, and in a low voice said, "What did the Mexica say?"

Syuxtun nodded toward the pyramid. "I asked him the way to the prisoner holding facilities, and he pointed to the pyramid." Then he said to Dea, as soothingly as possible, "They're not being led to slaughter. At least not yet." Then back to Zhuan, he said, "The pyramids are the way up. There's a lift that connects the top to the higher levels, and that's where the prisoners are being taken."

Zhuan responded with a short nod and, covering his mouth again, on the chance that someone might be watching, said, "All right, then. Let's get going."

As they neared the top of the pyramid, they got a better look at the surrounding cityscape, but the prisoners were nowhere to be seen, having already ascended in the elevator at the summit.

The pyramid they now climbed appeared to be only one of countless such structures throughout that level. They could be seen to the left and right, both "spinward" and "anti-spinward," and to the front, in the direction of the asteroid's far end, spaced on a regular grid every few hundred meters, disappearing at the "horizon" where the ground sloped upward and disappeared from view beyond the curve of the ceiling above. And from each pyramid rose a narrow pillar painted the same sky-blue shade as the ceiling it joined above, making them virtually invisible from the ground below. Evidently these pyramids, while designed to resemble religious structures back on Earth, were in effect nothing more than platforms used to bridge one level to the next. Their outward appearance seemed to be a matter of aesthetics rather than of function, since the elevators could just as easily go all the way from ceiling to floor, one assumed. This became even more evident when they reached the top and learned that the elevators did not in fact terminate at the pyramid's summit, but continued down into the body of the structure to service chambers hidden within.

Once they were high on the steps, about halfway to the top, Zhuan had decided they were far enough away from listening ears that they could converse relatively freely, remaining careful to keep their voices down. Their principal topic of conversation, as they neared the top of the pyramid, was how best to direct Yao and the demolition team to advance, having seen what they had so far of the city within the asteroid.

By now, Yao and his team would be preparing to exit the *Dragon* and carry the Dragon's Egg toward the heart of the asteroid. But before they left the relative safety of the vehicle they would wait for the report from Zhuan's team, who had been scouting possible approaches in their brief journey into the station.

Zhuan's and Dea's radios were safely tucked away under their worksuits at the small of their backs, leaving Syuxtun and Cai the only ones free to radio back to the ship. Making sure that the scrambler was set to encrypt and decrypt their transmissions, once they mounted the steps to the pyramid's summit and were able to inspect the controls and workings of the elevator, Syuxtun established communications with Yao, and relayed Zhuan's commands to him. Then, once Yao's confirmation was received, Syuxtun shut his radio back down, and the quartet rode the elevator up to the next level.

As the elevator started to climb, their subjective sense of "down" tilted somewhat in the direction of the far wall, the result of the station's rotational forces. They were alone in the elevator car, which didn't appear to be wired for sound, and felt free to converse for the moment.

"That was surprisingly easy," Cai said, smiling uneasily. "Who knows, maybe this'll be easier than we thought."

Zhuan thought to chastise the young man for inviting bad fortune by saying so, but it was too late to do anything about it now. Having said that things were easy, Cai was only ensuring that things would get much more difficult from here on. Or so Zhuan thought, and as the next few hours would show, he was far from wrong.

CHAPTER THIRTY-TWO

Yao prepped the demolition team, waiting for Zhuan's word. Somehow he'd wound up with only one of the crew's bannermen on his team, along with two of the guardsmen, the lumbering man-mountain Nguyen, and the slumbering oaf Paik. And while he was reasonably sure that Fukuda had received the standard bannerman microgravity training and would know everything he was saying by rote, he couldn't be as sure about the Green Standard guardsmen, and couldn't count on them having retained enough from his training sessions onboard the *Dragon*. And if they had, then a little refresher would do them no harm and would help to pass the moments until they set out.

"Which way is spinwards?" Yao asked, singling out Paik to answer.

The guardsman stifled a yawn, and shrugged.

"Come, this isn't a game, and our lives might depend on it," Yao said, steel beneath his words. "Now, which way is spinwards?"

Paik pulled a face, but pointed a gloved finger in the direction of the hatch.

It was the correct answer. "But how do we know?"

Paik began to shrug, then suppressed the motion. "Don't know. Just do."

Yao nodded, taking a sighing breath through his nostrils. "Your bones know if your mind doesn't," he said, not entirely unsympathetically. "Under centrifugal gravity, spinwards feels something like uphill, while anti-spinwards feels like it's sloping down." He pointed to the rear of the *Dragon*. "Face that way. Then turn your head quickly toward the hatch." He addressed the others. "All of you do it, you included, Fukuda."

"Oooh," Nguyen said, swaying slightly like a tree in a high wind. "The floor came up at me!"

Yao sighed, and nodded. They'd been experiencing something like the effect nearly every moment of the last nine days, and for days before that on Zhurong, but only noticed it when he pointed it out to them. "Yes, and if you do the same and turn to the right, you'll see the floor appear to slope down away from you. It's due to rotational effects. A soldier worth his salt can be dropped blindfolded into anyplace there's gravity and within a matter of seconds should be able to tell you whether he's on a naturally gravitating body like a planet or large moon, or on a station with centrifugal gravity, or perhaps even on a spinning ship moving through space. It's all to do with the fluids sloshing around in our ear canals. Now, the closer you get to the hub, the more pronounced the effect, which also helps you keep track of whether you've moving inward toward the hub or outward toward the edge."

Paik yawned again, and this time didn't bother to stifle it. "We've been over all of this, Yao. So what if I can't remember the whys and wherefores if I know which way is which? After all, it's not as if any of us is likely to survive long enough to be blindfolded and dropped anywhere after this, neh?"

Yao bristled, but before he responded with a stern rebuke, he caught himself. Paik was right, as much as the bannerman didn't want to admit it. Yao couldn't help trying to turn these men into proper soldiers, into bannermen, but there was little to gain from the effort. The chances were that all of them would be dead in short order, and all that was asked of the four of them at the moment was to survive long enough to get the fission bomb to the center of the station and set the timer. That required only a pair of strong arms, two functioning legs, and the good fortune not to get killed on the way. Knowing the effects of rotation on the fluids in the inner ear wasn't likely to be of any use to them, so long as they remembered "up" and "down," "this way," and "that way."

Looking at Nguyen, though, Yao realized that they'd be lucky to remember just that much, if that.

"Can't we just get on it with, already?" Fukuda said, twitching angrily within his matt-black pressure suit.

Before Yao could answer, he heard the ping of his jerry-rigged scrambler radio in his helmet, and with his tongue flicked the system to send and receive. "Yao here."

"Bannerman Syuxtun reporting," came the voice over the ether. The Athabascan's voice was clearly discernible, though something about the scrambler encryption-decryption routine left the pitch elevated, so that it sounded like a younger, almost childish version of the stoic man Yao had come to know. "Ready for your marching orders?"

The corners of Yao's mouth lifted in the shadow of a smile.

"Received and understood," Yao said, and toggled his scrambler radio into the off position. It would no longer transmit, but remain in a lower power state passively scanning for another incoming transmission, whereupon it would ping Yao once more. For the moment, though, his helmet was only filled with the sound of his own breathing, and the muffled noises that carried through his helmet's faceplate.

"Okay, men," he said, turning to face Fukuda, Paik, and Nguyen. "Here's the size of it. Personnel is scattered widely enough on the hangar floor that, with me scouting ahead, we should be able to get the three of you, along with the payload, out of the hangar bay without being noticed, so long as we move quickly and don't foul up."

Fukuda scowled, reading Yao's expression through the faceplate of his Eagle Knight armor. "Yeah, and then what happens?"

Yao returned the Nipponese's scowl, but nodded. "That's where the trouble starts. Just beyond those doors, it turns out, is a habitat, laid out like a city and fairly well populated. I might be able to make it through, so long as no one stops me and wants to have a long chat in Nahuatl, but you three"—he indicated their black stealth suits—"won't make it a half-dozen steps into that crowd before someone raises the alarm."

"So what do we do?" Nguyen asked, looking worried.

Yao pulled his most reassuring smile, for what it was worth. "The captain and the others saw ventilation panels set into the deck at regular intervals. Fresh air is cycled in and stale air is cycled out."

"The ventilation ducts would probably be in the ceiling, neh?" Paik asked, drawling.

Yao shook his head. "By pushing it through the floor they get the new stuff where they most need it, instead of pushing it down from the ceiling, where it would have to wait for the centrifugal gravity to pull it down to where it's needed. Anyway, there are access panels recessed next to some of the vents, for work-crews to gain access as needed, and that's going to be our way through."

"What, through the vents?" Fukuda sneered.

"Exactly." Yao pulled his fletcher from the holster at his side, checking the action. "A station this size would need good-sized ventilation shafts, so chances are we won't run into any difficulty maneuvering through them. And I'll be able to scout ahead and see where best we should come back up. There are elevator lifts that lead from deck to deck, the captain says, so all we need to do is get to the nearest of the shafts, catch an empty car and head up as far as we can go, and then we should be in business."

Yao paused, and looked around at the three faces before him.

"Any questions?"

Paik raised his hand, lazily. "Yeah, I've got one. Do we really have to do this? I mean, couldn't we just take the ship and head back to Earth?"

"Any actual questions?"

Yao waited for a moment, then slid his fletcher back into its holster.

"In that case, check your seals and fasteners, because we're about to head out."

Steersman Ang came to Yao, while the others wrestled the Dragon's Egg into a carrying position. The short man was dressed in a pressure suit, like the others, but while it had been tailored specifically for him by the Middle Kingdom artificers on Zhurong, still it seemed to fit him too snugly around his round belly, too loose around his arms and legs. The steersman moved awkwardly through the one-third Earth's gravity tugging at them, feet shuffling, both his hands wrapped around the handle of his flechette pistol, as though he'd be called upon to fire it unexpectedly at any moment.

"Bannerman Yao?" Ang began, his voice wavering. "Have you... have you got a second?"

Yao didn't, but nodded anyway. Too much was riding on the performance of each man, Ang included, for him to dismiss them cavalierly at this stage.

"I'm just…" Ang gnawed his lower lip between his front teeth. "I don't know about this." He looked around, nervously. "Do I have to stay here on my own?"

A faint smile shadowed Yao's lips. "Do you really want to go out there"—he motioned toward the hatch—"with the rest of us, out among all the Mexica?"

Ang thought for a split second, then shook his head. "No, I just…"

Yao nodded, and placed a hand on the steersman's shoulder. "I understand. You're right to be afraid. We are surrounded on all sides by our enemies, who would do us harm. But a duty has been handed to us, and we have no choice but to do it. If so, then the best that can befall us is that we succeed and survive, and the worst is that we die with honor having done what was asked of us."

The steersman's mouth twisted into a gross parody of a smile. "That's a great pep talk, there, bannerman," he said, chuckling ruefully. "You may have missed your calling, becoming a relentless fighting machine instead of a public speaker."

"Well," Yao said, laughing, "if I weren't a relentless fighting machine, who would be, eh?"

"Not me," Ang said quickly, sliding his fletcher back into its holster and holding his hands up, palms forward in an exaggerated defensive posture. "I'm quite happy being a coward and scoundrel, thank you very much. I'll just be here on the ship quaking in my rutting boots, waiting for the rest of you to get back." He paused, and glanced at the hatch, nervously. "I just hope no one comes knocking on the door."

Yao nodded, his jaw set. "Ang, that makes two of us."

Dressed in his captured Eagle Knight armor, Yao was the first off the *Dragon*, while the rest of the demolition team waited onboard for him to radio back the all-clear. He crossed the hangar floor, taking care not to walk too quickly, but to give every appearance of a ranking warrior casually returning to base for a bit of leave after a long foray into enemy territory. Of course, it was not a difficult pose for him to adopt, having been precisely in that position previously more times than he had fingers and toes. The only difference being the enemy, and the base to which he was returning.

Unlike Zhuan, Yao knew exactly what to expect from Xolotl, having carefully studied the estimates and proposed schematics provided by Agent Wu over the course of the last nine days. And where the Embroidered Guards' intelligence reports had been lacking, Yao had made inferences based on his own experiences. He had spent some years living along the border between Tejas and the Mexic Dominion, and had seen Mexic cities from close enough vantages that he had a fairly firm notion as to how Xolotl would be organized.

When the door leading from hangar to habitat opened—in reality two doors acting in concert, heavily shielded and strong enough to remain pressurized and secure in the event that either side lost internal pressure—Yao got his first glimpse of

Xolotl's interior, and though it matched his expectations in nearly every regard, there was one aspect of its appearance for which he had failed to account, one that would have been impossible to predict. The quality of the light which shone from the panels in the sky-blue-painted ceiling overhead, striking the brilliantly colored buildings below, their plaster-faced facades painted in bright reds and yellows and blues, reminded him of another city, glimpsed on another morning, at the moment when the sun first rose above the horizon and painted it in a prismatic kaleidoscope of colors.

It reminded him of Shachuan Station.

It brought a pang for Yao to realize that he hadn't thought of the Shachuan Station Massacre in some days, only reminded that morning when Zhuan had asked him about orders conflicting with conduct. He'd been so successful in losing himself in the minutia and preparations for the mission, en route from Zhurong, that he'd actually succeeded in forgetting the dark secret he had learned, that had set him on this road. Or if not quite forgotten, perhaps, then at least he'd managed to move it back from the forefront of his thoughts for a time. But discovering the prisoners on the Mexic asteroid, being led to slaughter, had reminded him of all of those innocents, the year before, who hadn't even had the luxury of knowing what dire fate awaited them at the hands of the approaching Mexic warriors. And if the commanders of the Eight Banners had not ordered Yao and his men to stand down and wait, he might have been able to rescue some of them, at least.

Well, he wasn't going to stand idly by and see innocents slaughtered again, whatever the circumstance, whatever the cost, whatever his orders. Could saving these prisoners somehow shrive him of the guilt he felt concerning his earlier inaction? Or do even some small amount to salve his pained conscience, after learning what he had of the reasoning behind the commanders' orders that the innocents not be saved?

Perhaps, and perhaps not. But either way, Yao was willing to spend his last breath and the last drop of his blood to find out.

With Yao standing guard, watching for gaps in the flow of pedestrians in the habitat beyond the hangar door, the other three members of the demolition team moved out, first Nguyen and Paik lugging the Dragon's Egg, which though relatively light-weight in the one-third Earth's gravity of the station was still an awkward load to maneuver. And then, once they had safely got through the door and down into the ventilation shaft that Yao had managed to open, largely hidden from view by the bulk of a large building painted in garish shades of yellow and red, Fukuda followed close behind, tensed and ready for action.

Once the three men were down the shaft, Yao made sure that their position was still unobserved, and then followed them down, closing the access panel after him.

The only flaw in their improvised plan was that the Mexic pressure suit which Yao wore did not share the same stealth capacities as the specially designed Middle Kingdom suits of the other three men. While they would be virtually invisible to any infrared scan of the ventilation ducts, Yao was not quite so well obscured from view. However, his was a suit designed for extended use in hard vacuum, which was to recycle as much of the suit's waste heat as possible to keep the wearer warm in the freezing cold of the void. By keeping the suit's internal temperature turned as high as possible, keeping the majority of the heat inside the well-insulated carapace, Yao would present a reduced thermal profile, with the warmest spot being the helmet's faceplate which, while tinted, still allowed more ambient energy to pass through than the reinforced materials of the suit itself. Of course, it meant that Yao was basting in his own juices inside the armor, and would have to keep his face turned away from any thermal sensors they happened to spot along the way, but these minor inconveniences aside, the resulting risk was an acceptable one, and was preferable to the alternative of traveling through the congested streets above, where his limited command of Nahuatl would be sorely tested, to say nothing of his only vague facial resemblance to the Mexic type.

And so the four men made their way further along the station, traveling deep within its very skin, the conduits of the ventilation system just large enough for them to pass two abreast. From time to time Yao climbed up to the access panels overhead, peering out into the streets above to chart their progress toward the nearest of the pyramid elevators. It was slow going, but so far they had not encountered any resistance, and no shots had been fired.

Yao knew, of course, that it couldn't last, but he was all for enjoying the easy stage of the operation for as long as it did.

Chapter Thirty-Three

"What am I looking at here, again?" Zhuan asked, keeping his voice low.

Syuxtun had explained, as they ascended in the elevator, that there were five principle decks in Xolotl. The number may have had some ritual significance, the Athabascan supposed, perhaps to do with the mythical five ages of the world in the Mexic creation story, with the current world being the fifth and latest. The religion of the Mexica was apparently filled with stories about the previous ages, or "suns" as they were called, named after the type of sun which shone down upon them. The present age, Syuxtun explained, was the Sun of Movement, in which the gods had perfected the formula for making men, so that they wouldn't melt into ash and fish when rain hit them, or move so slowly on giant legs that tigers would come to consume them, or be burned in flame, or be blown over the mountains by great winds and turned into monkeys. This Sun of Movement began when the great gods gathered at Teotihuacan, the place of dead gods, and the twin sons of the god of twos threw themselves into the flames which burned atop the high pyramid, and the sparks which flew out became the sun, and the moon, and the stars in the sky.

It was, Zhuan supposed, no more or less foolish than the creation stories of his own ancestors, who had believed that the first living being hatched out of a great black egg along with the heavens and earth, instead of life arising naturally on the Earth as the result of inexorable biological processes and the universe itself developing in much the same way, as philosophers now contended.

But even his brief tutelage in the belief systems of the Mexica had not prepared Zhuan for what awaited them when the elevator came to a rest.

"It is Fire Star," Syuxtun said simply, as though that explained everything.

The prisoner pens, or so the Mexic Jaguar Knight who had rebuked Syuxtun in the street had said, could be found on the innermost but one level of the station, where most of the rituals conducted onboard were carried out. It made a certain amount of sense—albeit somewhat morbid sense—to keep the prisoners near the places where they would eventually be sacrificed. And from what little Zhuan knew of the Mexic belief system, it likewise made sense that the rituals would be carried out near the heart of the station, for the greatest efficacy. The innermost level, doubtless, had not been chosen, since that close to the axis of rotation the centrifugal gravity would be considerably lower, and the tidal rotational effects markedly greater, such that it would be unnecessarily difficult on the ritualists, to say nothing of the poor prisoners. By positioning the prisoner pens and ritual areas on the next lower level, nearer the station's outer skin, the trade-off between diminished gravity and increased tidal effects would be kept within a more acceptable range.

So Zhuan had steeled himself, riding up in the elevator, for a possible gruesome scene at their destination. This would be a level on which any areas not needed for the station's physical operations—power plants, ventilation systems, and so on—would be given over to ritual purposes. And Mexic rituals almost invariably involved considerable amounts of spilt blood, as the black rust-like stains on the *Dragon* could attest.

Why, then, instead of the blood-soaked oubliette he had been expecting, was Zhuan facing a dainty and detailed miniature model of the red planet Fire Star, complete with tiny representations of Baochuan Prison and Fanchuan Garrison?

"I know it's Fire Star," Zhuan said in a whisper. "*Why* is it Fire Star?"

They were alone on the landing, looking out over the immense model. Even at such a reduced scale, this topographical model of the red planet's surface was immense, banded by walkways that ringed it like the oceans found on fanciful maps of the Earth made in the days before its surface was fully charted. The elevator they had just exited stood at what would be the south pole of Fire Star, and rose in a black pillar to join with the black ceiling high overhead, spangled with lights whose twinkling patterns matched the constellations as seen from the red planet's surface. There was the Lantern, there the twin stars of the Southern Gate, over there the Weaving Girl and there the Purple Luminous, all configured just a minute fraction differently than they would from the surface of the Earth, or from any point in between. This was the night sky as seen from Fire Star's surface at this hour, on this day, in this season. The lights above, Zhuan realized, must be positioned on tracks or some other mechanism which allowed them to be repositioned, in accordance with the movements of the actual stars in the heavens over the red planet.

"In the Mexic Dominion," Syuxtun explained in a low voice, "artisans and craftsmen, or *tolteca*, are highly prized members of society. This is because the Mexica believe that whatever the artist makes is itself an image of reality. And by building detailed replicas, and then effecting change directly to those replicas, they believe it may be possible to influence the natural world itself, and likewise effect change on the thing replicated."

"Hey, there's Shachuan Station," Cai said, pointing with a gloved finger, to a spot of red deep within the miniature Tianfei Valley. "But it's covered with some kind of snake thing."

"It's the Plumed Serpent," Syuxtun said, following Cai's gaze. "One of the Mexic gods. It's said that when the fifth age of the world began, the Plumed Serpent was given the task of peopling the world, and so gathered up the bones of the past men, ground them up, and bled on them from his member, and from the mixture the new men were born. The Mexica repay this debt by bleeding sacrificial victims in the Plumed Serpent's name."

"So that's why the blood-hungry bastards sacrifice innocent women and children?" Dea asked, disgusted.

Syuxtun shook his head. "Oh, no, that's just why they sacrifice to the Plumed Serpent. They actually sacrifice to any number of gods, with different reasons for each."

"Delightful," Cai said. Had he not been wearing the helmet in the shape of a jaguar's head, the faceplate closed, it was clear he would have spat, and as it was he was forced merely to grimace distastefully.

Zhuan drew himself up straight. "So the Mexic slaughtered countless innocent civilians at Shachuan, just to propitiate a mythical feathered snake?"

Syuxtun's expression darkened, and he shook his head. "No. Or at least, I imagine their first priority was the attack's military advantage. But then again, who knows? I've never really been able to understand the Mexic mind, so who's to say that the military objective was secondary, at that, and the principal motivation was the deaths themselves?"

Zhuan walked up to the edge of the landing, looking out over the familiar Fire Star landscape. It so closely resembled the planet's surface sliding beneath him as he orbited the red planet in the *Exhortation*, as he'd done countless times over the years, that Zhuan was momentarily disoriented by the frisson. Then he shook his head, as if to knock his brain back into alignment, and looked again. "It's wrong," he said.

"It's a rutting offense to nature, is what it is," Cai agreed.

"No, I mean it's *wrong*." Zhuan pointed to the miniature of Baochuan prison, which on closer examination was revealed to be surrounded by replicas of Mexic war engines, with a splash of Nahuatl glyphs painted across it. "They've got Baochuan extending further out into the base of the Great Yu Canyon than it really does. And look there." He pointed to the small outpost of Fuchuan, at the eastern end of the Tianfei Valley. "They've got the outpost in the right place, but there's what looks like a Mexic launch facility sitting right next to it."

"What the artist makes is an image of reality," Syuxtun repeated, by way of explanation. "They aren't representing Fire Star as it really is, but as they hope it will be. Those changes"—he pointed to the places that Zhuan had indicated—"must be future targets for Mexic strikes, and the miniature shows them as already having been taken and converted to the Dominion's use."

"That's a crazy way to run a war," Cai said, shaking his head.

"Well, it seems to have worked well enough for them so far," Syuxtun answered, his expression grim.

"We're wasting time with this rutting nonsense," Dea snapped.

"Dea's right," Zhuan agreed. "Besides, we're taking a chance talking so openly. Someone might…"

The rest of the captain's words were cut off when the elevator behind them opened again, and a ritualist strode out, his arms loaded with arcane implements. No longer alone on the landing, the quartet were forced back into their roles as prisoners and escorts, and the conversation was at an end. Syuxtun motioned toward the right, and the walkway that led around the perimeter of the immense model Fire Star. They continued on their way.

They moved for some distance through the level, past the Fire Star miniature. Fortunately, this level was more scarcely populated than the habitat level below had been, the province largely of technicians, priests, and ritualists, though sometimes it was difficult to tell which was which. In fact, as the controls and design of the *Dragon* had suggested, the disciplines of engineering and technology on the one hand, and mysticism and ritual on the other, were not clearly demarcated in Mexic culture. Nowhere was this more evident than in the entrance to the power plant control station.

Glyphs etched onto the floor gave directions and distances for key locales on the level, and Syuxtun related that the pictograms indicated that the prisoner pens could be found on the far side of the power plant entrance. As the four walked along, then, they expected to see some sort of doorway or archway, beyond which the station's engineering facilities would be found, but what they found instead was something entirely different.

This looked more like a temple entrance. Which, in many respects, it was.

Xolotl's power generation facilities were essentially a larger-scale version of the power plant on the *Dragon*, only monstrously larger, with turbines driven by water heated to steam by a nuclear reactor, which was located somewhere above them, near the asteroid's axis. But from where the quartet stood, one would never guess that something as mundane as a power plant rested within.

Two massive statues guarded the entrance, lifelike representations of men, bent forward slightly from the waist, their knees bent and their hands held out grasping before them; the figures were arresting, their fierce expressions disconcerting.

The one on the left was sculpted wearing a helmet which mimicked the shape of an eagle's head, with painted feathers covering his broad shoulders and arms, while the one on the right wore a helmet shaped like a jaguar's head, his body painted blue with black spots.

"The Mexic military is controlled as much by the priesthood as by their generals," Syuxtun said in a low voice. "Since Xolotl is a military base, and the power planet is the heart of Xolotl, they've made it into a sacred temple."

Dimly visible beyond the archway guarded by the two immense figures, they could see a vast space, and within the gloom were more such statues, but of even more gruesome design. The archway itself was lined with representations of human skulls along the inner edge, which on closer examination appeared to have been human skulls set into the concrete.

"Come on," Zhuan said, in a harsh whisper. "I don't want to hang around here any longer than absolutely necessary."

None of the others was in any mood to argue, and so they continued.

The glyphs etched onto the deck-plates indicated they had only a short distance to go before reaching the prisoner pens, when the quartet heard the sounds of a number of people approaching from the direction in which they were heading. They'd managed to get this far by avoiding contact with station personnel, and while Syuxtun had performed admirably in assaying the role of a Jaguar Knight when circumstances demanded that he speak with one of the Mexica onboard, Zhuan knew they were pushing their luck with each new encounter, and that it was only a matter of time before Syuxtun's bona fides were questioned or his authorization requested or any one of a dozen things that could go wrong. And then the game would be well and truly up.

The black-painted ceiling above still twinkled with artificial stars, which cast only a twilight glow onto the floor beneath, so that in the low light the quartet and the approaching Mexica had not yet come in sight of one another.

"That way," Zhuan said, indicating a nearby structure with his chin, urging Syuxtun toward it. It was a supply structure of some sort, like those they'd passed along the way, and though the doorway was low, rising only as high as their waists, it was open. If they moved quickly enough, they could duck inside, wait for the Mexica to pass, and then continue on their way to the prisoner pens when the way was clear.

The others understood the captain's meaning at once, and seemed no more eager than he for another encounter with the Mexica. As quickly and quietly as they were able, the four men hustled to the open door of the supply structure, and slipped inside through the low doorway. The close air inside smelled strongly of cleaning agents, and in the dim light the men saw that they'd found refuge in some sort of janitorial closet, brushes and brooms and mops stacked in profusion, along with buckets of caustic-smelling chemicals. It was hardly surprising, considering the amount of blood that must have been spilt on a regular basis in the nearby control station temple, that there would be a constant need for cleaning.

Zhuan and the others kept out of view as much as was possible, within the shadows of the supply structure. From beyond the open door, they could hear the approaching footsteps of the Mexica. There were a half-dozen of them, perhaps. And as the Mexica passed, they could just catch isolated glimpses of them, but only from the waist down, the view of everything above obscured by the low doorway. There were several Mexic warriors in armored pressure suits, if the legs were any indication, who seemed to be struggling slightly under some weight carried between them, followed by a priest or ritualist.

Finally, the procession passed by, apparently entering the control station temple the quartet had just seen. After Syuxtun stuck his head through the low doorway to check the surroundings and found them vacated, Zhuan ordered the men out of the supply structure and back on their way to the prisoner pens.

As they moved toward the prisoner pens, which the glyphs on the deck indicated were just a short distance ahead, Zhuan had Syuxtun radio back to Yao, to give the bannerman the location of the power plant control station they'd passed a short while before. Zhuan and Syuxtun agreed that the control station seemed a promising position to plant the Dragon's Egg. Not quite at the exact center of the asteroid, it was near the midpoint of its length, and connected directly to the reactor facilities which were positioned nearer the cylinder's axis of rotation. There was sufficient mass in all directions, Zhuan calculated, to prevent the resultant blast from simply venting into space, and the waves of concussive force would be sufficient to shatter to pieces any parts of the asteroid not caught up in the initial conflagration when the fission explosive was detonated.

Syuxtun relayed Yao's confirmation, saying that the bannerman reported that he and his team should be able to reach the control station shortly. It was hoped that the Mexic warriors and the ritualist who appeared to have entered the control station would have vacated by the time the demolition team arrived, but if not, Zhuan was confident in Yao's ability to deal with them.

CHAPTER THIRTY-FOUR

Bannerman Yao toggled his scrambler radio back to passive receive, and turned to address the other men.

"The captain reports that he's found the right spot for us to plant the Egg. That's the good news. The bad news is, there's two levels of Mexica between us and there, and time isn't on our side."

Fukuda scowled, and slashed the empty air before him with the blade of his saber, as if fencing with the shadows that lurked in the dim light of the ventilation duct.

"Why can't we just take the lift again?" Paik moaned, stretched out on the floor, propped up on his elbows. The steel bulk of the Dragon's Egg loomed beside him, looking bigger than it was in the gloom, while on its other side Nguyen sat crosslegged on the floor, his mouth hanging slightly open.

"We can," Yao corrected, removing his fletcher from its holster and checking the action, then loosening his saber in its sheath. He jerked his head back the way they'd come. "Just not that one."

It had been a close call. They'd ridden the lift up from the lowest level, having successfully avoided discovery as they moved through the crowded streets, Yao scouting the way ahead in his Eagle Knight armor, the others only emerging from the ventilation shafts when he'd confirmed the way was clear. They'd managed to get to the service chambers within one of the elevator pyramids, and from there into the lift itself. But their command of printed Nahuatl was only sufficient for them to enter the commands to make the elevator rise, not to prevent it from stopping if someone else pressed the call command, and so rather than riding it all the way to the top, which they presumed would be near the asteroid's core, instead the doors slid open on the next level.

There had been only two Mexic waiting on the landing, one of them a warrior in the armor of a Jaguar Knight, the other some variety of technician or ritualist. As soon as the doors slid open, the two Mexica had laid eyes on the three black-suited men in the car, and the steel sphere they carried, and their eyes had widened with surprise. The ritualist had opened his mouth, as if to call out an alarm, while the Jaguar Knight had reached for the obsidian club at his waist and rushed forward, already on the attack.

Fortunately, though, Yao had been ready, and before the ritualist had been able to utter a sound he lunged forward, driving the point of his saber into the man's bare throat. The movement left him momentarily vulnerable to the obsidian edge of the Jaguar Knight's club, but Fukuda rushed forward and parried the club's blow with his own saber. Then, while the Nipponese and the Mexic faced off against one another, warily, Yao casually unslung the rocket carbine from his shoulder and loosed a single round in the Jaguar Knight's direction. The self-propelled projectile slammed into the Jaguar Knight's chest carapace, knocking him off his feet and shattering the armor. It wasn't clear whether the projectile itself had penetrated into the Mexica's body, causing injury, but the point became academic when Fukuda surged forward and drove the point of his own saber down through the rent in the jaguar-spotted carapace. The Jaguar Knight twitched for an instant like a live butterfly pinned to a board, and then was still.

It seemed for a heartbeat that the incident had passed without anyone else noticing, and then Yao's keen hearing caught the sound of footsteps, even muffled by his helmet. Someone was running away.

"There!" Fukuda shouted, and pointed ahead of them.

It was another Mexica, clad in a simple white quilted mantle, a dozen or so meters from them and retreating fast. He'd evidently been approaching, had seen the altercation between the Mexica and the bannerman, and had seen the utility in taking to his heels before raising an alarm.

"I see him," Yao said. He chambered another round in his carbine and then raised it to his shoulder, but before he could fire the Mexica ducked behind a building-like structure, disappearing from view.

"Rutting dung!" Yao shouted. He turned to Fukuda, who now struggled to wrench his saber from the dead Jaguar Knight's body. "Get these two out of sight!" He indicated the two dead men with a curt nod, slinging his carbine on his shoulder and taking his saber in hand. "I'll take care of that one."

Without waiting for a response, Yao loped after the fleeing Mexica, his legs propelling him in long strides in the relatively low gravity of the station. The fleeing Mexica had got a considerable head-start on him, but Yao hoped that, even weighted down by the bulky Eagle Knight armor, he'd still be able to overtake him before he reached safety. This level appeared to be given over to various recreational facilities, if his first glance was any indication, and at this hour appeared to be largely unpopulated.

Yao rounded the corner of the structure behind which the ritualist had disappeared, hoping to catch some sight of him, but was surprised to find the man huddled just the other side of the corner, crouched low with his arms hugged to his chest.

For the briefest moment, Yao felt a pang of conscience at the thought of assaulting an unarmed man cowering in fear. It hardly seemed a proper act for a decorated soldier of the Eight Banners. He stayed his hand for the length of an eye blink, considering how he might bind and gag the man and secrete him somewhere out of sight, while Yao and his men completed their mission. But then Yao realized that, if he *was* able to complete his mission, then this unarmed ritualist and any number of others like him would be killed, just the same. And so, forcing himself to remember that this man might well have stained his hands with the blood of innocent Middle Kingdom subjects at sacrificial altars like that onboard the *Dragon*, Yao brought his saber down in a vicious stroke, the blade catching the man in the shoulder and not stopping until it had sliced several handbreadths in.

Hurrying back to where he'd left the others, his saber in one hand and the dead man slung over his opposite shoulder, Yao tried to remember that his cause was righteous, and that innocent Middle Kingdom lives might be saved through his action. But he still couldn't help feeling, at least for the moment, as if he were a common murderer, just like the men he now led. Perhaps he did belong with them, after all.

By the time Yao had rejoined the others, they had successfully moved the bodies of the two Mexica into the nearest ventilation ducts, without leaving any signs of the struggle. But while they had been moving the bodies, the elevator car had left without them.

"Why didn't you hold it on this level?" Yao asked, exasperated, tossing the body he carried through the open access panel, where it landed below with the other two.

"It's my fault," Fukuda said, while Nguyen's face took on a guilty expression behind his helmet's faceplate. "I thought it would take too long for one or two of us to move the bodies and open the access panel, so I ordered Paik and Nguyen to help me."

Yao glanced at the Dragon's Egg, which was on the floor near where Fukuda stood, a short distance from the open panel. "But you removed the Egg from the car...?"

"In case it got called to another level," Fukuda finished for him, answering Yao's unspoken question.

"Which it did," Nguyen said. His lowered his eyes to the ground. "I tried to catch the closing doors, but I was too late."

Yao scowled, but nodded. "You made the right call," he said to Fukuda. "But now we've got to wait for..."

"Hey, listen," Paik said, and pointed past Yao's back.

There were more footsteps approaching, a group of men sharing easy laughter.

"Damn," Yao swore. "Okay, into the shaft." He waved the other three men to hurry, first maneuvering the bulk of the Dragon's Egg down through the access panel, Paik going first and then taking the weight of it from Nguyen, and then the rest of them following after. They barely managed to get the panel closed behind them before the group of laughing men came into sight. The footsteps passed directly above them, heading toward the elevator pyramid.

"This isn't good," Nguyen said.

Yao quickly motioned him to be quiet with a sharp wave of his hand. But the Annamese guardsman was right. This wasn't good.

THE DRAGON'S NINE SONS

To make matters worse, from above they could hear the sound of another group approaching, and the laughter of those above turned to mocking derision of those who now approached.

"Okay," he said in a low whisper, just barely loud enough to be heard by those standing directly in front of him. "We can't afford to wait here for these people to move. Especially since when they go they're likely to take the elevator car with them, and we'd be stuck waiting for another. We've got to find an elevator that's not being used and take that, instead."

Sheathing his saber, after shaking the blood from it with a quick snap, Yao began to walk further into the dimly lit ventilation shaft, heading deeper into the asteroid.

After getting off the radio with Syuxtun, Yao at least knew where their destination lay. What he still didn't know, at least not exactly, was how they would be getting there. An elevator, surely, but which?

They made their way along the ventilation system, just as they had done on the lower level, with Yao heading up to scout for them from time to time. But so far, he had been unable to find a suitable elevator. Those that they passed were either too busy, or too near groups of people who gave no indication of moving.

Exploration had confirmed Yao's initial suspicions about this level's use. Here he passed men engaged in all manner of recreation and entertainment—including stalls where, behind curtains ringed with tinkling bells, they enjoyed the attentions of the purple-haired courtesans with the yellowed-skin and red-stained teeth.

Some of the entertainments were familiar to Yao. Men sat on reed mats around a board, throwing beans marked out as dice. Or they sang songs. Or they waited for their turn in the stalls with the courtesans, eager with anticipation.

Still others of the diversions here were completely alien to him. Strangest, perhaps, were the poles which rose two dozen meters or more from the floor, each with a rotating platform on top from which four ropes were suspended. One man stood atop the platform, beating a drum, while four other men each tied the end of one of the ropes to their ankles, and then leapt off, head first. The men, arms outstretched, spiraled down toward the ground as the platform above them turned, stopping only when their fingertips brushed the ground.

There was one of the entertainments, though, that was quite familiar to Yao, but alien just the same.

Venturing up from the ventilation shaft, careful that no one should see the Eagle Knight slip out from the access panel, he came across a ball court, where the players used only their elbows, knees, and hips to prevent a rubber ball from bouncing onto their side of the court, while at the same time trying to knock the ball through the ring mounted deep in their opponents' side of the court. The game had been a popular one in Tejas, in the years that Yao was stationed there. In Vinland, however, the players didn't observe the custom of the losing team's captains being taken prisoner and subsequently sacrificed by the victors.

Finally, Yao was able to locate an elevator close enough to a ventilation shaft for the other members of the demolition team to reach it without being spotted, and with few enough Mexica around that they were on likely to be interrupted getting the Dragon's Egg onto the elevator car.

As the others lugged the awkward load out of the shaft and headed toward the elevator pyramid, Yao kept a careful lookout. Luck appeared to be with them, so far at least, in that the disappearance of a jaguar knight and two ritualists had not been discovered, nor thankfully had their bodies which were now hidden in the ventilation shaft. As soon as the disappearance was noticed, or the bodies stumbled upon, Yao was sure that the alarm would be raised and that their chances of reaching the station's core unimpeded would become vanishingly unlikely.

The team managed to reach the innermost but one level without further incident. From here, things would be more complicated.

For one, here the ceiling was much nearer the ground, perhaps half as high as it had been on the last level, if not lower. And the ventilation was supplied not by ducts running through the floor, but through conduits in the ceiling overhead. As a result, the three men in their Middle Kingdom pressure suits would not be able to move stealthily through hidden ducts and shafts, but would need to proceed at ground level, along with Yao.

However, as they made their way forward, in the direction that Syuxtun had indicated, it became apparent that this might not present the insurmountable difficulty they had initially supposed. Unlike even the entertainment and recreation level, which was only sporadically populated, this level, which appeared to be given over entirely to ritual space and engineering, was virtually deserted, relatively speaking. And though the structures were widely spaced, not closely packed together as they had been on the habitation level below, there were still enough of them to offer ample places of concealment whenever Yao spotted Mexica heading their way.

They passed strange models and dioramas and statues, the ritual significance of which they could only guess at. From a distance, they glimpsed what appeared to be an enormous topographical model of Fire Star's surface at an incredibly reduced scale. There were statues of reclining figures with bowls held on their laps, and gigantic stone heads, an aviary full of live hummingbirds and a series of clear plastic cages containing butterflies in a dazzling array of colors.

There was what appeared to be a miniature version of one of the stepped pyramids, its sides pebbled instead of smooth, but as the four men drew nearer they realized that it was instead an immense rack on which were displayed countless human skulls, stripped of skin and muscle and viscera and bleached a blinding white. It was impossible to guess how many dead the skulls represented, but it would easily have numbered in the hundreds, even thousands.

"Come on, men," Yao urged, as the others paused in horrified disbelief at the macabre display. "We've got a job to do."

And with a renewed resolve they advanced, Yao feeling somewhat less like a murderer as they did so.

Finally, they spotted two immense statues, stylized portraits of a Jaguar Knight on the one hand and an Eagle Knight on the other, guarding a stone archway into a hulking structure.

"This is it," Yao said. He motioned toward the nearby structure.

When the Dragon's Egg had been moved safely out of sight, Yao checked the low door, which refused to open.

"This will have to do," Yao said with a shrug, then turned to address the others. "The captain said that a ritual party had gone in when his team was here earlier, so they may still be inside. If they are, we might have to fight our way in, but if they aren't, we can get this thing planted and be on our way." He turned to Fukuda. "I want you here with the bomb, just in case. Paik, you're with him. If it's clear, I'll radio for the two of you to bring the package in. If not..." He trailed off, and looked to Nguyen. "You're with me, big man."

"Yes, bannerman," the larger man agreed, nodding.

"Good luck, Yao," Fukuda said, as he and Paik took up their positions in the shadows of the low structure.

"Hopefully I won't need it, Fukuda, but thanks, all the same."

* * *

The two men approached the entrance without making a sound. Over the radio, Syuxtun had said something about the control station temple for the Xolotl power plant also serving as some sort of temple, but until he caught a glimpse through the archway Yao hadn't really understood what the Athabascan had meant.

Now he did.

Even before passing through the archway he could detect the copper tang of blood thick on the air, commingled with the smell of burning frankincense, and beneath them the chemical scent of bleach that could almost but not quite cover the odor of putrefaction and decay.

Yao could hear voices murmuring within, though from his vantage point he could see nothing of what lay beyond the archway but shadows and indistinct statues. He motioned for Nguyen to remain where he was, and slipped through the entrance, keeping out of sight.

Within he found a large four-sided patio, with four-petaled flowers scattered everywhere on the floor. The rear wall was dominated by a bank of controls, like a much larger version of the engineering controls of the *Dragon*, with dials and tells and readouts. The walls to the left and right were covered with brightly painted bas-relief sculptures depicting strange, grotesque scenes, while arranged before them were metal containers atop three-legged stands, containing sharpened animal bones and cactus spines which, even now, a pair of bare-headed warriors were using to pierce their own earlobes and tongues, spilling their own blood in auto-sacrifice to the gods. Near the entrance was a huge stone brazier carved in the imposing likeness of the Mexic rain god, in which burned the frankincense that Yao had smelled. And in the center of the flower-strewn floor, surrounded by a priest wearing the flayed skin of some previous victim and a collection of technician-ritualists and decorated warriors, was a large circular sacrificial stone, on which was carved the now all-too-familiar image of the moon goddess cut to pieces by the god of the sun. And tethered to the center of that stone was a young Han woman, stripped almost naked.

The woman's face was slack, her eyes half-lidded, and her mouth twitched in something almost like a smile. Based on this, and the way she swayed on her feet, it was clear that she had been drugged to keep her docile, before being brought here.

It took a moment for Yao to recognize what the woman clutched in her hand. It was a feather, which she held by the root like a soldier with his saber. To all appearances, she had been placed in this posture like a doll posed by a child.

As Yao watched, one of the warriors approached the sacrificial stone. He wore yellow armor, but no helmet, exposing his head which was shaved but for a braid which hung over his left ear. That, and the fact that his face was painted, the left side blue and the right side yellow, marked him as one of the Shorn Ones, one of the most prestigious sects of the Mexic warrior hierarchy. Shorn Ones were drawn from all of the Mexic warrior orders, and commanded the same respect and authority in the

Mexic Dominion's military that the highest generals held in Yao's Eight Banners.

The Shorn One stopped and planted one foot on the sacrificial stone, the other on the floor. In one hand he brandished an obsidian-blade-lined club, while his other held a shield, to the center of which was affixed a severed human finger. Yao had heard of the practice before, but had only seldom seen it. The Mexica, he had learned, held that the hair or middle finger of a woman who had died in childbirth could, if attached to a warrior's shield, make him invincible. The woman herself, on death, would have gone on to the Western Paradise, the House of Corn, and there become one of the goddesses who accompany the sun from its zenith every day down to the western horizon, where it disappeared from view and began its nightly journey through the dark underworld.

Facing the drugged woman with her feather, the Shorn One declaimed loudly, while the technician-ritualists moved to the reactor controls at the rear of the room, bleeding freely from holes poked in their arms and thighs with cactus spines. Then the priest in the suit of flayed human skin, an agent of the House of Darkness, began to chant, and the Shorn One stepped up onto the sacrificial stone with both feet, his obsidian club held before him.

With a sick feeling in his gut Yao realized what was about to happen. The Shorn One would engage in a mock combat with the sacrificial victim, who was allowed to put up a token resistance with the feather provided her. Then her blood would be used to satiate whatever hemoglobin sensors needed satisfying before the reactor controls could be operated, and whatever routine operation the technicians were involved in could be performed.

Yao tensed, drawing his saber, waiting for the right moment to move. He didn't have time to fetch the others, and as soon as he used the radio to call for assistance those within the temple would hear the sound of his voice and he'd be discovered. But if he were to save the woman from sacrifice, he couldn't leave to fetch them himself.

The Shorn One moved in slow, exaggerated motions. He brought the edge of his obsidian club near the drugged woman's bare arm, and gently pricked her soft skin with one of the black glass blades. The blood began to well, but if Yao leapt to her defense, then the mission be damned. The others could see to planting the Dragon's Egg once he was killed, but he would take as many of these blood-hungry bastards with him as he could.

"No!" bellowed Nguyen like a wounded animal, racing past Yao into the room, arms flailing. "I won't let you hurt her again!"

And then the matter was taken out of Yao's hands, and the moment for stealth was passed.

"Fukuda!" Yao shouted back over his shoulder, rushing after Nguyen with his saber in one hand and fletcher in the other. "We're all out of luck. Get in here, now!"

CHAPTER THIRTY-FIVE

Zhuan's team approached the pens where the prisoners were held. The six innocents they'd seen led from the hangar bay had apparently arrived long enough before them that they were already secured within, as only a pair of Mexic warriors in unadorned armor were in evidence, standing guard outside the entrance much like the giant statues stood watch over the entrance to the power plant.

The armor the warriors wore shared the same basic design as that now worn by Syuxtun and Cai, though lacking the ornamentation that indicated they had taken a large number of prisoners in combat. And with their heads covered by conical-shaped helmets, it was impossible to see whether they still wore the uncut queue of a student warrior, or if their hair was worn in warriors' scalp-locks. Either way, in addition to the obsidian-blade-tipped clubs each man had suspended from his waist, the two guards leaned on Mexic fire-lances. While the burning liquid magnesium that the lances sprayed in steady streams had been designed for use in the oxygen-poor atmosphere of Fire Star, it would burn well enough in the oxygen-rich air of the station to do a considerable amount of damage, especially to Zhuan and Dea, protected by nothing but the thin fabric of their worksuits.

Like most of the other structures on this level, the building which housed the prisoners was a simple structure of four walls surmounted by a flat roof, which under the spangled black ceiling overhead looked more like an isolated building on a city street than a containment facility onboard a station. Only the walls of the power plant control station rose as high as the ceiling overhead, with the other structures arranged in a grid pattern, albeit widely spaced. The nearest structures to the prisoner pens were a pair of stepped pyramids, from which elevators rose in black-painted towers to the ceiling above, but these were dozens of meters away in either direction. With any luck, the pyramids would remain untenanted throughout the coming encounter, but even if some Mexica were to exit the elevator just as Zhuan's team made their move, the sounds of the conflict would hopefully be so muffled by the distance that the noise would not carry.

It only remained to see if their ruse would work.

Syuxtun walked in front, with as officious and imposing a bearing as he could manage, while Cai brought up the rear, with Zhuan and Dea walking in the middle. They had paused in the concealing shadows of the nearest stepped pyramid before approaching, and the two men in civilian clothes had unhooked the stays on their worksuits and withdrawn the fletchers and radios they had hidden beneath their clothes at the small of their backs. Their radios were strapped across their chests under their worksuits, with tiny ear-buds hidden in their left ears, while the fletchers were slipped up their right sleeves. By walking with their arms crossed, huddled to their chest as if in fear or shivering in the somewhat cold air of the level, they were successful in obscuring the shape of the pistol through the fabric, and in hiding the outline of the radio beneath their worksuits. The concealment would not stand up under close scrutiny, but would allow them to get at their weapons and communication devices quickly, and since it wasn't known whether they would be able to bluff their way past the guards in the best of circumstances, the attendant risk was considered an acceptable one.

The moments leading up to the encounter were tense, not least because Zhuan and the others would only have the faintest idea what Syuxtun was saying to the guards, or they to him. And they could only hope that neither of the guards attempted to speak to Cai, who despite wearing the armor of a Jaguar Knight, understood only a bare handful of Nahuatl words, and none of them of any use in polite conversation.

Syuxtun called out, addressing the guards and raising a gloved hand.

Zhuan did his best to look like a terrified, dejected prisoner which, considering the icy hand of fear which gripped his insides, was not a terrific stretch.

He chanced a glance over at Dea, and saw that the younger man walked straight and tall, his chin held up and his eyes glaring defiantly. His arms were crossed over his chest, as Zhuan had ordered, concealing the radio and pistol, but everything else about his posture screamed that he was tensed and ready for battle.

The guard on the left straightened somewhat on hearing Syuxtun's call, and answered, while the guard on the right continued to lean heavily on his fire-lance, his expression looking bored through the slight tint of his helmet's faceplate.

Syuxtun spoke again, presumably responding to some question the guard had posed. He came to a stop a meter or so short of the entrance to the structure, and motioned for Zhuan and the others to stop.

The guard cocked an eyebrow, and after a sidelong glance to the other guard, looked back to Syuxtun. Then, he spoke again, somewhat slowly. Even though Zhuan couldn't understand the words, the tone made it evident that the guard was suspicious about something.

The guard on the right muttered something, his voice low and uninterested, and the guard on the left nodded, as though agreeing with some suggestion. Then, lifting his head somewhat and peering past Zhuan's shoulder, the guard called back to Cai, raising his voice slightly.

Zhuan tensed, having to restrain his impulse to look back at Cai, remembering that as a terrified prisoner he would have to remain cowed and motionless unless ordered to move.

Cai began to stammer, nervously, nonsense sylla-bles that sounded vaguely like Nahuatl but were meaningless.

The guard on the left turned to the other man, confused, and his meaning was evident, again, even if his words were not. *What did he say?* He looked back, clearly thinking that Cai was a crazy person, tightening his grip on his fire-lance. Meanwhile, the guard on the right began to straighten, clearly becoming convinced that something was amiss.

Syuxtun turned far enough to the side that he could glance over his shoulder at Cai, even with his peripheral vision somewhat obscured by his suit's helmet, and then raised his hands, beginning to address the guards in Nahuatl. Doubtless he was offering some explanation for why Cai was unintel-ligible, or some excuse for why they arrived without authorization or papers or some other bureaucratic requirement, or some other stratagem entirely. But it was impossible to know if it would have worked, for Dea of his own volition decided to try a more direct and conclusive approach.

The first guard was clutching his chest, eyes wide behind his faceplate, blood welling between his fin-gers, before Zhuan even realized that Dea had made a move.

The guard on the right, for all that he appeared to be lax and lazy before now, proved to be no slouch when action was required, and wasting no words swung up the end of his fire-lance and depressed the firing stud on its haft, sending a stream of burning liquid magnesium spraying out the other end.

Zhuan dove to one side, feeling the searing heat of the burning liquid as it passed. Dea leapt to the other side, the stream striking him on the left side and igniting the fabric of his worksuit. But though his clothing was engulfed in flames on his left hip, Dea didn't waste time or attention bothering about it, but squeezed the trigger of his fletcher and sent a stream of needle projectiles firing at the guard. The first of the frangible rounds hit the guard square in the faceplate and shattered on contact, not even scoring the reinforced glass. The next needle struck a little lower down, and pitted the helmet's faceplate. The next a little lower still and sent a crack spidering up the faceplate. And the next struck the guard in the throat, in the flexible joint where the helmet was joined to the pressure suit's carapace. The flexible material there was softer than the faceplate had been, and only a single shot was necessary to pierce it. The successive shots had been fired in less than three seconds, and by the time the spider-cracks were crawling up the faceplate, the guard began coughing up blood as the needle projectile was driven into and through his throat, piercing the esophagus and hitting the carotid artery, and in the next moment a spray of bright arterial blood painted the inside of the helmet, obscuring the guard's face entirely.

The guard on the left had only been struck once in the chest, and still listed on his feet, but as he sputtered, trying to catch his breath with one lung pierced by needle-shot to call out an alarm, Syuxtun drew and fired his own fletcher pistol, burying a half-dozen needles in the guard's chest. The next moment, the guard collapsed to the deck, almost dead.

So both guards were down, in a matter of moments.

Dea was climbing to his feet, using the cuff of his left sleeve in an attempt to swat out the flames which burned his left side, more irritated than concerned. From the looks of it, Zhuan thought it safe to assume the younger man had already sustained fairly serious burns to his lower abdomen on that side, unless the fabric of the worksuits was more flame retardant than he imagined.

Cai was on the ground, huddled into a tight ball with his arms wrapped around his head. With his fletcher in one hand, Syuxtun stepped back beside him and reached his other hand down to help Cai to his feet.

Zhuan couldn't help being surprised, not at Dea's quick action, or the suddenness of the attack, but at the clinical precision with which the Athabascan had dispatched the second guard, with no more hesitation than one would show when stamping on a spider crawling across a nursery floor.

Syuxtun looked up, once he'd helped Cai to his feet, and saw Zhuan's surprised expression directed his way. The Athabascan only shrugged, and said, "I am a follower of the prophet, captain, but I'm also a loyal soldier of the Eight Banners. Don't make the mistake of assuming that the one prevents me from being the other. I know how to do what needs to be done."

* * *

The two guards posted outside were the only ones manning the facility, the prisoners within safely secured in small cages, barred and locked. But the lack of any additional resistance didn't mean that there were not surprises awaiting the rescuers within.

The first surprise was who they found imprisoned within, and the second was who they did not.

"Where is she?!" Dea shouted, waving his pistol in the air, menacingly. "Where is Lei Xiaoli?!"

The girl whom Dea had raced to rescue, whom he had been forced to leave behind on Fire Star and who he saw again only a short while before in the Xolotl hangar bay, was nowhere to be seen.

"They... they took her," said an old woman, whom Zhuan recognized as being the first prisoner they'd seen marched off the troop transport.

"Where? Where did they take her?" Dea seemed a creature equally composed of rage and fear, close to raving.

It was clear none of those within the prisoner pens knew where she'd been taken. They clung to the bars of their cages like animals who had lost the will to attempt escape back into the wild. Zhuan had seen that look often, as a child, on animals who had been beaten once too often, any spirit driven from them, lacking even the drive to end their own lives.

Only the old woman and the other prisoners whom Zhuan had seen led off the troop transport showed any signs of vitality. The others, in their dozens, crowding the many cages within the prisoner facility, seemed almost dead.

Already Zhuan had known that fitting six prisoners onto the *Dragon* for a return voyage to Fire Star would be something of a stretch, even if most of the crewmen didn't survive to return along with them.

But dozens of prisoners, easily four or five times the number he'd come here expecting to rescue?

Either Zhuan was going to have to decide who would leave the station and live, and who would be left behind to die, or they were going to have to find a bigger ship.

Chapter Thirty-Six

Across the room, Guardsman Nguyen lay into the Shorn One with nothing resembling technique or tactic, only a blindly homicidal rage. Yao knew that, deep within the man-mountain's tortured mind, he was reliving that same moment from his youth, in which he'd arrived too late to save the woman he loved from a gruesome end. Having entered the control station temple behind Yao and seen the Mexica in the yellow armor drawing blood from the almost naked Han woman on the sacrificial stone, Nguyen's mind had gone back to that night, as it had done in the showers of Fanchuan Garrison weeks before. And just like that night when he had killed the guardsman who'd been in the act of raping a female member of the support staff, Nguyen would not rest until the Shorn One was dead, or he himself was, so long as he thought a woman's life was in danger.

None of this was proceeding as Yao had planned, but there was scant time for regret or recrimination. There were more than half a dozen Mexica in the room, warriors and ritualists, and if even one of them were able to raise the alarm and summon help, then the mission's chances of success would plummet, and the prospects of rescuing either the woman on the sacrificial stone or any of the other Middle Kingdom prisoners would all but vanish.

Yao opted for a mix of close combat and ranged attacks. With his saber in one hand, he fenced with the warriors who brandished obsidian clubs and knives, and whenever he had a moment's grace he fired off rounds of flechettes at the ritualists cowering by the engineering controls, dropping them one by one. When necessary, he rounded on the warriors and fired his fletcher at them from point-blank range, but considering the frangible ammunition and the armor that most of the warriors wore, in such close quarters his saber was the more efficient of the two.

So many of the warriors, particularly those who went bareheaded, were already bleeding freely from their lobes, tongues, and cheeks, having gored themselves on the sharpened bones and cactus spines, sacrificing their own lifeblood to their brutal gods, leaving it difficult for Yao to know when he'd scored a hit. But the warriors seemed hardly slowed by their wounds, and pressed their attack on Yao.

The bannerman felt himself almost overwhelmed by the superior numbers of the Mexica when Fukuda arrived, swinging his saber like a windmill's blade and firing his carbine one-handed, the rifle's butt resting on his hip. A single rocket projectile slammed into one of the Mexica who was advancing on Yao, knocking him off his feet, and since Fukuda didn't have a hand free to chamber another round he dropped the carbine to the ground, drew his fletcher from its holster, and squeezed off a continuous burst at one of the bareheaded warriors, whose forehead erupted in a red bloom as his skull shattered under the impact of dozens of needles.

Yao turned his attention to another Mexic warrior, who expertly wielded an obsidian club in one hand and a black-glass dagger in the other. The bannerman raised his fletcher to fire off a round, but the light-emitting diode in the handle glowed a baleful red, signaling that the pistol needed to recharge itself. A grim smile curled Yao's lip, and holstering his pistol he drew his own dagger with his free hand, raising his saber in the other, the tip dancing before him.

The Mexica lunged forward, sweeping his obsidian club in a sideways arc at Yao's head. Yao brought his saber up in time to block the swing, but the Mexica countered by driving forward his obsidian dagger. Catching the black glass on the edge of his own dagger, Yao batted the thrust away. The Mexica, his weapons on both sides held at bay by Yao's own in a tense struggle, swept out with one leg, trying to knock Yao's own from under him. The bannerman surged upward, pushing the Mexica's weapons away, and danced backward, just missing the Mexica's kick.

In the split-second it took the Mexica to recover his balance, Yao opted for a chancy maneuver. He flung his dagger at the Mexica's helmet, flipping end over end through the air. He knew that, in all likelihood, it would lack sufficient momentum and force to shatter the helmet's faceplate on impact, but the Mexica would doubtless be unable to control his reflexive impulse on seeing the knife spinning in the air toward his face and would flinch away. With the blade still flipping through the air between them, Yao lunged forward, taking a huge step toward the Mexica while driving forward the point of his saber, and just as the Mexica flinched from the thrown dagger, Yao's saber pierced the softer join between the Mexica's helmet and his chest carapace. The sword buried several centimeters into the Mexica's throat, and as the man's eyes widened and his mouth grew slack, Yao yanked the blade free, the point reddened with the dying man's blood.

Retrieving his dagger from the floor, where it had clattered after rebounding harmlessly off the Mexica's faceplate, just as Yao's saber had driven into his throat, Yao turned his attention to the rest of the room, to see how his companions fared.

Fukuda was making short work of the agent of the House of Darkness, who was armored only in a suit of flayed human skin. The priest defended himself with some skill, warding off Fukuda's initial attack with the same obsidian blade with which he'd doubtless ended the lives of countless sacrificial victims, but the longer reach of Fukuda's blade, to say nothing about the Nipponese's skill at wielding it, proved too much for the priest to handle, and a final sweep of Fukuda's blade cut him down where he stood.

Between them, Fukuda and Yao had accounted for all of the ritualists and nearly all the warriors in the room, leaving only the Shorn One in his yellow armor, with the severed finger affixed to his shield. Nguyen was clearly outclassed by the Shorn One in terms of technique and skill, since the man-mountain was freely bleeding from innumerable cuts on his arms, trunks, and legs, but the Shorn One had clearly discovered that the enormous guardsman could take an astonishing amount of punishment before admitting defeat. And Nguyen, for his part, seemed hardly to notice the cuts and gashes which rent the black material of his stealth suit, his faceplate shattered to pieces and his nose crooked and broken. He was intent on killing the Shorn One, for the sake of the young Han woman tethered to the stone, and was not about to let anything as trivial as the fact that he should by rights have no chance of winning the contest deter him from fighting on.

The battle was clearly taking its toll on the Shorn One too, despite the fact that he bore hardly any cuts. The effort required to keep Nguyen's grasping hands at bay was wearing on him. And so, it was with a visible strain that the Shorn One put all his energy behind a final blow, swinging his obsidian club two-handed in a wide arc and burying its obsidian blades in Nguyen's side. It must have pierced deep into the man-mountain's ribcage, and become trapped between the bones, for when the Shorn One tried to wrench it free, he found that the club would not budge, but remained stubbornly stuck in Nguyen's side.

Nguyen still bellowed with rage, saying to the uncomprehending Shorn One all of the things he would have said to that detumescent bureaucrat at the brothel, all those years ago. Sparing only the briefest of glances at the club buried in his side, Nguyen surged forward and took the Shorn One's shaved head in either hand. Then, locking eyes with the Mexica, Nguyen spun the shaven head to the side with a violent wrench and an audible crack. The Shorn One went limp, his sightless eyes rolling up in their sockets, and Nguyen released his hold on the shaven head, letting the Mexica fall to the floor in a heap.

The guardsman turned, finally seeming to take notice of the club buried in his side and the innumerable free-bleeding wounds and began to waver on his feet. He turned a fraction, until he faced the Han woman, who now knelt on the sacrificial stone, drugged and half-lidded, still holding onto the useless feather.

"I won't let him... hurt you... again," Nguyen said, with difficultly, and then toppled over backward like a tree felled by lumberjacks.

By the time Fukuda reached the guardsman's side, Nguyen was dead.

Yao didn't waste any time. He'd mourn Nguyen later, if he had the chance. For the moment, they had a mission to complete.

"Yao to Paik," he said, after tonguing his radio to transmit. "You ready to plant that egg?"

Silence was the only answer.

"Paik?" Yao repeated, more loudly, turning toward the temple entrance.

Still only static.

"Fukuda," Yao said, racing toward the door. The Nipponese was seeing to the Han woman, who seemed to have little understanding of what was going on around her.

"Hey, isn't this Dea's girlfriend?" Fukuda asked.

"Forget about her for now," Yao shot back, nearly at the door. "Something's wrong outside!"

Fukuda leapt to his feet and pounded after him, so that the two men cleared the temple and were back under the spangled black ceiling outside in moments.

A short distance off, near the structure behind which they'd left Paik, they saw a Mexic warrior stood over the fallen form of the guardsman, raising an obsidian club to deliver the killing blow, while at his side a Mexic ritualist bent over the Dragon's Egg, up to his elbows in the bomb's exposed innards.

The pair of bannermen didn't waste a moment in discussion, but raised their carbines and fired a pair of rocket projectiles at the two Mexica. The two targets crumpled to the floor as Yao and Fukuda raced over, their fletchers in hand and glowing green with full charges, ready to dispatch the Mexica if any life remained in them. The technician-ritualist had already stopped moving by the time they reached the site, but Yao emptied a half-dozen needles into the warrior's cracked chest carapace before he stopped twitching as well. Then Yao knelt by Paik to check the extent of his wounds, while Fukuda saw to the Dragon's Egg.

"Snuck... snuck up... on me..." Paik said, with difficulty, his lips flecked with pink foam, his eyes tearing with pain. The back half of Paik's helmet was staved in, and blood flowed freely from the back of his cracked chest carapace, pooling under him. "T-tired..."

Yao laid a hand on Paik's shoulder, and nodded.

"Go ahead and sleep, Paik. You've done your duty."

Paik blinked a shadow of a nod, and then closed his eyes, for the last time.

"Eighteen-rutting-hells!" Fukuda spat, stomping to his feet.

"What is it?" Yao said, jumping up to stand beside him. Looking down, he saw for the first time the extent of the damage to the Dragon's Egg. The top section of the steel sphere had been spun off, the sensitive inner components exposed, and Yao could see within a chaotic mess of wires and fuses.

"Well, *this* bastard"—he kicked the still form of the technician-ritualist on the ground—"obviously knew what he was doing. He's completely rutting destroyed the bomb's rutting timing mechanism and detonation controls."

"Which means... ?" Yao asked, sure that he knew the answer but needing to hear it from the demolitions expert himself.

Fukuda wrenched open his helmet's faceplate and spat on the floor in disgust. "With the electronics as wrecked as this, about the worst you could do with it is give someone slow radiation poisoning from the fissile materials at the core."

"You can't rig it to explode, even without the electronics?"

Fukuda shook his head, angrily. "It's worse than useless."

Yao raised the faceplate of his own helmet and took a deep breath, collecting his thoughts. Then he glanced back at the entrance to the control station temple, a plan beginning to form.

"So what are we going to do?" Fukuda said, exasperated.

"We're going to have to improvise."

Yao toggled his radio back to transmit.

"Yao calling the rescue team. Do you read?"

After a moment, the voice of Captain Zhuan crackled over Yao's helmet speakers. "Zhuan here."

"Captain, how close are you to the control station?"

CHAPTER THIRTY-SEVEN

Zhuan had already been en route to the elevator pyramid near the Fire Star model when Yao had radioed. He'd intended to lead the prisoners in a wide circle around the control station temple, in the event that the demolitions team was involved in a firefight there, but when Yao had radioed to say that he'd secured the station and needed the captain's assistance, Zhuan's team had been close enough that they could rendezvous there in a matter of moments.

It had been all that Zhuan could do to keep Dea with the rest of the team, when he'd discovered that Lei Xiaoli had not been with the rest of the prisoners. But when Dea learned that the girl had been found at the control station temple, and that Yao and the others had been able to save her from the altar, he'd been in a desperate hurry to reach her.

Yao hadn't said what kind of assistance he needed from Zhuan, but he had explained that while something had gone wrong with the Dragon's Egg, the Mexica didn't seem to yet be aware of their presence. Though it still seemed a near impossibility, they had managed to get this far into the mission without being discovered by the Mexica, and it seemed to Zhuan now, however unlikely, that there was a slim chance at this point that their mission might succeed.

When they reached the control station temple, though, Zhuan had to revise his opinion, for a number of reasons. First, it became apparent that they *had* been discovered, by more than a half dozen Mexica at least, to judge by the bodies piled in a disordered heap at the far side of the chamber, but that Yao and his men had been able to dispatch them before the Mexica had raised the alarm. Added to the two dead Mexica guards that Zhuan's team had left hidden in the prisoner pens a short while back, that meant a mounting death toll on their enemies' side.

But there had been a toll taken on their side, as well. Two members of Yao's team had fallen, the man-mountain Nguyen and the laconic Paik, who were now laid out along the opposite wall from the Mexic dead. Their crew of nine was now down to seven, the six in the control station temple and Ang onboard the *Dragon*. Seven, but with more than two dozen prisoners in tow.

"What's wrong with her?" Guardsman Cai said, as Dea rushed to the side of Lei Xiaoli, who had been made as comfortable as possible reclining on the floor, waiting for the effects of the drug to wear off.

"Drugged," Syuxtun explained. "It's a variety of fermented agave juice. More of a kick than the strongest spirits, or so I'm told."

"You wouldn't know, eh?" Cai said with a slight smile.

Syuxtun shook his head. "The Quran doesn't speak highly of alcohol, I'm afraid. Intoxicants, like gambling, are an abomination."

"What's the matter, beanpole?" Fukuda said to Cai, from the far side of the chamber, where he was busy reloading his fletcher. "Don't like anyone getting high if you can't see a profit from it?"

The color rose in Cai's cheek, but on seeing the sorry state of the woman cradled in Dea's arms, so nearly bled for the sake of the brutal and distant Mexic gods, he reconsidered. Shamed, he averted his eyes, and made no reply.

Fukuda, meanwhile, moved to join the captain and Yao, while the prisoners shuffled back and forth in the control station temple, unsure what was going on. The Nipponese was intercepted by a young boy, perhaps eight terrestrial years old.

"Sir?" the boy said, his voice high and piping. "Are we all going to die?"

Looking down and meeting the boy's eyes, Fukuda was brought up short, and a strange expression crept across his face, like a frisson of recognition. Holstering his fletcher, he knelt down and laid a hand on the boy's shoulder. "I can't swear to you that none of us will die, but I'll do my damnedest to make sure you and the others get away safely."

The boy nodded solemnly, and them moved off to rejoin the other prisoners.

"So where do we stand?" Captain Zhuan said to Yao and Fukuda, his voice low.

"The Dragon's Egg is cracked," Yao said, pointing to the mess of electronics spilling out of the steel sphere in the corner. "Irreparably."

"There's no way to get it to blow," Fukuda added.

"So that mission objective is a failure?" Zhuan said, without affect.

Yao shook his head. "Not exactly."

Zhuan cocked an eyebrow.

With a nod Yao indicated the engineering controls that lined the rear wall of the control station temple. "Those are essentially the same as the controls on the *Dragon*, wouldn't you say?"

Zhuan glanced over them. "I'd have to have Syuxtun translate the glyphs to be sure, but yes, they look like they follow the same design."

"Well," Yao answered, "what are the chances that we could force this system to enter the same sort of failure mode that almost cooked us en route from Zhurong?"

Zhuan's eyes widened fractionally, and he looked from Yao to the controls and back. "Kicking off a thermal runaway and meltdown," he said, with dawning understanding.

"Won't be as clean as the Dragon's Egg," Fukuda put in, "but it should get the job done."

Zhuan nodded appreciatively. "It certainly would, at that. The station's power generation facility is essentially the same as the propulsion system on the *Dragon*, you're right, but instead of providing thrust it propels turbines used to generate electricity. If we were able to stop the flow of propellant from the heating chamber to the turbines, and pulled out the control rods to let the reaction runaway in the reactor, then the heat and pressure would eventually build to explosive levels. A better option would be to cause a containment failure at the same time, getting the molten fuel in the reactor into contact with the coolant water. The steam explosion would be sufficient to crack the station in half, at the very least, and the meltdown would irradiate anything that survived the blast."

"That's what I'd hoped you'd say," Yao said with a slight smile. "So I've only got one question for you."

Zhuan raised an eyebrow.

"Can you show me how to do it? While you're getting the prisoners off the station, I'm going to stay back here and blow this place to pieces."

Fukuda went off to help the others get the prisoners ready to move out, and Yao and Zhuan huddled in the far corner, out of earshot.

"I'm afraid I insist, captain," Yao said, crossing his arms over his chest. "I must be the one to stay behind. You say yourself that there's no way to automate the failure mode, not when the Mexica might turn up at any minute to repair the system. Someone's got to stay here and enter the commands manually."

"Granted," Zhuan allowed. "But why must it be you? I have the most technical expertise of any of us, and you're the best capable of getting these people to the hangar in one piece. Why must you be the one to stay?"

"For my sins." Yao's voice was quiet, barely above a whisper. "It must be me, for my sins." He paused, a pained expression on his face. "What do you know about the Shachuan Station Massacre, captain?"

Zhuan's shoulders rose in a shallow shrug. "The Mexica attacked the settlement in large numbers, killed most of the inhabitants, and were driven away by the arrival of the Middle Kingdom forces."

Yao nodded, his expression grim. "That's the official account. And you've doubtless heard the line that the Mexica were heartless to attack a civilian outpost with no strategic significance, and that the Middle Kingdom authorities could never have dreamed that the enemy would stoop so low."

Zhuan allowed that he had.

"But what would you say if I told you that those same Middle Kingdom authorities, far from being surprised about the attack, had known about it long in advance, and had done nothing to prevent it?"

"It was some months ago," Yao went on, "that my unit and I chanced upon a large number of Mexic forces massing just outside Shachuan Station, deep in the Tianfei Valley. Taking cover, we radioed to command, informing them of our discovery and preparing to move in. But command instead ordered us to take no action, and to hold our positions. I thought they were addled, or that they hadn't understood our transmissions, or that they were joking... anything but that they were serious. I radioed again, and once more was told to hold position and take no action.

"If... if I'd been more of a man, I might have acted against my orders and moved in anyway. But I've never been anything but a dutiful soldier, and so I held my ground. Even so, I continued to radio, again and again, begging for permission to deploy and do at least some small part to protect the innocents in the settlement below, but each time my superiors repeated the order.

"My men and I were forced to stand by and watch the initial waves of the attack, during which countless innocents were killed. Finally, and only after the attack had been underway for what seemed hours, we received new orders. We were to divert away from the conflict to join with the main body of the Middle Kingdom forces en route from further up the Tianfei Valley.

"I... I try not to think about how many lives were lost in the hour that it took my unit to join the main column, and in the hour it took for the main column finally to reach Shachuan. But by the time we arrived, there were precious few lives left in the settlement to save.

"When the conflict was over, and the Mexica had withdrawn in victory from the smoking ruins of Shachuan, I vowed to myself that I wouldn't rest until I discovered the reasons why my unit had been ordered to take no action, when the worst that would have come of our deploying would have been our deaths, but in exchange for at least a handful of innocent lives saved. I started asking questions, and kept asking questions, using whatever influence or pull I had. And even when my superiors ordered me on three separate occasions to stop asking questions, I still pressed on, digging deeper, going higher, searching for answers. And finally...

"Finally I learned the terrible truth.

"My superiors had not allowed us to interfere with the Mexic attack because they had known in advance that it was coming. The Embroidered Guard had months before succeeded in decoding the cipher that the Mexic Dominion employs when communicating with their forces in the field.

"When these intercepted transmissions were decoded, or so I was told, they proved 'an invaluable resource to the forces of the Middle Kingdom.' They contained detailed information about troop movements, and security protocols, and even about the existence and location of this damned station. But it also contained something else. Detailed plans about an impending attack on Shachuan Station.

"You see, by the time of the massacre, the Embroidered Guards and the commanders of the Eight Banners and the Green Standard Army had known for weeks about the coming attack on Shachuan. It had been decided, though, that a move to prevent the attack would expose to the Mexic Dominion that their cipher had been cracked, and so the decision was made to let the attack proceed. The lives of the colonists in Shachuan, the reasoning went, were a price worth paying for the continued wealth of intelligence that would result if the Mexica continued to employ the compromised cipher.

"When my men and I chanced upon the Mexica in the process of launching the attack, the determination had been made that our intervention could be interpreted by the Mexica as the result of a compromised communication, even though I knew nothing about the damned intercepted transmissions at the time. If the Mexica suspected their communications had been compromised, then there was a chance that they would change all their security protocols, including the signs and countersigns that let us get onboard Xolotl.

"I was incensed, to say the least. I... I just wasn't sure how to respond. Should I break protocol and regulation by making this public, telling everyone what I'd learned? Should I quietly file a formal protest? Or should I simply resign my commission in disgust and return to civilian life?

"In the end, I needn't have worried. The decision wasn't mine to make. You see, my immediate superiors, who'd already warned me off asking those kinds of questions, had informed the Eight Banners commanders, who had in turn notified the Embroidered Guard. And it wasn't too much later that I found myself placed under arrest and dragged to Fanchuan for a disciplinary hearing. Only it wasn't a disciplinary hearing, after all, but an offer for one last chance to redeem myself by joining a mission to a secret Mexic base.

"So I joined this suicide run, my life and career wasted, and all because I wasn't man enough to step up and do what I knew was right. Instead I followed orders passed down by men I'd never met, who decided in their wisdom to sacrifice the very lives we were there to protect, in the name of some greater purpose.

"And that's why I must be the one to stay behind, captain. Because it's my only chance to redeem myself."

CHAPTER THIRTY-EIGHT

"No," Captain Zhuan said, forcefully. He crossed his arms, his jaw set. "I'll be the one to stay behind, and that's final."

Yao's eyes flashed, angrily. "And why? Have you heard nothing I've said?"

"No," Zhuan said, "I've heard everything you've said, and I sympathize. But I'm not going to sacrifice the lives of all of these people"—he waved an arm at the prisoners, who were starting to notice their raised voices—"because you want the luxury of a quick death to spare your damaged conscience."

Yao opened his mouth as if to speak, then closed it again, averting his eyes.

"Now, we're wasting time. I can't read these controls, and Syuxtun lacks the technical expertise to understand what he's reading. I'll need to have him translate them for me, and I don't have time enough to turn around and explain what to do, to you or anyone else. It's me or no one."

Yao looked up from beneath his brows, meeting Zhuan's eyes, and nodded. Then, after a long pause, he said, "Agreed."

Zhuan took a deep breath, and sighed.

"But we're going to need a bigger boat," Yao said, glancing at the prisoners. "That's a few too many to squeeze into the *Dragon*."

Zhuan nodded. "The troop transport that brought them was being serviced by the ground crews when we left the hangar. Unless it's already taken off again, which seems unlikely, it should be sitting there fueled and ready for you."

"Sounds as good a plan as any." As Zhuan moved to join the others, Yao followed at his side. "But you won't be able to do this alone, you know. Even if Syuxtun can translate for you quickly enough to come with us, you're going to need someone to watch your back. Once the Mexica figure out that we're here, which should be about the time we start marching through the habitat with a few dozen prisoners, they're probably going to try to retake the control station."

The others overheard the approaching pair, and Dea was the first to speak up.

"No offense, captain, but I'm going with Lei Xiaoli." He hugged the girl to his side, who was still shaking off the effects of the fermented agave. "I didn't come this far just to be separated from her again."

"Don't worry," Zhuan said with a faint smile, "I wouldn't ask you to do so. There needs to be some happy ending in all of this, somewhere."

"I'll stay," Fukuda said, stepping forward, chest puffed out. He glanced at the young boy who stood huddled with the other prisoners. "I ran away from a fight once, because I thought I wasn't big enough to win it. I'm not going to be doing that again."

Zhuan nodded respectfully to the Nipponese bannerman. "And I'm honored to have you."

"And I, captain," Syuxtun said, coming to stand beside Fukuda. "Any moment that these people are delayed diminishes their chance of escape. Better to let them depart and let me stay behind to translate for you, than to force them to linger while I read out the control labels for you now."

Zhuan had no desire to condemn anyone else to die needlessly at his side, but he couldn't question the Athabascan's logic. "Very well," he said, with some reluctance. Then to the others he said, "But no one else, alright?"

"Thank the ancestors," Cai said with an audible sigh of relief. "I was worried you were going to ask me to stick around, too."

Fukuda sneered. "Don't think you're getting off easy, beanpole. You've still got a whole station of Mexica to get through between here and the hangar, and that Jaguar Knight armor of yours isn't going to fool anyone if you're marching at the head of this lot." He motioned toward the prisoners.

Cai blanched, swallowing hard.

"Fukuda's right," Yao said. "We're going to need all the assistance we can get." He turned to the Nipponese. "Do you have enough ammunition to hold down the station?"

Fukuda checked the clips at his belt, and nodded.

Without another word, Yao went over to where they'd piled the weapons of the fallen guardsmen.

"I'll take that, bannerman," Dea said, when Yao held up Paik's fletcher.

Yao nodded, thoughtfully, and handed the holstered pistol over. Dea hung it at his left side, balancing the one at his right hip. Then, experimentally, he quick-drew both pistols at once, aiming at empty air. Then he spun both pistols on their trigger guards like a Tejas gunslinger, and slammed them back into their holsters.

With three more weapons to disperse, Yao canvassed the prisoners. Most were too dispirited to put up much resistance, he decided, whether armed or not, but several of the latest prisoners to arrive were eager to defend themselves, if need be. And so the young man and older man of the newcomers were each given one of the rocket carbines, and the old grandmother who'd first appeared at the top of the transport's exit ramp was given the other fletcher. The three prisoners were given a brief tutorial in the weapons' operations, less than was really necessary but better than nothing, under the circumstances.

Then, as Zhuan and Syuxtun went to work on the engineering controls, and Fukuda took up his position covering the entrance, it was time for the others to head out.

While Cai and Dea herded the prisoners, getting them ready to head toward the elevator near the model of Fire Star, whose pyramid on the habitat level was nearest to the hangar entrance, Yao came to stand before Zhuan.

The bannerman looked as if he were searching for the right thing to say. Finally, he came to attention and snapped off a salute.

"Captain Zhuan Jie, it has been an honor serving with you."

Zhuan straightened, and with a smile, returned Yao's salute with a somewhat lazy one of his own.

"You're a poor soldier at best," Yao went on, "but I've seldom known a finer man."

Zhuan's eyes stung, and he nodded, tight-lipped. "I've known one finer, at least, Bannerman Yao Guanzhong, and I'm looking at him."

Yao began to object, then thought better of it and nodded. "Good luck, Zhuan."

"And to you, Yao."

And that was the last the two men saw of one another.

When Yao and the others were on their way, Zhuan and Syuxtun went to work on the reactor controls, while Fukuda settled in to cover the door, his carbine across his lap and his fletcher in hand.

After a few minute's work, the captain and the Athabascan had worked out the essentials of the system between them, and Zhuan began formulating the correct series of commands to input to initiate the reactor overload.

"Seems pretty straightforward," Zhuan said, chewing the inside of his cheek nervously. "Still, I don't know that I'd be making much headway without you on hand to assist."

"I don't know," Syuxtun answered, conversation-ally. "You seemed to be picking up the fundamentals of the ideography on the *Dragon*'s controls well enough. Better than Ang, at any rate."

The two men paused, and looked at one another.

"Rutting dung," Zhuan spat, toggling his radio to transmit. "We forgot about Ang!"

As the radio hissed to life, the captain continued to set the switches in the correct sequence.

"Zhuan to Ang," he said, louder than was absolutely necessary. "Ang, do you read?"

A tense moment of silence followed, and the two men exchanged an uneasy glance.

"Ang, do you read?" the captain repeated.

Then, as if in response to his call, loud klaxons began to sound, reverberating through the control station temple, while in the ceiling overhead red lights began flashing. The station's internal alarm systems were sounding, and it didn't take much imagination to guess what might have set them off.

"Captain?" came the voice of Ang over the radio, breathless and strained, with the sound of gunfire echoing in the background. "You know, I was just about to call you…"

Steersman Ang had sat nervously on the bridge of the *Dragon*, waiting for the others to return. He'd removed the ill-fitting pressure suit, seeing little to be gained from keeping it on, and wore only his simple black worksuit. His shoulder ached dully, where Dea had needled him, and his palms were rubbed nearly raw with his incessant scratching. To pass the time he'd pulled out his set of loaded dice, and using his pressure suit's helmet as a bowl had rolled them again and again, practicing his skill at getting precisely the combination of up-turned faces that he desired.

The hours ticked slowly by, and aside from occasionally hearing Syuxtun radio to Yao over the scrambler radio in the helmet resting on the deck, there was no word from the others, and no sign of their return.

When he heard the pounding on the hatch, his first thought was that the captain had returned with the prisoners, and was unable to get it open. But then Ang had quickly realized that the captain would have radioed ahead, if he were heading back. And that if it was the captain, he'd likely have had no difficulty in opening the hatch in the first place.

Clutching his fletcher to his chest, Ang had crept down through the hatch to the lower deck, his heartbeat pounding like a drum in his ears. Terror gripped him, obscuring rational thought, or else he'd have thought to bring the scrambler radio with him, instead of leaving the helmet along with the loaded dice on the deck of the bridge.

It wasn't until he inched within arm's reach of the closed hatch that he could hear the muffled voices from outside. They didn't sound angry, more annoyed, but since Ang couldn't understand a word of their Nahuatl speech he couldn't say for certain. All that he did know was that unless the captain and the others had lost the ability to converse in Official Speech, whoever was on the other side of the hatch was no friend of his.

And then the hatch had opened.

The trio of Mexica who appeared in the open hatch weren't warriors, but regular technicians, a repair team in radiation suits. And they didn't carry weapons, but workman's tools. But Ang had scarcely bothered to wait to identify them.

With his fletcher held inexpertly in a two-handed grip, Ang squeezed the trigger and sprayed the open hatch with needle fire, indiscriminately. It was several seconds before he even managed to hit anything but the inner hull of the *Dragon*, seconds in which the Mexic repair team first gaped at him in shock and alarm, then turned to try to flee. One of the technicians went down with a handful of needles buried in his side, while another got several steps down toward the hangar deck before a spray of needles tore a red rill across his back. The third technician was lucky enough to fall backward, arms flailing as he toppled out of range, and then scrambled around the other side of the *Dragon* and out of sight before Ang could point the stream of needles in his direction again.

Ang had gambled that he might be able to wipe out the repair team before they raised the alarm, and buy himself some time before the station was able to send in armed troops after him. But as the two Mexica lay dying before him, the third one somewhere out of sight and shouting for help, Ang realized that he'd overplayed his hand, and that this was one roll of the dice that he wouldn't be able to cheat or bluff his way out of.

He seemed to move in slow motion, working his way back across the common area to the hatch which led to the bridge. To the bridge, where his rocket carbine and his scrambler radio were lying useless on the deck. Useless to him here, far out of reach, but less so if he were able to reach the bridge in one piece.

The first of the armed Mexica boarded the ship just as he began climbing the steps to the bridge, and fired off a stream of burning liquid magnesium that hosed the backs of his legs in flames. He managed to make it to the bridge without losing consciousness, and rolled back and forth on the deck to douse the flames, but by the time they were out his legs were badly burned, the charred fabric of his worksuit fused to the raw flesh, and the pain was so great he was sure he would lose consciousness at any moment.

Perhaps he did lose consciousness, at that, as it seemed only as long as one moment to the next before the ship was crawling with armed Mexica, and the station's alarms had begun to sound. He still managed to keep his grip on the fletcher, the barrel pointed at the hatch at the rear of the bridge, but Ang wondered bleakly if he still had the strength needed to pull the trigger.

Then the helmet radio had buzzed to life, and the faint sound of the captain's voice could be heard. It took painful moments to drag himself across the deck to where his helmet lay, and with a crooked finger he managed to reach in and toggle his own radio to transmit.

Then, over the sound of gunfire from below decks, as the Mexica began to fire at him up through the hatch, Ang spoke to the captain, relating what had happened.

* * *

The radio went silent after only a few moments, in which the steersman had related to Zhuan that he had been discovered on the ship by a Mexic repair team, and that armed warriors had now taken the ship and were about to reach the bridge. Then Ang's words were drowned out by rifle fire and the sinister hiss of fire-lances' burning streams, and then all went quiet.

"That's no way for anyone to die," said Fukuda from his post near the control station temple's entrance, his tone grave. "Not even a worm like Ang."

Zhuan nodded, while Syuxtun muttered a brief prayer for the dead beneath his breath.

"Come on," the captain said, shaking the moment from his shoulders and turning back to the reactor controls. "There's no time to waste, unless we want all the others to end up like him."

Chapter Thirty-Nine

The elevator car was barely large enough for Yao, Dea, Cai, and all of the rescued prisoners to fit, more than two dozen bodies crammed in cheek to jowl. But the alternative was to split their group into two or more parties, which Yao was sure would only increase their chances of running into trouble. They'd managed to make it from the control station temple to the model of Fire Star without encountering more than a handful of isolated ritualists, whom Yao had been able to dispatch in short order with rounds from his rocket carbine, or Dea with precisely placed spurts of needle fire. The number of bodies they'd loaded onto the elevator car seemed to trip some load limiter, and the car was now descending nonstop to their desired floor, the habitation level at the outermost deck.

But if they'd managed to make it this far without running into trouble, as soon as they marched out of the elevator car onto the city streets below—two gun- and sword-wielding Han in purloined Mexic armor and another in a Middle Kingdom worksuit, at the head of more than two dozen freed prisoners—the trouble would doubtless find them. Yao felt sure that alarms would be raised the moment their party was spotted on the crowded streets below, somewhere just before or after he and the others opened fire with fletchers and carbines on the assembled Mexica blocking their path to the hangar.

It came as some surprise, then, when a red light began flashing in the elevator car before they'd even reached the top of the elevator pyramid on the habitation level, followed in short order by a klaxon that set Yao's teeth on edge.

Yao had just heard the captain radio to Ang, and moments later heard the steersman's response, and so there was no question which of their number had been discovered. It was some small comfort that the captain was still at liberty to rig the reactor to meltdown, at least for the moment, but Yao found it difficult to find much solace in the fact.

"Well," Yao said, facing the doors as the elevator car slowed to a stop, the sound of the klaxon almost deafening in their ears. "So much for the element of surprise."

Then the car came to a halt and the doors slid open, and trouble, at last, found them.

Dea was the first off the elevator car, sheltering Lei Xiaoli with his body. The young bannerman didn't wait for any of the Mexica to notice their presence, but with a fletcher in either hand began firing into the crowd, trying to clear a path through the street to the hangar doors some hundred meters or more from the base of the elevator pyramid. Before the Mexica had even noticed the party of escaped prisoners descending the stepped pyramid above them, Dea had begun dropping Mexica—warriors, ritualists, student warriors, and courtesans—with precisely placed needle bursts, hitting each only as much as was needed to incapacitate before moving on to the next target.

Yao came next, at Dea's left, while Cai took up his position on Dea's right. The three soldiers formed the leading edge of a phalanx, with the two men and one old woman who were armed with their fallen comrades' weapons taking up positions covering the group's rear. Yao didn't like the idea of their flanks being so exposed, or their rearguard being composed of such inexperienced shots, but the intention was to drive through the crowd swiftly enough that they would outrun pursuit, which would mean that the bulk of the interaction with Mexic defenders would be ahead of them, and not behind.

Dea quickly thought better of firing simultaneously with both fletchers, and began with alternate shots, first with one and then the other and then the first again, so as not to deplete both weapons' charges too quickly. Even so, before long the diodes on both handles glowed bright red, and Dea shoved the fletchers in their holsters, one on either hip, and unslung his carbine, firing and reloading, firing and reloading, sending one rocket projectile after another in rapid succession, with only marginally less accuracy than he'd scored with the flechettes. As soon as the fletchers' diodes began to glow weakly green, he slung the carbine back over his shoulder, drew both pistols without a single unnecessary flourish, and resumed the cycle. Here he was not playacting, not acting the part of the gunslinger in the wild Vinland frontier, not fanning his hand needlessly over the pistols' reset levers for show; Dea was a machine, a precision instrument, with a single overriding preoccupation: to protect the woman who followed in his wake, and see that no harm came to her. Any other considerations were secondary at best.

Cai, for his part, seemed mostly concerned with saving his own skin. The remedial lessons and practice which Yao had forced on the young guardsman while they were onboard the *Dragon* had improved his marksmanship somewhat, but those gains were offset by the overwhelming terror which now gripped him. But while he had seemed principally concerned with his own survival when first descending the stepped pyramid, when he saw the massing Mexic warriors in the street below, and glanced back at the exhausted and defenseless prisoners who followed behind him, with nothing standing between them and the ritualists' black-glass blade except Cai and his companions, the young guardsman seemed to undergo something of a transformation. It was as if, in the span of a few moments, Cai had come to realize that his own life was not the only thing it was given to him to defend, and in fact that it might rank lower in the list than he would previously have guessed. So instead of merely targeting—however inexpertly or inaccurately—those Mexica who drew beads on himself alone, he began to focus his attention on any warriors who threatened the lives of the innocents in Cai's charge.

The phalanx of prisoners and rescuers advanced through the streets as quickly as they were able, movement varying somewhere between the pace of a slow crawl and a brisk walk, but while their progress seemed maddeningly slow, they were progressing, and so far without sustaining major losses. Their ranged weapons, the fletchers and carbines, in this setting meant that Yao and his men were able to keep the Mexica from moving to close quarters, and the fact that fletcher and carbine alike were essentially recoilless meant that they could continue to fire on the move, while the Mexica who faced them were forced either to employ fire-lances, which while deadly were only effective over short distances, or find locations where they could entrench to counteract the recoil of their standard firearms. And since there were comparatively few locations suitable for the Mexic rifles to brace themselves on the street—mostly along the outer walls of nearby structures—Yao and the others had the opportunity to concentrate their fire on those locations, and increase their odds of eliminating potential obstacles.

Still, it was not as if the prisoners and their escorts didn't sustain any injuries, or worse. The older male prisoner with the carbine fell, and somewhat gruesomely, when one of the rocket projectiles fired from his carbine inadvertently exploded while still within the barrel, turning the weapon into a shower of fragmentary shards and shrapnel within his arms. It was some small comfort that he died quickly, before experiencing too much of the pain his body would doubtless have suffered, as the firing mechanism of the carbine was driven up through the underside of his jaw, through the roof of his mouth, and into his brain, killing him instantly.

The other major injury was suffered not by one of the prisoners, most of whom escaped with at worst second-degree burns from the spray of the Mexic fire-lances, but by Cai, who caught a Mexic bullet in the femoral artery, while only a dozen or so paces from the hangar entrance. The constrictive material of his pressure suit acted to keep the blood from flowing too freely, but still the red ichor seeped from the rent in the suit the bullet had left, and Cai was able to walk only with one of the prisoners supporting him on that side, the guardsman's arm wrapped around this helpless stranger's shoulder.

Finally, the hangar door slid open, and Dea led Lei Xiaoli and the others through into the hangar, while Yao remained behind to cover their rear. The Mexica were regrouping in their wake, and the bannerman still had a fight on his hands to get the prisoners across the hangar and onto the transport without the Mexica following close behind and mowing them down from behind cover.

CHAPTER FORTY

With Syuxtun's help, Zhuan had managed to get all of the commands entered into the reactor controls, reordering dozens of switches in the enormous banks in precise sequence. The flashing lights and clanging klaxons of the alarm were grating, and served to disrupt his concentration, but too much depended on him remembering everything he could about reactor maintenance and potential failure modes from his days as engineer's mate on the *Jade Maiden*, all those years ago.

Then the Mexica arrived at the entrance to the control station temple, and there were even more challenges to his continued concentration.

The first that Zhuan knew of the assault was the muffled thump of Fukuda's carbine firing, followed by the whine of his fletcher sending a stream of flechettes through the air. There quickly followed angry shouts, and the bark of conventional rifles firing, and the sibilant hiss of fire-lances spraying burning magnesium.

At Zhuan's side, Syuxtun turned to look back to the entrance, his hand drifting to the fletcher holstered at his waist, but the captain kept his attention on his task. "Which are the switches that control the coolant flow, bannerman?"

Syuxtun yanked his gaze away from the entrance and back to the reactor controls. "Um... these." He pointed to a battery of switches at Zhuan's left elbow.

Not wasting time or breath with thanks, Zhuan shifted over and began to toggle the switches one after another.

"Captain?" Syuxtun said, his voice low, glancing over his shoulder at the entrance.

"Hmm?" Zhuan hummed, distractedly.

"Will you be needing my translating services for much longer? I'm afraid my attentions may be soon required elsewhere."

From behind him, Zhuan could hear the clang of saber rebounding off an obsidian club as Fukuda tangled with one of the Mexica who had managed to slip past the gauntlet thrown down by the Nipponese's fletcher fire across the entrance. From the sound of it, Fukuda was holding his own, but Zhuan knew that against the superior numbers of the Mexica it would only be a matter of time.

Zhuan nodded, and scanned his eyes over the reactor controls, searchingly. "Just one more..." he muttered, beneath this breath. Then, louder, he said to Syuxtun, "Remind me which were the controls for the containment system, again?"

Syuxtun's gaze darted back to the controls, and he pointed to a series of switches high and to the right.

"Thank you," Zhuan answered, shifting position. Then, with a sad sigh, he said, "I think that will be all, Bannerman Syuxtun, if your attentions are needed elsewhere."

"A little... help?" Fukuda called from the entrance, in considerable pain. He'd taken a number of blows in his contest with the obsidian-club-wielding Mexica, and while he was still on his feet, he wouldn't be for long.

Syuxtun nodded, and drew his fletcher. Before he moved off, though, he laid his free hand on the captain's shoulder.

"Those who believe and work righteous deeds, God will admit to gardens beneath which rivers flow, for God carries out all that He plans."

With a sad smile, Zhuan looked over, regarding the Athabascan. "Gardens beneath which rivers flow, eh?" He managed a chuckle. "That doesn't sound too bad."

Syuxtun nodded. "I hope not. We deserve it, I think."

Then the Athabascan moved off to assist in the defense of the control station temple, while Zhuan began entering the final commands to initiate the core meltdown and the associated steam explosion.

CHAPTER FORTY-ONE

Yao was in the process of loading the last of the prisoners onto the commandeered troop transport. Fortune had been with them, as the station's security protocols seemed to dictate that the defenders should concentrate their attentions on the safety of the station itself, and not on potential avenues for the attackers' escape. As a result, most of the station's personnel had been drawn away from the hangar and into the inner sections of Xolotl. Which was hardly good news for Captain Zhuan and the others attempting to hold down the control station temple until the reactor blew, but it meant that the obstacles between Yao's team and freedom were fewer than they'd otherwise have been. And it was really the only explanation for how they'd managed to get so many prisoners from the pyramid to the hangar without losing more of them to enemy fire. As it was, aside from the old man who'd died when his carbine had exploded in his hand, and a pair of women who were unlucky enough to stray too close to streams of burning magnesium, the rest of the prisoners reached the transport with only minor injuries. Bannerman Dea had taken a shot to the shoulder which, while it bled freely, did not appear to be life threatening.

Cai, though, had not been so lucky.

They'd found the troop transport unlocked and unguarded. A short distance away stood the *Dragon*, which was guarded by a pair of Mexic warriors in unadorned armor, but a few precisely placed shots with Yao's rocket carbines had taken the Mexica out almost before they'd noticed the group's approach. Yao had heard of Steersman Ang's end over his scrambler radio, so there was no point in entering the ship, but the bannerman couldn't help but feel a pang of sorrow at the man's passing. Ang had been a reprobate, a cheat, and a thief, but Zhuan had been right about one thing, at least: he was the finest pilot whom Yao had ever seen, though his skills had been hardly taxed in the course of their mission.

With Ang gone, though, and Zhuan back in the control station temple, it fell to Yao to pilot the commandeered transport out of the station.

Cai and the escaped prisoners who were supporting him on either side, one under either arm, were the last to reach the ship. As they approached, Yao was busy studying the controls of the gantry mechanism which had lowered the ship to the hanger floor. In order for the ship to depart, the gantry would need to be elevated again, lifting them up and away from the pull of the station's centrifugal gravity. And since they'd be getting no assistance from the station's tugs, the transport would have to rely on a combination of its own thrust and the gantry's launch mechanism to push them the rest of the way into the relative weightlessness near the hub, navigating through the hangar doors and into open space from there with her attitude thrusters.

There was a serious practical difficulty, however. The elevation gantry, which was essential in getting the transport launched, appeared simple to operate. The switches were labeled with many of the same glyphs which Yao had learned when familiarizing himself with the *Dragon*'s controls, allowing him to work out the operation with relative ease. However, Yao quickly deduced that the gantry could only be controlled from the hangar floor. And unless Yao was able to convince one of the Mexic ground crew to assist in their escape, one of their number would have to stay behind to operate it.

There was only one rational choice to make, but Yao was loath to force the burden on another unwillingly. To his relief, and perhaps to the surprise of both men, Cai proved to be a more generous spirit than any of them might have guessed.

"There's a problem, Yao?" Cai said, limping badly and leaning against the transport's hull, as the two prisoners climbed onboard. On the deck at his feet, blood already began to pool, seeping down his leg, and his face looked wan and pale.

"These are the controls for the gantry," Yao explained simply. "Without someone here to operate them, the ship won't be able to leave."

Cai didn't hesitate for an instant, but answered quickly, "I'll do it."

Yao narrowed his eyes, regarding the young guardsman carefully. "You realize that with the gantry raised, you won't be able to get back onto the ship?"

Cai shook his head, wearing a lopsided smile. "No, but I figured it'd be something like that."

The bannerman was thoughtful. "And yet you're willing to stay behind?"

Cai shrugged. "Look, I'm no physician, but I know people don't lose this kind of blood and still walk away from it." He gestured with a glance toward the sluggish river of red flowing down from the bullet hole in his suit's thigh. "Besides, I've never really amounted to much, anyway." He chuckled. "I'm not much of a soldier, I guess, but maybe this'll be one last prank I can play, only this time on the Mexica. What do you think?"

Yao returned the guardsman's smile, and nodded. "You're a better soldier than you think, Cai. A lousy marksman, but a better soldier, for all of that."

Cai leaned heavily on the gantry controls. "Sure, sure," he said, his voice wavering somewhat. "Now show me how to run this thing, will you? I'm starting to get a bit lightheaded, and not in a good way, so I'm not sure how much longer I'm going to be of any use to you."

Yao helped Cai shift around into position, and then began to explain the basics of the controls, wasting no more time on farewells. If everything was going according to plan in the control station temple, they were quickly running out of time.

CHAPTER FORTY-TWO

Zhuan was no more than halfway through entering the lengthy series of command codes when the next wave of the Mexic assault arrived. Working together, Fukuda and Syuxtun held them at bay, though with each passing moment their ammunition reserves dwindled, and their strength began to flag.

The captain did not look up from his labors, but was able to follow the course of the engagement by hearing alone, the whine and thump of the defenders' weapons, the hiss and bark of those borne by the attackers, the shouted challenges of the Mexic warriors and Fukuda's hoarse calls of defiance. If Syuxtun spoke at all, Zhuan didn't hear it.

Something shifted, and the exchange of fire changed tempo. The shouts of challenge in Nahuatl sounded closer, nearer to hand. Zhuan, unable to control the impulse, chanced a glance over his shoulder. In that glimpse, he saw enough to understand what had happened. It was a rush of warriors, throwing their bodies into the breach, sacrificing themselves so that some of those who followed behind might make it through the gauntlet and close with the defenders.

In that brief instant, before he turned back to his labors, Zhuan saw a group of Mexic warriors in their ornate armor, leaping over the bodies of their just-fallen comrades. Fukuda was rising to his feet to fend them off, while Syuxtun was falling back, firing on the attackers with his carbine.

Zhuan had looked for only the span of a heartbeat, for the duration between one eye blink and the next, but in that brief instant he saw Fukuda dispatch one Mexic with a vicious swipe of his saber, block the downward-falling club of another, and turn to lunge at a third. The Nipponese was a blur of movement, eyes wide and wild, a shout of defiance on his lips.

When Zhuan next chanced a look back over his shoulder, mere moments later, some dozen bodies lay at Fukuda's feet, each felled by his saber. But their numbers had proved too many in the end, as the Nipponese slid to the ground, bleeding and broken from the thrusts and blows of the obsidian clubs he had not been able to parry. Syuxtun could not move to help him, still needed to pick off the next wave of attackers with fletcher and carbine, and so Fukuda lay for a moment in the breach, along with the Mexic who had fallen before him.

But when the Nipponese spoke, spending his last breath in a dying gasp, it was not in defiance to the Mexic who had opposed him, or in prayer to some deity to receive him in death. It was spent calling out to his brother Keimi, begging for the forgiveness of a boy long since passed.

CHAPTER FORTY-THREE

Yao hadn't had a chance to strip out of his Eagle Knight armor, and so sat at the flight controls of the troop transport in full Mexic finery, his saber still belted at his side, his fletcher holstered on his other hip. On his orders Dea had taken the engineering controls, and while the younger man couldn't read Nahuatl anymore than he could speak it, Yao was confident that he could perform as directed, and so long as Yao could describe the appearance of the glyphs in question, Dea should have a reasonable chance of hitting the right controls. Dea refused to be separated from Lei Xiaoli, though, or she from him, and so she had been installed at the communicationist's station, strapped into place. They had no one to handle the navigation controls, but it wasn't as if Yao had a clear idea where they were going anyway. He'd try to contact Zhurong by radio when they were clear of the Mexic station, and hoped that one of the prisoners was adept enough with an abacus to help him plot their course.

The rescued prisoners had strapped themselves into acceleration couches in the lower decks, intended for use by Mexic troops in armor. Several of them had cast dark looks at the hatch leading to the prisoner pens on the lowest deck in which they'd originally come to Xolotl.

Yao spat a curse when it was discovered the ship refused to start, and glared at the sacrificial altar which hulked at the front of the bridge. He rose from his seat then hurried back out through the hatch, to the hangar deck where the two Mexic warriors who'd guarded the *Dragon* had fallen. One of the two guards was dead, bled white, but the other was still clinging tenuously to life, his erratic heartbeats pumping arterial blood through the wounds in his neck and chest. Without apology or ceremony, Yao yanked the dying man off the deck and flung him over his shoulder, then hoisted him up into the ship.

Once back on the bridge, Yao threw the dying Mexica bodily over the sacrificial altar, and then began strapping himself back into the seat at the flight controls. As the Mexic warrior's heart finally gave out, his final breath rattling through his teeth, his last lifeblood dripped onto the hemoglobin sensors. The tells on the controls went active, and the ship began to hum to life.

Yao scowled at the dead man draped over the altar. He'd dispose of the body once they were underway, assuming they made it out into open space.

On the hangar floor, Cai had performed his function admirably, getting the transport elevated high off the deck atop the gantry, and then positioning the craft so that its own thrust could push it up and into the essentially weightless region near the hub, halfway between the floor of the hangar and the opposite side which served as ceiling high overhead.

The ship shuddered out of its moorings, and attitude thrusters pushed it up and toward the hangar doors.

"They're closed!" Dea called from his station, his gaze fixed on the view beyond the forward ports.

Yao looked up from his controls, not wasting a breath on the curse that waited behind his teeth. The hangar doors, heavily shielded, were sealed tight, barring their escape.

"The captain's sure to blow the station any time now!" Dea added, sounding bleary from his loss of blood.

Yao needed no reminder. He loosened the straps holding him to his seat, and slid from the helm to the fire station. Puzzling only a moment to remember which glyphs indicated the firing mechanism, he loosed a stream of high-impact explosive projectiles from the turrets mounted on the transport's hull, exhausting the ship's supply in a continuous barrage.

The projectiles hit their marks, one after another, bright flashes against the hangar doors, leaving behind scuffed smudges when the puffs of black smoke drifted slowly away. But while the hangar doors buckled under the strain of the repeated impacts and explosions, they held fast.

The doors, though bowed, remained closed.

"Dea," Yao said, leaping back to the helm and grabbing hold of the restraints. "Engines to full thrust."

To Dea's credit, he only widened his eyes fractionally, and complied with Yao's orders without question or complaint.

Yao nosed the transport directly at the doors. "Brace yourselves," he shouted, to anyone who was listening. "And pray to whatever you hold holy that this works."

The transport juddered as it picked up velocity, heading directly towards the hangar doors.

Chapter Forty-Four

Syuxtun held the gap, using the bodies of fallen Mexica as a barricade from behind which he fired at any who ventured into the entrance, armed with Fukuda's weapons as well as his own. The chamber filled with acrid, greasy smoke, which rose from the bodies of the fallen that had been set alight by the subsequent attacks of the Mexica with fire-lances. The smoke drifted as black clouds in the strobing red lights of the alarm, searing the nose and stinging their eyes with tears.

Holding his carbine, crouching low, Zhuan remained by the controls, watching as the dials showed the reactor temperature reaching runaway levels. When the temperature spiked, and the melt-down began, he would toggle the final switch to vent molten fuel into the water coolant, triggering the steam explosion whose waves of concussive force would shake the asteroid to pieces. From time to time a bullet spanged off the wall above his head, and he would return fire, shooting off a rocket blindly through the entrance beyond Syuxtun's barricade of smoldering bodies. He wasn't sure if any of his shots actually hit anything, but it usually meant a delay of a few moments before another shot was fired in return, and it wasn't as if Zhuan had any reason to save the ammunition.

Fukuda lay where he'd fallen, near the entrance, sprawled over the man who'd killed him, who'd fallen to the Nipponese's blade before his own injuries had brought him down. Across the chamber lay the still forms of Nguyen and Paik, life long fled, looking almost as if they were slumbering side by side.

Somewhere beyond the ceiling overhead, there was the Xolotl reactor, which was mere moments away from core meltdown. The control station temple seemed to vibrate with the pent-up energy, propellant bottled up and not allowed to flow out and over the turbines. It could almost be heard, somewhere at the edge of hearing, a low-frequency rumble that presaged the coming conflagration. It was a familiar noise to Zhuan, but it took the captain a moment to place the sound.

It was the roar of a bear pouncing on its prey, claws out and teeth bared.

"Syuxtun?" Zhuan said in a low voice, but when he looked over he saw the Athabascan intent on the entrance, muttering prayers to his god beneath his breath.

The captain only smiled wearily, and nodded. He'd spent a lifetime outrunning the predators that had haunted his childhood dreams, the animals whom his parents had spent their lives training but could never quite tame. They'd terrified him, the bears, the tigers, the lions in their cages, and the young Zhuan had fled to space not only to chase romance and adventure, but to flee the terror that had gripped him since earliest memory. But space had proved only a temporary respite, as the fear had found him again when war had begun, and once more the growls of those untamed animals had haunted his dreams, the sound of them growing ever nearer.

To his surprise, though, Zhuan found that he wasn't afraid anymore. Having stopped and turned, at long last, he discovered that it wasn't a predator at his heels, but that in some strange sense it was Zhuan himself that was predator, and not the prey. It had merely taken him a lifetime to realize it.

The dial on the controls showed that the reactor had reached the critical point, and there was no turning back now.

With a growl rumbling at the back of his throat, Zhuan reached out and hit the switch, releasing the molten fuel into the water coolant. And then, before the explosion smashed his body to pieces, he opened his mouth, threw back his head, and roared.

Chapter Forty-five

As the transport collided with the buckled doors, the collision shook the ship badly, jostling the passengers, but with a straining sound of metal on metal that Yao could feel in his teeth, the hangar doors bent back, and the engine's thrust pushed the transport the rest of the way through. The transport's hull was scored, but remained intact, and none within were injured.

Yao had worried that there might be Mexic vessels already spaceborne that might try to impede them, but the only ships in evidence were those docked on the hangar floor back inside Xolotl, and none of them seemed in a position to take off any time soon. There was still a chance that one of them might be crewed up and launched in pursuit, but in short order those onboard the station had more to worry about than a ship of escaping prisoners.

The transport was a few kilometers away, only moments after clearing the hangar doors, when Dea pointed to the grainy screen on the console over-head. It was showing an image transmitted by a remote-viewing mirror mounted on the ship's hull and oriented toward the bow, pointed back in the direction they'd come, back toward Xolotl.

Yao wasn't sure what he'd expected. A fireball? A new star in the heavens as the station was con-sumed by flames?

The reality was nothing so poetic or dramatic, but no less affecting.

While those on the bridge of the transport watched, the roughly cylindrical asteroid of Xolotl simply *cracked*, approximately halfway along its length, like a snapping twig. And through the break poured a cloud of atmosphere that immediately froze into a crystalline cloud on hitting the cold vac-uum, punctuated here and there with debris, the largest of which was nearly the size of one of the stepped pyramids, the smallest of which may have been individual bodies.

And that was that.

Xolotl was dead.

The bridge fell silent, as they remembered those who had fallen, those who wouldn't be coming home.

Yao didn't speak. There was nothing to say.

Soon, he would fire up the ship's radio, and try to contact the commanders back on Zhurong. He'd need help in navigating this cumbersome Mexic transport through the black void back to Middle

Kingdom-held space, where they could transfer the rescued prisoners over to the authorities. And as soon as he did, Yao was eager to get back into harness and back down to the red planet's surface.

Success in the mission meant a full pardon for the survivors, both Dea and Yao himself, and a reprieve from the executioner's blade. But let Dea and his girl return to Earth, as Yao had no desire to take the proffered discharge, as well. He was a soldier, despite everything, and there was work still left to be done.

The war was still raging, after all, and there was no end in sight.

APPENDICES

Celestial Empire Chronology

Year in Western Calendar	Year in Chinese Calendar	Event
1424	Jia-Chen (Wood Dragon)	In the Middle Kingdom, the Yongle Emperor dies, and Zhu Zhanji, the Xuande Emperor, ascends to the Throne.
1460s		Treasure Fleet circumnavigates the African Cape of Storms and reaches the Atlantic. The Treasure Fleet opens water trade routes with the Europeans, particularly the Spanish and Italians.
1542	Ren-Yin (Water Tiger)	Treasure Fleet reaches the western hemisphere, making landfall on the western shore of the northern hemisphere, which they name Khalifah, in honor of the Muslim admiral of the Treasure Fleet.
1600s		The English begin colonizing the Vinland region, naming their first settlement Jamestown, in the colony subsequently named Virginia. At about the same time, Pilgrims fleeing religious persecution leave England and settle in Plymouth, to the north.
1600s		Powered flight is invented, when engineers of the Middle Kingdom marry Leonardo da Vinci's designs for a glider with a Han firework rocket. The vehicle is named the Flaming Crane.

1610	Geng-Xu (Metal Dog)	The Middle Kingdom ambassador to the court of the Grand Duke of Tuscany, Cosimo II, is given a telescope and a copy of Galileo's "The Sidereal Messenger."
1611	Xin-Hai (Metal Pig)	"Thy Saffron Wings" – A Middle Kingdom embassy is established in England, and the envoy is received at the court of King James I.
1644	Jia-Shen (Wood Monkey)	Beginning of the Clear Dynasty, when the Manchurians take Northern Capital.
1690s		Manchurian emperors begin to expand their influence militarily, both on land and on the sea. Constructing massive navies that dwarf even the innumerous ships of the Treasure Fleets, they begin a campaign of conquest in Indonesia, India, Arabia and Africa. By the end of the next century, parts of Europe are now under the direct control of the Dragon Throne.
1690s		Colonization of Khalifah by the Han begins.
1712	Ren-Chen (Water Dragon)	"The Sky is Large and the Earth Small" – A junior bureaucrat from the Ministry of War goes to the Eastern Depot to interrogate an old man who, in his youth, traveled with the Treasure Fleet to far side of the ocean and spent time among the Mexica.
1776	Bing-Shen (Fire Monkey)	The colonies of Vinland declare independence from Britain. The Commonwealth of Vinland is founded.
1790s		England and France fall before the Army of the Green Standard, and are brought beneath the banner of the Dragon Throne.
1800s		The Dragon Throne expands its control through Africa and the rest of Europe. By the end of the first decade of the century, all of Eurasia and Africa are under the control of the Middle Kingdom, with regional governors set up in each.
1820	Geng-Chen (Metal Dragon)	The Daoguang emperor ascends to the throne.
1843	Gui-Mao (Water Hare)	The Middle Kingdom's fleet launches an offensive on the southern continent of the western hemisphere, Fusang.
1845	Yi-Si (Wood Snake)	The independent state of Tejas is annexed by the Commonwealth of Vinland.

1850	Geng-Xu (Metal Dog)	The Xianfeng emperor ascends to the throne.
1853	Gui-Chou (Water Ox)	The Middle Kingdom's fleets cross the Atlantic and begin the process of invading Vinland from the east.
1861	Xin-You (Metal Fowl)	The Commonwealth of Vinland surrenders to the Middle Kingdom.
1871	Xin-Wei (Metal Sheep)	The Guangxu emperor ascends to the throne.
1899	Ji-Hai (Earth Pig)	The Mexica, the last significant power to resist the Dragon Throne, ejects any Middle Kingdom merchants or diplomats living within their borders. In retaliation, the Dragon Throne declares war against the Mexica, and the First Mexic War begins.
1905	Yi-Si (Wood Snake)	With their neighbors to the north (Vinland) and the south (Fusang) under Middle Kingdom control, the Mexica fall to the Army of the Green Standard. The Mexic War is done, and for the first time in history, a single power rules the whole globe.
1906	Bing-Wu (Fire Horse)	Aixinjueluo Pu Yi, the future Xuantong emperor, is born.
1908	Wu-Shen (Earth Monkey)	The Xuantong emperor ascends to the throne.
1924	Jia-Zi (Wood Rat)	"O One" – The Xuantong emperor views a demonstration of Proctor Napier's analytical engine, but Napier mysteriously disappears before the calculator can go into production.
1930	Geng-Wu (Metal Horse)	The Mexica drive the Han out of the Mexic isthmus in a bloody revolt, ending 25 years of complete global domination by the Dragon Throne.
1938	Wu-Yin (Earth Tiger)	The first unmanned orbital launch.
1940	Geng-Chen (Metal Dragon)	"Metal Dragon Year" – The first successful manned orbital launch.
		Aixinjueluo Pu Zhen, son of Aixinjueluo Pu Chieh (brother to Pu Yi) is born.
1952	Ren-Chen (water Dragon)	The Mexic Dominion begin their own space program.

1961	Xin-Chou (Metal Ox)	Construction begins on Gold Mountain and the Bridge of Heaven.
1962	Ren-Yin (Water Tiger)	First Vinlanders are brought to work on Gold Mountain.
1967	Ding-Wei (Fire Sheep)	Xuantong dies. Aixinjueluo Pu Zhen, the Shangsheng emperor, ascends the throne.
1970	Geng-Xu (Metal Dog)	Aixinjueluo Pu Ha Chi, son of Pu Zhen, is born.
1974	Jia-Yin (Wood Tiger)	The Mexic Dominion successfully launches a man into space. Their technology is built around a mixture of science and ritualistic blood sacrifice.
1980	Geng-Shen (Metal Monkey)	Bridge of Heaven is operational. It terminates in a simple orbital platform, not the grandeur of the later orbital city of Diamond Summit
1990	Geng-Wu (Metal Horse)	Early construction of Diamond Summit.
2000	Geng-Chen (Metal Dragon)	Aixinjueluo Pu Zhen dies. Aixinjueluo Pu Ha Chi, the Taikong emperor, ascends the throne.
2010	Geng-Yin (Metal Tiger)	Diamond Summit is operational. The Lunar Fleet begins ferrying material for the construction of the Cold Palace lunar base.
2015	Yi-Wei (Wood Sheep)	Cold Palace lunar base is operational.
2024	Jia-Chen (Wood Dragon)	"The Voyage of Night Shining White" – the Treasure Fleet sets off for the red planet, Fire Star.
2051	Sin-Wei (Metal Sheep)	"Line of Dichotomy" – During the Second Mexic War, a Bannerman and a Technician find themselves confined with a Jaguar Knight of the Mexic Dominion.
2052	Ren-Shen (Water Monkey)	The Dragon's Nine Sons – a group of Bannermen and Guardsmen set out to destroy the Xolotl asteroid base in a captured Mexic warship.

The Celestial Empire
Countries and Cultures

Country/Region	Name
China	The Middle Kingdom
South America	Fusang
Western North America	Khalifah
Central and Eastern North America	Vinland
Japan	Nippon
Korea	Choson
India	Hind
Britain	Britain
France	France
Germany	Deutschland
Ireland	Eire
Spain	Espana
Italy	Italia
Russia	Rossiya
Greece	Ellas
Turkey	Turkiye
Central America	Mexica
Middle East	Arabia

Culture/Group	Name
Black African	Ethiop
Native American (Western)	Athabascan
Native American (Eastern)	Algonkian
Indian	Hindi
Britain	Briton
German	Deutsch
French	Francais
Chinese	Han
Aztec	Mexica

AUTHOR'S NOTES

I'm the kind of person who won't buy a DVD if the only "Special Features" are trailers for other movies, and who always feels a little cheated when the last words in a book are "The End." I always like a little extra material to dig into after I finish a story, a peek behind the scenes.

With that in mind, I offer the following notes.

On the Celestial Empire

The world in which *The Dragon's Nine Sons* takes place is one in which I've set many stories and novels. Called the Celestial Empire, it is an alternate history in which China rose to world domination in the fifteenth century. In our own history, during the reign of Zhu Di, the Yongle Emperor, the Treasure Fleet under the command of Admiral Zheng He, a Muslim eunuch, traveled as far as India and the east coast of Africa, and possibly even reached the west coast of South America. The Yongle Emperor's successor Zhu Gaozhi, also known as the Hongxi Emperor, ordered the Treasure Fleet destroyed and all seagoing vessels outlawed, under the advice of Confucian officials who felt that the previous emperor's expansionist policies had robbed them of influence and power. From that point onward, China turned inward, and lost contact with its new-found trading partners across the seas.

The Celestial Empire diverges from our own history when the Yongle Emperor is instead succeeded by Zhu Zhanji, the Xuande Emperor, who not only continues to employ the Treasure Fleet, but expands its scope and mission. Before Christopher Columbus sets out to discover a new route to the east, dragon boats of the Treasure Fleet round the tip of Africa and arrive in Europe.

This final mission of the *Dragon* and of her crew takes place five centuries later, during the 52nd year of the Taikong Emperor, twenty-eight years after man first walked on the face of the red planet Fire Star.

On Sources

The sources on which I've drawn in fabricating the world of the Celestial Empire are too numerous to list, but those which were employed most often in the writing of *The Dragon's Nine Sons* were John Pohl's *Aztec Warrior: AD 1325–1521* and *Aztec, Mixtec and Zapotec Armies* (both from Osprey Publishing), *The Great Temple of the Aztecs* by Eduardo Matos Moctezuma (Thames & Hudson), *The Art of the Aztecs* (Hamlyn), and *Aztecs: Reign of Blood & Splendor* (Time-Life Books), and *Everyday Life of the Aztecs* by Warwick Bray (Dorset Press), all for details about Aztec life and culture; Abdullah Yusuf Ali's translation of *The Qu'ran* (Rahrike Tarsile Qur'an, Inc.), from which passages of the Quran have been loosely adapted; and *Ruling from the Dragon Throne* by John E. Vollmer (Ten Speed Press), for details on Chinese dress, Louise Levathes's *When China Ruled the Seas* (Oxford Paperbacks) and J.A.G. Roberts's *A Concise History of China* (Harvard University Press) for details on Chinese history, C.J. Peers's *Late Imperial Chinese Armies 1520-1840* (Osprey Publishing) for details about the Chinese military, and *Perpetual Happiness: The Ming Emperor Yongle* by Shih-Shan Henry Tsai (University of Washington Press) for his invaluable glimpse into the structure of Yongle's Embroidered Guard, which forms the basis of the secret police of the Celestial Empire. And finally, moving from matters historical to scientific, the JPL Small-Body Database Browser, which can be found online at http://ssd.jpl.nasa.gov/sbdb.cgi, is highly recommended for anyone interested in modeling the orbits of any asteroid, and especially of Amor-class asteroids like 137799 (1999 YB), which appears in the present volume disguised as the Directorate of Astronomy's Orbital Object 991216, otherwise known as Xolotl.

On Acknowledgements

I'd like to thank Lou Anders who commissioned the first Celestial Empire story, "O One" for his anthology *Live Without a Net*, and who inspired me to write more stories set in the world. I'd like to thank the various editors who have published stories in the sequence, helping me to map the world and its history in detail, including Andy Cox, Pete Crowther, Jetse de Vries, Gardner Dozois, Nick Gevers, George Mann, Sharyn November, and Sheila Williams. And I would like to gratefully acknowledge Solaris for the faith they've shown in the sequence by commissioning the present volume, and especially to George Mann and Christian Dunn for helping bring the project to fruition.

And, as always, I'd be remiss if I didn't thank my wife Allison Baker, without whose love and support my career wouldn't be possible, and my daughter Georgia Rose Roberson, who occasionally lets me decide what we'll watch on television.

Chris Roberson
Austin, TX

ABOUT THE AUTHOR

Chris Roberson's novels include *Here, There & Everywhere*, *The Voyage of Night Shining White*, *Paragaea: A Planetary Romance*, *X-Men: The Return*, *Set the Seas on Fire*, *The Dragon's Nine Sons*, and the forthcoming *Iron Jaw and Hummingbird* and *End of the Century*. His short stories have appeared in such magazines as *Asimov's Science Fiction*, *Postscripts*, *Interzone*, and *Subterranean*, and in anthologies such as *Live Without a Net*, *The Many Faces of Van Helsing*, *FutureShocks*, and *Forbidden Planets*. Along with his business partner and spouse Allison Baker, he is the publisher of MonkeyBrain Books, an independent publishing house specializing in genre fiction and non-fiction genre studies, and he is the editor of anthology *Adventure Vol. 1*. He has been a finalist for the World Fantasy Award three times—once each for writing, publishing, and editing—twice a finalist for the John W. Campbell Award for Best New Writer, and twice for the Sidewise Award for Best Alternate History Short Form (winning in 2004 with his story, "O One"). Chris and Allison live in Austin, Texas with their daughter Georgia.

Visit him online at *www.chrisroberson.net*.